THE FOUR SONYAS

by Vladimír Páral

Translated from the Czech by William Harkins

A Garrigue Book/CATBIRD PRESS

Translation of *Profesionalní zena* © 1971 Vladimír Páral

First English-language edition.

CATBIRD PRESS, 16 Windsor Road, North Haven, CT 06473.
Our books are distributed to the trade by
Independent Publishers Group.

The translator acknowledges his indebtedness to Michaela
Harnick and Peter Kussi for their help in solving problems
in this translation. He would also like to thank his editor,
Robert Wechsler, for all that he added to this translation.

Library of Congress Cataloging-in-Publication Data

Páral, Vladimír, 1932-
[Profesionální zena. English]
The four Sonyas / by Vladimír Páral;
translated from the Czech by William Harkins.
1st English-language ed.
p. cm.
"A Garrigue book."
ISBN 0-945774-15-X: $22.95 (cloth)
I. Title
PG5039.26.A7P713 1993
891.8'635--dc20 92-30413 CIP

Characters and Pronunciation

SONYA CECHOVA *Chaick'-oh-vah* (heroine, her last name is the female form of the word for "Czech")

ZIKMUND HOLY *Zeek'-moond Hoh'-lee* (lives in **Usti nad Labem** (n. L.) *Oos'-tee nahd'-lahb-aim*, or Usti on the Elbe; **Ziki** *Zee'-kee*) **Aja Hola** *Eye'-ah Hoh'lah* (wife of Ziki)

WOLF ZAHN and **BERTA ZAHNOVA** *Vohlf* and *Bare'-tah Zahn* (Ziki's henchpeople)

VOLRAB and **VOLRABKA** *Vohl'-rahb* (Sonya's guardians, and managers of the Hotel Hubertus in **Hrusov** *Hrroo'-sohv*; Sonya calls them **Uncle** and **Auntie**)

ALOIS HUDLICKY *Al'-oh-ees Hood'-lich-kee* (postmaster near Hubertus; married to **Sarka**)

SAMES *Sah'-mesh* (forest ranger near Hubertus)

SROL *Shrol* (veterinarian near Hubertus)

BEDA BALADA and **LISAVETA BALADOVA** *Bay'dah* and *Lee'-sah-vay-tah Bal'-ah-dah/doe-vah* (Prague intellectuals summering at Hubertus)

PETRIK METELKA *Payt'-rzheek May'-tel-kah* (dyer at Hrusov Cottex)

RUDA MACH *Roo'-dah Mahk* (itinerant laborer and Sonya's first beau)

JARUNKA SLANA *Jah'-roon-kah Slaw'-nah* (Sonya's best friend, **Jaruna**)

ALENA BERKOVA *Ah'-lay-nah Bare'-koh-vah* (wife of pharmacist **Ph.Dr. Berka**, also Ph.Dr., summering at Hubertus)

JAKUB JAGR *Yah'-koob Yahh'-ger* (name of father (retired staff sergeant) and son (engineer at Usti Cottex, infatuated with Sonya)) **Zlatunka Jagrova** *Zlah'-toon-kah Yahh'-grow-vah* (Jakub Jr.'s sister, **Zlatus** *Zlah'-toosh*) **Kamila Ortova** *Kah'-meal-ah Ore'-toe-vah* (Jakub Jr.'s fiancée and neighbor)

JOSEF HNYK *don't bother* (the Hubertus drunk and informant)

MANEK MANSFELD *Mah'-nake* (mysterious stranger from Prague, **Manuel, M.M.**)

LUBOS BILY *Loo'-bohsh Bee'-lee* (Zlatunka's fiancé)

LANIMIR SAPAL *Lah'-nee-meer Zahh'-pal* (engineer at Cottonola in Usti, would-be writer)

VIT *Veet*, **CENEK** *Chay'-nake*, **LUMIREK** *Loo'-mee-rake*, **PAVEL ABRT** *Pah'-vayl Ahb'-ert* (the Cottonola bachelors)

IVANKA *Eve'-ahn-kah* and **BARBORKA** *Bahr'-bohr-kah* (the Cottonola bachelorettes)

MARIE JUNKOVA and **PETER JUNK** *Mah'-ree-ah* and *Pay'-tair Joonk* (Cottonola couple)

ANEZKA SBIRALOVA *Ahn'-ayzh-kah Sbeer'-ah-loh-vah* (Cottonola dorm housekeeper, **Sbiralka, Grannie**)

BERTIK LOHNMULLER *Bear'-teak Loan'-mool-air* (Ziki's coin supplier)

KRYSTOFEK *Kree'-shtoe-fake* (Jarunka's pet boy, **Krystof** *Kree'-shtohf*)

JELINEK *Yale'-eh-nake* (chef at Usti Cottex and Sonya's first boss there)

KAZIMIR DRAPAL *Kaz'-eh-meer Drahh'-pal* (librarian at Usti Cottex and Sonya's boss)

LUDVIK LUDVIK *Lood'-veek* (head of production at Usti Cottex and Sonya's boss, **L.L.**; his wife is **Zora** and his daughter is **Lanka**)

LADI TRINGL *Lahh'-dee Trreen'-gull* and **IVOS RYBICKA** *Ee'-vohsh Ri'-beach-kah* (L.L.'s assistants, **L.T.** and **I.R.**)

IDA PAPOUSKOVA *Ee'-dah Pah'-poh-oosh-koh-vah* (L.L.'s secretary, **I.P.**)

ARNO RYNOLT *Ahr'-noh Rree'-nohlt* (head of Cottex adjustment center in Prague; his wife is **Anna Rynoltova** *Ah'-nah*)

JOSEF NOVAK *Yoh'-sef Noh'-vahhk* (Anna's son)

VLADIMÍR PÁRAL *Vlah'-de-meer Pahh'-ral* (author of this novel)

BOOK ONE
SONYA'S HOTEL YEARS

The airy bluish folds of the second-floor lace curtains of Villa
Cynthia, built in the era of Art Nouveau and since then
modernized several times, each time more expensively (the last
time, last year, for an even hundred thou), came together with
a firm tug of the cord and formed a continuous veil, a signal
for the two below to conceal themselves in their designated
places and remain there on guard and motionless, no matter
what might happen in front of the villa's grilled entranceway.

Zahn nodded his head zealously as a signal to the window
above that he'd got the point. His wife, Zahnova, set down her
black suitcase, lined on the sides and corners in light-colored
leather, right next to the inward-facing side of the stone lantern
by the door, all precisely according to the scenario and so that
the entire scene could be viewed more easily and completely.
Both nodded their heads once more to the one above them,
obediently and joyfully (they both detested Aja), and disappeared into the entranceway, which they double locked, leaving
the key in the lock so that it would be impossible to dislodge it
using a similar key from the outside.

Engineer Zikmund Holy (49), tall and slender, clad in (first-
class) tailor-made trousers of fine-combed, light-beige wool,
and an exclusive chocolate-colored shirt made of natural silk,
with a sulfur-yellow tie magnificently displayed on a barely
discernible tummy, withdrew from the window and walked
noiselessly over the purple Turkish rug to the ebony glassed
sideboard; with the skillful, silent movements of a single hand
he unlocked and let down the massive door: on the counter thus
formed he placed a simply etched glass taken from the upper

section of the mirrored shelves and drew out and uncorked (always with a single hand) a bottle of Tarragona spiced wine, in one motion he poured his noontime dose into the glass (precisely the same—a finger's breadth below the top of the glass—as any other day) and with alpaca-lined tongs (always with a single hand) he lowered a circlet of lemon onto the surface of the wine. Aja will be surprised. But if she looks hard, will she be able to see anything from there? She won't look, of course, but let's hope we can hear her angry cries (and later, perhaps, her begging) through the casements of the side window, opened for just this purpose.

Unfaithful wives have been stoned, buried alive, immured, or at least whipped half-naked at the pillory — the unfaithful wife Aja Hola would in a very few minutes find a locked house and a suitcase full of her things standing next to the lantern to the left of the door. She won't take a good hard look, she'll curse. Vulgarly. At most she'll beg a bit . . . and we'll have a good view of that from here, through the lace curtains. Of course, the curtains could be opened, making the view somewhat more colorful, with sharper contours. Two, three, no more than five minutes of ecstasy. Zikmund took a sip of his drink.

What will follow? A small tug-of-war over the divorce, but not too much. He'll cope easily, as he has done twice before. If Aja's cheeky, I'll put the screws on. If she dares come here again, the Zahns will work her over in the garage. As they did that time with Marie. And then he'll be free. Chess, the mountains, and detective stories with iced champagne. And no more marriages again, ever. At most some sort of pick-me-up . . . something young, foolish, and obedient. Aja's room will be vacant. How many beautiful young girls will thank him for it . . . and oblige. Followed by ten hours a day of sleep, and playing with the cat.

Down the street, on the other side of the low metal fence with sharp points on top and stone pillars (the whole thing rebuilt for 8,600 crowns), came Aja Hola in a red dress with wildly huge white dots, white sandals (340 crowns), a white shopping bag (420 crowns) over her shoulder, tan and on the whole very pretty for her twenty-eight years, with a head of hair (her permanents cost 50 crowns a piece, but then who really knows how much, and hardly as often as she claims, as she has claimed until today), effectively disheveled from artfulness, recently experienced bliss, neglect, or to be provocative perhaps? I have prepared a little surprise for you, my love, and Zikmund took another sip, again a very small one. What mattered to him most was that today his noontime dose of Tarragona should last him until the soup arrived, as any other day.

Aja comes through the gate and walks along the main drive. He looks at his wristwatch (2,350 crowns) just at the moment when she ought to catch sight of her suitcase beneath the lantern. She tries the door. Again. She fishes for the key in her handbag. But somehow the key doesn't fit, of course. She's a bit confused now. Zikmund takes another sip.

"Mr. Zahn!" Through the open casement of the side window Aja's rapid breathing can be heard perfectly. In the entryway, Mr. Zahn hears, but doesn't listen.

"Mrs. Zahnova!" In the kitchen, Mrs. Zahnova rejoices silently.

Those two are marvelous. Their fifteen years at the Cynthia have been excellent training for them. They're perfect.

Aja steps back from the door and stumbles over her suitcase. "Ziki!"

Her eyes don't actually goggle, but her anger plays according to the script. Zikmund draws back the curtains so that she can see him easily from below. Behind the closed window he takes a sip. Let's wait now until she starts to beg.

"Ziki, are you playing some sort of crazy joke?"

Aja's face is turned upward. This is how I wanted it, dear. Behind the window Zikmund raises his glass as in a toast, but he doesn't drink, he only grins.

"Ziki, at least open the window. I'll explain everything — Ziki!"

Aja's lovely, tanned face is turned upward. It shines only on the temples, as it does after love-making. . . go down, let her in, tell lies again for a while, avail yourself once more of her tanned face with the moist temples on the white damask cushion—

"Ziki. You can't do this to me. . ."

I can do what I like. The momentary weakness passes, Zikmund looks at his watch and then again out the window. Aja opens the suitcase and then slams it shut again. Will she beg? Or will she carry on?

"Don't imagine that. . . I've got my papers and all my things in there . . . Ziki! This can't happen so suddenly. I'm going to the police!"

Her papers and documents are all bound in red in a pocket of the suitcase, and the police will find a house locked and silent. So now get the begging part over with and then clear out. In eleven minutes it'll be time to have my lunch.

"Ziki. Ziki. Please. . ."

Aja's lovely pleading face with its moist temples . . . now it's perfect. Zikmund closes his eyes with pleasure and permits himself—Aja had long since ceased to interest him—a glance at the golden ring and silver flesh of the circlet of lemon swimming in the warm brown wine.

Noiselessly he drew back from the window and refrained from facing it even when its glass broke behind his back, noiselessly he left the room as the stone quietly rolled across the purple rug and came to rest between the white lions and the stylized grapes. Zikmund left the room, cautiously stepping over the stone thrown by Aja's hand. He left the room with the unfinished drink, and by closing the door he filtered out the sound of Aja's curses (particularly coarse), on the staircase he found absolute quiet and slowly he descended the stairs to the entrance hall.

"She's gone now," said Zahn, and he would have laughed if that had been respectful.

"This evening change the locks on the front door and the gate."

"Preparations have already been made, sir."

"From now on, everything has to be locked. How about the ignition?"

"But you've already taken the keys. We could change it, but it wouldn't look pretty. I'd rather arrange a hidden switch for the electrical system; that would be useful, for instance, when we park in Prague overnight."

"Good. You're both off till Monday."

"Thank you, sir."

"Berta can serve lunch now."

Sitting alone at the long table in the ground-floor dining room, paneled in Finnish larch, Zikmund stirred his bouillon and egg and just before taking the first spoonful finished his noontime Tarragona.

Following lunch (veal cutlet *nature* with herb butter, cherry compote, grated roquefort cheese) and an hour's siesta (absolutely dreamless, save that just before waking he saw the tantalizing image of an unknown girl kneeling in a long children's nightshirt, a view from behind, but only a few seconds or so), a hot-and-cold shower, a good rub with a towel, in the entryway Zikmund took a packed weekend suitcase from Berta Zahnova, in front of the garage he got into his car (a low-to-the-ground, blue-black British Triumph), already started up by Wolf Zahn, its engine warm, gas tank full to the brim, oil full to the top line, and the battery charged, on the street he shifted into second gear and right away into third as he drove through Klise, Usti's ritzy section, and then the Vseborice prefab housing on his way to the concrete highway to the north, he shifted into fourth gear, switched on the radio, below Decin Castle he crossed the bridge over the Elbe, and after a further, pleasant fifty-minute drive up mountain roads to the resort town of Hrusov, at the foot of steep ridges, in the vicinity of Cottex Plant No. 08, along the main—and only—street on which, right behind the drugstore, there is an open field alongside a real log cabin, in the center of the round square a red gas pump and grass sprouting up out of the pavement, on the less frequented spots (especially the square) Swedish clover blooms purple, but everything is clean and the sharp air has the perfume of water.

OUR FIRST FLORICULTURAL EVENING proclaimed a handmade placard at the gate of the Hotel Hubertus, and Ziki drove into the hotel courtyard, the manager, Volrab, hastened to open the car door (he never failed to do this), his wife Volrabka wiped her hands on her apron and already she was rushing to carry his suitcase up to room No. 2, which is reserved in our name for the entire year.

Not a single customer in the bar, Zikmund took a seat at his table by the window. From the kitchen doorway the waitress, Sonya, smiled at him.

"The usual!" Zikmund shouted across the room, and in a businesslike manner he scrutinized Sonya, who leaned over the refrigerator, stood on her tiptoes to reach some glasses on the top shelf, carefully poured out the dry vermouth, and ran to the kitchen for a circlet of lemon.

Hair thick, long, passionately red, skin taut, fine, gleaming, shining green eyes, not even nineteen yet, beautifully developed, an erect carriage, breasts placed far apart, delicate shoulders and a delicate waist, a flat stomach underneath the tightly laced apron, long thighs and long legs . . . first-class stock, daughter of a brilliant surgeon and self-taught aesthete who, after a successful Prague practice, had built a villa here big as a castle and who, like a village squire, raised his daughter not for work but for marriage. But he died prematurely, his villa was turned into a dental clinic and the orphaned Sonya taken on as a housemaid, one who was now to be grateful to the Volrabs for a bed in the Hubertus kitchen, though she was shamelessly exploited by these two nimble fatties. She will give thanks on her knees, with her hands clasped.

Sonya spread a napkin over the metal tray, underneath his glass, and before coming out from behind the bar she pulled back her apron, smoothed her hair, and again smiled prettily. Created for a sensitive connoisseur. She would oblige. A little girl to be played with. When she's good, she'll get stockings and she'll be permitted to play the piano. And when she's bad, she'll be whipped.

"Sonya. Last time you told me you wanted to get away from here at any price. I have a nice room for you . . . everything you need."

The Hotel Hubertus' FIRST FLORICULTURAL EVENING (MUSIC — SINGING — RAFFLE two posters promised, both of them designed by Sonya employing bright crayons she still had from school, one she nailed up on the front door of the hotel, the other on the door of the post office at the Hrusov train station) filled the bar for the first time on a Sunday since the appearance of the local magician Tonik Magik three years before. The manager's wife, Volrabka (a sweaty slippery ball), was in the kitchen diluting the wine and turning out individual servings of salami. The music and singing were provided by Sonya (wearing a new green silk dress — it was the first time she'd ever appeared in the bar without her apron!) playing the ancient piano to frequent applause. At midnight Volrab (a sweaty slippery ball) drew the last of the second barrel of beer and declared the raffle open.

A total of seven customers had, for three crowns apiece, purchased tickets (pages from last year's desk calendar), to which the management of the hotel had added a free carnation (Volrabka had propagated two whole beds of these from a one-crown seed packet), and now Sonya was making the rounds of the tables with a basket containing the collected tickets covered with a napkin and the first (and only) prize (a horribly synthetic Metropol Dessert Wine, product of the Jilemnice starch factory, suddenly withdrawn from sale the year before last). Ticket No. 3, belonging to postmaster Alois Hudlicky (a pale, shy little man wearing lenseless spectacles), was the winner.

"And now our deserving postmaster will take the first and foremost prize of our Carnation Soirée, a bottle of the finest Cinzano Very Special French vermouth — may we have applause—" Volrab thundered in his whiskey bass, Alois Hudlicky bowed distractedly, Sonya smiled prettily, the customers clapped, and Volrab went fluently on: "—and in addition to the first prize, we are adding a further delicacy, our little Sonya, just come closer and you, Postmaster, come up here, sweets for the sweet, a kiss from our little Sonya — may we have some applause—"

Sonya kissed Alois Hudlicky on his sweaty bald pate, the bar filled with applause, and she stuck his carnation into her low neckline and then smiled prettily, the applause intensified. "We want one too—" the forest ranger, Sames, shouted (a fifty-year-old bearded bachelor), "we've paid for the flowers!" and the applause became thunderous, "For every — flower — a buss!" the white-haired veterinarian Srol chanted till his face turned red, and the whole bar lent its support.

"In view of the wishes of the honorable public, instead of a single carnation, we shall reward you all as a favor from our Hotel Administration, one sweet kiss — Sonya, come closer, and you, gentlemen, come up according to the number of the ticket you've drawn, and each of you will get applause as well—" and Volrab admitted each gentleman by number.

No. 1: The hunchbacked blacksmith at Cottex (his tall, beautiful, icy spouse followed his movements from and to their table with great distaste) — Smack!

No. 2: Beda Balada (an intellectual from Usti nad Labem, summer guest of the Hubertus, in Room No. 3) — Smack!

No. 3: The veterinarian Srol (at his table his silent spouse gazed at the tablecloth, after thirty-seven years of married life she did not dare say anything to him.) — Smack!

No. 4: Petrik Metelka (a bachelor colorist at Cottex, whose ears turned red at the moment he fulfilled his secret desire) — Smack!

No. 6: Ranger Sames (with his two thumbs and index fingers he cruelly stretched Sonya's face along its vertical axis, so that he might enjoy the so-called *kiss-and-pinch*) — Smack!

And No. 7: Ruda Mach (from his table Jarunka Slana, Sonya's

best friend, grinned at him, she had come to take leave of Ruda forever and spend her last night with him) — Smack! and Smack! (twice in all) and already shouts from the bar: "What's up?!" "Just one!" "Every one should get two!" To this Ruda Mach answered — Smack!

"How people work out their repressed ideas. . ." whispered the pharmacist Berka, wearing dark glasses (upset that he hadn't bought a ticket), his spouse (who also had a university degree) also in dark glasses (they were summer guests, in Room No. 6).

"But the girl really is quite chic," Alena Berkova said.

During No. 6's buss, Engineer Ziki Holy suddenly got up from his unfinished vermouth (carrying three losing tickets inside his jacket), and soon after him, a mysterious guest wearing dark evening attire disappeared inconspicuously.

"Innkeeper! Where are the rest of the tickets? I'll buy another three!" Ranger Sames shouted, and impatiently he readied his thumbs and index fingers.

"Let's have them here! I'll take five!" shouted silver-haired Srol.

"I'd like a couple more, too, Mr. Volrab," Petrik Metelka announced softly.

"I'm sorry, sir, but our raffle is quite finished and I must bring it to an end," Volrab thundered.

"Then let's have another round!" "There couldn't have been only seven tickets!" "I didn't get any!" "One more!"

"That's enough!" Volrab roared so loudly a thick blue vein broke forth in the middle of his bulging forehead, he struck the bar with a bunch of keys and, in the resulting silence, added good-naturedly, "Look here, gentlemen, closing time has long since come and gone. My wife and I are both very much obliged to you, but still you can't ask us to go on serving carnations at only three crowns apiece, when things are going to pot and for half an hour now no one has ordered so much as a beer. You have to agree, 'When there isn't any money, the show isn't very funny!'" And once again he struck the bunch of keys against the bar, and then once more. "Or does somebody wish to order something, perhaps?"

And so Ranger Sames ordered another small portion of salami, "plain" (and again he started rubbing his thumbs and index fingers together), the venerable Srol took it into his head to request "another large portion of your headcheese," but only when the bachelor Petrik Metelka ordered champagne did Volrab consent to go on, and at once he took firm charge of the proceedings.

"Ladies and gentlemen, kindly excuse me, but I shouldn't have to run back to the kitchen for each crappy little request. Mr. Hudlicky, you haven't eaten anything yet! Let's have two portions of real Hungarian salami, and then a bottle of French white, how 'bout it? And Mrs. Sarka'll have Italian salad and Mr. Srol salami with wine and Mr. Sames wine with salami, I'm already off to place the orders and there'll be more carnations. When there's money—you've got it!—the show is funny!"

At the piano, Sonya had turned pale and was smiling feebly, Volrab pushed into the kitchen, sent Volrabka to the garden to pick carnations, and (while Volrabka crawled about the garden with a flashlight in her teeth) skillfully cut the small portions of salami by a good third, he poured one glass from the bottle of wine and then filled the bottle up again with tap water, corked it again, and liberally doused the salami with paprika, pepper, and salt.

The carnations went like hot cakes, gentleman after gentleman got up from his table (in response to Sonya's fervent pleas, Uncle Volrab at last consented that she merely receive kisses and no longer give them) and the bar resounded without respite with Smack! Smack! Smack!

"I'll wait for you in the room, dear," Ph.Dr. Berkova said in a grating voice to Ph.Dr. Berka, the happy possessor of two carnations (all night long slaps could be heard coming from Room No. 6).

"Aren't you ashamed, it's so vulgar and base—" Lisaveta Baladova said in anger to her (for many years impotent) spouse

Beda, who grasped six carnations in his sweaty hand. "I shall hold her as long as I can, to protect her from this mob," the intellectual replied with dignity.

Into the bar stormed the young engineer Jakub Jagr (the guest in Room No. 4, who was attached for a month to the Hrusov branch of Cottex) with a suitcase in his hand. He dropped it rather than set it down, and rolled his eyes at the frantically kissed Sonya.

"What are you doing to her—" he groaned.

The heavy garage door banged shut so that the interrogation—two men growling at one another across the silhouette of the car—would be secret.

"What is your Sonya like?"

"She's. . . She's beautiful."

"Ha! Hmm! Nonsense. Her age—"

"Nineteen."

"Hmm. Height—"

"Five feet six."

"Hmm. Is she fit?"

"Completely. And wonderfully. . ."

"Hmm. Nonsense. How do you know?"

"If only you could see her for just a moment."

"Ha! Hmm! Nonsense. What can she do?"

"Everything."

"Nonsense. Education?"

"None actually, but. . ."

"Ha! Hmm. So what can she do?"

"Cook. Wash clothes. Make beds. Play the piano and sing."

"How can she earn a living?"

"She can be a waitress, a telephone operator, a salesgirl, a babysitter. . . the best thing would be a hostess. But I would be happy to take care of her myself. . ."

"Nonsense. Are you fond of her?"

"I'm mad about her."

"Nonsense. More than about Kamila?"

"That's something different. I've known Kamila for many, many years and I've got used to her."

"So marry her!"

"But when I love Sonya— do you understand? Even though I've known her only a couple of weeks. I'm fond of Kamila. But I love Sonya and I can't live without her!"

"So marry her!"

"Dad — if I could just bring Sonya home to live with us."

"You've got to choose one or the other. No woman's worth very much, but still you've got to choose. Make up your mind and then bring the better one home. I mean the one who's less bad. End of conversation."

Pre-war staff sergeant Jakub Jagr (51, father) energetically passed his hand over his short gray crewcut and set off at a brisk pace. (Now he's disappearing into his room, where no one dare follow him, and in the evening he'll go out to the garage to hear Jakub's vital decision.)

In torment, the young engineer Jakub Jagr (25, son) pressed his sweaty forehead against the windshield of the car. The one who's less bad.

According to Jakub's valuation tables, the comparison between Kamila and Sonya came out as follows:

Physical Characteristics:
Sonya (perfection)	100
Kamila (completely acceptable)	75

Character Traits:
Sonya (the ideal woman)	100!
Kamila (self-conscious, quiet, indifferent)	55

Erotic Attraction:
Sonya (maddeningly beautiful)	100!!!
Kamila (we've known her since childhood)	45

Education:
Sonya (never finished *gymnasium*)	20
Kamila (chemical engineer)	80

Living Conditions:

Sonya (poor as a churchmouse)	0
Kamila (a villa and all the property; the sole heir)	100

Social Status:

Sonya (a village orphan, exploited by grasping relatives)	0
Kamila (a member of the cream of society of Usti nad Labem)	100

Kamila totals 455, Sonya 320. But *Education* can be upped to 100 (in Sonya's case), while *Character Traits* (in Kamila's case) show a tendency to deterioration (as can already be seen). And what are all Kamila's 455 points compared to the glowing 100!!! of Sonya's beauty — and if *Love* for Kamila is 100, then love for Sonya must be at least 10,000.

The strong June sun at noon on Sunday beat down upon the young engineer when he emerged from the darkness of the garage, and with dark wet crescents under his armpits he trudged through the baked yard, from the door of the white villa his mother looked at him, but didn't dare ask him anything (Jagr women wait silently for the men's decisions), Jakub lurched through the corridor, with both her legs his sister, Zlatunka, swiftly stopped the motion of her rocking chair, but then went right on rocking (Jagr women are silent even when they want to scream), Jakub avoided the insistence, rage, and despair of his sister's eyes, ran upstairs to his room on the second floor, and double-locked the door behind him.

On the hygenically clean floor protected by a polymer enamel coating, a tightly-woven, firm, thin carpet *bouclé*, bright blue in color (but darkened near the window by the thousandfold marks of a naked, exercising body), metal furniture and a narrow metal bed with a thin, hard mattress, dazzlingly white bed linen, on the wall a spring exerciser for the biceps, a sculpture of a tiger's head, and two walls covered with bookcases holding a good 355 square feet of technical books, scifi, and mysteries.

Beyond the graceful swaying of the radiant tops of apple and cherry trees, in a similarly beautiful garden, the very similar villa of the Jagrs' neighbors, the Orts, whose daughter Kamila was looking forward to her wedding, as were all the Jagrs and all the Orts, for all was long since decided and readied for the joy and prosperity of the two neighboring houses: the newly-weds Jakub and Kamila will get the luxurious second floor of the Orts' yellow villa, while for Zlatunka and her fiancé the luxurious second floor of the Jagrs' white villa will be vacated, and so the thus united families will live together forever, as in a fairy tale. . .

(Beyond the graceful swaying of the radiant tops of apple and cherry trees, Kamila Ortova is standing in the second floor of the yellow villa, by the window with cream-colored curtains — behind her a large cabinet crammed with her trousseau, the most expensive damasks and the finest linens with red mono-grams in the corners, the family silver in leather caskets, and crested china — if Jakub doesn't whistle at the garden gate today either, then it's all over for him).

All I have to do now is go downstairs and shout, "I'll marry Kamila!" And my parents will be glad and Zlatunka will be glad, all I have to do is cross the garden and whistle at the Orts' silver-gray garden gate, the elder Orts will smile benignly from their garden table, Kamila, smiling too, will rise and walk to-ward me along the pebble walk *I would run to meet Sonya*, with Kamila on our Sunday walk to Strizov Forest *just as so many hundreds of Sundays before, WITH SONYA IT WOULD ALL BE FOR THE VERY FIRST TIME,* by the old oak Kamila will turn her face and passively let it be kissed, *kneeling I would kiss Sonya's knees,* my wedding to Kamila is set for August, the wedding guests will dance on our lawn under Chinese lanterns and in the evening in our bedroom on the second floor Kamila will stand in front of the mirror and slowly begin to remove her wedding veil, *I would see Sonya reflected in that mirror and burst into tears,* Kamila's sweaty face in the maternity ward where my child will be born, *Sonya's sweaty face in the maternity ward where my child will be born,* care for the child would take so much of

Kamila's time that she would cease to care for herself, *Sonya will still be beautiful at forty,* Kamila would start getting bored, and me too, *I will love Sonya forever. . .* Now I know that I would not really be happy with Kamila, I REALIZE AT LAST THAT IT IS SONYA I WANT—

The nervous tension of the past few weeks was suddenly swept away by intense happiness, and the young engineer lay down on the floor, groaned, and then, turning on his back, his hands behind his head, he dreamt for hours on the firm blue carpet.

Not until the approach of evening did Jakub get up decisively and pack four white shirts in his suitcase (normally two would have sufficed) and, after a brief hesitation, he added two more, from his secret cache inside the dust jacket of Dorothy L. Sayers' *Murder Must Advertise* he drew out his entire "emergency" cash fund of 2,700 crowns (normally 300 would have sufficed, taken from the envelope marked "Official Travel") and he stuffed it into his black breast pocket, with a dry feeling in his throat he spread out on the suitcase an elegant pair of shorts made of sparkling scarlet silk (when I bought them, a week ago now, I didn't think about Kamila at all—) and quickly he snapped the suitcase shut and now he was marching and now he was galloping down the stairs.

In the hallway, his father, mother, and Zlatunka looked up from their canasta. Three spreads of cards barely fit among the glasses on the black-stained oak.

"You haven't been to see Kamila today," his mother remarked into the rigid silence (the twenty-year friendship with the Orts next door is turning into bitter, life-long warfare).

Zlatunka jumped out of her rocker, ran out the door, and banged it behind her (her fiancé will have to begin looking for an apartment at once).

Without a word Jakub quickly walked straight to the garage and stood there with his face to the wall until he heard his father's footsteps behind him and the banging of the heavy garage door.

"I hear—" the staff sergeant barked in the gloom.

"Sonya!"

"Ha! Hmm! Nonsense. Is it definite?"

"Absolutely."

"Hmm. Good. Kamila was a fine girl — but she doesn't have the spark. I approve."

"Dad — you really mean—" Jakub turned around and ran toward his father, if the narrow lane between the wall and the car would have permitted, he would even have (the Jagrs never kiss, as a matter of principle) *kissed* him.

"And that Sonya of yours — has she got the spark? Sure! I'll be able to tell from far away, from the way she walks. You can tell with a horse or a woman. Hmm! Ha! Ha! Bring her here on Saturday!"

"Of course, by all means. I'd be happy to. . . except. . . she may not want to."

"Ha! Hmm! Nonsense. I want to see her. If she's got the spark — Ha! Ha! Ha!"

"Now that I'm certain, it will all go quickly. I'll have a chance to talk with her this evening—"

"A chance to talk with her! Hmm! Nonsense. Men don't talk with women. Are you a man? Well then! You must conquer her!"

"Yes, Dad."

"No long drawn-out rigmarole! All is fair in love and war— ha! Everything! You understand? Ha! Ha! Ha!"

"On Saturday I'll parade Sonya before you."

Jakub Jagr left via the garden and then, his face rigid, he walked past the fence and the Orts' silver-gray garden gate. Ort, his wife, and Kamila were sitting at their garden table, silent and flint-like.

(Kamila's face became rigid and her fine white fingers crushed a corner of the yellow tablecloth, even though it was woven with the red monogram that you chose, Jakub Jagr, tonight will be the last time I shall weep — *it's only that we're too close to one another here, don't you agree? But for that reason we will meet again many times, and under different circumstances* — and Kamila's face hardened again.) As if on shards crackling under his feet Jakub took the shortcut across the grassy slope that for so many years was my path and yours, Kamila, *we always used to kiss under this oak tree,* and suddenly moisture forced its way into Jakub's eyes, this our beloved green vale will never again be what it was, as I will never again be a boy, the tears pour over his cheeks and burn, from time immemorial LOVE, WOMEN, SEX, MARRIAGE meant the same thing as Kamila, and breaking up with Kamila suddenly seems the same as amputating my feet. —*Darling Sonya, appear and lighten this my last moment of unhappiness,* but from my shoulderblades wings are already budding — there's nothing for a legless angel to do but fly.

From the longest platform at the Usti train station there's a wonderful view of the Elbe rolling on toward the ocean, and in the final rays golden dust was dancing (Kamila had already ceased to exist), with his suitcase Jakub marched along the concrete platform, and the bright smoke of the Orient-Express made him suddenly feel wonderful, he recalled that he'd had nothing to eat since breakfast and at a kiosk he bought four cold green meat patties and a pocket flask of brandy with a bakelite stopper.

The train rushed across the mightily flowing river and on its rippled surface the fateful day was perishing magnificently, Jakub chewed the meat, gulped down the brandy from the bakelite, and thought of Sonya, she IS wonderful, but she must be stripped of those base habits of the waitress and the maid, of laughing at anyone who buys a glass of beer, of flirting with deliverymen for free, the wife of Engineer Jakub Jagr must be respectable and must have CLASS, to re-educate Sonya toward this end means to reduce her to the molecules from which a new personality can be erected—

It is only a short stroll from the little Hrusov station through the village to the Hotel Hubertus, even shorter at a brisk gait, and out of breath Jakub barged into the hotel with his suitcase—

the suitcase which he now dropped rather than set down in the doorway to the bar:

Sonya at the piano in a green dress and around her drunken jubilation and shouting, scumbag after scumbag took her in his arms, pressed her to himself, and shamelessly licked both cheeks, arms, shoulders, and her neck — and Sonya did not *defend* herself in the least, Sonya even *smiled* — and from the bar her guardian Volrab watched and *laughed* — from the kitchen doorway her guardian Volrabova *laughed* at the sight — and Volrab signed up more and more scumbags and guffawed at the entire company.

"What are you doing to her?" groaned Jakub.

"It's a floricultural evening." the ebullient Ph.Dr. Berka informed him. "Wouldn't you like to have a kiss too? For a mere three crowns in the local currency, and that girl really puts on a performance! Get your change ready and join the line there by the counter."

Sonya's pale face and green frock kept disappearing behind the red, sweat-streaked napes and the unbuttoned jackets of the scumbags, and reappearing after a frightfully muggy smacking of lips, with her dress woefully rumpled and on Sonya's face yet another damp red stain, Sonya's pitiful smile — or was it a smile of pleasure?! — one customer would take her whole face in his hand, the next one would hook her face with his elbow and then slide his free hand over the contours of her body—

Jakub rushed out of the bar into the cool night, it's only a short stroll from the Hotel Hubertus to the station, even shorter at a mad dash, beyond the station there's nothing but a dark meadow and woods, with his suitcase in hand Jakub ran through the darkness of the woods, stumbled on roots, and ran on and up all the way to the crest of the mountains, and in the glassy gleam of the moonlight, lying among the black skeletons of trunks uprooted by a tempest, he wept bitterly.

Infinitely later, toward morning, he got up and knocked on the door of the sleeping Hotel Hubertus, under the stars, so clear here because they're so close, and only the murmur of the mountain stream answered out of the night's coolness. Jakub set down his suitcase and with both his fists he began to hammer away at the poster that began with the words FIRST FLORICULTURAL EVENING.

With a lit flashlight in her hand Sonya came at last to open the door, over her long nightshirt a shabby greatcoat (a very fat gentleman's) and barefoot on the cold stone floor . . . you wanted to weep for her.

"Sonya, I love you! I really do! And I've decided to marry you."

Sonya rubbed her bare ankles against one another and smiled prettily at Jakub.

"Sonya, you can't stay here another day. I'll find you a job and a place to live. And then I'll take you home with me, to Usti—"

"Uncle and Auntie won't let me go."

"Sonya! You must come with me. I love you. Today I broke my engagement for your sake. I can't live without you. Do you hear? I love you!"

Sonya took a step back, away from Jakub, the cone of light from the flickering flashlight shone on the contours of her waist, the bend of her elbow, the curve of her neck beneath the cascade of glittering liquid copper hair, 100!!! Sonya's beauty soared to a score of at least 100,000, Jakub reached for her and pressed her against the wall, suddenly he lurched, blinded by the shining lens pressed to the bridge of his nose, and already she had torn free of him, then the rattle of a key in the lock and Sonya's laughter behind the locked door.

As if beaten up, Jakub crawled to the hotel entrance and in his room No. 4 he slammed down his suitcase. When he opened it, the red silk of the shorts lying on top struck him a vicious blow below the belt.

With clenched fists Jakub marched across his bare room, and when he began to feel cramped there, he marched up and down the nighttime second-floor corridor on the red coconut matting past the doors of the hotel rooms, MEN DON'T TALK WITH

WOMEN, *are you a man?* I haven't been, Dad, but now I will be (from room No. 6 slaps and a woman's cries), YOU MUST CONQUER HER (from room No. 5 the "Big Beat" of consummated love), ALL IS FAIR IN LOVE AND WAR—

Jakub flew down the stairs to the ground floor, on the way he fingered his breast-pocket wallet crammed with its emergency 2,700 crowns, *wouldn't you like to have a kiss too? For a mere three crowns that girl really puts on a performance! Get your change ready and join the line* — when she's given so much, then why not me too, again Jakub fingered the wad of banknotes over his heart, *no long drawn-out rigmarole* and I'll buy that girl 900 times running.

The front door of the hotel was locked and so was the door to the kitchen, of course. But not the toilet for the bar's customers (crumpled carnations on wet paving stones) and Jakub crawled through the narrow window and jumped down into the darkness of the courtyard.

The kitchen window was wide open and from the inside, through the complete darkness, shone an odd, narrow, zigzag chink stretching across the room, suddenly it moved, swelled up, and then zigzagged again, evidently the floricultural evening was still in progress — no matter, I too will up the stakes—

Jakub swung through the window, crept toward the transverse, chest-height strip of light, and inserted one hand into it, he was grasping a featherbed from beneath and firmly he yanked it off: underneath the featherbed, lying on her stomach in her long nightshirt, Sonya was reading a book by the beam of her flashlight.

"Listen here, Mr. Jagr!" she hissed.

"Forgive me, Sonya, I just thought that. . ."

"Shh! — You have no business thinking! Get right out of here!"

"I can't leave, Sonya, till you promise me. . ."

"Shh! — I'll promise you tomorrow, but now get out or you'll wake Uncle!"

"I could spit on that fat, vile, no-good—"

"Shh! — Jakub . . . go away!"

"Sonya, you're so wonderful and beautiful and—"

"Shh! — Let go of me, or— Shh!"

"Sonya. My love—"

"Shh!"

After a little jostling, Jakub felt Sonya's soles on his chest, he leaned toward them and was kicked so hard he stumbled and knocked over a chair. Sonya slipped out of bed and ran to another door.

"Stop or I'll shoot!" Volrab's voice could be heard from that direction.

"My husband's got a gun!" Volrabka shrieked from the same direction.

(The exhausted Sonya had hardly been able to stand on her feet when her Uncle Volrab pushed old man Srol, the final participant in the FIRST FLORICULTURAL EVENING, out into the night. A total of 126 carnations had been sold.)

"Our pantry's been cleaned out," Volrab rejoiced, "and the cellar too."

"I'd never have thought we could get rid of that potato salad from last Thursday," whispered Volrabka, touched. "It was a big success, my darling, big as a building!"

Volrab cut his wife a huge hunk of bread and spread it thick with lard, Volrabka threw two half-pound sausages on to boil for her husband, at once they began to eat and at the same time count their take (greasy, gleaming fingerprints on the crumpled banknotes), which exceeded their wildest dreams (and the greasy kiss-marks of their gleaming, greasy lips), with her fingers Volrabka fished fried pork rinds out of the pan, dipped them in salt, and tossed them smack into her gullet. Volrab opened a large container of Spanish sardines, salted the entire contents and, without even a slice of bread, ate them off his knife, incessantly chewing he drew four beers, gulped them down, and then two more (Sonya drank a glass of milk and before going to bed she aired out and cleaned up the bar) and then they all went to bed.

"For tomorrow evening we'll make a walnut cake with peanuts and margarine, a whipped-cream cake with eggwhites, and ice cream with powdered eggs," Volrabka dreamed while Volrab unfastened her bra.

"With those canned herrings I'll make real Parisian rolled anchovies, and with last year's currants I'll make 'Extra Special' Swedish punch," Volrab rejoiced as he crawled under his featherbed.

"To think that we even sold that potato salad from Thursday. . ." Volrabka whispered, entranced, her hands behind her head.

"We had a fine soirée, that's for sure. And the next one will be much finer. Success after success!" Volrab addressed the darkness.

"I still don't feel sleepy," Volrabka snickered, and she pinched her husband hard on his fat hip, "How about it, you devil?" and again she gave her husband a mighty pinch on his hip.

"But it's time to make sleepy-bye, darling," Volrab grumbled, rolled over, and peacefully fell asleep.

Volrabka went on snickering a while (she was thinking of those delicious war years, of our old Hotel Globus across from the Usti railway station, of the brisk trade in the bar and in the guest rooms whenever a train arrived from the front or a boat anchored in the harbor, there were times when even Mme. Wohlrab herself was pressed into service for the warm young bodies of those starved beautiful boys from the Navy and the Wehrmacht) and then she too fell asleep, happy that they had sold Thursday's potato salad.

Suddenly awakened by noise from the kitchen, the door of their bedroom violently thrown open, and on the threshold a dark figure.

"Stop or I'll shoot!" roared Volrab, and he rolled out of bed in search of a poker.

"My husband's got a gun!" Volrabka screamed, and in no time her hand was equipped with a long knitting needle.

"Uncle! Auntie! It's just me!" cried Sonya. In the twinkle of an eye the Volrabs were standing on the alert like cranes (the nights at the Globus had been wild ones whenever a train arrived from the front or a boat anchored in the harbor) on both sides of the bed, he with his outstretched poker, she with the pointed end of her needle projecting forward (employees can do ugly things sometimes).

"It was only Engineer Jagr coming to get something," Sonya explained breathlessly.

"And you let him in?" asked Volrabka.

"He came in through the window. I was airing out the kitchen."

"So run then and get that window closed!" Volrabka screamed, and she turned to her husband: "What could he want so late?"

"But you know, my darling, what the young man might want from our Sonya."

"But that's vulgar — why, he didn't even come to our evening!"

"Sonya darling, have you closed the window? . . . And the front door's locked? Well then, come and go beddy-bye between the two of us, you know we won't give you up. . ."

"But there's no point in. . ." Sonya started to object, but then stopped herself (one didn't make objections to the Volrabs).

And the Volrabs placed Sonya between them in the marriage bed, almost tenderly, without Sonya it wouldn't have been a success and that potato salad would have gone to feed the pig, with their hands they kept reassuring themselves in the dark that they really had Sonya (at the same time appraising how well she had developed, just right for a colonel from the General Staff wearing an order of laurel leaves, swords, and diamonds), and they fell asleep full of their cares, which were by no means small ones considering the fragile nature of the goods (but we know very well how to deal with such things).

That Sunday morning, on the second floor of the Hotel Hubertus in Room No. 5, face to the wall, Ruda Mach slept in the nude and beside him Jarunka Slana, dressed in Ruda's shirt (her back supported by a pillow propped against the headboard), she was smoking his cigarettes on an empty stomach and swallowing her tears.

The last time, the end, never again. Ruda's brown face, drenched by the rain, and his laugh when he picked her up on the highway, a waterlogged hitchhiker just kicked out of her house . . . in nothing but the outfit she happened to be wearing . . . and his rough hands running through her hair to wring the water out of it, then along her chin, her neck, to warm her up faster . . . and later on that night, and for hours now in this room and long after love-making was over his hot palms went on warming her frozen soles. Could it really have been no longer than two months?

With Ruda love unfortunately has no continuation. He knocks about hotels, everything he owns in a single suitcase, when he needs a girl he puts himself out and can be quite charming. But in the morning he gives her the boot—the beast.

He's just an animal. But a young girl needs a husband, a place to live, and security—

With a snarl Ruda turned over on his back and began to snore quietly. In ever widening golden trapezoids the morning sun moved toward a guitar which hung next to the scuffed-up door.

Farewell, my love, whispered Jarunka, and tears dripped onto her breasts, why do things in this world never go the way a person would like them to — and stubbornly she tried to think of her fiancé, Dr. Lubos Sedivy, of the new, cosy little apartment on the eighth floor of a new building. Of the new blue gown hanging in her closet, of the reception hall rented for the wedding, and the row of garlanded automobiles in front of the Palace Hotel, but Ruda Mach snoring louder and louder made these highly artificial images collapse and Jarunka ran her damp cheeks along his cool skin, scraping against his growing beard, and she swept his face with her hair until finally he woke up.

"Hi, love," yawned Ruda, without even glancing at her, he took a quick look at his watch, which he never took off, and already he was on his feet, he stretched at the window until his joints cracked, and then placidly and powerfully he broke wind, then drank down half the water in a tin pitcher, splashing the remainder on his face and neck and shoulders, the running water shone on his rough brown back, a hard, mobile sculpture of muscles and tendons, and it shone like mercury in the dark growth on his chest.

"Hand me my shirt," he growled, and as he pulled it over his wet body, the fabric marbleized. "So get going already," he growled impatiently and with rising anger. He always wakes up in a rage and he has never known how to say goodbye.

A final look at Ruda's room, the green bed, the scratched-up guitar on the wall, the never closed closet door, and then already the cold stairs down (when I climbed them I might have experienced all the love of my life) and in the bright morning glare in front of the Hotel Hubertus Jarunka had to lean against the dew-covered railing.

"Well, so long," said Ruda.

"I could wait for you until you come back this afternoon."

"There's no sense dragging things out any longer."

"What else do you have to say to me?"

"Have a good time."

"I never had so good a time with anyone as I did with you — and I never will."

"Hell, you act as if I were leaving you, and not you me. Jesus, are *you* getting married, or am I? Well, don't bawl any more, girlie . . . Well, so long."

And Ruda leapt over the railing (silvery droplets of dew rolled down the metal poles like tears) and already he had gone, from the meadows below the tracks mist was rising and the wind drove white shreds of paper past the red gas pump, Ruda thrust his hands into his pockets, started to whistle, and walked off through the summer morning, a fellow who knew how to make every girl happy, but once he'd made it with her didn't know where to go from there.

While Jarunka Slana went on weeping in the hotel kitchen with her best girlfriend Sonya, Ruda Mach was walking through the entryway of Cottex Plant No. 04 (a good-natured Old World building that looked like vanilla ice cream with whipped cream on top, geraniums at the windows and a red star on the roof, a meadow in front, a mountain stream in back, and beyond that nothing but forest up to the sky), at the red-and-white barrier he pinched the gatekeeper on her mighty backside, and before she had stopped squealing with fright he was out in the meadow pinching a young lab assistant on her rosy little posterior and rumpling the front of her too loose-fitting white labcoat, he threw his shirt into the bleaching room, in the course of two beers he lined the rest of the chlorinating basin with alkaline-resistant tiles, he was unusually adept and the work whistled through his fingers, he went into the office to give a piece of his mind to the time-and-motion spies, in the director's office he mortally offended Director Kaska as well as the technical inspector from the Usti branch, Engineer Jakub Jagr, in the lab he again rumpled the lab assistant and sent her out for a pound of bloody headcheese, meanwhile he stuck into his pocket four sample skeins of the finest Egyptian cotton called *mako* (far more delightful than toilet paper) and went to sit for a bit in an outhouse overlooking the Jizera River.

(". . .but what if you had to choose between unreliable love and marriage to a Ph.D. who has his own apartment with central heating, a balcony, and a car!" cried Jarunka Slana in the Hubertus kitchen, drawing her knees under her chin, still in tears.

"Love, nothing but love!" Sonya said decisively as she attacked the potatoes energetically with a scraper.)

The outhouse on the river only had three sides, in place of a fourth there was a view of the valley from the circular opening one sat on, Ruda Mach pulled out of the back pocket of his lowered trousers a brass-bound wallet, spread out his pay and his papers on his bare knees, and buried himself in administrative work.

As a trained insulator and specialist in alkaline- and acid-resistant pavings, tiles, putties, glues, special cements, brick-work, and paints, Ruda Mach always found well-paid work wherever he took it into his head to go. Most of the year he worked in the great industrial complexes of Northern Moravia and Eastern Slovakia, where there's good company and a fellow has a fine time, but when the meadows blossom he would head out with his school map on a tour of places where so far he had never been. And the heads of small factories stuck away in charming tourist sites would outdo one another in their bids to the experienced specialist, who could do by himself as much as a whole gang could, they replied with costly express telegrams to his scrawled notes written with a carpenter's pencil, they sent him their own cars to pick him up at the station and they were glad to pay for his hotel rooms.

(". . .because Ruda Mach has a white liver," Jarunka sighed across the hot stove with such emphasis that Sonya dropped her ladle into a casserole of boiling goulash soup.

"A white liver—" Sonya repeated with horror, "What does that mean?"

"It means that as a man he's simply fan-tas-tic—")

In the great industrial complexes of Northern Moravia and Eastern Slovakia women are scarce and unavailable. Ruda Mach loved girls and had a burning need for them.

When he had thoroughly counted his pay (he was an expert at complex special pay rates and knew them better than any bookkeeper did), he stuffed the roll of banknotes into the crammed compartments of his wallet, got up, made use of all four skeins of cotton, in the lab he packed his mouth full of bloody headcheese and then in the bleaching room by noon he had finished a day's worth of work, he hurled heavy shovels

full of wet insulating material into the wire netting high above
his head, at a fast tempo and without a single pause, more the
sporting elegance of a handsome naked body exerting itself
than a construction worker's drudgery (joy from using one's
muscles along with joy from letting them relax, and joy from
food, from making love, from cold water and from sleep, Ruda
Mach had felt one or another of these joys continuously
throughout his thirty-one years), at last with a fine trowel he
smoothed out the solidifying mass into rounded shapes (he was
thinking of a girl's body and of joy), perfectly and with tenderness (a touch obedient to the material and with joy), then he
stepped back from his work and with his head bent toward one
shoulder he appraised it: it was good and it was finished (joy).

(". . .and keep an eye on him. Understand?—" said Jarunka,
and Sonya avoided her penetrating gaze, she bent over the
chives on her chopping board and the skin on her neck turned
red — both girls held their breath for a moment in a special
tension in which sympathy was strangely mixed with envy, and
pleasure with pain — it lasted only a second and already Sonya
was chopping her chives again and Jarunka was continuing to
rinse her reddened eyelids with strong tea. The girls no longer
had anything to say to each other and in a little while Jarunka
Slana was hitchhiking to Usti to get married.)

The factory meadow ended at the confluence of the millrace
and the river, in a wild triangle of never-mown prairie, buried
in yard-high grass, Ruda Mach lay on his stomach and, his eyes
closed, placidly devoured what was left of the bloody headcheese wrapped in greasy newsprint, then he lazily stretched
his front paws (rough as a tire and beautiful as a javelin-
thrower's) and with his face on his hands he slowly closed his
eyes, he felt wonderful, and when Ruda Mach feels wonderful
he starts getting bored. For amusement he rolled over on his
back, and when his fat wallet started to pinch him in the hip he
rolled over again as he had been before, pulled his wallet out
of his back pocket, held it firmly in his teeth, and with his bare
elbows he parted, bent, and broke off the grass in front of his

nose until he'd made a clearing two feet square; on this he carefully laid out his wallet.

Bound on the corners with brass strips, the smudged leather was stretched taut with compartments jammed fat as a box of candy. The right or "business" half was stuffed with pay slips, hotel bills, urgent telegrams from directors, a thick wad of hundred-notes, already stamped blank forms, and court summonses.

The left or "pleasure" half was taken up mostly by his sixteen-times-folded school map, and crammed in its folds and in the leather were postcards from pals with more in the way of signatures than actual messages, and long-drawn-out letters from girls, a photo of a half-naked black girl from *Youth World*, and photos of girls with the marks of small-town photographers on the back and brief texts such as *Never forget, Hanka,* or *With love from Ph.Dr. Zdislava Tanningerova-Boricka,* a fragment of an envelope with a red Sierra Leone stamp, a colorful coaster from the Munich brewery Olympiator with a tiger licking up beer foam inside a circular caption, *Was der Tiger unter den Teiren ist der Olympiator unter den Bieren,* and a calendar for an entire year on one side of a waxed card. With a fingernail Ruda scratched out last Sunday's date till it was illegible (for the part of the year that had already passed, there were only dug-up strips), he put the calendar back into the "pleasure" side, the wallet into his trousers and, chewing on a stalk of grass, he turned over once more onto his back, now waiting only for the honking of the siren.

At the tiny swimming pool (a couple of minutes from the plant) he was again lying on his stomach in order to view the Hrusov summer visitors, but his boredom only increased, none of the men could possibly be compared to him and none of the women aroused any stir of feeling in him, so then he rolled around in a cool fishpond, chewed on reeds, dived, reemerged, and snorted when he ran into the floating green water plants, again he was lying in the grass in the sun and then again in a frantic crawl he rushed across the pond like a typhoon, a whirlwind of spraying water, foam, swirling mud, and bits of grass, twigs and tattered leaves.

Lazily Ruda trudged through the empty, glowing streets leading to the Hotel Hubertus, on the gates of which the poster from yesterday's Floricultural Evening was still lit, in the empty bar he at once ordered two beers from Sonya, one for thirst and the other for pleasure, the other one he pushed aside with just the dregs left and ambled up to his room No. 5 and, just as he was, with his boots still on, he collapsed onto his freshly-made bed, he was extremely bored (suddenly he longed for the bustle of the crowded dorms of the great industrial complexes of Northern Moravia and Eastern Slovakia, where a fellow never feels sad), suddenly he got up and went to sit by the window with his guitar, for an hour perhaps he strummed morosely (used as he was to hard sixteen-hour shifts and then the rest of the night playing cards, he felt physically almost a captive of this sleepy hotel room, his muscles twitching restlessly like a stallion kept too long in a stable), already this feeling had faded, he roared in anger, slammed his guitar down on the table, slammed himself down on the bed, and when he felt his brass-bound wallet against his hip, he quickly sat up and opened it on his knees.

From the "pleasure" side he drew out his old school map and the calendar, with his finger he traced a road along the mountain chains shown in brown (he was fond of mountains), looking especially for mountains which had a lake (he suddenly felt a longing for a lake, any sort of lake), until he discovered a promising blue oval located on one side of a dotted brown mountain (2,500 to 3,000 feet above sea level), and on the other side a ring with a dot inside it (a town of 5,000 to 10,000 inhabitants), there it would be no problem finding specialized work for Ruda Mach and already he was reaching with his finger for the calendar (suddenly resolved to get the hell out tomorrow morning).

Just then, outside the door, a woman's scream, the smashing and clanging of metal, Ruda sprang out into the corridor — in her green dress from the Floricultural Evening Sonya was kneeling on the floor and collecting broken dishes on a tray.

"This will get me another licking," she sighed.

"Naturally, I will pay for everything," Engineer Ziki Holy said in a grating voice, he was standing in the open door of Room No. 2 across the hall, "Come in, please, inside, just for a second, and I'll give you some cash."

"I'd rather get a slapping from my Auntie!" said Sonya.

"Come back to my room and you'll get the money right away. We really can't stand here in the corridor—"

"That's a pile of horseshit and all for some stupid crockery," said Ruda (he had no love for engineers), "I'll give you a century note, Sonya, without the horseshit and right away. Come on in—"

With her tray full of broken crockery Sonya crossed the hall to Room No. 5 and on the threshold Ruda clapped a hundred-note on the tray and bared his teeth.

"What did that old fogey want?"

"He claims he's sick, but actually he's shamelessly healthy."

"But you'd shake up a dead man three days buried. Just think how you sent those old fogies off their rockers yesterday."

Sonya rubbed her bare ankles against one another and smiled prettily at Ruda (and imperceptibly she closed the door behind her).

". . .it's because you're such a pretty girl."

"Prettier than Jarunka?"

"Don't give her a second thought. She's not important."

"She told me lots of things about you."

"I'll bet a lot of it was made up."

"I don't think so. Are you still fond of her?"

"I like her and I don't like her," said Ruda, sticking to the truth.

"And now you're going off to find another one—"

"Maybe so." (In the circle with the dot something would be sure to show up.)

"So you don't like it here anymore?"

"What would there be here for me to like?"

Sonya rubbed her bare ankles against one another and smiled prettily at Ruda. Ruda slowly pushed her hands, which were holding the tray, away from her body (as if unveiling her) and slowly he looked her over from her flaming red hair all the way to her tiny ankles and naked, delicate little toes, Sonya opened her mouth just a bit and it was as if she had stopped breathing (he made a mental note of this), nakedly she endured Ruda's eloquent gaze, which bored straight into her eyes, then her lips, her shoulders — until she drew the tray back to her breast again (as if resuming the veil), but she remained in Ruda's room (he made a mental note of this) and her green eyes illuminated her (he had never had so beautiful a girl).

Ruda slowly drew Sonya to himself, softly kissed her hair, and then pushed her from his room. Again he reached with his finger for the calendar and again on his school map he found the small blue oval of the lake, he sighed (but the lake will still be there a thousand years from now) and crammed it all back into his wallet, shoved the wallet back into his trousers, and with his guitar resumed his place at the window (his mind suddenly made up).

Hotelier Volrab was most pleased when he woke up alone, from the kitchen the sweet sounds of pots cooking and his wife singing, there's no denying the fact that I haven't lived in vain in this world and I've had my share of experiences too, Volrab twisted pleasurably underneath the warm featherbed and snickered softly (he was recalling the delightful war years, with our old Hotel Globus across from the Usti railway station, the brisk trade in the bar and in the guest rooms whenever a train arrived from the front or a boat anchored in the harbor, there were times when, early in the morning, even Herr Wohlrab himself had to go upstairs to the guest rooms and the fresh, sweet, drowsy flesh), he reflected with pleasure on yesterday's success and full of zest for life he woke merrily to Monday morning, on the kitchen table he was greeted by a liqueur glass of rum for his digestion, a big mug of white coffee with the skin of the milk on it, and a mighty wedge of sponge cake spread with strawberry jam and covered with sweet cream, with his mouth still full he set the day's menu with Volrabka and gave Sonya a whole list of tasks, the girl had to flit hurriedly through the kitchen, the bar, and the pantry, "And don't forget to bring in some parsley—," when you don't keep close supervision, the workforce may get fidgety, "—and scrub the bar and change the light bulb in the hallway!"

"I'm not real sure, you devil, whether I can wangle Spanish cutlet out of this," Volrabka announced, sticking her finger into a plate full of green strips of meat.

"How many days has it been?"

"Sunday, Saturday, Friday, Thursday, Wednesday, Tuesday—" Volrabka counted on her fingers.

Beef could last all of twelve days at the Volrabs' (since thirteen is an unlucky number). On the first day beef was served up as "steak," and if it didn't sell it was offered a second day as "steak." If it still hadn't sold, it was brought out on the third and fourth days as "Moravian pot roast." When even that failed to sell, it would be served on the fifth and sixth days as "Spanish cutlets," in case of further failure, on the seventh and eighth days it would be made into "Mexican goulash," then on the ninth, tenth, and eleventh days it would be served with something else as "homemade stuffing," and finally, on the twelfth day, the unsuccessful meat would be put through a grinder and end up in soup as "liver dumplings," and this would always sell.

"—it's the sixth day," Volrabka counted, "but the meat's a tiny bit out of sorts."

"Day 6's always been Spanish cutlets," Volrab said matter-of-factly as he left the kitchen, "so pepper and scent it well and the ladies and gentlemen will be kind enough to gobble it all up."

He glanced into the bar, where Sonya was on her knees scrubbing the floor, he assigned her the added task of polishing the spigots, he turned on the tap and served himself a beer,

which he drank with gusto, in the hallway he ascertained that
Sonya had already changed the light bulb, and he went out into
the yard in a very good mood. For a time he stuck sunflower
leaves through the wire of the rabbits' cage and, moved, he
began to push them tenderly into their pink snouts, he glanced
in at the chicken house, and in the sty he tickled Emil the pig
behind the ears for a while, both of them snickering, he gave
Emil a sugar cube and then just stood for a while in the
sunlight.

A low blue-black car drove into the yard and came swinging
to a stop right beside him, it was Engineer Zikmund Holy
coming back from his morning swim.

Ziki rolled down his window and beckoned with his finger
for Volrab to come over.

"For some reason you walked out on us early last night,"
Volrab trumpeted while making a polite bow. "Perhaps our
Floricultural Soirée wasn't quite to your taste?"

"It certainly wasn't," Ziki said icily. "Listen, I will be a little
bit ill this afternoon," by extending his hand in a commanding
way he assured himself of Volrab's complicity, "let's say at
exactly five o'clock. The bar's just about empty then, so you can
send Sonya up to my room with tea. And if she doesn't quite
get back in five minutes' time, you can do without her for a bit.
Let's say half an hour."

"Of course, sir, I've no objections, but begging your pardon,
the girl is supposed to bring up tea twice in the space of five
minutes—"

"All right, let's say I'm ordering Sonya for half an hour."

"I've no objections, sir, of course, I'm just wondering what a
girl would have to do in all that time. Pray, don't be angry with
me, you know I'm just a stupid country yokel—"

"I want Sonya to read to me," Ziki grinned and started the
engine again. "Put it on my bill," and with his brights on he
drove into the garage.

Volrab hurried down the corridor, rubbing his hands together, in the kitchen he affably permitted Sonya to prolong

saying goodbye to her friend Jarunka Slana — nevertheless, she may not stop working for a moment — and he rushed Volrabka to their bedroom, behind the closed door they had a long discussion, most of which consisted of figures: "Fifty is too little—" "You can't insist on all his savings up front. It's only the first time, after all—" "At the Globus it was never less than twenty marks, and that was two hundred crowns—" "But those were Protectorate marks and the girls had some skills, after all—" "Well, sixty at least—" "How about eighty crowns then—"

In the afternoon, at half-past four (only Ruda Mach was hanging around the otherwise empty bar; he was already supplied with his two beers, he would order a third towards evening), the dumbfounded Sonya was commanded to put on yesterday evening's green silk dress, Volrabka took pains combing her hair, and Volrab personally took charge of tightening her apron from behind.

"You're so good to me, Auntie and Uncle," Sonya was astounded and touched by their unprecedented concern, "and all this for serving tea to Mr. Holy. . ."

"Be nice to him, Sonya," Volrab said earnestly. "Very, very nice. You understand . . . he's important to us. He's our very best customer!"

"If you're very nice to him," Volrabka said in a sudden burst of inspiration, "you can wear that dress for every day."

"Yes, yes. . ." Sonya gasped and clasped her hands.

"And for our next evening you can sew a new one," Volrabka went on, "a pink one. . ."

"Better a white one," Volrab said.

"A young girl looks best in pink. . ." Volrabka was in her youth again.

"But white means she's innocent, and that always makes the biggest splash," said Volrab.

"Come here, Sonya," said Volrabka, and she pulled her toward herself. "I hope you still *are* innocent," and when Sonya bent her head in confusion, Volrabka raised it with her finger and insisted: "Well? I asked you a question!"

"Yes, Auntie," Sonya whispered, blushing.

"You haven't done anything with any man?" Volrab needed the information.

"No, Uncle," Sonya whispered, blushing.

"Even with Mr. Jagr?" Volrabka was truly concerned.

"No, Auntie," Sonya whispered, blushing.

"And never with anyone else?"

"Not even once?"

"No, Uncle. No, Auntie," Sonya whispered, blushing.

"Well then! You certainly couldn't do that sort of thing for us, for everything we give you: a place to live, clothing, shoes, food, drink, heat, good manners, security. . ." Volrab counted it all off on his fingers.

"Just remember how you came to us. A few rags of clothing and a few books in your suitcase and a pair of shoes, they were worn out anyway and one stocking had a big hole in the heel. . ." Volrabka reminisced.

"In a nutshell, with a bare ass," Volrab summarized.

"And now, here with us, you've got everything," Volrabka moralized.

"Yes, Uncle. Yes, Auntie," Sonya whispered, turning pale.

"Well then. You see that we give you good advice, and you have to be careful with the men folk," said Volrabka.

"But not with the men we recommend, 'cause we give you good advice," said Volrab.

"Take Mr. Holy, for instance. He's a most respectable gentleman," said Volrabka.

"He has a car, a villa in Usti big as a castle, and so much money he could take a rake to it," said Volrab.

"How many girls would be happy if such a respectable gentleman came to see them in their room. . ." Volrabka was reminiscing again, but she caught herself right away: "if they could serve tea in his room."

"Mr. Holy is a fine gentleman and we would have nothing against your being nice to him in the best way you know how," said Volrab.

"He'll tell you what to do and how," said Volrabka.

"So be as nice as you can to him," Volrab summarized.

It was five o'clock now, so the tea tray was loaded quickly for room No. 2. "But this tea is old and Mr. Holy always insists on having fresh tea—" Sonya grew frightened.

"But he said five on the dot and five it is, he'll have to drink it somehow," said Volrab.

"And two sugar cubes will do for him," said Volrabka, and in a flash she removed two cubes from the four on the tray.

"So go now, Sonya," said Volrab, "and be very nice to the gentleman, and if there's any sugar left over, bring it back, my Emil's so fond of sugar."

While Sonya scurried away with the tray, Volrab went back to preparing a chicken and Volrabka to preserving strawberries, but their heart was not in their work, both looked up quickly when Sonya finally returned, and they were horrified at the broken crockery on the tray. But when the girl smiled. . .

"I knocked straightaway at old Holy's door—" Sonya began her account, but Volrabka quickly put her hand over Sonya's mouth and tactfully silenced her.

"We aren't interrogating you about anything, Sonya."

"You're mature and an adult and a clever girl, and you your-self know best that you want to be successful," Volrab said quietly.

"I just wanted to explain about the hundred-crown note—" Sonya tried to explain, but Volrabka's hand prevented any fur-ther explanation.

"And you can start work on that white dress right away," said Volrabka, "and I'll peel the potatoes for you today."

"And here's something for you, for your success, buy your-self some candy," said Volrab, from his wallet he took out a five-crown note, put it down on Sonya's tray, picked up the hundred crowns from Ruda Mach, and crammed it into his wallet and the wallet into his pocket. Next he took the sugar cubes for Emil the pig.

Touched, Sonya thanked her extremely kind Uncle and

Auntie for taking care of her and for the very first money they had ever given her, and then she started to collect the broken crockery. Her red hair sparkled on her tender shoulders, and over them sparkled the four eyes of the Volrabs.

So tall in her sheer (the effect of hundreds of washings) nightgown which stretched down to her toes (a castoff from Volrabka; 3-5 Sonyas could fit in it), she was making up her extra-high bed in the kitchen of the Hotel Hubertus (the bed was at the height of Sonya's breasts, because Volrab had inserted three cast-off mattresses which it pained him to throw out), my bed is that of a fairy-tale princess, only instead of a pea underneath the mattresses there were eighty concealed, uninventoried cans of Spanish sardines, which Uncle Volrab liked so much, under the top mattress she placed a novel she was reading (the Volrabs forbade Sonya to read at night because it spoiled her eyes, her skin, and her figure) by Armand Lanoux, *When the Ebbtide Comes*, borrowed from the Hrusov Public Library (every Thursday Sonya went there to borrow one), over the made-up bed she threw a retired billiard cloth covered with cigarette burns and three retired plastic tablecloths (to protect the mattresses against kitchen fumes), on top of them a lace bedspread—Auntie always enthuses about beauty—on the bedspread an earthenware bowl. She stepped back from her work and with her head leaning toward her shoulder she evaluated it critically: it looked horrible, but how much better it was than sleeping next door between the Volrabs (after the hit she made with Ruda Mach's hundred-note, Sonya was once again allowed to sleep by herself in the kitchen), but even this bed doesn't belong to me nor does the nightgown, I don't have anything I can call my own . . . all I have is the faith that one day my prince will come and take me away from here.

> *Clean up the kitchen*
> *And scrub up the floor.*

Scrub up the bar
And the corridor.
Dust the tables and then the chairs.
Spigots and taps must glisten bright!
Polish good, Sonya, up and downstairs.
Bedrooms, bathrooms, and kitchen don't shirk—
Hard-working girls aren't afraid of work,

Uncle Volrab's work instructions set to rhyme contained 52 verses, and the poet persisted in adding additional lines.

Making up the rooms is the finest hour of the day. From the corridor with a pail, mop, and two rags, Sonya would climb the staircase up to the second floor. A broad hallway goes up the middle of the second floor; on the left it ends with a window that looks out on the backyard, on the right it ends with the white door of the largest and most luxurious room, No. 1, which Volrab called the BRIDAL SUITE (although nothing "bridal" had ever taken place in it: room No. 1 had remained permanently without occupants).

From the staircase, the left side of the corridor appears very short, with the two cream-colored doors of the bathroom and the WC, and then just the window. On the right side are rooms Nos. 6 and 5 (with windows facing the courtyard), opposite them the three cream-colored doors of rooms Nos. 4, 3, and 2 (with windows facing the street), the last of which adjoins the Bridal Suite.

Volrab's instructional ballad makes cleaning the WC the first assignment. ("—so you can have the nasty part taken care of right up front!").

To wash the toilet nicely,
The handle polish too,
First raise the lid precisely.

What can a girl do, whose father, unfinished *gymnasium*, and student love affairs have in seventeen years taught her nothing but a few French, Russian, and Latin phrases, to sing, to dance, to play the piano and the harp, to make light cheese pastries to be eaten with wine, to ride a horse, Ovid and *Anna Karenina*, to embroider silk stretched tight on a tambourine and French kissing, to polish old silver and make flower arrangements, to stop nose bleeds and greet customers in the entryway, to change a record or a diaper, $E=mc^2$ and to iron a shirt by spreading it out both ways over the ironing board, the powers that drive history, to teach children to speak, to behave as required, patiently or aggressively, to tend a sick person, to smile prettily at and listen to men?

But then Father died when I was barely seventeen (my mother even earlier), leaving our beautiful villa, but along with it nothing but debts, and of course the dental center needs the villa more than me, and so I am most grateful to Uncle and Auntie for my high bed with its sardines, where I'm warm and don't go hungry, for all this I give my all (the very first day, Uncle Volrab took my suitcase just because it appealed to him), I can always get married even without the villa and without my father, the famous surgeon, and of course without the suitcase, only I'm sorry I didn't finish *gymnasium*, and there are too many verses in Volrab's poem:

> Grease its joints with vaseline,
> So it won't squeak anymore—
> Scrub the porcelain with Super-Clean.
> Bathrooms, toilets, and kitchen don't shirk—
> Hard-working girls aren't afraid of work,
> And dance around it as if in crinoline.

Ahead of her schedule, Sonya locked herself in the bathroom. She had three wonderful times each day: her nightly reading, cleaning the bathroom, and—for the last two months—cleaning room No. 5.

Before the water had filled the tub, Sonya carefully hung up her dress (since Monday the one made of green silk) on the bakelite hook on the wall and examined herself critically in the mirror. I'm not exactly awful-looking and that for women is always extremely important, that's what we told one another when, day before yesterday, we last talked to Jarunka Slana (she always took a bath here before going to see Ruda Mach), we're a lot like one another, as all young girls are a lot alike, only what I do with what I have is somehow more provocative—I suppose more conspicuous and more to the point—and for that reason less proper (I don't really care, but Jaruna does envy me), and I have an unpleasant suspicion that this will bring me a great deal of trouble— (but perhaps not *only* trouble—). But there's no question that I have better skin than Jaruna's (it's because Grandmother rubbed the foam from fresh milk on my face) and Jaruna has thousands of freckles on her face (I don't have a *single one*). And that's why men are so interested in me (I'm interested in them too), only I won't settle for just anyone. Because I want nothing less than the IDEAL MAN.

Refreshed, happy, in good cheer from the ice-cold water, with her pail and her broom Sonya danced down the hall past the window and slipped right into the cream-colored door No. 4 opposite:

> Hard-working girls are beloved by the Lord—
> They start with No. 4 for their reward.

With the exception of the Honeymoon Suite, all the rooms in the Hubertus were exactly the same, each one had the same double bed and wardrobe, a night table, and an identical chair with an identical table covered with a lace tablecloth (Volrabka enthuses about beauty) and on it an earthenware bowl (Volrabka bought them by the dozen from a traveling salesman so she could get the thirteenth free, those not used were stored away in the kitchen under Sonya's bed) and on the identical washbasin a mirror.

From the point of view of cleaning up, No. 4, Jakub Jagr's room, would have seemed ideal: there was nothing in it to clean up. The only evidence that anyone lived here was his toothpaste and toothbrush—she was not allowed to open wardrobes or drawers—who would have guessed that such an orderly young man, who polishes his shoes like a mirror every day and goes to bed every night precisely at nine, would break into the kitchen to declare his love and attack me so that the poor orphan had to take refuge in her guardians' room — but still that was more amusing than reading Armand Lanoux with my flashlight under the covers.

So Jakub loves me and he's a quite acceptable young man, quite good-looking with his straw-colored hair, blue eyes, rosy girlish skin, and athletic figure . . . but to clean up his room is nothing short of a horror story or detective novel:

For starters, he leaves four boobytrapped hundred-notes in a drawer, and then letters sprinkled with salt (to see if I'm reading them. I always read them—nothing interesting—and I sprinkle salt back on the top envelope), there's candy in a bag that's clearly been counted (there are always exactly eight pieces!) and he likes to mark the wardrobe door and the suitcase (nothing interesting inside) with a hair. Only his hair is quite shiny.

With the tip of her tongue and much delight, Sonya removed Jakub's shiny hair from the wardrobe door and expertly investigated the closet: this time he's brought white shirts, not only that, but six of them! That's on my account. And those fancy red silk trunks are also new — you can see that by the price-tag from the store, good God, how he has planned his campaign against me! Otherwise nothing interesting.

Carefully Sonya examined Jakub's suitcase and found a shiny hair attached, this time on the side. Sneaky! In the suitcase a pile of magazines with questionnaires and tests which were intended to show if HE and SHE would make a happy couple. In the left pouch questionnaires that have already been filled in (Jakub brought them to the bar and Sonya had to fill them in while she was serving customers) and in the margins in four colors of pencil, Jakub's countless subtotals, glosses, marginalia, exclamations, queries, and diagrams. In the right pouch questionnaires and tests newly prepared for further interrogation of Sonya (nothing interesting).

But what is it that Mr. Jagr has arranged for me next, the test claims, TELL US WHAT MAKES YOU LAUGH AND WE'LL

TELL YOU WHO YOU ARE. For instance, joke No. E2: Relaxed and enjoying himself, a young man is smoking a cigarette in bed. Beside him his girlfriend is lost in reverie. "You know what," she says, "we ought to think about getting married, don't you agree?" The young man: "You're right, dear, but who would marry either of us?" Sonya laughed at this (4 points), banged the suitcase shut, replaced the hair on the side of the suitcase, and turned to read the white sheet of paper that had been placed on the end table.

I LOVE YOU AND WANT TO MARRY YOU.
J. J.

Sonya closed her eyes halfway and walked slowly toward the mirror, she stood in front of it for a while and smiled prettily at herself:

Sonya Jagrova—

— — *"Good day, Mrs. Jagrova. How are the children?"*
"You know, as long as they're healthy."

— — *". . .we've always considered you a member of our family, Sonya, as our very own daughter!"*
"Yes, Mr. Jagr. Yes, Mrs. Jagrova."

— — *"It's nine o'clock already — throw that novel away—"*
"Yes, Jakub. Yes, dear. Yes—"

Sonya breathed on the mirror and rubbed it with a dry rag, she rinsed out Jakub's cup, he can keep his Kamila—the one you call "My beloved" in your letters, and she calls you "Darling," she washed Jakub's washbasin (already painstakingly washed), I won't surrender my virginity to you, Engineer Jagr.

A careful chambermaid never stops,
And after No. 4 to No. 3 she hops.

Room No. 3 was like a pigsty, with suitcases open on the floor and clothing tossed about, on the table mushrooms were drying and on the chair three shoes and across its arm one suspender — in bed on an enormous pile of all sorts of bedding (they even required three extra blankets!) Beda Balada (an intellectual from Usti) was lounging in striped pajamas, reading a thick tome and munching on cherries (he spat the pits on the floor).

"Just listen, Sonya, what the philosopher Yang-chu had to say about life," Beda called enthusiastically, and already he was reading: "Half of time is taken up by childhood and senility. Almost half of the half that's left man sleeps away all night and dozes away all day. Almost half of what's left is squandered on illness, pain, and sorrow. I don't believe that from what is left you could find a whole hour of complete satisfaction. So what's life for?" Beda stuck two cherries in his mouth and repeated gloomily: "So what's life for?" And contemptuously he spat both pits on the floor.

"If you don't get out of bed, I can't clean up your room."

"Leave it the way it is. Why disturb the natural flow of things. . .?"

"If you really don't want the room cleaned—"

"Throw away that rag and open up your soul. Only Buddha, the Light of Truth, can lead you to the infinite ocean of divinity which we call Atma. Buddha dozes in your body unutilized," Beda leaped agilely out of bed and placed his big white right hand on Sonya's shoulder, "if he is supported by the will, he will release the divine force of Kundalini, which dozes in the form of a coiled serpent at the lower end of the spine — you, Sonya, have it somewhere around—"

With her wet rag Sonya pushed the scholar's groping hand away and, laughing, ran out into the hall.

Room No. 2 had been rented for the entire year to Engineer Ziki Holy, this gentleman could obviously afford to pay twenty-two crowns a day for his room even though he came here only a few times in summer and in winter just for the weekend — this gentleman had shown his true colors when I brought him his tea yesterday at five . . . he was wearing a robe and that's it.

But Mister Ziki adapted extremely well to the Hubertus dearth. With pleasure Sonya strode on the soft purple carpet made of sheepskins (Ziki had brought it from home, of course), carefully dusted the remarkable gong made of beaten metal (once at night it resounded through the entire hotel), and couldn't restrain herself from fondling Ziki's ostentatious playthings: the set of silver goblets in a travel case of black leather and red silk, costly chased vials—on the shelf beneath the mirror a whole perfume shop—on the table in blue leather a large manicure set with golden scissors, on the window sill a travel mirror with a leather calendar and an array of bottles with wine labels like fairy-tale banknotes, he even has his own special sugar, carved cubes shaped like the four card suits in red and blue, in the wardrobe a lot of wonderful sparkling things in cases—all leather—and on a pile of elegant shirts made of natural chocolate-brown silk there lay, like a coiled serpent, a woven whip made of painfully yellow leather.

With horror Sonya banged shut the door of the wardrobe, she quickly finished her cleaning, but once again, trembling, she opened the wardrobe; the end of the frightful sulfur-yellow object seemed slightly darkened, as if worn—

The preceding weekend his wife Aja Hola had slept here, she liked to sleep till noon and could even sleep the whole day through, that beautiful suntanned woman with intense black eyes. "Pour me a little from that bell-shaped bottle and come drink with me—" he told me that past Sunday. Ziki has bright gray eyes like the ash of a fine cigarette, but yesterday they suddenly turned yellow and began to burn. If I have to serve him tea again, I'll call on Mr. Ruda Mach . . . But what if Mr. Mach goes away?

On the table a cream-colored envelope marked SONYA. Inside three hundred crowns and Zikmund Holy's card, on the back of the card: "100 crowns for Room No. 5, the rest for you. A room in Usti is reserved for you until 7/15. Z."

Sonya helped herself to the two hundred crowns (curious that after two years without a single crown I've suddenly got some money: yesterday five crowns and today two hundred already) and she shoved them into her bra.

Then she closed her eyes halfway and walked slowly toward the mirror, she stood silently in front of it for a while, and (with a facetious look at the crystal and the golden bottles of Paris perfume) she smiled prettily at herself:

Engineer Ziki's newest flame—

— — "Miss, do you wish to take the one with pearls or the one with emeralds?"
"Wrap them both up and send me the bill."

— — "Sir, your room is No. 105. And yours, Madam, is No. 106. I am your obedient servant, and I wish you a good night."
"Send a bottle of bubbly up to 106. Very dry. And a masseur at eleven in the morning."

— — "You're leaving this evening. Your suitcase is at the station. And that cream-colored envelope on the desk is for you."
"Yes, sir. You've been most kind to me, sir."

Sonya breathed on the mirror and rubbed it with a dry rag, she rinsed out Ziki's cup, I don't want to have anything to do with you, Mister Ziki, you horrify me, she cleaned his washbasin and with the tip of her rag she danced over the bottles: I will not surrender my virginity to you, sir.

Sonya crossed the corridor diagonally, in the direction of the stairs, and stopped in front of room No. 6 (no key for it). Inside, the voice of Ph.Dr. Berka (raised an octave): "If you don't stop that I'll get up and let you have it—" and simultaneously the voice of Ph.Dr. Berkova (raised two octaves): "If you keep driving me crazy, I'll get up and turn you into a slobbering little wretch—"

Sonya turned the handle (locked), knocked loudly, and called: "Shall I make the room up now?!"

"For God's sake, let us sleep some more," and "For God's

sake, is it morning already? Get out or I'll shoot you!" the married Ph.D.'s. raised their voices simultaneously. OK, they can clean up after themselves for all I care. Cleaning up after them is like trying to bind sand into bundles.

Sonya smoothed her hair down over her temples and, holding her breath, entered Room No. 5.

There was a special scent here—not of perfume and leather as in Ziki's room, and certainly not of boot polish and soap as in Jakub's—it comes from the rumpled bed, fleeting as the odor of all his things, there is a strong odor of leather, but of skin as well . . . and instead of perfumed soap, there is something in it like what wafts up from a cold stream of water. And of course the smell of tobacco (that most of all), but also something like fresh hay, and something from a stable . . . perhaps a horse's mane? And the smoky smell of a campsite and something like the sun beating down on felled young pine trees. Definitely the smell of grass — no, it's blueberries! And of burning leaves. . . And then something metallic, the way old polished brass would smell. And of blood . . . And a thousand more things can be smelled here, and the whole effect is a rich cranberry tart, a total mystery. That special smell in here is the smell of a man.

Sonya picked up object after object and they lingered in her hands before she put them carefully back in places she herself had chosen for them, here in Mr. Ruda Mach's room I don't give a damn about Uncle Volrab's verses and I arrange the inside of the wardrobe every day (Mr. Mach doesn't stick his hairs on the wardrobe door, but then he doesn't have anything in it that wouldn't be nice to pick up and stroke), in fact poor Mr. Mach doesn't have much of anything.

A handsome dark suit on a hanger marked HOTEL SUVOROV.

Two torn shirts of checkered flannel (one green and yellow and the other gray and blue — I prefer the latter).

Two handsome white shirts.

A black leather tie mounted on rubber.

Two pairs of shorts, both red.

Seven pairs of socks, which he washes in the sink (sometimes I do it for him but how am I to find them, Uncle Volrab, when he throws them, say, into a suitcase), and often he tosses them in the wastebasket.

Not a single handkerchief! (They're the first things I would buy for him.)

A magnificent Italian sweater, but there's a burn-mark at chest-level. And that's the entire list of what Mr. Ruda Mach has in his wardrobe. But what might he have if he could only learn to save a bit (or if someone saved for him . . . possibly a woman. . .)! But each payday he treats the whole bar, hauls girls around in a cab which he has to summon from as far away as Jilemnice (he pays the return fare as well), and buys the kids he meets ice cream and lollypops—just as yesterday he calmly gave me a hundred-note for the broken crockery—and the girls and the kids adore him . . . But when he was lying here sick, not a foot stirred to come and help him.

He is terribly alone. That business with Jaruna Slana, that wasn't anything, Jaruna says she loves him, but she's only come here on Sunday evenings, and only for a fling (but he too carried on without her, and how!). And she was getting ready to marry Dr. Sedivy! There's no doubt Mr. Mach needs someone to take care of him.

And when he's alone he must feel sad. When Mr. Ruda feels sad, he sits at the window and plays his guitar. And he plays his guitar every evening. To himself. . .

Sonya laid out the mattresses on the window sill, and the rug, from which she knocked the dirt off, and she dusted the box springs (Uncle Volrab's verses don't mention these things, so I've made up a verse of my own) and, after prolonged reflection, she made Ruda's bed with delight, as one makes a rum-cake, if only there weren't so many of those girls, the ones he'd had in the past two months, how anxiously they'd climbed the stairs and waited in front of the locked room while Mr. Mach was still at the plant, and then their joy which sounded down the long corridor (very weakly, of course. But a few times Sonya heard it at full volume when, holding her breath, she put her ear to the door of No. 5), and their happiness when they kissed Mr. Ruda early in the morning. . . How their eyes would shine! And how much soda water they would drink before breakfast.

Sonya took the cream-colored envelope from Ziki, with the remaining hundred-note, and placed them on the table along with Ziki's card with its invitation to his villa in Usti, just so Mr. Ruda could read it all. Maybe he'll get the drift of things. . .

Sonya closed her eyes halfway and walked slowly over to the mirror, she stood silently in front of it for a long time and then she smiled prettily at herself:

Sonya Machova—

— — *with him by taxi to Jilemnice and on beyond to Spindleruv Mlyn, dancing on the glass floor and then on the night train drink beer with the conductor from the same bottle*

— — *sit with him the whole evening by the window and feed the fire with fragrant branches*

— — *make tea for him (never grog!) and give him medicine with a spoon. Stop his nosebleeds and fevers with a cooling compress. And do flower arrangements for him*

— — *sing when he plays the guitar and laugh all evening long*

— — *sit in the corner, look at him, and embroider on silk with a tambourine for a frame*

— — *with a large bag go shopping for two and bake light cheese pastry to eat with wine*

— — *pick up his pay. And iron his shirts*

— — *give him French kisses*

— — *and teach our son to say "Daddy"*

Sonya smiled into the mirror, then rinsed out Ruda's cup and shaving brush, ran its damp bristles along her chin and then, laughing, washed the washbasin and joyously leapt out of room No. 5.

The final room on the floor, No. 1, was called the Bridal Suite (two windows and glass doors onto the balcony, stylish white furniture, a tall mirror in a white frame, and a white double bed beneath a white canopy). Sonya went into room No. 1 and quietly locked the door behind her.

From the corridor Sonya's sudden shriek, the smashing and clanging of metal, Jakub Jagr rushed to the door — in her green dress from yesterday's "Floricultural Evening" Sonya was kneeling on the floor and collecting broken dishes on her tray while, in the door to his room, in a bathrobe, Ziki Holy towered over her — *What was she doing in his room?*

"Come back to my room and you'll get the money right away," said Ziki — *he wasn't wearing a shirt under his bathrobe.*

". . .I'll give you a hundred-note, Sonya, with no bullshit and right away. Come in," said Ruda Mach in the doorway of his room, No. 5, and without any hesitation Sonya went in — *What will she do in his room?*

Quietly Jakub shut the door to his room, No. 4, and with his temples glistening with the cold sweat of dismay he stared at himself in the mirror: derailed, capsized, and crushed . . . never would I have believed I could ever end up in such a state. It's the end of Kamila, that peaceful relative of mine, the end of the fairy tale about the wedding of two neighboring villas in the green vale of childhood. . . What can we put in place of that? Yesterday, Sunday night, Sonya refused me, and now on Monday afternoon, in two minutes' time, Sonya goes from one man's room to another's . . . and the most terrible thing is that I love her just the same and even more, I don't understand myself anymore, but I do grasp one thing: at the age of twenty-five I've suddenly learned that love of a man for a woman exists and how crazy it can be.

Engineer Jakub Jagr suffered in front of the mirror, quite

involuntarily he glanced at the steel stopwatch on his wrist and quickly he took hold of himself (he was a technician), in a flash he estimated Sonya's arrival at Mach's room, No. 5, at 5:26 P.M., he opened the door to the hallway just a bit and simultaneously watched the door to room No. 5 and the second hand. At 5:32 Sonya left room No. 5, a bit anxious as if disturbed, and a bit disheveled (of course, this could have occurred earlier, in the time *before* 5:26, in room No. 2) and she rushed downstairs as if something had upset her.

Jakub quickly went up to the door to room No. 2, in the keyhole unfortunately a key, so that the view was practically nil.

"What is it?!—" Ziki said icily in the suddenly opened door — *he was now wearing a shirt under his bathrobe.* Jakub stayed bent over and said in a controlled voice, "Pardon me. My battery rolled over this way—" and he knelt in order to look for it more easily. In the triangle formed by Ziki's legs he could see a strip of the violet fur (!) carpet and on the visible slice of the table an open bottle of Cinzano Bitter, *is that what he drinks at teatime* (as served by Sonya before 5:26)?—

"It hardly could have rolled into my room," Ziki snarled, and he banged the door shut.

The lock on Mach's door, No. 5, was without a key, it's true, but through the hole he could see nothing but a swinging leg (evidently Mach was sitting at the window). He could hear a powerful strumming on a string instrument right up to the end of his eavesdropping, 5:53.

5:57 P.M. to 12:10 A.M. Sonya works in the bar. The usual customers, everything's normal. Ziki dines on chicken with mushrooms (not on the menu) and a wedge of cheese, he drinks heavily (a large bottle of wine plus a small one, plus two double cognacs), indifference toward Sonya, coolness from Sonya, he leaves at 8:37. Mach dines on warm sausage (not on the menu) and two beers (he doesn't finish the second one), special attention toward and from Sonya, he leaves at 9:04. Volrab behaves as usual.

12:12-12:21 Sonya shuts down and cleans up the bar.

12:22 Sonya cleans up and airs out the kitchen.

12:41 Sonya goes to bed.

12:42 Volrab fortifies the inside of the kitchen window with a crossbolt and a padlock.

12:46 the Volrabs turn out the lights in their bedroom.

12:49 a feeble light turns on in the kitchen (evidently Sonya's reading flashlight).

1:33 darkness in the kitchen.

1:34 heavy snoring in Mach's room, No. 5.

1:34 a dim light goes on in Ziki's room, No. 2.

5:54 Mach leaves for Cottex.

6:02 Sonya cleans up the kitchen, with the window still locked and barred.

6:29 Ziki leaves in his blue-black Triumph, license no. UL-81-51.

6:52 at the front gate of Cottex, Mach punches in (No. 171): arrival 6:00 sharp.

On the instructions of the Usti directorate, Jakub Jagr was making a complex technological inspection of the Hrusov branch factory No. 08. In less than four weeks he had uncovered some 72 irregularities (broken rules, inadequate use of labor during working hours, inadequate and even nonexistent gate controls, dripping from the roofs onto dyed material, a high rate of wear of manganese from the friction rollers through which the material passed, smoking in the towcloth storeroom), while the branch director, Kaska, made excuses with increasingly embittered humility.

"Could you find a job in your plant for a nineteen-year-old girl comrade?" Jakub asked him.

"Of course we could, Engineer Jagr, you just have to say the word," Kaska said eagerly.

"One where she would be dry and warm and have lots of light."

"Of course, I'd be delighted."

"But you haven't asked me what her qualifications are."

"I was just about to ask, what qual. . ."

"None at all. She didn't even finish the *gymnasium*. But she knows how to tackle a job."

"Right away, as soon as you send her to me—"

"And you'll have to find her a place to live. From the day she starts."

"I can manage that somehow, I'll do my best."

A telephone inquiry made to the secretary of the MNV ascertained that Sonya Cechova was in fact registered as a permanent resident at the Hotel Hubertus, but her employment was not on file. In view of her age (19) it would be possible to declare her current social status, from the legal point of view, as a "person evading work responsibilities," possibly even as a "parasitic element."

11:31 Mach in the bleaching room, 1:02 in the lab, 1:18 he headed off to an unknown spot in the vicinity of the factory.

The security guard sent out to look for him found him lying in the grass by the confluence of the factory millrace and the Jizera River.

According to relevant documents, via the directorate of the Usti factory, Cottex branch 08 paid to Engineer Zikmund Holy, the principal specialist in industrial water management at USVLH in Prague, address Usti nad Labem, Vilova 26, for the first year of use of his patent No. 338269, "Purification of industrial discharge water through its biological modification" up to 12/31 of the past year a payment totaling 108,653.92 crowns (with prior approval from the ministry and USVLH). According to a memo from the accountant J. Metelka, Ziki would have royalties from Cottex plants Nos. 06 and 09 as well, from Metex 111, 112, 113, and 114, Lina's chief plant, and Chemolin B, which would be even larger, and the total would evidently exceed a million crowns for the current year. Further, J. Metelka's memo informed them that Engineer Z. Holy is disliked for his arrogant behavior and universally feared for his connections.

2:00 Mach walks past the gatekeeper of Cottex 08 on his way (he says) to the town swimming pool. On his way home from Cottex, Jakub bought candy (4 crowns) and pink letter paper with envelopes (4 crowns), because today is Tuesday and in four days, on Saturday afternoon, I will take Sonya home.

That afternoon in the bar (when Volrab went to the cellar to tap the beer): "Sonya, I love you. . ."

Sonya rubbed her ankles together and smiled prettily at Jakub.

"Sonya, you must leave here at once. Tomorrow morning—"

"Uncle won't let me."

"I've found you a nice job at Cottex, where it's dry and warm and there's lots of light. And you can have a room the very day you start! I'll lend you money for the first few days. And on Saturday I'll take you and show you our home—"

"Uncle and Auntie would never let me," said Sonya, but she smiled prettily at Jakub.

(Shortly after, in the corridor, while Volrab was coming back from the cellar:)

"You are surely aware, Comrade Volrab, that as manager of this enterprise you are violating both the letter and the spirit of the applicable group of proclamations, decrees and procedural regulations concerning the management and mobilization of the work force in a border area and the preferential treatment due them in border-area factories—"

"What— what— what's that you say?" Volrab was frightened by the long sentence, so much so his forehead was bathed in sweat. "I haven't done anything, Mr. Jagr!"

"Your *very* distant relative Sonya Cechova is, in the eyes of the law, a parasitic element. *Immorally exploited*, I should add."

"But Sonya lives with us just like our own daughter!"

"How much do you pay her every month? And where do you deposit the tax money?"

"But Mr. Jagr, how can you say that when we're one big happy family?"

"I'd say it wasn't like that *at all*, the way you live together here. And you should be aware that *procuring*, too, falls under the *criminal* law."

"You've given me quite a start, Mr. Jagr! And what law does

it fall under when you climb into windows to get at innocent girls in their beds? Like last Sunday, huh?"

"You can still escape scot-free if you let Sonya go as soon as possible to take a job at the local Cottex plant. From the point of view of state interest and the preferential treatment of border-area factories—"

"Sonya has a job with us and with it free lodging, food and clothing — on Sunday she got a new silk dress and now we're making her another one — shoes, food, drink, heat, good manners, and security. Security, Mr. Jagr, so wild hooligans don't climb through her window at night and crawl into her bed!"

5:57-12:08 Sonya works in the bar. The usual customers, everything's normal. Ziki is still away. Mach dines on two sausages with horseradish (not on the menu) and two beers (he doesn't finish the second one), still special attention toward and from Sonya, he leaves at 9:11. Contact established with the local informant (their everyday customer Josef Hnyk) at a cost of two large beers and two small rums. Volrab watches like a hawk.

12:09-12:19 Sonya shuts down and cleans up the bar.

12:20 Sonya cleans up and airs out the kitchen.

Out of the darkness of the hotel courtyard two bright cones of light, Volrab with a flashlight in one hand and pitchforks in the other, Volrabka with a flashlight and a hoe, and their uproar:

"What sort of bum is hanging around out here!"

"Help! Thieves!"

"You hooligan, thought you could get our Sonya by hook or by crook! For the second time, even!"

"My husband will tell the police and will write to your management about it!"

"I'll teach you a thing or two about those laws of yours!"

12:30 they were still making a to-do.

In his room, No. 4, Jakub was writing on the first of the four pink sheets he'd bought that day:

"Sonya, I love you. Be ready to go. On Saturday I will take

you and show you our home. J.J." He placed the note in full view on the table and weighted it down with the first of the four candy boxes (cognac-flavored creams).

On a postcard of Hrusov the usual news to his father (like every Tuesday, so that it reaches Usti on Thursday. And on Saturday I'll bring Sonya home). "Everything fine. On Saturday I'll arrive with Sonya at 4:40 or, if nec., later. Yours, J."

After taking care of his correspondence, the young engineer spent more than forty minutes gazing out the window at the stars.

Starting on Wednesday, things took an unexpected turn.

5:12 a blue-black Triumph with the license number UL-81-51 drove into the hotel courtyard, carrying Ziki and an unknown woman.

Ziki argued with Volrab for a while. Then the unknown woman stepped out of the car with a black suitcase of strange, oblong form and disappeared into the kitchen.

She remains there hour after hour.

The local informant, Josef Hnyk, identifies the unknown woman as Berta Zahnova. From the abundance of Hnyk's talk (four large beers and four large rums) and by means of digressive, non-leading, and repeated corroborating questions, it turns out that Berta Zahnova, several times incarcerated, is a servant at Ziki's villa in Usti, where she lives with her husband, Wolf Zahn, arrested for murder, a crime which Ziki's lawyers succeeded in getting reduced to manslaughter. In consequence, the Zahns are rightfully grateful to Ziki and evidently bound to him through subsequent, shadowy events, so that they act as his gorillas.

Berta Zahnova remains in the kitchen hour after hour, until nightfall.

SONYA MUST LEAVE HERE AT ONCE — under these circumstances, even at the risk of a kidnapping charge.

On Wednesday, shortly after eleven, Ziki and the chief attorney left the conference of factory directors being held in the mirrored salon of Usti's Palace Hotel, by a palm tree in the foyer both men, laconically and to the point, said what they had to say and shook hands with a smile, the chief attorney sat comfortably in his official limousine and Ziki did the same in his (the two large black cars parked at the hotel entrance differed only in their license numbers).

"To the town square," Ziki gave the order to his chauffeur, and during the two-minute ride there he considered that he actually had nothing to do here till the end of August, in the calendar window of his platinum British datamatic stop-watch he read "3/3/July," and in his thoughts he put aside his business affairs.

At the square he had his chauffeur open the door, and while stepping out he pointed down with his thumb and then crooked his index finger (i.e., "Wait here, I'll be back in half an hour").

He entered the local branch of the State Savings Bank, asked for ten thousand crowns at window No. 4, the teller filled out a pink withdrawal slip and Ziki signed it in the lower right-hand corner, looked at the cards of his four checking accounts (a total of over 800,000 crowns. And roughly the same amount would come in before the end of the year), sat for a while in an armchair holding the stiff cardboard call number in his hand (in his thoughts he put aside his financial affairs), when they called his number he crossed to window No. 1, picked up a packet of hundred-notes, without counting it he stuck it into his breast pocket and went out into the heat of the square.

He entered the city courthouse, in the third-floor corridor in front of the offices of the government notary he sat down on a leather sofa alongside Bertik Lohnmuller, from whom he took a matchbox, inside of which a twenty-dollar gold coin shone against a background of blue velvet, Ziki balanced it in his hand, bit into it, passed a fragment of touchstone around it, nodded and dropped the coin into his pocket, returned the box to Bertik and paid him thirty-six hundred crowns (ridiculously cheap), asked about some sapphires (not in yet), listened to news about a gold Spanish four-doubloon piece and placed an order for it, then for any number whatsoever of gold Roman solidi, fixed their next meeting for the following Wednesday, and went out into the heat of the square.

He had the chauffeur open the door and said, "Home," and half reclining on the rear cushions he looked out, bored, at the hot streets of the city of Usti. On Vilova Street the chauffeur downshifted to third and then into second as he drove through the open gates of No. 26 and through the garden up to the garage of Villa Cynthia, where Wolf Zahn was polishing the windshield of the blue-black Triumph with a chamois cloth.

Ziki dismissed the chauffeur and looked quizzically at his Wolf.

"Mme. Aja was here," Wolf announced.

"You don't say."

"She wanted to go up to her room."

"That's interesting."

"She wouldn't be talked out of it."

"That's typical of her."

"I finally had to lay a hand on the dear lady."

"What did you use?"

"A blackjack."

"Won't it leave marks?"

"I threw a tarp over the lady."

"Be as careful as possible until the divorce decree is announced! How about our room?"

"The cage is ready for the canary."

With Wolf behind him Ziki went up to the second floor, in the pale blue bathroom he undressed with Wolf's help and permitted himself ten minutes of ice-cold shower, then Wolf unscrewed the shower head and lashed his master into condition with the forceful stream, and finally a hot shower (it prolongs the effect of the cold).

Naked, Ziki passed through the corridor to the dressing room, where he put on cream-colored shorts, a chocolate-

colored shirt (both made of cooling natural silk), beige trousers
of light, loosely-woven wool and, in front of a mirror, he
carefully tied his sulfur-yellow tie.

He entered the room with the bay window, walked noiselessly across the purple rug with its white lions and stylized
grapes, with the skillful, silent, economical movements of a
single hand he unlocked and let down the massive door of the
ebony sideboard: on the counter thus formed he placed a
simply etched glass taken from the upper section of the
mirrored shelves and drew out and uncorked (always with a
single hand) a bottle of Tarragona spiced wine, in one motion
he poured his noontime dose into the glass (a finger's breadth
below the top of the glass) and with alpaca-lined tongs (always
with a single hand) he lowered a circlet of lemon onto the
surface of the wine (relishing as he did so the view of the yellow
circlet and the silvery rim submerging into the warm brown),
he took a sip and glass in hand went to take a look at the canary
cage (a recollection of Aja's tan face with the moist temples and
the way she shrieked).

"Good morning, sir," Berta Zahnova greeted him in the "little
room" (white furniture, a thick yellow rug sewn from sheepskins, no heavy or sharp object anywhere, the door and window
without handles, and outside the window a concave grill).

"It's all in working order," Wolf said from over by the
window.

"But what if she were to break the glass," Ziki said, and he
took a sip of his Tarragona.

"She could only break the inside pane. Outside, there is a
wire which lowers a metal shutter immediately and then— Do
you care to try it?"

"Later," said Ziki. "Is Berta ready for the trip?"

"Yes, sir. Would you care to see it before lunch?"

Ziki nodded, Berta trotted off downstairs, and when Ziki
descended after her to the hall, he found her waiting for him
by her open, oblong suitcase. With her hands she moved aside
a few pieces of underwear and took out a silvery pair of double

bracelets (a toy from the London Woolworth's: children's hand-cuffs which Wolf had provided with a real lock).

"Hands—" said Ziki, and when Berta held them up for him, he set his glass of Tarragona down on the ivory table and snapped the cuffs around her wrists.

"My wrists are a little bit too thick," Berta said apologetically when Ziki had trouble taking the handcuffs off.

"That's OK. Gag—" said Ziki with his glass again between his fingers, and from underneath her garter Berta drew out a chamois pouch soaked in kerosene.

"Chloroform—"

"Here, sir," Berta pointed to a bottle labeled GURKEN-MILCH. "And I'm also taking—"

"That will do. You may serve lunch."

Sitting alone in the ground-floor dining room paneled in Finnish larch, Ziki stirred an egg into his bouillon and before taking his first spoonful he drank up the rest of his noontime Tarragona.

After lunch (steamed boneless chicken with cashew nuts, chilled pineapple, a wedge of cheddar cheese) and an hour-long nap (absolutely dreamless, except shortly before waking a tantalizing image of Sonya Cechova kneeling in a long children's nightgown, a view from behind, the whole thing last-ing no more than a couple of seconds), an ice-cold then a hot shower, toweling off, in the hall Berta Zahnova was already waiting with her oblong suitcase, when she caught sight of Ziki she got up at once, waited until he passed by her, and at a distance of three paces followed him to the garage, where Ziki got into the already started up blue-black Triumph, Berta got in beside him and placed her suitcase on the back seat.

"You must have forgotten this in the pocket of the trousers you wore this morning," said Wolf Zahn, and in his fingers he held the gold twenty-dollar piece.

"Stick it in my pocket," said Ziki, pulling out with one hand on the steering wheel and the other on the mahogany gearshift.

Wolf ran alongside the car, stuck the coin in Ziki's pocket, and banged the car door shut.

On the street Ziki shifted into second and then right away into third, he drove through the ritzy quarter of Klise and the Vseborice prefab development, heading toward the concrete highway to the north, he shifted into fourth, turned on the car radio, and looking straight ahead he recapitulated:

"The main thing is to keep your eyes open. The hardest will be to watch out for Jagr."

"Engineer Jakub Jagr, young, blond, room No. 4," Berta said nimbly.

". . .he's a mooncalf, but an unpredictable one. One night he climbed into her window, and then he spied outside my door. But, of course, the most dangerous one is Mach."

"The bastard in No. 5."

". . .and don't let the Volrabs out of your sight."

"Count on me, sir."

Below Decin Castle, Ziki crossed a bridge over the Elbe, shot through Decin, and turned sharply up a hill, at a railway crossing the red lights had begun to blink, it would still have been easy to make it across the tracks, but Ziki stopped and waited until the barriers had dropped into their cradles. The train didn't come for a long time.

"We've got beautiful weather," Berta took the liberty of observing.

Ziki didn't answer, he put his hand in his pocket and played with his new coin until the barriers went up again.

> *Last she must clean the Bridal Suite,*
> *And the cleaning work is all complete.*
> *Then Sonya's got to wash the staircase too;*
> *Don't spare the soap and keep your hands*
>   *like new.*
> *But remember, and the kitchen too don't shirk—*
> *Hard-working girls aren't afraid of work.*

Thus, Volrab's poetry laid out the plan of the hours of that particular Tuesday, and tirelessly, without a pause, Sonya scraped potatoes, polished shoes, beat eggwhites, scratched Emil the pig, watered the gladiolus, irises, and (on Sunday night thinned out) carnations, sliced liver for the soup, cut dumplings with a thread, cleaned cucumbers and Uncle Volrab's pipe (when I'm married that skill will come in handy), sugared tarts, poured the soup and carried it out to the customers (maybe someday I'll be the chef at the Paris Ritz) and smiled prettily at every one of them, took the leftovers out to Emil, washed the dishes, polished the billiard cues and, for the first time that day, before spending her afternoon in the bar, she had a minute to catch her breath, and already Jakub Jagr was rushing in.

"Sonya, I love you!" he said in the doorway (a quite good-looking boy, that Jakub, with his sincere blue eyes) and: "You must leave here right away. Tomorrow morning!" (I'd be most happy to, except that you may not be the real prince I'm waiting for) and: "I've found a good job for you at Cottex!" (but there's work everywhere and I can earn my keep) and even: "On Saturday I'll take you and show you our home!" (any girl would be happy to hear that, but Uncle and Auntie would never let me go).

In the corridor outside the bar, poor Jakub had a nasty run-in with Uncle (on account of me. Wonderful!), they screamed at one another so that I didn't have to put my ear to the door to make out every word.

"Just so you know, Sonya," Uncle snorted with rage, downing beer after beer, "Engineer Jagr says you're living here with us as a parasitic element — but if I ever nail him again in the yard at night, I'll give him some bodily injury he'll never forget! Hooligan! Stupid clown!"

Jakub has good intentions toward me, I'm sure, but he's brought me more trouble than help, since his visit on Sunday night Uncle locks my window every night — do they even do that in prison?

"Sonya, you really didn't do anything with Mr. Jagr, nothing at all? You know you can tell me *absolutely* everything. . ."

"I've already told you I didn't, Uncle! Not even with Ziki. . ."

"I didn't ask you about him. But how about Mr. Mach — don't you fawn on him more than is necessary for a respectable girl in a respectable bar?"

"You must have dreamed that."

"If only I had! Why in heaven's name didn't you give him the beer I drew for him?"

"Because Mr. Mach knows dregs when he sees them, whereas Mr. Hudlicky will drink absolutely anything, as you very well know."

"If only I did! And the way you brought him fresh salt straight from the bag. Just get it into your head that I'm going to keep my eye on you!"

"With Ziki too?"

"Good God, call him Mr. Holy!"

"But yesterday in the room he asked me to call him Ziki."

"He meant when you're alone in the room with him — otherwise don't get ideas in your head. You know he's our best customer. And no vagabond laborer like Mach. You can get somewhere with Mr. Holy, if only you'd be nice to him. But if you're nice to that fix-it man, he'll fix you up with twins before you can close your eyes."

"Yes, Uncle."

So now when I'm working, Uncle doesn't stir from the bar and doesn't take his eyes off me — he even leans over the counter to have a better look whenever I wait on Mr. Mach — and whenever he has to go to the bathroom (which is quite often) he knocks with his keys on the kitchen door, and then Auntie watches me until he returns.

Ever since the Floricultural Evening more people have been coming (and I know why!). Petrik Metelka (the young colorist from Cottex with the red ears) orders a bottle of champagne just for himself (he doesn't know how to drink it, he only orders it because he's afraid of Uncle) and he stares at me without letting up. Postmaster Hudlicky stares at me from the next table (he keeps sticking out his tiny chest, but it isn't much to look at) and Uncle serves him nothing but dregs. The veterinarian, Srol, strokes me on the backside every time I bring him Egyptian white wine (made especially for him by Auntie out of cider and mentholated spirits), he adds bicarbonate of soda and when he burps he strokes me on the backside again. But then I've got Mr. Ruda Mach. . .

How all their eyes shine when they stare at me, they'd kiss again without a second thought. They all pretend to be tigers, but all of them (except for Mr. Ruda) are rabbits, even the great Mr. Ziki snapped shut like a jackknife when yesterday in his room I scalded his shameless paw with boiling water from the teapot, I'd never have done that to Mr. Ruda — *even if he were to reach for you WITH HIS PAW?* — Mr. Ruda hasn't got paws, he has beautiful, tanned, powerful hands, like a real live man. And Jakub Jagr watches it all from his table and keeps writing it down in his notebook — all I'd have to do is stamp my feet and he'd run off again. Rabbits is all they are.

I'm glad Mr. Ruda Mach is here, just in case there's some sort of row (if only there were a row. . .), it's good to have a real live man around. And so I always serve Mr. Mach the very best of everything (he so needs someone to take care of him), yesterday I talked him out of ordering the "homemade stuffing" made with eleven-day-old meat and instead I served him warm smoked pork, from which I cut the best slice (if Auntie had seen me!), and how he enjoyed it! And today, instead of the Mexican goulash (which has been growing moldy in the casserole for two days now) Mr. Ruda will get the fresh sausages that Uncle set aside (there'll be trouble when he doesn't find them!), and beer that's clear, just as it ought to be. There's no doubt that Mr. Ruda looks at me too, but it's nice the way he looks, just like looking at a girl he likes (even I know that), and it's certainly permitted and it's certainly nice, isn't it?

Sonya smiled prettily at Ruda Mach while she was serving Srol's fourth "Egyptian white," and all of a sudden Dr. Srol stroked me on my backside a bit too hard (behind the bar Uncle was arranging the cigarettes in the display case so he didn't see a thing), then Dr. Srol jumped up on his chair (Uncle was still arranging the cigarettes) and squealed "Ow!" and stroked his own backside for a change.

Mr. Mach had given him a well-planted kick from behind, through the opening in his chair. Uncle (suddenly the cigarettes were sufficiently arranged) boomed from behind the bar: "What does Mr. Mach want?!"

"Nothing for me," Mr. Ruda laughed. "But this old gentleman seems to want something you haven't got on the menu!"

Mr. Ruda Mach is the first person here who's stood up for me. And when after some time Uncle went off to the bathroom (Mr. Srol was still stroking his own backside, drinking his poison, and following it up with bicarbonate as if it were bread)—Auntie watched me in his place—Mr. Mach suddenly ordered a bottle of No. 12 (because he knew that to get it I'd have to go to the cellar), and when I was on my way back with it Mr. Ruda was waiting for me in the corridor (I *knew* he'd be there) and marvelously he stroked my hair.

"Don't be afraid, Sonya," he said softly. "And if you need anything, all you have to do is ask."

"You're very kind, Mr. Mach."

"Or just wink."

"Yes, Mr. Mach."

And again he looked at me in such a special way, just as he had when he gave me the hundred-note for the broken crockery, actually it wasn't exactly a proper look, but perhaps someone who helps you has a right to look at you that way. . .

I could have endured his gaze till midnight, but just then Uncle came out of the WC and let me have it: what was I doing hanging around out here?

"I sent her down for a bottle of No. 12!" Mr. Ruda said loudly.

"All of a sudden," Uncle grinned. "You always used to say it was doctored."

"And it is! But not as much as your beer! The tubes that bring the beer up from the basement must be mixed up with the plumbing!"

"Well, well, well, maybe things aren't so bad after all," Uncle muttered (he doctors everything he lays his hands on), he chased me into the kitchen and started into me right away, once again he charged me for everything since the year 1905 and didn't even forget the hole in one of my stockings (though the stocking was from the suitcase he had taken away from me on the very first day).

"I'll never ever do it again," I lied, and then I sniveled a bit so he would give me some peace (anyway, he couldn't deprive me of that wonderful moment in the corridor).

> When the last guest leaves our hostelry,
> Clean up the bar and bring me the key.
> Then go to the kitchen and continue your work,
> It likes to be clean as you like to be fed.
> A working girl knows she can never shirk,
> She dusts and cleans and then goes to bed,
> Crosses herself, and then sleeps like the dead.

Uncle and Auntie went out to the yard late tonight and I'm waiting for them to come and place the bar over my window, and I'm also waiting for them to disappear into their bedroom, I'm always waiting for something and most of all for *my prince, who one day will come and take me away from here—*

But it's not a fairy tale I'm waiting for.

WHAT I WANT: human things. An orderly and satisfying life. To be happy. Someone who likes me and whom I like. My own husband, and to have children with him. Decent work. To have clothes to wear and to never be hungry.

WHAT I DREAM ABOUT: To sit by my very own fireplace with a fire blazing away. To dance on the deck of a steamship at night in the Indian Ocean. To see Mount Everest. To walk with my lover on a slippery path in the rain and the March wind. To be certain.

WHAT I FEAR: war, hunger, torture, death.

I may think about men too much (a tiger's always better than a rabbit) and I may read too many novels. But most likely I'm a normal girl who believes life can be as beautiful as Heaven and that love is the bridge up to it.

Long after midnight a sudden shouting from the yard: "What sort of bum is hanging around out here?!" Uncle cried out. "Help! Thieves!" Auntie cried out in harmony, "You hooligan, thought you could get our Sonya by hook or by crook—"

So once again Jakub was standing under my window. Who would have expected this of such a decent young man, who polished his shoes like a mirror every day and who went to bed every evening at 9:00 sharp. Or of Mr. Ziki, who had such a beautiful wife, Aja. Or of Mr. Ruda Mach, whom all the girls from the entire republic longed for — *that beautiful moment with him today in the corridor.* How his eyes shine when they look at me (he can look at me as long as he wants)! I have an inkling that something is going to happen to me. If only it would happen soon—

When the Volrabs came back from their nighttime sortie into the yard, after numerous admonitions ("Yes, Uncle," "Yes, Auntie.") they checked the bar on the kitchen window and disappeared into their bedroom with all the keys, and when their muttering had finally quieted down, Sonya turned on her flashlight and under the featherbed read on in Armand Lanoux's novel, *When the Ebbtide Comes:*

> . . .Naked, fair-haired women with great fixed and watchful eyes were walking . . . perhaps to some cruel rituals. . . The hairy pudenda of the beautiful sacrifices betrayed their animality in contrast with the innocent purity of their faces. . . Flowers growing up through cracks in the polished floors . . . all this placed these melancholy young ladies in the role of the priestesses of Sigmund Freud, if not Sacher-Masoch, exquisite sleepwalkers flirting with rape, which was emblematized by the young, faultlessly dressed gentlemen, evidently indifferent, buttoned up in their green frock-coats, with derbies on their heads.

I have an inkling that something will happen to me soon. That a man will come. When he comes, something has to happen. The man is supposed to build a house and for this the woman will make him happy.

My prince and my lord, come—

"People are no good, Emil," Volrab complained to the pig during their sweet early-evening fondling session in the pigsty, and he gave him a good scratching behind the ears, "just when you're beginning to get somewhere, they pull out their switchblades. Take that engineer Jagr, for example: we serve him all sorts of special dishes and we pamper him all sorts of ways — and then he tries to steal away our Sonya, and threatens to have the law on us in the bargain!"

"Hrr-hrr," the pig said to that.

"You're right, he's nothing but a white-collar clown. But then take that fellow Mach: a day laborer who doesn't order anything at the bar, and he lies in wait for our Sonya in the corridor. Is it for him we bring her up and cultivate her like a flower?"

"Hrr-hrr."

"You bet. We'll wipe the floor with him. Like we did with those other gentlemen, right? And we'll keep an eye on Sonya, and every Sunday there'll be a floricultural evening, success after success, and you'll live to see the day the Hubertus becomes the Grand Hubertus, with neon signs and red coconut matting from the staircase out to the gate. . . Here, Emil, I've brought you sugar, take it and make yum-yum—"

"Keek-keek," the pig rejoiced, but all of a sudden the blast of a siren as for a fire. . .

In the middle of the yard Engineer Holy's luxury sedan was still rocking on its springs, so rapidly had he come to a stop.

"Hey, manager! Your best customer's here—" the engineer says through the window, lording it over, of course. And beside him sits that old witch Berta Zahnova — pray to God and cross yourself.

"I've brought Berta with me in case I need her here. You can charge me as if for an extra bed."

"Most certainly, sir, that will be eight crowns a day, since your room is first category and de luxe—"

"Ever since that floricultural evening of yours strange things have been happening here. A man doesn't feel quite safe here!"

"That's because our customers all run after Sonya. Just last night Mr. Jagr was trying to get at her by climbing through the kitchen window — and it was the second time he tried that!"

"You have to keep a close watch over that girl!"

"We've got a bar across the window, but when the customers are all so wild about her—"

"I've got an idea. Why don't we have Berta sleep in the kitchen with her—for greater security. Just for a couple of days."

"But after all. . . that would. . . There isn't another bed there."

"You can work that out somehow. I'll pay well for it."

"But we'll still have to charge the same as for an extra bed in your room, since there aren't any tariffs for sleeping in the kitchen, and since your room is first category and de luxe, it would still come to eight crowns, since—"

"I'll pay twenty-five."

"I ought to talk it over with my wife."

"Later, I haven't got the time now. And you can ask her what she'd like me to bring her from London on my next trip."

London has many things a woman likes ("I'd be quite happy, sir, with a few bottles of that Scottish grape-pomace brandy.") and so Berta Zahnova (an old acquaintance from the Globus, former citizen of the Third Reich and a large-scale procuress of our poor Protectorate girls, whom no one ever set eyes on again) was bedded down in the kitchen.

Volrabka and Zahnova embraced one another and kissed each other noisily, Sonya was ordered to prepare white coffee, to whip cream, to add fresh vanilla to the finest sugar and to cut slices of marble cake (made in three layers: plain, chocolate, and pink), both ladies recollected in sentimental fashion the delightful war years when they were still called *Gnädige Frau* and *Madame* and when business was still booming and there was still some sort of order, until midnight they prattled together (Berta Zahnova was sitting in the corner behind the stove) and over the pots and pans they called to one another:

". . .and you remember Emma, that wall-eyed redhead—"

"How could I forget her, she got married to an American Negro. And Oberstleutnant von Goltz—"

"He was killed at Minsk."

"Dicke Trudi works in Usti now as a shithole hag and she drives a broken-down Opel from East Germany."

"Is there any chance you know something about our little Lieselotte? She was like a daughter to me. . ."

"Why, those fellows on the steamship bought her, they sailed around with her for five days, and then she jumped under a train at Decin."

"Help yourself to another piece of cake, it's fresh."

At midnight the ladies opened a bottle of Griotte Morella and in half an hour's united effort they licked it all up. Then they decided that Berta would sleep in the same bed with Sonya, in the kitchen.

"But that's really not necessary now," Berta said when Volrab was placing the bar over the kitchen window.

"You'll both go beddie-bye better," said Volrab, forcefully closing the padlock and conspicuously sticking all the keys into his pocket. "Secure is secure."

"But if something— during the night—" Berta said.

"All you have to do is knock. Wifey and me, we're light sleepers!" Volrab told Berta, and as soon as he had shut the bedroom door, he hissed at Volrabka: "You hear? She wanted to have the window open!"

"Why would she?" Volrabka was surprised.

"Why, maybe to smuggle Sonya up to No. 2 during the night."

"That would be a dirty trick — after that marble cake and the Griotte, and I had fresh vanilla added to the sugar . . . But if anyone's capable of it, Berta is. . ."

"She's capable of anything! Why do you think Mr. Holy's planted her here with us?"

"Good Lord, how these times corrupt people! Nothing's the same as it used to be . . . there's no style or chic. And charm doesn't even exist anymore."

"So long as that witch is here, sleep with one eye open!"

Berta Zahnova sat down in the corner behind the stove and, except when she was spying on people, she stuck it out there all day long. Volrab was uneasy under her keen surveillance, he crammed his pockets with sugar and with an open can of Spanish sardines he walked peevishly around the yard, eating sardines with his fingers straight from the can (unsalted and without lemon they taste like boiled tripe), he fed the sugar to the pig and spoke to him reproachfully.

But Emil soon infected him with his good humor. Volrab stood for a while in the sun, just so, and already "ideas were beginning to come to him": he resolved to feed Emil fishmeal (so he grows nice and fat) and to give Sonya a bar of his private stock of pink soap (so she smells nice), she shouldn't use laundry soap any longer or spread lime for the chickens (so their eggshells are nice and thick), and Sonya should make that dress out of the white material with the canaries on it, like a wedding dress, white has always been the biggest hit, and let in the gray Belgian rabbit.

All of the Volrabs' merchandise was tender and succulent — Volrab was enthroned behind his beer tap until midnight, he watched Sonya closely while he pondered over marketing, Ranger Sames can pick up over two-and-a-half thousand and whatever else he can manage to steal in the woods, just once he could send me a brace of pheasants or a side of venison, and how would it hurt him if just once he were to send his women out to pick bilberries for the Hubertus—or cranberries! Mmm!

"Sonya, serve our forest ranger the strongest beer we've got."
Venison is nothing without cranberries.

Mr. and Mrs. Balada from No. 3 are the picture of
bureaucratic poverty, you can't get anything out of them. Petrik
Metelka is a fine customer with his daily bottle of champagne,
but watch out for the adolescent in him! He'll go and shoot
himself in the head some day, and then there'll be trouble!
"Sonya, offer Mr. Metelka the Parisian salted almonds!" "The
peanuts, Uncle?" "I said Parisian almonds, and take him two
packs!"

Postmaster Hudlicky is good for nothing, with his sixteen-
hundred crowns and his old lady Sarka, demanding as a Turkish princess, for an hour now he's been sitting over his first pint
while the bar's been filling up, I'll have to give him a small
warning so he won't be an inconvenience here. But that animal
doctor, Srol, knows what makes a good customer, "Another
small bottle of that Egyptian, Doctor, what do you say? Sonya,
can't you see the Doctor doesn't have anything to drink!"

The phone rang, long distance, and Pav, the dentist from
Jilemnice, was inquiring if it were really true that the Hubertus
was offering kissing evenings and if there were any truth to the
rumor that it had booked a belly dancer, "Something like that,
Doctor," Volrab said into the mouthpiece and he promised to
reserve a table for Sunday evening, for Dr. Pav "and two other
gentlemen." "But be here at eight o'clock sharp, 'cause with the
crowds we get it's hard to hold reservations—" said Volrab and,
spellbound, he hung up the phone, they were already calling
from the district capital. . .

"Sonya, when you have a free moment bring some cardboard
from the kitchen, cut each sheet in four, and write nicely on
each one RE-SER-VE in big letters, the final E has a reverse
accent, you know, because it's *French!*"

And Volrab drew a beer for himself and, touched, gazed at
Sonya's calves, success after success, like way back when at the
Globus whenever a train arrived from the front or a boat
anchored in the harbor, on each table a sign RESERVÈ.

When, on Wednesday evening, Ruda Mach entered the bar and caught sight of Ziki (for the first time since the day before, the day he had found the cream-colored envelope in his room addressed to Sonya, Engineer Zikmund Holy's card inside, and on the back of the card: "100 crowns for Room No. 5, the rest for you. A room in Usti is reserved for you until 7/15. Z." and a hundred-note), the first thing he did was carefully close the door behind him.

Then he walked slowly over to Ziki's table, unhurriedly he pulled out of his rear trousers pocket his brass-bound wallet, took a hundred-note out of it, and stuck the wallet back in his pocket. Then he unfolded the bill on his palm, cleared his throat with a rumble, and slowly, deliberately, and thoroughly spit on it.

The bar grew noisy and excited. Sonya put her hand to her mouth and turned pale. "What does Mr. Mach want?" Volrab roared from behind the bar.

With icy calm Ziki plunged his spoon into his bouillon, Ruda Mach crumpled the bill into a sharp little ball and hurled it between Ziki's eyes. "Just so you don't lose it!" he said, and he continued to tower over Ziki's table.

The paper ball lay dead on the tablecloth. Ziki made an imperceptible movement with his left shoulder while drawing forth from his briefcase a small pistol, and he aimed it quite visibly at Ruda Mach's stomach.

The silence in the bar kept growing heavier and heavier. Then Ruda Mach laughed and said: "Are you going to squeeze it or aren't you? Before my legs start to ache!"

Ziki's gaze and the barrel of his brown pistol dropped slowly to the tablecloth.

"I don't have a pistol," said Ruda Mach, "but come out to the yard if you want to fight it out with me. But you don't, do you. Well then, tuck your pistol away and make yum-yum with your soup like a nice fellow."

Ruda Mach went and sat down at his table (the bar was humming, Ziki put the pistol back in his pocket and made yum-yum with his soup, Volrab wiped the sweat from his brow and drew a pint of beer from the tap). Sonya slammed her tray down on the bar and ran to Ruda's table.

"Give me a beer," said Ruda Mach, and he smiled handsomely into Sonya's green, dilated pupils, which flashed with everything a young girl can feel (he made a mental note of this).

"Yes, Mr. Mach—" she sighed, and she smiled at him beautifully.

Where the Cottex meadow ends at the confluence of the mill-race and the river, in a wild triangle of never-mown prairie, buried in yard-tall grass, his eyes closed, Ruda Mach was finishing his Thursday lunch (blood sausage wrapped in newsprint), then in a five-square-foot clearing among the stalks he spread out a fascicle of technical documentation from Director Kaska ("Reconstruction of the bleaching room. 4/3, B/6. A battery of rinsing vats.") and he took his carpenter's pencil to the blueprints (he didn't like them) and drew things the way he would like them to be (it looks as if I'll be staying here a little bit longer).

On his way back to the bleaching room along the river bank, he pulled out of the grass an entire plant of splendidly blooming wild poppy. He sat down on some beams in front of the joiner's, plucked the firmest bud, cautiously freed it of its silky red petals (these will be the body and the skirt) and with his fingernails he pinched the bud so that less than an inch of stem was left (this will be the neck), then from the middle of the biggest flower he tore away the green seedhead fringed in black and he punctured the stalk beneath it (this will be the head), set the head on the neck, put the finished doll on his palm, and carried it off to the lab.

"Hey, that's really nice," said a pretty young lab assistant.

"Keep it down," said Ruda Mach, he took a matchbox from the table, poured the matches out on the table, and asked for "a swatch of cloth, any cloth, as long as it's beautiful."

The lab assistant eagerly brought some swatches, Ruda didn't care for any of them, only when he leafed through the costly sample book of the firm of Ciba International, bound in leather and printed in gold on wonderful, heavy Bible paper, and came to a page covered with jagged rectangles of silk dyed *Victoria-blau 2G* did he tear one out, make a bed in the matchbox, and carefully place Sonya's doll in it (for baby clothes he used *Silver-grey* from Du Pont de Nemours, made of tussah silk).

In the bleaching room he threw off his shirt and, sparkling with sweat, worked mercilessly on his battery of rinsing vats until the end of the shift.

Just before the second shift it started raining. Ruda Mach jumped over puddles on his way to the gate and in pouring rain (how nice the water smells—) he ran to take shelter in the doorway of the pharmacy. From each drop that fell on the granite pavement, a silvery fountain exploded, Ruda Mach breathed deeply, gazed at the shining pavement, and looked forward to having Sonya.

The alarm watch (Ziki's gift from the London Woolworth's) on Berta's wrist, which while she slept lay underneath her head, began on Thursday morning at 5:15 (yesterday Volrabka told her that Sonya wakes up at 5:30 and so she set her watch fifteen minutes earlier) to rattle right in her ear. Berta turned it off right away and lay motionless in the dim light alongside Sonya, who was breathing regularly.

The brightening square of window was barred and pad-locked, Volrab had, the night before, conspicuously taken the key together with all the other keys to the kitchen and the bar. Berta grinned (yesterday's Griotte was still working pleasantly in her veins) as she considered the sequence of today's tasks.

Sonya stirred in her sleep, embraced a corner of the pillow (the little one has pretty elbows), and mumbled something, like lightning Berta put her ear right up against Sonya's lips, but she couldn't understand a word, and again Sonya rolled over and faced the wall. Berta looked at her English watch—5:23—so we better get up, we've got a lot to do today.

With her knees and elbows (she had to move them only an inch or so) she began to poke Sonya's body until the girl finally woke up.

"Good morning!" said Sonya (the finest moment to evaluate the girl is the moment of her awakening, and the little one looks good even when she first opens those green eyes of hers).

"Good morning," Berta Zahnova smiled at her bedmate and then Sonya (lying against the wall) crawled over her to get out of bed; simulating gestures of helping and getting out of the way, Berta felt her over like a true connoisseur (first-class material) and while the naked Sonya was washing herself in the sink, she looked her over like a specialist (a fine piece, Mr. Holy will be most satisfied).

"Your boyfriend must really go for you, Sonya."

"I don't have one, Mrs. Zahnova."

"Don't tell me, such a beautiful girl—"

"Really I don't, Mrs. Zahnova."

"Mr. Holy told me you were the most beautiful girl in the Giant Mountains—"

"Ziki likes to kid around. Why doesn't he bring along his wife, Aja?"

"Don't you make out better without her?"

As soon as Sonya had left the kitchen, Berta ran to the door, placed her ear against it, and followed the sound of her footsteps, why isn't the little one going off to clean up the rooms? Berta rushed to the bolted window, but just as she was bringing up a stool (damn Volrab!), Sonya returned and caught sight of her: she had re-entered the hotel through the garden entrance with a white gladiolus in her hand (come on!).

As soon as she could hear Sonya's footsteps going up the stairs, softly but like lightning Berta pounced on Sonya's things: some hand-me-downs (washed to death), worn-out shoes, under her mattress a novel by someone named Lanoux, but where are her personal documents? Evidently the Volrabs are keeping them to hold the girl in their clutches. But how is it possible that the girl should have so pitifully few things? After more searching Berta found in the bottom layer of mattresses (on the springs beneath it was nothing but Spanish sardines, which meant that old Volrab was also a thief) a flat candy box (cognac-flavored creams), in it two hundred-notes and a five-crown note (apparently all of her cash-on-hand and capital) and a few letters from someone named Jarunka, nothing but the silly prattle of two girls, but there were two other letters which will be of interest to Mr. Holy.

On the first (a white sheet of office stationery) in hand-printed letters: "I LOVE YOU AND WANT TO MARRY YOU. J.J."

On the second (pink stationery, on the envelope just a single word: SONYA, an envelope without a stamp or a postmark, apparently delivered by hand): "Sonya, I love you. Be ready to go. On Saturday I will take you and show you our home. J.J."

"When I glanced into the bar last evening," Berta told the Volrabs after breakfast, "it seemed to me that I saw Engineer Jagr, from Usti, one of those youngish blonds."

"You did see him, and he is from Usti," Volrabka said with her mouth full.

"A hooligan," Volrab said with his mouth full.

"By any chance, is his name Josef?"

"Jakub."

So J.J. is Jagr from room No. 4.

When Sonya came back from cleaning the rooms, it did not escape Berta's notice that in the kitchen the girl was up to something around her bed, and then she saw Sonya quickly take something out of her empty pail and stick it under her mattress (we know where she put it and that it can't get away from us).

"I'm going out to get some air—" Berta mumbled, and she went noisily down the corridor, nimbly removed her slippers at the end of it, ran quickly up to the rooms (on the way she went over Engineer Holy's plan in her mind), and once she got her bearings (the plan was as precise as the engineer himself) she pushed her way into room No. 4 without making a sound:

In the wardrobe gleaming red shorts suitable for a nightclub acrobat, still with their price tag ("PRICE 76,—") and several white shirts of second-category quality. In the suitcase crumpled newspapers, color pencils, and official stationery with the Cottex letterhead. In the night table two blank pieces of pink stationery (just like the one under the girl's mattress) and two more candy boxes ("Blue Dessert" and chocolate-covered cherries). Satisfied, Berta left Jagr's room after less than two minutes (her speed was so great she failed to notice Jakub's checkpoint hairs on the door of the wardrobe and on the suitcase).

Room No. 5 was that bastard Mach's: a vagabond's room right down to that banged-up guitar on the wall. Under the washbasin freshly washed socks were drying, he had probably managed to do this before leaving for work, but certainly he hadn't managed to put in a vase that disgustingly fresh white gladiolus from the hotel garden!

Two minutes later (after five short raps) Berta was already making her report in room No. 2 across the way:

"She wakes up at half past five. She's very nicely developed. You'll be satisfied with her, sir. At night the Volrabs lock all the doors and bolt the window, they take the keys with them to their bedroom. I have a feeling they're watching me. She insists she's a virgin. She's reading a novel by someone named Lanoux. She asked about Mrs. Aja and she took the liberty of calling you Ziki. She has practically nothing at all. Her papers are evidently kept by the Volrabs. Volrab stores sardines in her bed, nearly a hundred cans of them. She corresponds with someone named Jarunka, but it's nothing more than the silly prattle of two girls. Jagr, in room No. 5, wrote her that he loves her, that she should be ready, and that on Saturday he would take her with him and show her to his parents."

"This Saturday?" asked Ziki, and he dipped a biscuit in his 'early morning tea.'

"The letter wasn't mailed and has no postmark. I think Jagr writes her fairly often and leaves the letters lying around his room, where she finds them while cleaning and takes them off to hide under her mattress. Today she got another one, I'll let you know about tomorrow."

"How about Mach?"

"She took him a white gladiolus from the garden."

"Does she give any other customers flowers?"

"Apparently not Jagr. The others are still asleep."

"Have a look at their rooms when you get the chance. It wouldn't be a bad idea to turn Jagr and Mach against each other somehow."

"Count on me, sir."

"Go on acting as usual. Stay in the kitchen. If I need you, I'll order *hot milk with rum*."

"I understand, sir."

Quietly Berta Zahnova went back across to room No. 5, after brief consideration she took a razor blade from the shelf beneath the mirror and slit all the strings of the guitar hanging on the wall. She crossed again to room No. 4, where after a brief search she came across Jakub Jagr's small yellow swimming pass (with a photo from his childhood no less), crossed again to room No. 5, and dropped the pass on the floor right by the door, silently she ran downstairs, nimbly put her slippers back on, crossed the yard, then sat down in the kitchen at her place in the corner behind the stove and said:

"You've got beautiful flowers in the garden. Mr. Holy would certainly appreciate having some in his room."

"Can do," said Volrab. "Sonya, hop out to the garden and drop off a bouquet in No. 2."

"In our hotel we used to place a bouquet in every room every day," said Berta.

"Yeah, in those days folks had *altogether* better manners," said Volrab, "but the socialist price guide doesn't mention bouquets. And even seed packets can add to your overhead, you know."

During the day, Berta frequently nodded off (conversation with Volrab bogged down somewhat, and Volrab was never especially polite), so that by evening she was again quite fresh, and when Sonya called into the kitchen, *"One hot milk with rum for table number two!"* in ten seconds Berta was leaning over Ziki's table in the bar.

"Mach slipped her something small, a matchbox or the like," whispered Ziki.

"Count on me, sir."

The next morning at five o'clock, in room No. 2, Berta announced the text of another pink letter from Jagr ("I love you and on Saturday I'll take you away"), his next box of candy (assorted liqueurs), and another white gladiolus for Mach (nothing of interest in the rooms of the other guests). "And this is what Mach gave her in the bar—" and Berta set down on Ziki's table a large matchbox (so-called family size), on its yellow label a red crab extended its claws, inside, a child's doll made from a wild poppy.

"Telephone Wolf from the post office," said Ziki over his 'early morning tea,' "have him come Sunday afternoon with the van. Have him load on the medium-duty gear."

On Thursday afternoon, upon returning to his room, No. 4, Engineer Jakub Jagr was alarmed: for the very first time Sonya has broken into my wardrobe — the hair is torn away from both sides of my suitcase as well . . . did she act out of mere curiosity or from a new-born personal interest? What do I actually know about her psychological motives and mechanisms—

With the suitcase open on his lap Jakub passionately re-examined his previous evaluations of Sonya's replies to his psychotechnical tests, as for instance to the question: *Do you respond to a new experience a) pleasantly, b) energetically, c) depressively, d) with much agitation,* Sonya had underlined *a) pleasantly,* although this could indicate nothing more than the curiosity of a hotel maid, but on the other hand, to the question on another test, *Would you be interested to know what color ties your fiancé prefers, before you marry him?* Sonya had replied *YES*, an answer that could wonderfully mean—

In the midst of his dogged concentration on the contents of his suitcase, Jakub suddenly realized that something was out of place (the young technician was known for his precise photographic memory) and immediately detected what it was: his swimming pass had disappeared from the suitcase, a yellow card with his photo on it—

He instantly embarked on a comprehensive survey, standing on the chair he examined the wardrobe from above, then he pushed the wardrobe and the bed away from the wall, inch by inch, on his knees, he tested the possibility of the floorboards coming unstuck, he scrutinized the drain in the sink, the windowsill, even the facade within an arm's-length radius of the window, and he unscrewed the globes and bulbs of the chandelier—nothing. But why would Sonya take his swimming pass . . . BECAUSE IT HAS MY PHOTO ON IT—

The door of his room flew open and in burst Ruda Mach, he carefully closed the door behind him and said: "By any chance did you lose this—" and in his hand was my swimming pass with my photo on it.

"I was just now looking for it. . ."

"Do you remember where you left it?"

"It's always in my suitcase. . ."

"So you don't remember?"

"I'm absolutely certain it's always in my suitcase—Ow!!—"

This last was Ruda Mach grabbing Jakub by his hair, with a vigorous tug he pulled Jakub's head forward to his knees and led him (this hurts more than crawling on your knees, and even more than the usual method of being dragged along the floor by your hair) the whole way down the corridor to his own room, No. 5, where he flung him ("OWWWW!!—") onto the floor and pointed with the swimming pass to his guitar hanging on the wall, with its slashed strings dangling like the hair of a hanged hippy.

After more swearing and prolonged explanations culminating in a solemn oath with two fingers raised, Ruda released Jakub with the words: "Well, I really don't know why you would have done it. But then *who* could it be?"

Who and why and WHAT CONNECTION DOES IT HAVE TO SONYA— Jakub whispered to the mirror in his room (for the second time already his wet washcloth had grown warm in an effort to relieve his tormented head), of course it wasn't Sonya who'd cut the guitar strings, it was as if some gang was beginning to take over the hotel — Day after tomorrow I'll take Sonya home.

Technical operation in the form of a rehearsal:

(Jakub walked downstairs to the ground floor) here at the foot of the stairs I'll wait for Sonya, I'll kiss her and take her out through this gate (Sonya has the key: she unlocked it for me that awful Sunday evening) and I'll take her by the hand (in our other hands we'll both be carrying suitcases) quickly across the meadow shortcut (or down the street, depending on whether it's day or night) to the train station (Jakub took the meadow shortcut to the Hrusov station and checked the time on his steel stopwatch: 9 minutes. Via the street it takes 13 minutes) at a time as far as possible linked to the train's departure (on his pocket calendar Jakub had already checked off the train times according to the glassed-in posters at the station: *5:42, 6:37, 7:44, 14:11, 15:26, 19:31, 22:16* and he had rechecked them according to the posted Czechoslovak Railways timetable), "take one last look—," I'll tell her, and Sonya will surely be touched, I'll be tender toward her and I'll leave her to think her thoughts, but when we get out at Martinice (*6:03, 6:58, 8:05, 14:32, 15:47, 19:52, 22:37*) I'll try to make her laugh, at the Martinice station we can have a glass of wine (tomorrow I'll buy a bottle of good red and two collapsible cups, a fifth box of candy for the trip) and then by express (R 151, R 47, R 242, R 93) along the Elbe to Usti and by taxi to our home. . .

5:57-12:10 Sonya works in the bar *beautiful enough to drive one mad with her long, firm, slender legs. An erect, royal Madonna with a halo of strawberry-blond hair. Eyes like moist, warm emeralds. That silvery laugh of hers* — and she belongs to that orangutang Mach and that brute takes note of it and brazenly laughs in Sonya's sunlight, Sonya herself has admitted him into her radiance. . . Tarzan Mach slowly draws a large matchbox out of his pocket (so-called family size), plays with the box with his plump, dirty fingers (on its yellow label some sort of red spider), suddenly he snaps his fingers (at Sonya!) and in a second Sonya is next to him (how she obeys him!) and that bison Mach sticks the matchbox into her apron . . . How greedily and yet how proprietarily he feasts his eyes on Sonya . . . And how easily Sonya bears his gaze—

But what can there be in that box? I don't know, but I do — I've read heaps of crime novels and I always understood cravings for gain, security, power, and pleasure, even sheer boredom or indifference as psychologically explicable motives for murder — now I suddenly realize that it could also be mere jealousy. Even jealousy not based on a thing—how they smile at each other, Beauty and the Beast!—even, so far, jealousy not based on a thing. For if a greater evil is prevented, murder is necessary and logical.

12:11 A.M. (tomorrow is Saturday already, when I have to take Sonya home) Jakub began to pace back and forth in his room, No. 4, he decided to stay up until morning, when Sonya would come to clean his room, so he could talk with her, on the third (the next to last) pink sheet of stationery all he wrote was: "I LOVE YOU AND I AM WHOLLY YOURS — JAKUB," he placed the letter on the table and next to it the third box of candy ("Blue Dessert," the next to last one, and tomorrow I'll buy a fifth for the trip) and for ninety minutes he looked out the window at the stars.

"Sonya!" Jakub said the moment Sonya came in to clean his room in the morning. "I love you and I want to marry you. Tomorrow I'll take you and show you my home."

"Uncle and Auntie would never let me," said Sonya, but then she smiled prettily at Jakub.

"But you can't stay here — it gets worse and worse every day."

"You're right about that. Especially now that Mrs. Berta's sleeping in my bed—"

"It's horrible, what they do to you here . . . Sonya. We must leave tomorrow. Put all your things in a suitcase—"

"A small shopping bag would do for my things. The little kind that children play with. And I don't have a suitcase, Uncle took mine away the very first day I came here. . ."

"Don't take anything then, I'll buy you everything you need and everything you want. We must leave tomorrow! The local to Martinice, the express to Usti, and a taxi to our home. . ."

"That would be nice, but—"

"You'll love our house. It's in a green valley at the base of Strizov Mountain, I'll take you for lovely walks. It's all white and we'll have the second floor just for the two of us, in front there's a garden with beds of gladiolus and roses and a wicket gate overgrown with roses leads to our apple and cherry orchard . . . At the end there's a bench I had an urge last spring to paint green, but for you I'll make it white. . ."

"That would be lovely . . . Oh, Jakub . . . when I don't know yet what's going to happen to me. . . Something's definitely going to happen—I have an inkling, you know—but I don't know what . . . So I'm asking you before it happens to me . . . Sometime later say all over again what you said to me this morning. . ." And Sonya ran out into the corridor and locked herself in another room.

Jakub walked back and forth from the window to the door, she's gone before I had a chance to give her the letter and the candy, Sonya hadn't said YES, but she hadn't said NO either, it sounded like MAYBE— *but do women ever say YES? YES IS WHAT WOMEN MEAN WHEN THEY SAY MAYBE—*

When an hour later he heard Sonya's footsteps, Jakub ran out into the corridor and gave Sonya the candy and the pink letter. "I understand you and I'll wait till you decide—" Jakub blurted out, just then the door to No. 3 opened and Beda Balada, in his shorts, began to listen with great interest— "Thanks," Sonya whispered, she smiled prettily at Jakub, dropped the candy box and the letter into her pail, threw a rag on top of it all, and ran downstairs.

Jakub had been pacing back and forth in his room, No. 4, for scarcely five more minutes when suddenly from the corridor the quiet rustle of footsteps and it stopped in front of my door . . . is it Sonya coming back to look through my things—or perhaps to upgrade her MAYBE to a YES—

Endlessly and without a single squeak, my door handle descended — is this the way she was coming to declare her love? . . . Jakub quickly slunk away into a corner and like a criminal hid behind the criminally opening door. Berta Zahnova slipped into the room and silently shut the door behind her.

Without the slightest hesitation and with terrible deftness she opened my wardrobe, with her left hand she jerked out one of my white shirts, in her right hand there was suddenly a butcher's knife, she picked the shirt up by its collar to her eye-level, pierced it through the shoulder blades, and then with a vigorous cut she slit the back all the way down, threw it on the floor, and reached for another one of my white shirts.

"You old bitch!" roared Jakub, and he leapt out at Berta Zahnova.

The woman kept her cool, all she did was look down at the ground.

"What's this all about?" cried Jakub.

"Pardon me, there's some misunderstanding—I must have gotten the room numbers mixed up."

"So you cut up shirts in other rooms? Maybe the one where you cut the strings of a guitar? And why did you take my swimming pass to room No. 5?"

"I don't know what you're talking about. I'll say it again: I got the room numbers mixed up. How much did that shirt cost?"

"A hundred and fifty crowns. So what was that pass thing all about?"

"I don't know what you're talking about," said Berta Zahnova, who had been fumbling in her apron for some time, and suddenly she pulled out two hundred-notes, placed them on the edge of the washbasin, with her knife in her hand she passed close to the dumbfounded Jakub and, before he could get hold of himself, opened the door with a lightning-like motion and disappeared like a ghost.

While his anger froze (or did it grow and become more productive), Jakub picked up the two hundred-notes and in his other hand he grabbed his Foreign Legion dagger (purloined by his father and ceremonially turned over to Jakub on his eighteenth birthday) and went to settle matters right in the lair of the gang leader.

The key was sticking out of the door of room No. 2, just the way Sonya had left it after cleaning, Jakub unlocked the door (the room was empty, Ziki always drove to the swimming pool before breakfast) and without hesitation he opened the wardrobe, a pile of elegant shirts of chocolate-colored silk smiled out at him provocatively, Jakub fastidiously swept a short, painfully yellow whip off the top of the pile, picked the first shirt up by its collar to his eye-level—for a whole fifth of a second he admired the softness and marvelous texture of perfect Japanese weave (he was a textile engineer)—pierced it through the shoulder blades, and then with a vigorous cut he slit it all the way down, threw it on the floor, and then reached for another, pierced and slit, and then a third, a fourth, and finally the fifth and final one.

Then he stepped over the pile of rags (the Japanese really know how to make silk!) in order to place the two hundred-notes on Ziki's table. But there was already something on Ziki's table.

On Ziki's table there was a large matchbox (so-called family size), on its yellow label a red crab stretched its claws toward the English words, THE RED CRAB. Inside the box, under a swatch of silver-grey tussah silk, on top of another swatch of acetate silk dyed *Victoriablau* 2 or 3 G was a doll of the kind village children make from wild poppy flowers — it was Tarzan Mach's matchbox.

The entire hotel in the hands of Ziki's gang, and Tarzan Mach (that game with the pistol in the bar on Wednesday evening was nothing but camouflage) is another of Ziki's gorillas, specially hired for use against Sonya, GANG AGAINST SONYA, *and I alone must defend her*—

But engineers are special people (as when they reached the moon), Jakub looked at his steel stopwatch and began a comprehensive examination of room No. 2 (he was a technician).

Wonderfully refreshed, Ruda Mach came back on Friday evening straight from the swimming pool, his hair still wet, to his room, No. 5, and on his table found a letter (in this hotel *everyone* had gone nuts):

> *Dear Mr. Mach!*
> *The strings on your guitar could only have been slashed by Mrs. Berta Zahnova, who's been living in our kitchen. She works for Mr. Z. Holy of room No. 2 and I know that she's now following me into all the hotel rooms.*
> *Yours,*
> *Sonya Cechova*

Ruda Mach looked at his guitar, its strings hung on the wall like intestines (but the world's full of new guitars), he threw Sonya's crumpled letter into the wastebasket and went to have dinner in the bar.

Behind the bar, Volrab had a poker face, Ziki was looking as if nothing in the world could interest him so much as his soup, Jagr eyed me as if I'd just been released on parole, that fellow Metelka poured champagne into himself like water, and from all the tables the stares of bigwigs and high livers from that stinking Usti (where I wouldn't even spend an hour), only Sonya smiles at me prettily — what's up?

It's Sonya. That kind and beautiful girl, whom they treat here like a goat at the annual market fair. But she deserves far better treatment. Something should be done for her (and when Ruda Mach comes to the conclusion that something should be done, he does it, at the latest the next second).

The next second, Ruda Mach walked straight over to Sonya, took her head in both his hands (and Sonya raised her face to him), and gave her a nice kiss on the forehead and—so that everyone would know that she'll be mine—he kissed her beautifully on the lips.

By popular demand of the guests and the hon. public
OUR SECOND FLORICULTURAL EVENING
Hotel Hubertus
MUSIC - SONG - RAFFLE WITH FLOWERS
Starring the ever-popular Sonya Cechova
Admission 6 crowns   Begins at 8:00 P.M.
20 crown Minimum

On Sunday evening Volrab read the poster up on the gate of his hotel again and again, Sonya had really done a good job with it, in five colors yet, only the admission fee could easily have been 8 crowns and the minimum at least 25 . . . we know how to raise prices, and when customers pay money, the show will sure be funny!

With delight, Volrab read the whole poster two more times, all the way from "By popular demand. . ." to "20-crown Minimum" and now he was hurrying to look over the bar for the last time before the great soirée, all the tables were still empty (today we don't open until 8:00 P.M.) and the hall was festively adorned: between the chandeliers were festoons of crepe paper left over from the firemen's ball (at a loss of 200 crowns, since around midnight Ranger Sames had dragged in eight more pickled forest rangers, who brawled like bulls), on the walls three clusters of brown-glass Christmas ornaments left over from the Cottex 08 Christmas party (at a loss of 300 crowns, since the kids gobbled up everything without paying a crown, and eventually they tipped the Christmas tree over onto the billiard table), and two Chinese lanterns left over from our *First Formal Dance* (at a loss of 400 crowns, since except for the musicians—they were paid the 400 crowns—only three customers bothered to come, and between them they ordered all of five beers and headed home), on every table a clean white tablecloth and napkins even, and on each table a white sign RESERVÈ. . .

Volrab sighed with happiness, drew himself a beer, and mulled over the strategy to be employed in the upcoming match: by the door the Baladas from No. 3, that wretch of a clerk who orders a small beer in the bar and then enjoys a bottle of co-op rum in his room — I'll show you, you riff-raff, by 9:30 you'll have gobbled up two skewers of meat with veggies and then at least two ice creams at 4 crowns apiece, I'll show you what you've got to order when you go to a soirée!

For young Mr. Metelka it will be Parisian bubbly, Parisian almonds again, of course, and our top special appetizer, Parisian rolled anchovies (from that can of herring) . . . nothing but Paris for your bare ass, dearie!

Postmaster Hudlicky won't be coming tonight, who would have believed what a champion of diet food he is — but then how he twitched when I hinted that we wouldn't be counting on him to come this time . . . That's it, fellow, don't come here at all, when you haven't got the wherewithal!

Veterinarian Srol has a lot of class, his table RESERVÈ right by the piano to give him a good view, and right off he'll cut into a double portion of pork on a spit with lots of veggies and his Egyptian white wine.

For Dr. Pav and the other two gentlemen from Jilemnice bubbly on the table before they realize where they're at, and then the menu right away, they're big shots and the crème de la crème of our soirée — next to them the smith from Cottex won't look so hot, he's an expendable customer, but he knows his liquor, while the gentlemen from the district capital like it best when they can swill and soak for free. . .

Ranger Sames—what a customer he is! If just once he'd send over a brace of pheasants or a side of venison — and a bucket of cranberries . . . mmm! But he better not pinch Sonya so much on the cheeks tonight, or the girl's capital value might wear out too quickly.

Vagabond laborer Mach—nothing but trouble! He can't be reasoned with, he's likely to belt someone . . . But bear in mind, you tramp—you won't sit here till midnight sipping just two beers!

Ph.Dr. Berka and Ph.Dr. Berkova, they hardly eat a thing, but they do like to drink, so no problem. And next to them Engineer Holy from No. 2 has already ordered his dinner, only real Italian vermouth will serve his needs (he'd know another kind right off, yes he would), and for him I give up my own Spanish sardines *Mallorca* . . . we'll work it all out on the monthly bill, Engineer!

Engineer Jagr, that hooligan and blithering idiot, is an extremely unattractive customer . . . but to keep him away from dinner would be ill-advised, for he would again threaten to go to the district authorities. So let him peek—perhaps through a magnifying glass—at our honest hospitality, but he better not lay a finger on Sonya!

And one chair in the corner (and the Bridal Suite!) were reserved by telephone from Prague — could it be the one who sat here last time through the entire gala? — Yeah, it's all getting to be a pretty big deal.

Flushed with creative effort, Volrabka was in the kitchen circling about her original creations: a hazelnut cake made with Sana (the own dear sister to butter!) and peanuts (it was cut a little crooked, so the slices that could be served were called *Turkish Hazelnut Delight*), a whipped-cream cake made with eggwhites (it had risen beautifully, and the leftover beaten eggwhites were tossed onto last year's cookies moistened with drops of vinegary apple juice and presto! a tray of *Baden Slices*), and an *Omelette 'Surprise'* (batter made from powdered eggs, filled with strawberries preserved in liqueur, and then browned until it becomes a little crumbly), beaten eggwhites, chopped peanuts, and—what no one could have expected—dried prunes soaked in French Alpa, which does wonders to refresh your feet).

Volrab "deigned to create in meat" and fabricated such specialties as *Garnished Platter Grand Hubertus* (circles of sausage with scraps of smoked ham, tomatoes, mustard, and chopped peanuts), *Chef's Secret* (beef rolls filled with circles of sausage and chopped peanuts), and *Hamburg Pilot Fish* (circles of sausage with onions, peppers, chopped peanuts, and vinegar, and for a spicy effect on the palate a little of the hydrochloric acid used in the bathroom).

"And now put paprika, pepper, and salt on everything!" Volrab eagerly ordered.

"But Uncle, it's already so black with pepper, as if I'd emptied a whole ashtray on it," said Sonya.

"You can never have too much pepper," said Volrab, "but you have to work it in underneath, like this—" and with his fat fingers he turned over the circles of sausage, powdered their tummies with pepper the way you powder a chafing infant, and thus galvanized he turned them over again.

"Are there enough flowers?"

"I think there are, Uncle, see—"

Sticking out of six metal buckets under the kitchen window were bundles and sheaves of carnations, irises, and gladiolus, in all more than half a flower wagon.

"And now, Sonya, pour hot water into the basin and take off all your clothes!" Volrabka commanded, and he began to prepare the main course. She soaped and scrubbed Sonya, who stood naked in the basin of water on the floor, until Berta Zahnova climbed out of her corner behind the stove and nimbly gave her a hand.

The women raised Sonya's arms and legs and scoured them all over with a washcloth, a sponge, and a brush, then they rinsed her with the entire contents of a garden pail, rubbed her with a towel until she turned red, perfumed under the armpits, on the breasts, and behind the ears, dressed her in the new white gown, combed her, sprinkled her with cologne from Volrabka's wedding silver-and-crystal flagon, massaged the cheeks until they were rosy, a drop of vinegar in each eye to make them sparkle ("a pity we don't have any atropine," Volrabka sighed), and on the lips they rubbed white machine oil ("It would be a waste of good lipstick, since it would be gone right away," Volrabka explained).

Sonya took the skirt in her fingers and in front of the kitchen window, enchanted, she whirled about in the most beautiful dress she had ever worn in her life.

Volrabka's eyes filled with tears and, touched, she whispered: "She's like a little bride, our girl is. . ."

And Volrab, moved to the point of blowing his nose, said with feeling: "It's as if we were marrying off our own daughter. . ."

> *Madelon, pour me some wine,*
> *Let's be very merry,*
> *Germany's in decline,*
> *Now we have them to bury.*

sang Sonya, wearing her white dress and playing the piano in the bar, on her lips the repulsive taste of machine oil, intended to prolong my kissability, and under my eyelids the vinegar burns so my eyes'll sparkle — all so the gentlemen will buy plenty of tickets, which Uncle is now preparing at the bar . . . with what pleasure he uses his thick, fat hands to count those tickets to my lips . . . How much longer must I be grateful to him?—

"After a delightful musical overture we will go on to our first drawing — there will be more drawings and each of you will get your share in this the floricultural lottery of our second floricultural soirée!" Uncle Volrab announced, and he came out carrying the tickets (pages from last year's calendar). "Each ticket is a mere five crowns, and with each ticket the management gives gratis a charming flower and, as a special favor, the administration throws in, entirely free, a kiss from our beautiful

Sonya—Sonya, come here and let the gentlemen see—for a mere five crowns three favors right off and every ticket a winner—"

Sonya got up on the piano (that increases the gentlemen's willingness to buy, but I have no desire to smile at them, even if they all buy tickets of admission to my favors, even those given gratis. Dr. Pav and the two other gentlemen from Jilemnice, Mr. Beda Balada from No. 3 and Ranger Sames, the unknown man in the tuxedo who had reserved a table and the Bridal Suite by telephone from Prague . . . isn't he buying any? But then why did he come — Mr. Mach is buying a ticket and the smith from Cottex is impatiently waving a five-crown note.

Why then am I hanging around like a gingerbread heart at a fair, waiting to be bought? — do I really want to know? Or do I get a kick out of the men in the bar? Is it fun for me? Or do I merely consider it part of my vocation and my job?

This and that and this and that. Actually, I am four persons: besides the ordinary Sonya I am also *Sonya-Marie* (quiet, gentle, defenseless, and happily subservient), next *Sonya-Marikka* (provocative, bold, risk-taking, wild), and then *Antisonya* (she always tells the unpleasant part of the truth). And those four girls quarrel and fight inside me and it's always the one who is on top at the moment who pushes me in some direction, usually where I don't even want very much to be. . .

"So smile prettily, Sonya, and we'll begin the first drawing!" Uncle Volrab called to me, he handed me the covered basket containing the tickets and applauded loudly.

I reach under the cloth, pull a piece of paper out of the basket, and hand it to Uncle.

"The first winner is No. 6!" Uncle calls out. "Let the lucky winner come up promptly—Sonya, come closer—"

The first lucky winner is Mr. Beda Balada from room No. 3, he hands Uncle his coupon, receives a pink carnation, and now he's standing right in front of me. I can't avoid kissing him, but it's hardly something to rejoice about— ("It's your job—" whispered *S.-Marie*. "Get it over with, there's a lot more of that waiting for you," grinned *Antisonya*) —so in my job as Sonya I kiss him very modestly on the forehead.

In the second drawing, the hunchbacked smith from Cottex wins my favor, and after him comes Jakub Jagr, holding No. 8 . . . a really good-looking jock of a boy, with hair like yellow silk, sincere blue eyes, and the well-scrubbed, rosy skin of a young girl. . . "*You'll like our house,*" he had said to me day before yesterday. "*It's all white and we'll have the whole second floor to ourselves, in front is a garden with beds of gladiolus*—BUT THAT'S WHAT I BRING MR. RUDA—*and roses and through the gate overgrown with roses is the way to our apple and cherry orchard . . . At the end is a bench which I painted green last spring, but which I'll now paint white, for you. . .*"It isn't a little thing Jakub is offering me (it's what a 100% *S.-Marie* would deserve) —why doesn't Mr. Ruda Mach offer me a white house in a green valley. . .

"Sonya, if suddenly something should happen, say all of a sudden the lights should go out, sirens should sound, and something like snowflakes started flying about—don't be afraid—I'll manage things for you—" Jakub whispered hurriedly, "but the best thing would be if you would go inconspicuously out into the corridor, I'll be waiting for you down at the foot of the staircase, the last train leaves at 10:16 P.M., it connects with the express R 93, and then I'll bring you home by taxi—"

"How wonderfully good you are to me. . ." *S.-Marie* smiles at Jakub for me.

But Uncle is applauding me impatiently, he wants to sell me so many times today — and so the ordinary Sonya at once reaches into the basket for a ticket, in my haste I draw out three at once, they're all crumpled together, Uncle gives me a nasty look but he's already announcing:

"The next winners are numbers 10, 11, and 12, please come up, lucky gentlemen—Sonya, come closer—"

The lucky gentlemen are Dr. Pav and his two friends from Jilemnice, to correct my *faux-pas* (that's all the French I know, except for *Bonjour, Je vous aime,* and *Merci* — and of course *l'amour*) as the fiery *S.-Marikka* I kiss all three heads in a row.

The holder of No. 3 (horse doctor Srol) deserves *Antisonya,* but that contrary girl is always hiding at the rare moments when I would like to be her.

And with ticket No. 5 Mr. Ruda Mach rises from his table, HOORAY! (all four Sonyas in me called this out together), and now he's coming up for his kiss, tall, frank, everything about him is brown, his thick dark hair and his good dark tan. *Handsome.* . .

And a real man among all these rabbits, he fears nothing and no one, not even Mr. Ziki's brown revolver. The first person here who ever stood up for me. And he can be tender as well . . . that pretty doll he made me out of a wild poppy—how could I ever have lost it? And when, on Friday evening, he kissed me in front of everyone here (like nobody ever!), it was not only beautiful (like nothing ever!), it was in front of everyone, that's the most beautiful part of it and so terribly important.

At his table now, Jakub is covering his face with his hands, so Jakub is suffering, Jakub, who offers me a white house, a wedding, and a whole life together . . . what does Mr. Mach have at his disposal? How easily and quickly he parted from his girls forever, after all the happiness they'd had together — and how many of those girls has he brought here . . . Could a mere four Sonyas suffice him for the rest of his life? Which of the four would he put up with the longest — and which would he need the most? Does he need any of them at all?

Mr. Ruda Mach's lips silently say YES, and in response all four Sonyas kiss those lips.

"I'm not crazy about anyone kissing you but me," says Mr. Ruda Mach.

"Me neither. But I can put up with it a bit longer. . ."

But once again Uncle is already applauding me impatiently, that kiss must have struck him as indecently long — and possibly too good for just five crowns . . . Uncle's given me

another nasty look and then hastily—as the always prepared
S.-Marikka—I divide my restrained favors between tickets Nos.
7 (a from room No. 6) and 4 (the forester Sames, who pinches
and smells).

Ticket No. 9 is the property of Mr. Ziki, in no hurry he walks
toward me through the tables, an extremely elegant (today for
the first time he isn't wearing that brown shirt and that loud
yellow tie. . .) and rather terrifying gentleman. Is he carrying
that brown revolver in his pocket? (*S.-Marikka* thinks that Mr.
Ziki has something about him that's quite special, perhaps even
cruel, but strangely fascinating. . ."His wallet, maybe?"
Antisonya grins. *S.-Marie* is frightened of him.)

Mr. Ziki kisses coldly, but perfectly.

"In my house in Usti I've got a beautiful room waiting for
you," he says drily. "With a view of the garden."

"Uncle and Auntie would never let me go," *S.-Marikka* chirps
flirtatiously.

"I could take care of that in five minutes."

"Would Mrs. Zahnova and I still sleep in the same bed?"

"Zahnova lives on the ground floor and she would obey you
like a dog."

"It's a deal!" *S.-Marikka* laughs. "But first I want a pretty
lady's pistol. And a platinum anklet!"

"If we leave today, you can get the weapon by lunchtime.
And the anklet before dinner in Prague."

The smile *S.-Marikka* gave to Ziki contained many promises,
and now we have the last drawing of the first series: Petrik
Metelka skulks forward with blazing ears for a little buss from
me . . . how ashamed he is, and for no reason, actually he might
be the best of them all, not only because he's the youngest, but
also because he's the purest, the sort I might have deserved —
and liked the best. . .

Before the second series Uncle orders "a small musical interlude for the beauty of the ear and right after it we'll go on to
the second round, sit on the stool, Sonya, and give us that one
about the star!"

And Sonya sat on the piano stool, raised her eyes to the ceiling, put her fingers on the keys, and sang:

After dusk has fallen,
When it's growing late,
I sit outside on the bench
Beside our garden gate.
I look up at the heavens,
I look up at my star.
Where are you, where are you, my star—
Where are you, where are you, my star. . .

At his table, in torment, Jakub covered his face with his hands while Sonya was kissing Ruda Mach, writhed with anger while she was kissing Ziki, and suffered during young Metelka's turn ABSOLUTELY UNBEARABLE — once more with another ticket in his hand he went up to invite Sonya to leave with him by the last train of the night, and if she cannot or will not, I will put an end to this disgusting masquerade:

First of all, unscrew all the fuses in the corridor. Using a flashlight in the darkness that follows, activate the civilian defense alarm on the roof. Pull the fire extinguishers down from the wall, release their safety catches in the corridor, open the door to the bar with his foot—but the people will already be running out of there—and fire at them a full dose of freezing flakes of CO_2.

Jakub felt for the flashlight in his pocket and just then Wolf Zahn came into the bar wearing a black leather jacket, he looked about lazily and went over to sit down at Ziki's table, the gangster has come to tell his boss that everything's ready—

What had the GANG AGAINST SONYA prepared? 5:11 Wolf Zahn had driven up in a gray van, license No. UL-91-91, he parked it in the yard and then didn't budge, so that until now an investigation was not feasible — now he clearly comes ready for action—

Now that an investigation was feasible, Jakub got up from his table and, inconspicuously, with his hands in his pockets, sauntered out to the corridor, silently ran down it (while taking stock of the electric fuses and fire extinguishers filled with CO_2) and in the darkness of the yard he took the long way around to the right (because it faced away from the windows of the kitchen and of the Volrabs' bedroom) side of Zahn's van.

The front and back doors of the van were locked, of course, but now was no time for technical niceties or even common decencies, Jakub wrapped his fist in his handkerchief, knocked out the side window, and made his way into the back of the van.

From the kitchen window very little light reached here, but it was still more than enough to confirm the very worst: on the floor of the van lay a folding metal stretcher, to which four leather straps had been fastened—for tying down a victim—next to it a tarp and two blankets, so no one could hear Sonya screaming when they tied her down—

In the corner, in a metal receptacle packed with excelsior, a glass 25-liter carboy, upon opening it a gust of ammonia. Releasing 25 liters of ammonia would incapacitate all living things over a space of more than two acres — along with carefully placed explosives and hand smoke-grenades of the series RDG, it was enough for a paramilitary squad to capture a town.

Right by the door a small canister, when you unscrew the top you can smell the sweet, heavy scent of chloroform—evidently for one-on-one combat. Beside it a ball of silk parachute wire, a truncheon—so the captive would give in as soon as possible. . .

And here we have a license plate numbered PB—that's Pribram, isn't it—PB-26-52, for quick concealment in case of detection . . . and on the front seat, just like gangsters: black stockings to pull down over the face, 3 pairs of dark glasses with convex lenses, 2 hypodermic needles, 2 vials of hypodermic solution.

As soon as Volrabka had gone out of the kitchen and into the bar to cut, in person, her "hazelnut" cake (made of the cheapest grade of peanuts and stale Sana), Berta Zahnova sprang from her corner behind the stove, ran through the kitchen, and shut the door to the Volrabs' bedroom behind her.

Mr. Holy wanted her to find our girl's citizen I.D. (to have it ready in case in five minutes' time we may feel like going to Usti), Zahnova drew out of her apron a small but effective flashlight in the form of a fountain pen (a gift Ziki had bought at the London Woolworth's) and she began systematically to search from corner to corner, under the beds, in the pillows, in the night tables, in the wardrobes — she drew up a chair and with the flashlight in her teeth examined Volrab's papers piled right up to the ceiling.

> *I look up to the heavens*
> *I look up to a starrr,*
> *Where arre you, where arre you, my loovelyy*
> *starrr. . .*

Volrab crooned happily with his hand on his glowing brass pipe as he affably watched how carefully darling Volrabka was setting the nut cake down . . . a cube of Sana, a pinch of flour, chopped peanuts, baking powder, and three yellow sherbet-powder tablets, and how the ladies and gentlemen lick their chops over it, Mme. Baladova takes two pieces at three fifty per, chink-chink, I've got the whole cost sheet for the cake at home and what's left is pure, clear profit, Mme. Baladova also takes two pieces so she doesn't look like a skinflint, it's the ladies who have to put up a good front at a soirée, and so thanks for your seven crowns, my good lady, chink-chink: I'll write it down in my accounts — it will be like Silesian headcheese with bacon, mmm! And Ranger Sames raises his thumb and then his pinkie, that means a beer and a small beer chaser, chink-chink, it's already being drawn for you,

> *. . .Wherre arre you, wherre arre you, my*
> *loovelyy starrr. . .*

after an aperitif pastries do just fine, Ranger, and then there'll be *Garnished Platter Grand Hubertus* at eleven, chink-chink, and at midnight I'll bring out the *Hamburg Pilot Fish*, covered with hydrochloric acid, for a fiver, chink-chink, after which we'll serve wine—'cause the beer will have run out by then, hi-hi—and century-old monk's brew.

> *. . .Wherre arre you, wherre arre you, wherre*
> *arre you. . .*

Jakub crawled out through the broken window of the van and in the cool of the night breeze he was wiping cold sweat from his forehead when he caught sight of a little light dancing inside the Volrabs' bedroom.

Forward leaps and then slowly along the wall to stretch his head, protected by his bent forearm, toward the bottom of the window frame — in the darkness of the bedroom a small point of light right below the ceiling and once you accommodate your retinas you could see Berta Zahnova with a flashlight in her teeth grubbing wildly through some papers. . .

Why didn't you turn on the light, Mrs. Zahnova? . . . And what could you possibly need so urgently just now? . . . Is this Ziki's surprise attack on the Volrabs? No question. Either Volrab doesn't belong to Ziki's gang, or Zahnova and Volrab belong to rival gangs in Ziki's underworld. . .

But now Sonya's at stake, and the freight in Ziki's van and Zahn's presence in the bar dictate prompt action, at whatever cost. . . Even at the cost of establishing hitherto unimaginable (and then imaginable only for as long as the campaign takes!) contact—

Jakub burst through the corridor and flew into the bar right up to the counter, on catching sight of Volrab he stifled his disgust—that bald, repellent swindler who exploits and now prostitutes my Sonya—only with a stubborn effort of his will (only for as long as the campaign takes!) and out of breath he informed Volrab about the plots against Sonya, ". . .in that van they have everything prepared for tying up, gagging, torturing, and rendering her unconscious. . ."

"I'm surprised," Volrab answered with equanimity, "that you forgot about your authorities and took it upon yourself to break into a strange car — Hey! *Wherre arre you, wherre arre you, my loovelyy starr. . .*"

"I'm telling you again: Engineer Holy and his people are preparing to kidnap your ward Sonya, and the penalty for such a felony—"

"More of your authorities, huh! Pardon me, but why would Engineer Holy try to kidnap Sonya when all he's got to do is ask me and I'll give her to him myself — *Wherre arre you, wherre arre you. . .*"

"You already sent her to his room, didn't you? So excuse me for bothering you, I'll take care of things some other way!"

". . .*Wherre arre you — my loovelyy starr. . .*"

"Maybe you'll be more interested to know that at this very moment Berta Zahnova is in your bedroom with a flashlight in her teeth, plundering your papers up on top of the wardrobe."

"*Wherre arre you. . .* What's that you say? I haven't got any papers. . . Berta! Darling, come here right away. Forget that cake and get a move on—"

The Volrabs flew into the kitchen and a moment later a cry reached the bar, then a dull thud (as if somebody had fallen off a chair) and a growing hubbub.

"I just want to go on enjoying myself like this a bit longer," Ziki told Wolf Zahn, entertaining himself by watching a circlet of lemon swimming in a glass of *Gancia* white vermouth, he clinked the ice against the side of the glass and took a sip. Then he leaned back lazily in his chair and played with the twenty-dollar piece in his pocket (he clinked it against his pistol).

I'm simply enjoying myself. Why in this miserable hotel? An easy twenty-minute drive and I can be almost a mile above sea level (you can't do that in London, in Paris, or in Rome, Madrid, or New York) and the mountains do me good. The only problem here is how to spend the evenings . . . but I probably could import some entertainment. Mass tourism has already destroyed the Côte d'Azur and Rome, in London everything has become hopelessly expensive, New York is vulgar to the point of tears, and Paris is now only for the swindling of stupid tourists. Those tedious, cliché-ridden cabarets in Pigalle . . . I much prefer a private show: the Hotel Hubertus enveloped by clouds of ammonia.

I've worked a long ten years and I've worked hard enough, I should say. I simply have enough of everything. The worldwide sex craze bored me before it got off the ground. Mass duplication precludes true arousal. All I want is a little kitten to play with. When someone has a surplus of free time—and I've nothing to do till September—he gets a little frivolous.

"Ready?" Ziki asked his Wolf.

"Yes, sir. I'll cut the telephone wire, activate the ammonia, and before it starts coming out I'll set off a few explosives. I'll toss out some RDG, and under its cover I'll bring her to the car. Can I tie her up?"

"Only if it's necessary. — Get out as soon as you can and send me a telegram."

"When do we launch the attack?"

"As soon as I say IT'S STUFFY IN HERE."

Ziki had noticed Jagr's argument with Volrab at the bar, and it seemed he had heard his own name. He picked up his glass of *Gancia Bianco*, consoled himself with the sight of the yellow rim (yellow excites me) and the silver wheel of the lemon circlet swimming in the pale golden wine, and took a sip, it seemed to him that in the harmony of tastes he recognized a foreign note, and he carefully examined the front and back labels.

Of course: on the front, under the white letters *GANCIA*, the royal crest (of the House of Savoy?) and a row of gold medals earned at world fairs, there was a painstakingly depicted picture of the winery in *Canelli (Italia)* — but on the back, all the way at the bottom, under the words *Délicieux, s'il est servi "on the rocks" et un zeste de citron* a sudden blow between the eyes: *Produit par Vinoprodukt, Zagreb*—

In silent laughter Ziki leaned back in his chair, in this bar nearly everything's a fake . . . Volrab is simply a genius at all kinds of doctoring. What sort of face will he put on when he finds guaranteed, 100% RDG under his feet?

As soon as Volrab returned from the kitchen to the bar (sweaty and flushed), he started to sell tickets for the second drawing in an obsequious fashion (Ruda Mach could not stand obsequiousness) to the "dignitaries" (Ruda Mach could not stand dignitaries), to those district clowns from Jilemnice and to the dandy from Prague, then to Ziki Holy, then to the local clowns, and finally to the summer guests from Usti, and when for the fourth time Volrab turned his back on Ruda as he passed by his table (Ruda could not stand people turning their backs on him), he caught Volrab by the elbow, pulled him toward himself, bought ticket No. 23 (poor girl—how many tickets does that blithering idiot still have?) and rejected a broken carnation (I have enough of Sonya's in my room already).

In her long white dress, Sonya (if ever I should happen to get married?. . .) got up from the piano, drew a ticket from the basket, Volrab, the idiot, called out No. 21, and the first clown from Jilemnice rushed up to lick her over, with disgust Ruda Mach twisted on his chair and looked up at the ceiling so he wouldn't have to see.

Volrab, the idiot, called out No. 17 and Ruda Mach went on gazing at the ceiling (his jackknife was opening in his pocket) and then the idiot called out No. 23, that's me.

Ruda got up, stepped forward, tripped over somebody's foot, and fell on the floor, he shot glances all around him and saw Wolf Zahn, who was guffawing into his mug — the heavy had stuck out his stump and upended me. Ruda sat up, looked around, then quick as lightning seized the leg of Zahn's chair, jolted it a trifle in his own direction (tipping it backwards) and then in the opposite direction, propelling Zahn right into Ziki's lap, he brushed his hands off on his knees, rose, and went up to Sonya to claim his kiss.

"Things here are beginning to go downhill," he told her after the kiss (which was like sugar candy).

"Yes, Mr. Mach," she told him (he had never had such a beautiful girl before).

"Sonya, it would have been better if you had cleared out of here while there was time."

"But where, Mr. Mach?" There was something like an invitation in her voice (he made a mental note of this).

"Somewhere out. . ."

"By myself I'm afraid." The invitation in her voice increased (he made a mental note of this).

"I'd go with you, if you'd like."

"That might be wonderful, Mr. Mach. . ."

"It will be wonderful. Give me a kiss."

And Sonya did—twice on a single ticket—and what a kiss! (he was making mental notes of everything) and the scarecrows in the bar began to grouse loudly. Volrab (he won't try anything on me again, and if he does—!) quickly called out the next number, 15, and the smith from Cottex marched quickly up to Sonya (it's okay when it's a pal) and now the scarecrows quieted down.

Jakub covered his face with his hands, so he wouldn't have to see Mach (ticket No. 23) kiss Sonya — he was letting his hands fall to the table when he heard the fall of a body. And when Mach whirled Zahn into Ziki's lap with such acceleration that the two crooks and the chair crashed to the floor, a whole series of new combinations rushed through the young engineer's head.

Evidently Mach does not belong to Ziki's gang, they're not putting on a show—and what purpose would it serve anyway?—and so the pistol scene Mach vs. Ziki on Wednesday evening wasn't camouflage either, but further evidence of the rivalry Ziki-Mach. Evidently that was why Ziki had armed himself. . .

Mach kissed Sonya and then Sonya kissed Mach a second time in such a way that Jakub's head was swimming . . . But at that moment Sonya's safety was at stake . . . even at the cost of establishing a hitherto unimaginable (and then imaginable only for as long as the campaign takes) contact—

While the hunchbacked smith was still kissing Sonya, Jakub raced between the tables to Ruda's, and before the newly chosen ally even had time to sit down, Jakub invited him to "step out for a tête-à-tête."

"We'll dish it out in the yard," Mach said cheerfully, "and may the best man win—" and when the two young men got outside in the dark, Mach asked Jakub seriously where he wanted to be laid out.

"I don't want to fight you—" Jakub blurted out.

"That's too bad, I was really looking forward to it—"

"—but there's something I have to show you. . ."

Jakub led Mach to the side of the gangsters' van, crawled through the open window, and then, as proof, showed Mach one piece of terrorist armament after another, the charges, the RDG smoke bombs, the ammonia, and the chloroform. . .

"They brought all this just for that poor girl. . ." Mach growled, "but the fact is that there's a bit too much of that stuff for just a weekend. Why would that scarecrow. . . that idiot act so idiotically, like in a movie?"

"He wants to take Sonya away, and she doesn't want to go."

"You bet she doesn't want to. But these things . . . they must cost some money, just the two cars. . ."

"When somebody makes five thousand a month plus another million a year—"

"And how do you make that many crowns?"

"Holy read somewhere that you can purify the refuse water of textile mills biologically by releasing it into a convenient meadow. So he had it patented and now one textile mill after another discharges its water into a meadow. And we've got lots of textile mills."

"Engineers are all crooks! Every single one of them!"

"It's actually a good thing, it saves hundreds of millions in purifying apparati, which we haven't got in any case, it preserves the purity of the streams, it keeps the ecology pure—"

"Well, OK, I'll read up on it sometime. But engineers are still crooks. Anyway, it's high time we did something here."

"What do you suggest?"

"Hm. . . Look, run over to the shed and bring back a few wedges. You know what a wedge is?"

Jakub brought back a few pieces of wood and meanwhile Mach had ripped two iron poles out of the fence (which was now leaning a bit). Then without a word the young men pounded the wedges in under the right wheels of the car until they had elevated it a bit on that side. Then both of them grabbed the fence poles and, using them as levers, planted them under the right side of the van and pushed on them until the car turned over onto its left side, and the falling glass crashed and clinked.

"You already know your way around the inside," Mach said to Jakub, "reach in there and get a screwdriver for the wheels."

Then Mach unscrewed the right rear wheel, which was sticking up in the air, and with Jakub he took it off, the work whistled through their fingers (they were both technicians), and while Jakub rolled the dismounted rear wheel toward a ditch, Mach took the screwdriver to the front wheel.

Honoring the latest winning ticket (No. 13, Ranger Sames and the "pinching" kiss) Sonya moaned with pain when that forest bear buried his claws into her cheeks, claws which, with their bristles, resembled—

"Uncle, call an intermission or I'll collapse right here—"

"Well, well!" said Uncle Volrab, and he gave me a nasty look, "maybe you're not really made of sugar!" Then he clapped and announced a "brief musical interlude."

With burning cheeks I sit down at the piano, what can I play for these gentlemen who haven't come looking for music? . . . I can play and sing my favorite aria, Senta's from *The Flying Dutchman* (where has Ruda Mach gone?).

But already during the first bars the gentlemen are buzzing away, if only Uncle would ask them for a bit of silence, I look at them imploringly, at least a little bit of silence for my music—

"Keep those smoochers to yourself, they hurt my ears—" Uncle screamed at me — he's already pretty indifferent to me, why must he be cruel as well? — he just joins the crowd, eager to tear me to pieces. . .

And "Uncle" (Mr. Volrab is a *very* distant relative) hawks his demands at me and already he is impatiently starting up my auction again, with one fat, fleshy meat-hook he is handing out carnations, gladiolus, and roses, which I watered all summer long, and with the other fleshy, fat meat-hook he's sticking five-crown coins and notes into his pocket, the price of my flayed face, the smith buys two carnations, Ranger Sames five irises, then suddenly the mysterious gentleman in the black suit stands up (the one who came from Prague and took our Bridal Suite) and he buys every single one of the sixteen roses, pays Volrab a hundred crowns, and won't accept the change. . .

Who could it be? The mysterious gentleman with the sixteen roses is suddenly standing in front of me, and his silvery tie is glistening.

"Make him sit down!" yelled the gentlemen in the bar. "Why, they haven't even called any numbers yet." "If him, then anyone!—"

The mysterious gentleman presents me with the bouquet of roses, and when I accept it from him—now I must kiss him sixteen times—he abruptly bends over, touches my hand with his lips, and vanishes from the bar.

"Now, now, gentlemen, calmly and one at a time. Otherwise there'll be disorder!" Mr. Volrab calls out.

"I'm buying all the tickets that are left!" Mr. Ziki calls out.

"That would be pretty expensive!" Mr. Volrab calls out.

"I'm paying in dollars!" Mr. Ziki calls out, and he holds up a silver dollar.

But the gentlemen in the bar aren't about to put up with this, each tries to outshout the other, they shove Volrab away from the tubs of flowers and take the tickets themselves, a crush and shoving and the struggle begins with the overturning of the tub of gladiolus, black shoes crush the stalks and elbows jab bellies, all of a sudden I find myself in the middle of a circle of men, besieged and taken captive — their eyes are so close to mine that I can see everything in them as in a mirror, Ranger Sames is waving a bowie knife, the kind used to take on a wounded beast, Petrik Metelka is tossing me onto the rear seat of his motorcycle and with a roar of the engine he is heading out into the dark, the smith carries me high over his head into a dark room and toward a roaring fire, Balada is casting Hindu spells on my spine, Mr. Ziki is looking on with a sneer as Zahn and Zahnova drag me to their low, dark automobile, and Volrab is sticking the American coin in his pocket, *where is Mr. Ruda Mach?*—

Jakub drags me across the nighttime meadow toward the station and shouts out to me the timetable of train departures, then he shoves me into his room, No. 4. Ziki pulls me by the hair through the corridor on violet sheepskins to room No. 2 and a brass gong rings out over the entire town, all the men from the town run toward the hotel, they come riding in taxicabs from Jilemnice and flying in from Prague, the Hubertus has an endless corridor with a thousand rooms and I am dashing from door to door, *they* are bargaining, laughing, haggling, and putting me on the block for five crowns, for a roll, for an old newspaper, for a burned-out match, and Volrab and Volrabka are dragging down the stairs a laundry hamper full of silver dollars—WHERE IS RUDA MACH?—the customers are staring at me, biting me all over, cutting flesh from my bones and throwing it away — for this I kiss each of them on the cheek, that's my job here and my vocation.

"Run up to my room, I keep the key under the doormat—" Ruda Mach shouted right in my face. — HE'S COME BACK. HE'S COME TO PROTECT ME! — "and double latch it behind you!"

The next moment Zahn threw him down on the floor and jumped on him with both feet.

When Ruda Mach and Jakub Jagr (both of them out of breath and with hands a bit besmudged) came back to the bar and saw the crowd surrounding Sonya, they hurled themselves into the battle raging around her.

Ruda Mach flung aside the veterinarian Srol and told Sonya to run away — the next moment Zahn grabbed him from behind, threw him on the floor, and jumped on him with both feet. Jakub struck the hunchbacked smith with a perfectly executed hook, but the smith merely shook it off, pressed Jakub against the wall, and started to hammer him just the way he worked in his smithy.

Ranger Sames pushed Volrab onto the piano and his skull came in for some more karate chops from Ziki's hand, the forester roared with pain and threw himself on Ziki like a maddened buffalo. Ziki defended himself coldbloodedly, alternating Japanese wrestling techniques with English ones, and soon he was back on the attack. Ph.Dr. Berka struck Dr. Pav on the head with a billiard cue, while the provincial intellectual Beda Balada crawled under the table, his wife Lisaveta was slapping one of the gentlemen from Jilemnice, and Petrik

Metelka was marking the face of the other with the broken neck of a champagne bottle.

A bruised Volrab pulled Sonya out of the bar, but the warring horde rushed after him into the kitchen, Volrab and Volrabka attempted to abscond with Sonya into their bedroom, but spiteful Berta Zahnova inserted her puny leg at just the right moment from behind the not quite closed door, then with her shoulder she opened it wide and the battle poured out over the entire floorplan of the hotel.

Volrab started hitting his customers with a poker, but they quickly bent it and gave chase after Sonya.

"Leave our little girl alone!" Volrabka squealed, and she stabbed the customers painfully with her knitting needle.

"Leave me my daughter!" Volrab shouted with the awesome voice of a tragedian.

Berta tried to tear Sonya away from Volrabka, and when she failed, she bit Volrabka on the back of her hand, with her needle Volrabka stabbed Berta's shoulder muscle and hissed: "That's for my little Lieselotte, the one you bartered away—"

Ziki trod once more on Ranger Sames's neck, wiped his hands off with his perfumed handkerchief made of natural chocolate-colored silk, and assessing the entire situation with a glance he called out in his sharp, shrill voice: "IT'S STUFFY IN HERE!"

Zahn tore himself free of Ruda Mach, cut the telephone wire near the bar, ran out into the yard, cursed to no avail at the sight of the overturned van (though he had been schooled to face much worse situations), pulled out the carboy of ammonia, dragged it into the front hall, unstopped it, turned it over with his foot, and ran for the smoke grenades.

Just as Wolf Zahn was cutting the telephone wire near the bar, Jakub Jagr freed himself from the blacksmith's pummeling and broke the fuses out in the corridor. With his flashlight on, he ripped the fire extinguisher off the wall, released the catch, and icy flakes of CO_2 began to shoot out into the darkness.

The smith from Cottex threw the smoking RDG out the

kitchen window and with a double hammer (clasp your hands firmly over the head and slide them down the face of your opponent) he floored Wolf Zahn. Ziki tried to defend his grenade-man with a magnificent 'uppercut,' but precise British technique in a free-for-all in the dark was not quite the right thing, the smith grabbed Ziki like a sack of potatoes and hurled him out the window into the yard. Just then the postmaster Alois Hudlicky, his left sleeve torn, walked into the kitchen.

Meanwhile Ruda Mach bitterly fought his way to Sonya and grabbed her away from the Volrabs. Volrabka parried with her knitting needle, but Sonya grabbed the weapon away from her and planted it in her aunt's belly in a very gruesome and quite determined fashion.

Volrabka went into shock from "my little girl's" sudden mutiny, Ruda Mach raised Sonya over his head with both arms and ran toward the door. At the bedroom door Volrab made a heroic stand, he took a knee in his stomach, tossed away his bent poker, and stretched his short arms toward Sonya, but she was too high up and all he could do was pull one white sandal off her foot. "He's kidnapping my little girl—" he wailed and roared and groped for her kicking feet until Sonya struck him him hard between the eyes with her bare heel.

"Et tu, my daughter!" Volrab cried out.

With Sonya still above his head, Ruda Mach ran out into the corridor. At the foot of the stairs, illuminated by the light of the moon, stood Engineer Jagr, his suitcase in one hand and a stolen kitchen knife in the other, "Sonya, should I kill him?" he cried out.

"No," cried Sonya.

"The last train has left already, but I'll phone from the drugstore for a taxi to Jilemnice—"

"No!" cried Sonya.

"I'll kill him!" Jakub cried out, and he thrust the knife toward Ruda Mach.

"No," Sonya said. "It's him I want."

After Sonya's abduction the battle spread to the yard and the garden, the guests of the Second Floricultural Evening pulled the rest of the flowers out of the ground and, although there were only a few of them left, they tore up the winter onions, the parsley, the garlic, as well as Volrab's beloved horseradish, even the bricks (which the connoisseur of horseradish had buried in the ground to hold back the sprouting of his favorite bulbs), they let the pig go free and chased it around the yard (poor Emil was so worked up he ate glass shards from the van, and in the morning he kicked the bucket), they knocked over the rabbit hutches, took eggs from the henhouse and threw them at one another, and broke through the half-tumbled-down gate and into the neighbors' gardens, whose owners, dressed in long flannel (in the Giant Mountains the nights are cold even in July) nightgowns ran out with flashlights, lanterns, candles, as well as rakes, pitchforks, shovels, poles, and shotguns (in the Giant Mountains a good quarter of the population have gun permits and the rest hunt without bothering to get one). The first shots went off in the night.

At that very moment in the smoke-filled, carbon-dioxidized, and ammoniated kitchen stood Sarka Hudlicka, the wife of the postmaster (clutching in her hand the sleeve torn from her husband's jacket) in the retinue of the local chief of police.

"The fuses," was the chief's first order, and when the lights came on in the kitchen he shook his head at the field of combat, stepped over the trampled "whipped-cream" cake on the linoleum, tramped on the crackling peanuts, swept from a chair the disfigured remnants of the *Baden Slices*, moved a tray of *Turkish Hazelnut Delight* out of the way, sat down, and opened his notebook. "So it's the same as last time?" he asked matter-of-factly.

"How can you talk like that, Major; nothing happened today. It's just that the customers got feeling a bit lively," Volrab said stalwartly.

The next moment Beda Balada fell off the stack of mattresses on Sonya's bed and the Spanish sardines poured out onto the linoleum.

"Perhaps, but let's take a look at that." The chief looked over at Beda.

"I had a headache and so I decided to take a little rest. . ." the intellectual whispered apologetically, and he massaged his aching coccyx, right near the place where the divine force sleeps in the form of a coiled serpent.

"Yes, that's the complete and absolute truth, Major," Volrab lied courageously. "Mr. Balada, he's a scholar, and I offered him the opportunity to rest there for a while."

"So then nothing actually happened?" the chief asked.

"Nothing at all, and everything's in complete and absolute order," Volrab spoke valiantly, and with his foot he accidentally knocked over a plate of *Hamburg Pilot Fish*, from the surface of this delicacy emerged a few green bubbles of hydrochloric acid.

"So you won't make any claim for damages?" the chief asked, looking with interest at the many cans of scarce Spanish sardines.

"Not a single crown," Volrab whispered heroically, and with difficulty he leaned on his bent poker. "They're all our customers, as dear to us as our own daughter. . ."

"And your girl, Sonya Cechova?"

"She is also in complete and absolute order—"

When Ruda Mach carried Sonya upstairs to his room, No. 5, he sat her in a chair, sat himself down on the bed, placed his hand on his stomach, and said: "Whew—"

"Did something happen to you, Mr. Mach?"

"Yeah. That bruiser Zahn kicked me right here—whew!"

"Can I make a cold compress for it?"

"No. But you can make me some hot grog — but where'll we get the rum?"

"If you think that will help you. . ."

"I never take any other kind of medicine. But I'm out of rum."

"Just a moment, Mr. Mach," said Sonya, and she slipped out into the corridor, for a second she listened to the row going on down below, rushed into Room No. 3 and, with a bottle of rum belonging to the Baladas, she ran to the bathroom, turned on the water heater, filled a white enameled pitcher with fresh water, and carried it and the bottle to Room No. 5.

"You're incredible." Ruda Mach rejoiced and nimbly sat down on the bed, tenderly I poured and mixed his grog in his toothbrush cup (the one I had cleaned out this morning).

"Wonderful medicine," Mr. Mach eulogized after drinking half the cup, and then he replenished it from the bottle with straight rum. He drank another half a cup and again replenished it with rum, right up to the lip.

"Don't you take it a little too strong?"

"That's just so it won't be too hot," said Mr. Mach, he drank up another half a cup and again filled it up from the bottle.

"But it must be cool enough by now. . ."

"This is Jamaican-style grog, Sonya, and Jamaica is an island in the tropical Caribbean Sea — it's real hot there, you see."

"And there's too little water," I said as Mr. Mach drank half a cup and poured himself another — so that with half a toothbrush-cup of water he had gone through a good half of the Baladas' bottle.

"There's plenty of water in the tropics, Sonya, in a year the rainfall can easily reach thirteen feet. Only that water is full of terrible diseases," said Mr. Mach, and now he was drinking straight from the bottle without diluting it (it didn't matter anyway), then he lay down on his back, closed his eyes, and said:

"Can you stay here till morning?"

"I don't know . . . I'm scared to go downstairs by myself . . . But on the other hand. . ."

"Don't be scared—we've got two beds here. G'night!"

"Good night, Mr. Mach."

Mr. Mach turned his face to the wall and in a minute he was asleep. In another minute he began to snore softly.

When his sleep resembled that of the dead, I crawled carefully into the other bed, still fully dressed, propped up my back with a pillow, and brought my knees up under my chin. What will happen to me next?

Outside the door (I had double-locked it and left the key in the lock) traffic kept up until morning, steps going up and down the staircase, doors banging, insults and quarreling (in the turmoil the Baladas' rum bottle could have been carried off by anyone in the world), sometimes even blows, and only come morning was there dead silence.

Hour after hour I sit on the bed beside the snoring (now quite strongly) Mr. Ruda Mach and I gaze at the opposite wall, at his guitar with its strings cut, and golden squares of trembling sunlight glide infinitely slowly toward the door. *What should I do?*

Thank Mr. Mach for his protection (it's *marvelous* . . . only I wish he wouldn't snore so much) and go back to "Uncle" Volrab's verses, to unending toil from half past five in the morning to half past twelve at night, to go back to the bolted kitchen window and to sleeping in a single bed with that witch Zahnova — they're watching every step I make so I won't get away from them again. And how will Auntie greet me after I pricked her with her knitting needle, and Uncle after I kicked him in the forehead. . . Why, they aren't really even relatives of mine—

"Hi, hon," Mr. Mach yawned, and he didn't even look at me, he squinted at his wristwatch (which he never took off, even to sleep!) and already he was up out of bed, he stretched by the window until his joints cracked, then poured cold water into the jug, drank half of it, and poured the rest over his face and neck and shoulders until the flowing water glistened on the brown muscles of his body, which he carries as if it were one brown, firm, resilient muscle—strong. And beautiful. . .

"Hand me my shirt—" he growled, and he pulled it onto his

wet body (the water marbleized the fabric) and then "So what's with you?" he asked.

"I don't know. I'm scared to go downstairs to the kitchen . . . But then, on the other hand. . ."

"Well, don't be scared then and stay right here. I'll be back this afternoon."

"I'll wait for you."

"What will you do all that time?"

"What do women do? . . . I'll wait until you come home from work."

"OK then. Here's something for your breakfast. So long then."

Mr. Mach put fifty crowns on the table, went out into the corridor (I immediately double-locked the door) and in a few seconds I caught sight of him through the window as he jumped over the railing in front of the hotel and walked on, from the meadows below the train tracks mist was rising and the wind chased white scraps of paper around the red gas pumps, Mr. Ruda Mach stuck his hands in his pockets, started to whistle, and walked off into the summer morning. . . Is he the prince who will take me away from here?. . .

Because otherwise WHAT WILL HAPPEN TO ME NEXT—

I don't have a watch, all I know is that suddenly I have an ocean of time on my hands. I'll clean everything up for Mr. Mach (what will I use?), but that won't take very long. I have to stay here in this double-locked room (I can hardly go out with just one sandal): the first morning of the freedom I've longed for. . .

After a while steps in the corridor and then Jakub Jagr leaves the hotel, white shreds of mist chase around him and Jakub walks on . . . if I were to open the window and call, he would take me away by local train, express train, and taxi to their house, *to the house that is all white, and we'll have the second floor to ourselves, in front of our house is a little garden with beds of gladiolus and roses and through the gate overgrown with roses is the way to our apple and cherry orchard . . . At the end is a bench which*

he painted green last spring, but which he'll paint white now, for
me. . . Jakub walks off into the summer morning.

More time passes, ten minutes or a year, and from the end
of the corridor (from the Bridal Suite) I can hear steps, it's him
— a black automobile drives out of the courtyard, the gentleman from Prague who gave me sixteen roses and didn't ask a
thing in return, except that he (as if he were the first man ever)
kissed my hand.

The black car turns around and stops all of a sudden, the
mysterious gentleman gets out—did he leave something in his
room? No—and he looks into my window right at me and goes
on looking, even after I've jumped behind the window curtains,
and now he even bows to me and now he blows me a kiss —
as if he knew I was still looking at him from behind the
curtains. . .

And then another year, or ten minutes, and jolting out of the
yard is Mr. Zahn's gray van, good and battered now, with Mr.
Zahn inside, good and bandaged, and beside him Mrs. Berta
Zahnova with a bandaged shoulder. Aren't they going to stop
and come up after me with a ladder? What could I do . . . just
shout a little — Thank God they're gone.

Then Mr. Ziki drives out in his low sportscar, I notice a white
package on the empty seat next to him, that's his cold lunch (up
to now I've always prepared them), that means he'll spend the
whole day in the mountains. Would Mr. Ziki *still* want to buy
me a lady's pistol and a platinum anklet *now*?

After a moment, heavy steps, they stop in front of my door
and a mighty snorting before the voice and the knocking
announce the presence of Mr. Volrab.

"Sonya, are you in there?"

"No!" And I wouldn't let him in for anything—

"Look, darling, we've been waiting since morning for you to
come to your senses, but it's past nine, the work's bogged down
in the kitchen, and none of the rooms have been cleaned!"

"I won't do your cooking and your cleaning anymore, Mr.
Volrab. I'm giving you my official notice!"

"But that's just what I'm here to inquire about!"

"Jakub told me that I'm not even registered as living here. So why should I cook and clean the rooms, when I'm not even living here?"

"But what will you live on, huh?"

"For starters, on what you owe me for two years' work, of which you've given me only five crowns so far, out of Mr. Mach's hundred-note. All the rest of it—Mr. Volrab—you still owe me!"

"Owe you, shmoe you, you're meshuga! Remember how you arrived at our home. A few rags and books and two shoes—the others were all worn out—and one stocking had a hole on the heel. All of it rattled around in a tiny suitcase—"

"—which you stole from me the very first day. Bring it here right away! With my pay for the last two years in it!"

"—and that's not mentioning all the other things we've given you during those long, long years: a place to live, clothing, shoes, food, drink, heat, good manners, security. . ."

"Fine security! You sent me to Ziki's room and yesterday you set twenty wild men on me!"

"But it's not so terrible if our gentlemen guests are just a tiny bit lively—we paid for it more than you did—why, they're all just like our own little children, and sometimes children take vacations—"

"I haven't had a single vacation in two years. Not even a day off! Not a single free Sunday! So now I'm taking two vacations, two days off, and a hundred free Sundays!"

"But darling, a delusion's got hold of you . . . It's not like that at all, and anyway, everyone loves you and is crazy about you. You'll be a whale of a success now . . . And then remember that I'm your father and your mother!"

"And Volrabka?"

"Why, she's your mother and your father, too!"

"So then I've got four parents, right! Look here, Mr. Volrab, my parents are dead . . . and the two of us are *very* distant relatives, okay. What are you actually . . . the brother-in-law of

my great-grandmother's cousin? But that isn't the point, Mr.
Volrab! Bring me my suitcase, my other sandal, and my pay for
the last two years. Right away!"

"Sure, you think it's plain as der Tak, my darling. I happen
to be your legal guardian, appointed by the court!"

"And I happen to be an adult, of age, and that's absolutely
that!"

"You'll have to explain all that to the district court in
Jilemnice, which is where I'm having you carted off in a jiffy!"

"I'll send my husband there on my behalf."

"What's that?!—"

"You were always asking me if I'd had anything to do with
a gentleman. I really didn't, never, not with Jakub, not with
Ziki—honest! At least not until yesterday. Since last night—"
and then I sighed to make the lie sound completely spontane-
ous, "Ruda Mach and I are like husband and wife!"

"For Heaven's sake, Sonya, what you're saying is dreadful—"

"Nothing dreadful about it, just the opposite. Ruda Mach is
my husband and I am his wife. And as long as you won't give
me my suitcase, my sandal, or my wages for the past two years,
I won't say another word to you. And if you go on bothering
me, I'll tell my husband to whip you like a horse!"

"But you wouldn't do that, Sonya, my precious darling. . .
Not now, when the bar's been wrecked by those villains, the
kitchen's upside down, the garden's trampled, the fence's
knocked over, the rabbit hutches're toppled. . . And do you
know the most horrible thing? My Emil's dead. . ."

"That pig was more your relative than I was. And now don't
bother me—I have my *own* problems."

"Darling Sonya, come downstairs, there's a lovely breakfast
waiting for you and everything's forgiven. . ."

"Clear out, or my husband will slaughter you and you'll go
join your pig!"

And that's how I proclaimed myself the wife of Ruda Mach.
I am now the wife of Ruda Mach. My husband has gone to

work and left money for me to go shopping. So then, Mrs., what are you doing babbling with your crazy neighbors?

Sonya began to sing and to unstitch the flounces from her white dress (I'll sew them on again for evening wear, so I have to buy a needle and a spool of white thread). Then she put on her only sandal, picked up Ruda's empty suitcase with one hand and with the other some crumpled old newspaper (that's to show people I'm carrying the other shoe to the shoe repair), and so I set out on my first shopping trip for my family.

So Hrusov had its second sensation in a short period of time, people stared, even stopped short on the street, Sonya greeted each of them and to each she smiled prettily.

First of all bread, "Is it fresh, Ma'am? My husband won't eat stale bread!" (how that widow in the bakery stared at me!) and then salt, a good two pounds of it, one has to have salt in the house.

And then four ounces of sweet butter to go on the bread, "Is it fresh, Ma'am? My husband would chase me out if it wasn't!" (how Mrs. Dvorakova in the dairy store gaped at me!) and then ten dekas of the finest cheese (I'll teach my husband about nutrition!), and next door, at the butcher's (how he gawked!), ten dekas of imitation salami (because a man can't do without meat, after all. . .) and at the produce shop two pounds of lovely tomatoes.

How wonderfully it's going . . . as if it's what I'd been born to do. But now it's my job and my vocation. . .

Now some tea and half a pound of sugar (but no more grog, my love, it makes you snore too much) and a needle and white thread for my wedding dress. And for you, two lovely white handkerchiefs (I meant to buy them a long time ago, my love) and for me a pair of sneakers on sale, so I won't have to run around town for you barefoot (some day you'll buy me golden slippers for the ball, won't you?). For the last six crowns a child's harmonica, since they've ruined your guitar . . . so you can play when you're sad (but that won't happen as long as I'm around) and I can sing along with you.

Waving the suitcase elatedly, in her new, glowing white sneakers, she climbed the Hubertus staircase to her own room, No. 5, in the corridor Ph.Dr. Berkova from No. 6 stopped her and lost her temper:

"Isn't anyone going to clean this place today?"

"They haven't cleaned my room either. We'll have to complain to the management!" I said to her, and I banged the door behind me. The help here sure is awful!

Home now, Sonya took off her sneakers (at home I can go barefoot so the first shoes given me by my husband will hold up longer), she found a chewed remnant of Ruda's carpenter's pencil and on the border of the newspaper, employing the tip of her tongue, she totted up in a beautiful script the accounts for her first shopping expedition:

Sneakers	13.00
Harmonica	6.00
Needles and Thread	2.00
2 Handkerchiefs	8.00
Tea and Sugar	4.00
Bread	2.90
Salt	1.30
1/8 Butter	5.00
10 dks Salami	3.10
10 dks Cheese	2.70
Tomatoes	2.00
TOTAL	50.00

Then I cleaned up the entire room (like never before) and then did nothing but wait for my husband to come back home from work.

What else should I do . . . now there was nothing to do but GET READY FOR MY WEDDING—

Sonya threaded the eye of the new needle with the new thread, sang softly, and began sewing the flounces back on her white wedding dress.

From six in the morning till noon the half-naked Ruda Mach

lined the thiosulfate vats in the Cottex sulfur bleaching room, ate his pound of headcheese for lunch and, using a fine trowel, smoothed out the hardening cement in oval forms (thoughts of Sonya and joy), perfectly and tenderly (the touch of smooth material and joy).

"I need to speak to you," said Jakub Jagr, approaching him from behind.

Ruda Mach stood up in his vat and turned toward Jagr. "I'm listening," he said.

"It's important to me that Sonya is well," Jagr said.

"To me too," said Ruda Mach, and he passed his palm over his bare, sweaty chest.

"I wanted to take her home, show her to my parents and be betrothed to her. But she's in your room now. Is she going to stay there?"

"That's certainly the way it looks."

"Does she want to remain there?"

"That's certainly the way it looks."

"Tomorrow I shall go away from here and it is not likely I shall ever return. I would like to ask you to give her my final regards."

"OK."

"We two are not likely ever to meet again. I shall say good-bye now. Be good to her. . ."

"OK. So long."

And Ruda Mach turned his back on Jagr (glad that he had carried it off so smoothly), knelt down again in his vat, and with his fine trowel smoothed out the smooth material (thoughts of Sonya, beauty, and joy), then tossed the trowel aside and smoothed the cement with his bare hand (joy).

When the shift was over he lay for a while in the grass in the sun, like a typhoon he plowed his way a few lengths of the swimming pool in a wild crawl in a savage whirlwind of spraying water, foam, whirling mud, and pieces of grass, twigs, and torn leaves.

With his hair still wet he passed through the glowing streets on his way to the Hubertus, where right at the door that idiot Volrab tried to stop him.

"My dear, respected Mr. Mach," he babbled, "you are my dearly beloved guest and I am as fond of you as I would be of my own son . . . but when are you going to send our little Sonya back home?"

"You'll have to ask her that. She's an adult."

"But our little child is so foolish still! And when you've got so much influence over her . . . And between us fellows—you don't really want her hanging 'round your neck?"

"Look, chief, don't worry so much, and run down to the cellar for a bottle of beer. Bring me two of them while you're at it!"

"As her legal guardian, appointed by the court, it's my job to worry about her! So what's going to happen to my ward, Mr. Mach?!"

"I haven't had time to think that over yet, chief."

"So he hasn't had time to think that over yet! But to seduce her, that you've managed in a matter of seconds, huh?"

"Tell me before I belt you one, idiot: who told you I seduced Sonya?"

"She told me so herself, Mr. Mach! Herself!"

"Balls. She couldn't have said that."

"That's what she said this morning when I had a word with her."

"It was Sonya who told you I seduced her?!"

"This morning my dear Sonya told me that she and you are like husband and wife! And then she said it again: you are her husband and she is your wife. I've got witnesses to that, being as how Mrs. Berkova and Mrs. Baladova heard every single word she screamed at me through the locked door. Mr. Mach!"

"OK, so run and get me those two bottles of beer — and make sure they're good and cold!" said Ruda Mach, and he went upstairs to room No. 5, where Sonya was standing in her white dress, she rubbed her bare ankles together and smiled beautifully at Ruda.

On the table a garnished plate of sliced salami, cheese, and tomatoes, and slices of fresh bread, and in a little pot swam some nice, dewy butter.

"Great," said Ruda, and he sat right down to eat.

"But that was supposed to be our dinner. . ." said Sonya.

"OK. We can have it for a snack and go out for dinner," said Ruda, and he reached for some salami.

"Don't get angry at me, Mr. Mach, for buying these sneakers with your money — Volrab won't give me back my sandal . . . But I kept a good account of everything. I even had enough left over to buy you a present, but that I'm saving till dinnertime. . ."

After their snack, a walk to Saddle Meadow, where the grass is dense and magnificent, and there's a view of the central range of the Giant Mountains, then a swim in a forest pond and, hungry as wolves, joyfully back to dinner at the hotel.

With arms ceremonially linked Ruda and Sonya walked into the bar (and the bar stared: they were a handsome couple), Ruda seated Sonya at his table and then said casually over his shoulder (but they could hear it even in the kitchen) across two tables to Ziki:

"Look, Mr. Holy, or whatever your name is, give Sonya up forever, get me. Or I'll fix you up for some surgery."

"Much obliged, Mr. Mach," Ziki said in his clear, sharp if slightly shrill voice. "I'm only interested in girls who are *intact.*"

Ruda Mach clenched his fist (but Sonya quickly took it in her hand), glanced at Sonya ("Don't mind him, I beg you, *please.* . ." she whispered and blushed) and so he didn't and he left his fist in Sonya's nice, warm hand.

"Would you like fizz water today?" was all he said.

"I would, Mr. Mach."

After dinner, in their room, No. 5, Sonya gave Ruda her present, the child's harmonica. Ruda was happy and at once began to play song after song on it.

"Sonya," he said softly. "Why did you tell Volrab that lie today, that we had made love together?"

Sonya rubbed her bare ankles together and smiled beautifully at Ruda. He looked at her. He had never had such a beautiful girl before (or such a determined or such a brave one).

Both got up at the same time. Slowly Ruda put his harmonica away and put his hand on the top button of Sonya's white dress.

"Do you want to stay with me, Sonya?"

"Yes, Mr. Mach."

"Call me Ruda."

"Yes, Ruda. That's what I want."

Late at night Sonya quietly got out of bed (Ruda was already beginning to snore lightly), slowly walked barefoot to the window, and pressed her burning forehead against the cool glass. From now on I am completely, absolutely, and truly the wife of Ruda Mach.

It happened so suddenly and so abruptly that I didn't even realize quite what it was my husband was doing with me. . . It was as if I had missed out on one of the most grave and weighty moments in a woman's life . . . But no matter, it had already happened. Next time I will pay more attention to what I'm doing.

It had to happen, but still I am a bit sorry it did . . . How beautiful it was *before* . . . why couldn't that beuaty last longer . . . a week longer . . . a month . . . Why must the May of cultivation and the June of rapid growth of our love be so brief . . . and why must July's harvest come so soon. . .

I have lost something forever. But I have gained something new in its place and it is strong and very special: the feeling that I belong to my husband — with my whole self, with all I have, everywhere, forever. That I have nothing but him and what he gives me, that all I am is only for him and that all we have we have together.

Our Honeymoon:
When we wake up in the morning, we kiss, we eat breakfast,

we kiss, and then Ruda goes off to work. The eight hours of separation go by swiftly, since I'm with Ruda all the time, even when he isn't right here with me. That's why I do everything thinking *of* him and *for* him.

I have a new, bigger shopping bag made of shiny leather and I like to go shopping — this is my job now, for Ruda, and my vocation, I test the bread with my finger, jab the tomatoes, and handle the heads of cabbage. The Hrusov women soon got used to me, and now we give each other advice on vegetable oil, goat's milk, and salads made with rhubarb and chicory, and they advise me about what I'll need to do when a baby starts kicking inside me . . . And together we lit into the butcher when he denied having any lungs and hid them behind the counter.

At home I clean up, then wash and sew my husband's things—how they needed it!—and every time I go shopping I bring him back something new, a shirt, two handkerchiefs, or shorts. I like to hold his things, and when there's nothing to repair, I can at least caress them for a while.

Ruda brings home with him a racket, confusion, laughter. With his hair wet (he goes straight from the factory to swim in the town pool, but really more to rest, because he works hard in the bleaching room) he hammers on the door and throws me a piece of raw meat wrapped in bloody newsprint. No one has cooked for him for a long time and invariably he brings something back from the butcher's that he's especially fond of. He swings onto the bed, then he's right back up on his feet, he jostles me, neighs, pulls me by the hair, and chases me around the room, we laugh, he makes me angry, but I can't really get angry at him, he pulls me down on the bed, we laugh and play like a couple of kids.

Then he looks me over again and again, measures the length of my hair, which is almost as long as his forearm, and the size of my waist, which is 23 inches, he passes judgment on what I've bought, works out the evening menu, criticizes my hairdo, sticks his nose into my things and grabs one thing after the other, tries out my lipstick and bra, douses himself with my

cologne, praises the skirt I patched together from cheap remnants—I like that—licks the cut on my knee and tells me I'm
beautiful — how lucky I am.

Afternoons we climb up to Saddle Meadow, where the grass
is dense and magnificent, and there's a view of the central range
of the Giant Mountains, my husband loves the mountains, we
gaze together at the foothills reddened by the setting sun and
Ruda tells me about the South Sea Islands (which he's found on
maps and in magazines) and he likes me to tell about the
gladiators in classical times, and about Renaissance Rome, and
especially about the voyages of Columbus, Cortez, Magellan,
and the British pirates, which I remember from *gymnasium* days
and from what I've read in novels, then we go swimming in the
forest pond and at dusk we slowly return to the hotel.

We eat dinner in our room, Ruda bought a double hot-plate,
I've largely given up a balanced diet (milk, cheese, vegetables,
tea) in favor of meat, and we eat at least two pounds of it every
day—Ruda eats three- quarters of it himself—and he likes to
eat it with his hands. Then he plays his harmonica and I sing
for him, and soon we go to bed and we're together, absolutely
together, I feel his body as my own, but both bodies still possess
so much mystery, and I go to sleep after he falls asleep, with
my ear on his firm chest, I put my arm around him and we
breathe together in a single rhythm.

In the morning I get up first, to make his breakfast and help
him dress.

"Hi there, geisha—" he laughs at me while he drinks the tea
I serve him and him alone, I eat only after he's gone (Ruda
thinks Japanese are the ideal women).

"'Yes, sir,'" I smile at him (as I would to a captain who's just
sailed in from the South Seas).

We kiss, and as soon as he leaves (as soon as I can no longer
see him from our window), I throw myself into my work, and
there's certainly plenty of that — I have more new verses to
learn:

The orangutan, with his plate of beef,
Eats and drinks beyond belief.
His monkey wife must feed him well,
Oh, poor thing, she goes through Hell!

His monkey wife is lucky.

For I have a husband, and he is all I have, do, desire, think about, and am . . . he is my job and my vocation.

I want to learn everything, to perfect myself, and to achieve the highest level, to achieve mastership, champion status, the scepter and the crown—

Ruda read to me with relish from *Youth World* (from an account of "a great Chinese dinner" in a perfect sixteenth-century Imperial Palace in which, amid some 108 courses, they served pike stuffed with mouse drumsticks and slugs à la Great Mandarin) about Japanese women, that "it may well be cruel, but a Japanese woman is brought up from childhood to believe that she must prepare for her toiling husband a life in which he can spend his free time resting, with a maximum of relaxation, calm and pleasure."

"And aren't I a 'toiling husband?' " he called to me.

"My duties as a geisha will be strictly kept," I promised him (and took a vow on it).

Japanese women are pure *S.-Marie* types, and of all the four Sonyas, *S.-Marie* is the one I like the most (*S.-Marikka* is more of a dream, while *Antisonya* is as repulsive as cold toes). But of course we don't live in a sixteenth-century Imperial Palace, and instead of stuffed pike we eat potato goulash and potato pancakes, and mouse drumsticks run under our bed at night.

I would like to help my husband earn money. And for my own sake I would like to work — not like at the Volrabs', but in a factory: genuinely, honestly, and with dignity.

Ruda is solidly against it, and so without telling him I asked the Cottex gatekeeper to let me into the bleaching room after Ruda had gone in himself.

The Cottex bleaching room is bigger than the Hrusov church,

more resonant than its organ, everywhere, hanging on the walls, from the ceiling, over the doors, or simply in the air are porcelain loops out of which endless strings of wet cloth pour out in all directions and at all angles upward, downward, parallel, and crisscross.

Wearing only the pants from his overalls, Ruda was kneeling in a kind of pit, puttering around in wet cement — that was my first impression. But after a while I realized that my husband was carrying out an unbelievable number of tasks all at once, now as a bricklayer and then as a carpenter, now with metal and then with a brush, all in all it looked the way I imagine sculpting to be, for isn't art just that many professions all at once?—and isn't that what art is all about? . . . So many tools —a shovel, a saw, wirecutters, a crowbar, the sort of mallet pavers use, even a fine confectioner's spatula — and how many things he takes in his hand: bricks, cement, boards, planks, angle irons, poles, bars, clamps, cramps, and wires . . . he picks it all up, each differently, but everything *with joy* . . . that's how statues are made, and that's how I found the key to my husband, who likes to eat with his hands. . .

From *Youth World* he reads to me (at home I was leafing through the magazine again) that "the European is always quick to turn up his nose at anyone who eats with his hands. Alas, we forget that for the sake of our proclaimed hygienics and esthetics we pay no small penalty. For we are poorer in one precious sensory perception, which results from direct contact with our food. . ."

And then Ruda threw away his confectioner's spatula and smoothed the wet concrete with his bare hand, like he does my body at night ("we are aware," I read at home in *Youth World*, "how strongly we perceive, by contact with our hand, the tempting coolness of an apple, the soothing softness of bread, and the intimate warmth of a potato baked over an autumn fire. . .")

With his firm, gleaming chest my husband breathes deeply

(as he does when he makes love to me) and he smooths out the wall he has just created . . . he is *handsome* and I LOVE HIM—

I also want so much for him to belong to me, and I would most gladly walk at his side, to be his in front of all Hrusov and all the world, but unfortunately Ruda doesn't like to walk arm-in-arm with me (it is, after all, a public embrace, permissible yet beautiful!), "like a well-fed bureaucrat on a Sunday stroll with his family before their tarok game—" he faults me for this, but it means a great deal to me—

I don't mind if he gets angry at me sometimes, but it did scare me when one evening—all of a sudden, out of the blue— he sat down by the window and played his harmonica for an hour . . . a kind of music for which there are no words and for which none of my songs are suitable. It scared me that he was playing only for himself — just as he had before we began living together.

Feverishly I started to think: what will his Japanese *S.-Marie* do now? *S.-Marikka* advises us to draw him out of his melancholy, to provoke him roughly and fervidly— "Is the gentleman fed up with you already?" *Antisonya* grins. "Anyway, how much longer can he stick it out with you in this hole? A week? Maybe all of two? But when he does pull out—*it's unavoidable*—will you go with him? OK, but will he take you with him?" And *Sonya Undivided* suddenly broke into tears.

Ruda sighed, put me down on the bed, and consoled me the way he likes to console me. And in his hands I responded—the way a radio responds when you turn it on. How humbled I am by the happiness he showers on me so lavishly and with so little effort . . . and how enslaved. A man, he knows how to rule, I—in my womanly vocation—know how to submit.

"But that can't be all there is — it wouldn't be enough!" *S.-Marikka* is angry, even furious.

"And you'll turn him off while you're at it. You're too stereotypical, darling," *Antisonya* grinned.

However, *S.-Marie* praises me and exhorts me to patience, tenderness, and faith.

And Ruda wipes away my tears with his cheeks (they scratch me and I kiss them) and with his sculptor's hands he warms my heels, which in my grief have turned cold and stiff, to cheer me up he crawls across the floor on his knees, I bump into him and we're laughing again and we're smitten again and we make love and everything is as it should be again.

Somehow I got around to mentioning my best (and only) friend Jarunka Slana (who had had an affair with Ruda), and Ruda remembered her at once. How he came to life . . . and every recollection—and there were a lot of them—was like a blow with a cat-o'-nine-tails, the whip his favorite British pirates used on their slaves.

"But you have to admit that I'm better than Jaruna—" I tried to turn it all into a joke.

"Stand up," he commanded me like the captain of a slaver, and then he compared us like a connoisseur, as if we were both standing there in front of him. One beside the other. . .

And so next morning I wrote to Jaruna special delivery, asking how to deal with Ruda. And Jaruna answered special delivery: "Being with him is really wonderful—you know that yourself. Only he'll never marry you. And that's actually for the best, because to be his wife would be incredible hell."

"That's just what I've told you all along," *Antisonya* grins, "and anyway, poor thing, notice that so far Mr. Mach hasn't said a single word about marriage."

S.-Marikka is furious and she suggests I try to make him jealous. And *S.-Marie* cries . . . I cry with her.

But that's just when I'm alone; when Ruda comes home, I put on a happy face for him. He tosses me the bloody meat and pulls me by the hair, after shaving he drenches himself with my cologne, chases me around the room, and pulls me to him — and I love him more and more, even when he snores, even when he picks his nose, even when (and because) he eats with his hands, I love him more and more, till it's unbearable—

It seemed (I still don't have a watch) that Ruda was coming home from the factory and the swimming pool later and later, until I finally learned that he goes from the factory and the swimming pool to the local bar and talks there *awfully* long with Hnyk, his drinking buddy from the bleaching room — what could *he* have to say that's so much more interesting than what *I* have to say?

And so today I am standing with my shiny leather shopping bag, which contains swimming suits, a snack, and a blanket from the Hubertus (so he'll be more comfortable with me) at one forty-five in front of the Cottex gate. There are other *Maries* there waiting for their husbands: Mrs. Astrid Kozakova (Kozak brought her from Norway), who has five children (Kozak likes to take a drink now and then), Mrs. Dvorakova (Dvorak runs away from her at least twice a month), Mrs. Hnykova, the wife of the Hubertus barfly . . . representing the *Marikkas* is the Moravian Sekalka, a brave fighter who, as soon as she sees "that skunk of mine," grabs him by the sleeve and drags him home as her lawful plunder . . . Another one who waits with us is the tiny, beautiful Alzbeta, whose husband, as soon as he catches sight of her, runs out of the crowd to her and kisses her right away. . .

We are standing in front of the gate waiting for our husbands. We have kerchiefs on our heads, for since the middle of August cold winds have been coming down from the mountains even in early afternoon.

Where the Cottex meadow ends at the confluence of the millrace and the river, in a wild triangle of never-mown prairie, buried in yard-high grass, Ruda Mach was finishing the lunch Sonya had packed him (two slices of bread and viscous cheesespread and two sour summer apples) and with his fingernail he scratched out the next day on his calendar. August is on the run, yeah, after July it's always August and already this summer's going down the tubes.

Lazily he stretched his front paws and, with his face buried in them, slowly closed his eyes, he felt absolutely good (and when Ruda Mach feels good, he starts getting bored). Waiting for the siren, he thought about taking a swim and about having a beer with that joker Hnyk.

In front of the entrance, in the crowd of women (they were all wearing kerchiefs, just like old women), there was Sonya (also with a kerchief on her head).

"Why the hell are you hanging around like a spy plane," he grumbled.

"I couldn't wait for you any longer."

"But I'm going to the swimming pool now."

"I'll come too. I brought a snack and a blanket. . ."

"If you want," he grumbled.

From then on Sonya hung around in front of the entrance every single day, packed for a picnic as if for a family with five brats . . . but the water was already too cold for swimming. The mountains are beautiful, but the summer will desert them too soon.

The day came when the line of vats to be scrubbed out came to an end.

"Our sincere thanks to you, Comrade Mach," Director Kaska told him, "you have delivered some first-class work here. . ." And so forth and so forth.

"What have you got for me now?" Ruda asked the director.

"We didn't expect you to do things so quickly and so well . . . Obviously we've still got heaps of work for you, but the planning boys haven't got it all put together yet. But don't give it a thought, you can take today off—with pay—and tomorrow morning we'll talk about what comes next."

"So tomorrow morning I'll be in at six."

"Eight will be just fine. Your bonus is ready now . . . enjoy it!"

It was just nine o'clock in the morning. Sonya had packed bread glued together with some kind of watery cheese—what does she think I want with cheese all the time?—and another sour apple . . . Work ought to get its just desserts—

Ruda Mach stood in front of the gate (in his back pocket that

1,500 bonus) and looked at the white highway (I start doing time again at two . . . didn't she say she had to go to the hairdresser's?) and listened to the tooting of the local train leaving for Jilemnice and Martinice, it's gone already, too bad (he could have had a nice little outing. . .), he gazed again at the white highway and thought about all he could do in the space of five hours, at which point a truck went past, Ruda waved as was his habit, and the truck-driver turned on his directionals, hit the brakes, stopped, and opened the door.

"Where are you going?" Ruda asked him.

"To Liberec," said the driver.

"Great, I've never been there," said Ruda Mach, and he climbed into the cab (Sonya was going to the hairdresser's, anyway) and already they were on their way.

A guy always has it good on the road and the truckdriver was a great guy, on the way, in Vratislavice, they unloaded some rugs, then they ate some tripe soup that was sharp as a knife (a helluva lot better than Volrab's pig swill, and he doesn't let you cook in your room, either), and already there was stony white Liberec set out on its green slopes like a cake on a table.

"Damn, from this distance your Liberec doesn't look too bad!" Ruda Mach delighted.

"Just wait till you see it close up!" said the driver, and he began to describe the fun you could have at the Nisa Dance Hall and the fun at the Green Tree, the fun at the Town Hall Café (where the girls are), the fun at the Grapevine Bar and the fun at the People's Restaurant in the park, and then he let Ruda out on the main square.

The town hall there is enormous, historic, and just opposite, on the second floor, is the Town Hall Café, the one with the girls, at a tobacco stand that shone like a goldsmith's, Ruda bought a pack of Egyptian cigarettes called Simon Arzt, its tobacco was as yellow as chanterelle mushrooms and its smoke was sweet and blue, he rubbed his hand over his rough chin and turned into a barbershop that looked like a café. Damn, the barbers here are women, this is a new experience for me, and what women . . . here was a chick right out of a picture book (the guys in Ostrava would really go crazy!) and I end up with one who's all oil and water.

"With steam and birch twigs, or without?" said the prissy miss.

"The whole works. Whatever you've got—" Ruda Mach smiled at her.

"I give manicures too," the prissy miss grinned, "but that comes to twenty-five c-r-o-w-n-s, young man!"

"I just happen to have that much and enough left over for bubbly and two silk stockings, young lady!"

"Two stockings!" she said and then came out with a contemptuous "Fffff!"

It doesn't matter, I'm doing better at home, Ruda Mach rejoiced (right now Sonya must be sitting at the beauty parlor, I'll give her a hundred crowns to pay for it) and steamed, shaved, trimmed, massaged, rubbed with cream, perfumed, and powdered, Ruda drank a small Hunter's Brandy on the ground floor of the Town Hall and then, refreshed, went out into the street.

This here Liberec is really great — Ostrava it isn't, but then it's cleaner. And they've got streetcars and there's a theater . . . well, but any decent town has all those things.

And look, ads just like in Ostrava: they're looking for brick-layers, masons, even insulators. How much could I make: 2,500-3,000, that would do, *hiring allowance 1,000, housing allowance 500, uniform allowance 300, non-resident allowance 17 a day —* Christ, that would all be in your pocket before you even picked up a shovel! *And for singles, lodging right away, for couples up to 6 months' wait* . . . Christ!

In the wine-cellar Ruda devoured four "tartar sandwiches," made with raw meat, onions, and lots of pepper, and drank a glass of wonderful Hungarian Fortuna "bubbly." Here they even pour champagne into glasses — what a nice racket they have!

And at the travel bureau an enormous poster showing a

blue-blue sea with cream-colored whitecaps and it said: *Only one seat left for our week-long trip to the Costa del sol . . . 1,350 crowns per person.* I've never been to the seashore, never been on a plane — and I've got those 1,350 right here in my pocket. . .

All of a sudden Ruda felt warm (it was hotter here than way up in Hrusov), and to avoid wasting time he took a taxi "to the best swimming pool you've got!"

And it was enormous, behind a dam a big blue lake with cresting waves just like at the seashore . . . And the babes there, Christ, all of them blondes in pointy bikinis with cigarettes in their painted fingers, one of them wore a gold necklace in the water. . .

With all this Ruda developed a thirst, went back by streetcar (when was the last time I jumped on a trolley!) to the city, and tossed down a double Hunter, it's a very powerful aperitif, and now that's enough monkey-business, time for yum-yum and then back home again.

But as if out of spite, in front of the butcher's was a musical instrument shop the equal of which could not be found in Kosice or even in Ostrava . . . and in the window an entire forest of guitars.

Ruda barged into the shop and tried out guitar after guitar, absolutely happy he strummed one after another and at last paid 920 crowns for the most expensive one in the shop.

He would have liked to set himself down somewhere and strum away the whole evening — but he had to go back to Hrusov — meanwhile the Hunter was doing its thing, and Ruda barged into the butcher's, they've got warm salami here, that's great! He propped his new guitar against the white tiles of the counter and ate, as an experiment, twenty dekas of salami with two poppyseed rolls—salami as thick as your leg—then fifteen dekas without any rolls, then ten more dekas with one roll, then another ten dekas without any rolls and, to finish things off, another fifteen dekas without.

Salami like that—and it was the real thing!—deserves the best beer there is, and around the corner is the Plzner Beer-house, Ruda sat down at the corner of the bar and downed one beer after another (where would that lunatic Volrab dig up a keg of real Pilsner!), relishing its creamy foam, he put the third mug down on a coaster and unbuttoned his shirt all the way down to his navel, and after the fifth he started to strum his new guitar, in a little while (by then it was getting dark outside) the whole bar was singing and the whole bar was sending Ruda drinks for free, then things started getting a bit confused, someone pushed someone and then someone took me off somewhere (the way things are I can't make it home and it's pitch dark), that someone was some sort of woman or maybe there were two of them, we were sitting in some sort of kitchen, or whatever it was, and of all things I seem to remember a funny sort of table covered with oilcoth with violet birds on it, and I woke up in the morning on someone's sofa.

The women were actually three in number and all ugly as Monday morning, and their kitchen stank like a stable. Ruda checked his wallet (it's lucky for them they didn't rip me off!), took his guitar and, since the door was locked, crawled out through the window over the toilet, jumped down on the garbage can, dusted himself off (it didn't help much), and took a long drink from the pump in the backyard.

And then get on home — with his guitar Ruda trotted through sleeping Liberec, at eight I've got to see the Cottex director, two fellows loading cans of milk told him that the Jablonec trolley connected with the main highway going north, Ruda rode the streetcar out to the edge of town and at the turnaround jumped down from the platform onto the highway, which he liked and which turned out to be the right one.

On a truck hauling sausage casings he got as far as Korenov and above a cheerful little stream he waited for another connection, the highway at the end of summer had a quality that touched his heart, Ruda played his guitar and gazed at the wet stones and the ferns golden in the morning mist.

A great guy in a funeral van set Ruda down right by the gate of the Hrusov Cottex — how is it that now it seems so tiny . . .

Ruda clocked in at 7:42 and slowly finished smoking a Simon Arzt above the white rocks of the Jizera falls.

"I hope you had a fine day off, Mr. Mach," Director Kaska said in his office, he coughed and stuck into his mouth a contraption for asthma, a rubber balloon in a tube (mountain air does have its limits).

"So what have you thought up for me, Director?" asked Ruda Mach.

"Well, you see, the planning people are drawing up plans—I gave them their orders yesterday, so it will take them roughly a week—but I have something special for you, something quite nice. . . You know, it's my own little dream, one I've never had time for so far, but now that we've got you with us. . ."

"So what did you dream up for me, Director?"

"You see, we've got women working in the bleaching room and you know what they learn in the kitchen — if they put salt in their dumplings instead of sugar, pigs can still manage to eat them, but when they mix acid with lye in the bleaching room, you have a mess on your hands that costs you ten thousand. And that's just the job I have for you. In a word, pick your colors and paint all the pipes in the bleaching room: blue for water, green for alkali, red for acid, white for steam, yellow for gas. . ." "Purple for air, right?"

"We don't have any air pipes in the bleaching room. . ."

"That's a pisser. I'd paint them purple with green dots and orange stars and for each vent I'd add a guardian angel with golden hair and rosy cheeks. . ."

"Then the job doesn't appeal to you—"

"Painting pipes— at our plant in Ostrava apprentices do that. And only when there isn't any regular scutwork for them to do!"

"I'm really sorry, I was so looking forward. . ."

"When I take on a job, it's got to be a real job! No scutwork for Ruda Mach, Director!"

"Well, whatever you say, but it's too bad. . . Of course I can pay you an average wage for the few days it will take the boys from planning to work things out, and in the meantime you can simply take a breather. . ."

"And gather cranberries and sage for an infusion to clear out my lungs—no!"

"Stick around and I'll find you something else. . ."

"Oh, sure. I'll go pick up the paints. Write out a requisition for it."

"That's really fantastic, Mr. Mach, you've made me very happy! You'll see what pleasant work it will be, and how grateful our girls and women will be to you. . ."

Ruda picked up the paints and began to mix them in the bleaching room, beginning with red. When he opened the can of thinner, he was overwhelmed by that awful stench of chemicals, a real pisser, yuck! With disgust he painted a few yards of piping, and when the fumes of the thinner (in Ostrava they issue us masks for this kind of work!) filled his lungs, in rage he threw down his brush and went to "air himself out" on his meadow.

Where the Cottex factory meadow ends at the confluence of the millrace and the river, in a wild triangle of never-mown prairie, buried in yard-high grass, Ruda Mach smoked a Simon Arzt from the Egypt of the pyramids, sphinxes, and the date palms from the Nile and the Red Sea, the warmest of all the world's seas (the mornings are already cold and it's all downhill from here), his brassbound wallet open in front of him he scratched out the next day on the waxy face of his calendar and reflected on the now dug-up furrows of the time spent in Hrusov (and on the untouched columns of untouched days).

Then he counted his money (it's enough, and I won't save up for a dump in this place), and out of the "pleasure" section of the wallet, like a sword from a scabbard, he produced his school map, folded sixteen times (and out tumbled a postcard from his pal Pepa from Iraq, that's down there somewhere near Egypt, hey Pepa, why didn't I go there with you. . .) and he spread the map out on the grass. The blue ovals of lakes, scattered over the republic like kiosks at a fair, smiled at Ruda, the Liberec lake isn't even here and it's so big, what about this one or that one over there or this one here (he suddenly felt a longing for a lake, any sort of lake), anyplace there's some decent work for Ruda Mach, I'm still a bit too good to wield a brush, Director, just make sure the girls in that bleaching room of yours show up for work, Ruda thought a little about Sonya, such a young girl, with her whole life ahead of her, lazily he stretched out his front paws and with his face propped on them thought with pleasure of his new guitar (his mind suddenly made up).

I felt really bad when by half-past two all the men had come out of the Cottex gate — and Ruda was not among them. Until the gatekeeper finally told me that he had gone off hitch-hiking somewhere. . .

"He needed to go somewhere," says *S.-Marie* "and he'll certainly bring us back a lovely present, a pleasant surprise. . ."

"Just so the surprise won't be *un*pleasant," *Antisonya* grins, "and just so he *does* show up—"

S.-Marikka is angry, furious.

I lay by the swimming pool for an hour or so (glad I didn't have a watch: I would have looked at it so often that I would have gone out of my mind) and I kept lifting my head to see if he was coming. . . My husband didn't come. From the pond a chill passed through the yellowing grass of the fleeting summer, and that melancholy feeling like long ago, the sorrow that my holidays were coming to an end. . .

Following *S.-Marikka's* advice I ate both my lunch and Ruda's. (*S.-Marie* didn't approve of this and *Antisonya* taunted me, saying that only aging has-beens stuff themselves to dull the pain) and all at once it occurred to me that Ruda was probably drinking his beer in the bar already, so I ran back to the Hubertus — in the bar Hnyk was guzzling beer all by himself. So Ruda must surely be waiting in the room and grinning about the present he brought me . . . in the room just *Antisonya* grinning at me out of the mirror.

I tried to calm down and then, at the usual hour, I prepared our dinner (cheese croquettes with spinach). . . My husband didn't come home at the usual hour, nor by nightfall (lucky I don't have a watch!), he left me alone all night.

An entire night with the four Sonyas was terrifying.

I stayed in bed almost till noon. . . why clean up, shop, wash, cook — why bother to get up at all?

But that's my job here and my vocation! And so, with everything at home ready as it should be, at two o'clock I stood with the other women at the Cottex gate, and when the siren blew and the men began to come out, I even smiled—

And that's obviously why Ruda came. My husband— but how awful he looked, his clothes were rumpled and his sleeve ripped — he laughed and showed me his new guitar.

"It doesn't matter at all, at least I had some peace and quiet to look after things at home. . ." S.-*Marie* answered on my behalf.

"Next time I'll take you along," he promised.

Something has happened to my husband. Of course Ruda can't be expected to do menial labor like some sort of apprentice. A small plant like the Hrusov Cottex can't offer Ruda what he needs to feel fulfilled. And obviously we can't go on living in a hotel forever. But something *else* has happened to my husband.

I brushed off his rumpled clothes and sewed his sleeve, Ruda joked for a while as always, but then grew serious and sighed:

"You women are all like angels. . . Hm. But if I had wings, I'd fly with them. . ."

I was extremely kind to my husband (not even the slightest hint of reproach!) and later that evening I even ran out for a bottle of rum for his grog (which I never liked to prepare) and Ruda drank the grog again what he called "Jamaican" style, like our first night together, when everything was still innocent, pure, and full of expectation. . .

Ruda had gotten drunk in Liberec (I know everything about him) and now he's drinking again. . . but is alcohol the thing that happened to my husband? With fright I realized that it was something else. . . something even worse for me.

Late into the night Ruda sat at the window and played his guitar (he'd suddenly forgotten the child's harmonica I'd given him) and he kept talking on about his South Sea Islands, where one day he would sail and make his living repairing motorboats and water skis, all day long on the white sand of the beach under the sun, now and then he would pluck a coconut from a palm tree, cut into it with his machete (he showed me how), and drink its cool, delectable juice, then eat the creamy pulp — and one could live that way all year long. When he finally fell asleep, I wept: there was no room for me in those South Sea islands of his. . .

My husband kept going to Cottex, and every day he came home from work more enraged, one day out of rage he painted his entire arm purple and then grabbed at me horribly, like a zombie. . . He sat in the bar till it got dark and the rest of the time he spent at the window playing his new guitar.

And so I had to get a hold of myself, get the better of my feelings for my husband's sake—that is my vocation—and beg him to find work somewhere else. And work for me as well.

Ruda didn't answer and kept on going to Cottex. Until one day he brought home his pay, gave me a thousand crowns, and said, "Tomorrow I'm leaving."

"Good."

"Wait for me here. As soon as I land something, I'll write you."

"I'll wait for you."

"I will write to you."

In the morning I made him tea for the very last time (and I didn't cry: that is my vocation) and came down with him to the front of the hotel, where I felt so weak I had to lean against the cold, dewy rail.

"You're great," my husband said to me.

"I love you."

"I will write to you."

"I'll be waiting."

"So long," said Ruda Mach, and he left, his suitcase in one hand and in the other his new guitar, from the meadow under the railroad tracks a dense white mist rose up as far as the highway, Ruda began to whistle and vanished into the whiteness, my first husband.

No letter came from Ruda.

At 3:50 P.M. Engineer Jakub Jagr walked past the fence of the garden next door, the Orts', with its silver-gray gate, and he walked through the blue gate into the Jagrs' garden and entered his house.

On the hallway his mother and his sister, Zlatunka, glanced up at him from their rocking chairs (his father would come here from his room at 6:45 sharp).

"How's work?" asked his mother.

"Nothing special," said Jakub.

"You've got a letter," said his mother.

"The address is complete, but written by somebody who must have been plastered," said Zlatunka.

From the table at the foot of the staircase Jakub picked up the newspaper (his father had read it between ten and eleven o'clock and in the evening it had to be returned to him for his documentary clipping) along with the letter postmarked Hrusov, went upstairs to his room on the second floor, and double-locked the door behind him.

For a full minute he looked around his room (the tightly-woven, firm, thin carpet *bouclé*, bright blue in color, but darkened near the window by the thousandfold marks of a naked, exercising body, metal furniture and a narrow metal bed with dazzlingly white bed linen, on the wall a spring exerciser for the biceps, a sculpture of a tiger's head, and the flat planes of two walls covered with a good 355 square feet of technical books, scifi, and mysteries), and fully absorbed in his unusually flat dagger, he cut open the envelope (the writing did indeed testify strongly to the writer's use of alcohol) of the letter from our paid informant in the bar of the Hotel Hubertus:

To the Right Honorable Engineer Jagr!
   Heartfelt greetings. This morning Ruda Mach deserted your Miss Sonya, quit his job at Cottex, and he's already cleared out of here. Heartfelt greetings and send me at least 50 — Thanks!
                              Heartfelt greetings!
                              Josef Hnyk

   or send me 75 instead   Heartfelt greetings!

Slowly Jakub walked over to the window and looked blankly out at the tops of the apple and cherry trees, towering beyond them was the golden family stronghold of the Orts (so far Kamila Ortova has not attempted to officially break off our engagement), Ruda Mach picked Sonya like a cherry and now he's spat out the pit.

So once again Sonya is free as a pit on the ground, *but a new tree can grow from a pit on the ground,* Sonya with her strawberry-blond halo of hair and with eyes like great fiery emeralds IS NOW FREE FOR ME— I promised her our house and Sonya said: *"Sometime later repeat to me what you said this morning. . ."* That sometime later has NOW ARRIVED—

Jakub ran around the room for a while, then lowered himself onto the floor and, lying on his back on his firm blue carpet, his hands behind his head, he dreamed for a good hour — he spent another hour visualizing how it would be.

Suddenly he rose, his mind made up: SONYA WILL BE MY WIFE. And I will make a wife out of her—even from the wreckage. It's even better from wreckage, and it's best of all from nothing but molecules of pure womanhood. . . Jakub Jagr's mate will have CLASS.

Jakub plunged into the study of his thick diary and on its pages made a series of observations using four different colors of metal pencil, then in black he filled out a money order in the amount of 65 crowns, to the order of Josef Hnyk in Hrusov, and wrote a short note to the latter:

> *Mr. Hnyk:*
> *Thanks for the report, by post I am sending you an increased payment. From now on send a detailed report every day. I am raising your pay by 25%.*
>
> *J.*

and to the same mountain town, in red pencil on pink paper:

> *I love you and I will come for you.*
>
> *J.J.*

At 6:15 P.M. Jakub followed his father to the garage (it is a Jagr woman's place to follow the men's decisions and nothing more), banged the heavy garage doors behind him, and placed himself on the left side of the vehicle (his father always stood on the right).

"You received a letter from Hrusov!" the sergeant said in the dim light.

"From my informant, Hnyk. Sonya is free," Jakub announced.

"Ha! Hm! Nonsense! Then that fellow has already left her—"

"Ruda Mach has broken his employment contract and cleared out. . ."

"Hmm! Then he didn't stay very long with her—Hmm!"

"He wasn't a suitable partner for Sonya. Sonya has potential for class."

"Ha! Hm! Nonsense. What if he's made her a child?"

"I don't believe it. Anyway there are methods—"

"Phooey! Phooey! Remember: never anything contrary to nature. Phooey!"

"Certainly, Dad. But with Ruda Mach's lifestyle, paternity is decidedly not in his interest. . . And he would know how."

"Hmm. Only if she knew how as well. If she's got the spark — ha! Ha! Ha!"

"We'll find out everything. Meanwhile, what's important is that the two of them are no longer together."

"But how long can she hold out—ha! And if she's got the spark — ha! Ha! Ha!"

"We'll get there before anybody else."

"So you still want her?"

"Head over heels. Totally. More than ever before."

"Ha! Hm! Nonsense. She's got to have the spark if she gets you so hot and bothered—ha! Ha! Ha!"

"Dad, I love Sonya."

"Ha! Hm! Nonsense. You won't make your mother happy—but never mind. Zlatunka will be furious — that at least will give her some fire. My own daughter doesn't have the spark—hmm! Enough. What do you propose?"

"We will bring Sonya here in this—" and Jakub banged on the roof of the Jagr family van.

"Ha! Hm! Nonsense. You're talking about kidnapping?"

"Precisely."

"And if she doesn't go along with it? If she's got the spark — do you know what a devil like that can manage? Ha! Ha! Four men couldn't hold her down — ha! Ha! Ha! Ha! Ha!"

"I've thought it all out. We'll plan it as a military action."

"Ha! Ha! Wonderful! No long drawn out rigmarole! A night attack! All's fair in love and war—ha! All's fair! Ha! Ha! Ha!"

"If Sonya doesn't go along—out of concern for her relatives, her neighbors, her friends—we can help her *save face*: we'll tie her up, drug her if we have to. I'll bring chloroform tomorrow.

"Bring ten yards of laundry cord! A backup can of gasoline! Good flashlights! A spare battery! An extra line of communication with Hrusov! By telephone!"

No letter came from Ruda.

Every day I stayed in bed a little longer, until I wasn't getting up till after nine, when the mail comes, and when a letter from Ruda might come like an electric shock treatment—but no letter came. However, Jakub Jagr did write me: *I love you and I will come for you.*

The long walks of an abandoned wife. It rained almost every day. I bought a cheap loden coat and wore it with the collar turned up, and I wore the sneakers from Ruda along the wet, shiny black asphalt as far as Rokytnice, as far as Pasky, as far as Korenov, and towards the New Mexico Motel, across the river is Poland. . . whenever a car came by on those narrow roads I turned my back on it and climbed down (so I wouldn't get splashed) into the ditch, where fragrant grass and gleaming ferns grew in great abundance.

I still had almost a thousand crowns from Ruda, so I could permit myself all sorts of things. I spent lots of my time shopping (I'll never buy myself a watch), nothing but inexpensive sweets, milk, and eggs (so that the thousand crowns would last as long as possible. . .), and my friends sighed over me and pushed gifts into my hands, from Mrs. Astrid Kozakova a white Norwegian sweater with white sheep on the front (and some sort of arrows coming down from the neck), from Mrs. Dvorakova a kilo of boiled cranberries, from Mrs. Hnyk a bag of dried linden flowers, from Sekalka a yard of gleaming Moravian sausage and a used men's umbrella, and from pretty little Alzbeta a string of wooden pearls which her boyfriend had crafted at home on a lathe.

In the next-to-last house on the road to Rokytnice lived a woman who read Tarot cards for three crowns. She asked me in (it was pouring buckets and Sekalka hadn't given me the umbrella yet).

I sat in the fortune-teller's kitchen, the oven kept us warm, its fire glowed through the cracks, her sick husband was lying in bed staring up at the ceiling. I had to make three stacks out of the deck of cards, using only my left hand (the hand nearest my heart), the fortune-teller gave her husband tea to drink (while he drank he watched me, then he kept looking at me and smiling) and she foretold "much trouble, but also much joy, a sudden trip and then right away another one, no more happi-

ness with a strong brunet, nor with a young blond, only with
the fifth man will contentment come. . .," oh my, she took three
crowns from me and her husband waved when I left (later I
bought him a children's harmonica for six crowns, and on my
next walk there I gave it to him, and every time I walked along
the road to Rokytnice I heard the sound of a harmonica coming
from the fortune-teller's house.)

I love you and I will come for you, Jakub wrote me every day—
no letter came from Ruda—and Volrab asked me, "So, I mean,
how are things going?" I'd like to know that myself, Mr. Volrab.

The last time I went out to Saddle Meadow, the mountain
peaks were lost in the clouds as if they'd gone off somewhere
into the sky and vanished. It rained interminably. The grass by
the swimming pool had turned yellow, the pond shivered with
cold and with the circles made by falling raindrops. It rained
interminably.

With my old men's umbrella I would walk the wet asphalt
as far as Korenov, sometimes to the Polish frontier — but the
next afternoon I was always in front of the Cottex gate. We
women would greet one another in silence and wait. . . Then
the siren would blow and the men would come out.

Women and girls would come out as well . . . The next
morning I got up at five (anyway, I'd been up since midnight
from the noise) and by six I'd already gone in the front gate. In
the office they made me wait a whole hour, but then Director
Kaska apologized very nicely and personally took me on a tour
of the plant.

I'd already seen the bleaching room, that's more for men
(although women do work there and I'd like to be one of them),
the rest of the place was just enchanting: the room where they
make starch is wet, but lively as a swimming pool in summer,
girls splash and shout at each other, the radio's on, and the
foreman, Mr. Pohoraly (a handsome man), very nicely asked me
to stay ("until you retire") and then winked at me out of the
corner of his eye. I'd like it here!

The adjusting room is actually like one enormous office, dry, warm, clean, and bright, women in white sit behind long tables and their work is like what they do at the post office. I'd like to work here too!

But the most beautiful is the drying room, a large warm hall bathed in the rosy glow that comes from the jaws of the drying machines (big as buses), girls in nothing but bras and shorts, always two by two, feed the machines rolls of wet fabric and help its teeth bite into the edges of the cloth, and from then on the machine does everything itself, it slowly swallows the wet cloth and out of the other end (a good way off) it slowly rolls up the dry cloth, which smells of ironing and home, of childhood and mama. . . Always two by two, half-naked girls raise each roll with an elegant movement of their arms and their entire bodies, they're beautiful in the rosy glow — it's a ballet! — here they dance their job and their vocation.

This is where I want to work!

"Gladly, of course," Director Kaska smiled at me, "right away, perhaps tomorrow. Come at six A.M., bring your I.D. booklet, and you can start at once."

"My I. D. booklet?. . ." But I don't have one, Volrab took it away from me the very first day I came to the hotel—

"It's just a formality," the director smiled, "so we'll look forward to having you! And please give my greetings to Comrade Engineer Jagr. . . it's important to me, I thank you!"

"My I.D. booklet—," I said to Volrab at the bar, and I opened my hand, "right away, nice and fast!"

"It's not so easy, Sonya," said Volrab, and quietly he drew himself a beer.

"Is it *my* I.D. or *yours*?! Well?! Right away, on the double! Tomorrow I start work at Cottex!"

"As your lawful guardian and legal fiduciary, I won't give it to you—"

"You won't?! I'll go to the police right away!"

"And you'll stay there. Until they haul you off to the district court in Jilemnice and then to prison. So go ahead—and count on my giving you what-for at the hearing!"

"But it isn't possible that— After all, it's *my* I.D. . . ."

"It is, and I'll give it to you in person—"

"Uncle! I beg you. . ."

"—only when you've worked off the debt you've run up here!"

"*I*'ve run up a debt with *you*? No, *you*'ve run one up with *me*—two years' pay. . ."

"Quit singing that same old tune, my dear, or you'll work me up into a froth! You have a long record of going through food, clothing, light, and heat. . . you've run up a bill for an even four thousand."

"I've never seen that much money in all my life. . ."

"But I'll give you a fair chance to work it off. If you'll come back, I'll pay you . . . ahh . . . five hundred a month!"

"I make a thousand in the drying room!"

"That'll be the day. Well, just so you can see how much I love you . . . I'll pay you . . . ahh . . . seven hundred a month, even if it ruins me!"

"So that would be four thousand two hundred at the end of six months."

"Right on the nose. And then you can go off to Cottex and in a year you'll be running the place."

"And you'll really pay me seven hundred cash every month?"

"On the first of every month!"

"That'll be the day! In two whole years you paid me just five crowns — and that came out of a hundred-note *I* brought *you*— no! I won't let myself be exploited again!"

"Just as you wish, my dear. Go and think about what you owe me. It's exactly four thousand . . . and every day twenty-two crowns gets added on, for room No. 5."

I dragged myself up to my number 5 (how long can I go on paying twenty-two crowns for my room, that's six hundred sixty crowns a month just for lodging), in my soaking wet loden coat I collapsed on the bed and bawled for hours, then I just wheezed for a while, what will I do all night. . . Before they pulled down the shade in the store, I had just enough time to buy myself a bottle of rum.

Back "home," I went right to the bathroom to get hot water out of the heater, I filled the flowered pot halfway (I'd bought two of them with Ruda's money, along with saucers, plates, and a teapot—why didn't I think to buy regular shoes instead of sneakers!—in my vocation as a wife I was just an apprentice. . .), I topped it up with rum from the bottle, drank half of it, and then filled it up with rum "Jamaican style" . . . in an hour I didn't give a damn.

Next morning my head felt ghastly, I thought that right then I could have been dancing freely and professionally in the drying room at Cottex — and so I went on gulping grog and luckily fell asleep, waking up just before two in the afternoon— *time to go to the gate and meet my husband.* I bawled and gulped some more.

But I couldn't go back to sleep and the rum was all gone, I threw my still wet loden coat over my shirt and in my eternally wet sneakers I ran out for another bottle . . . but it was Saturday and the store was closed. There was nothing left but to buy my consolation at Volrab's bar (with its twenty-percent markup).

"So we've got thirty-seven plus seven forty, that makes exactly forty-four forty," Volrab counted happily, but he pushed away my hand and the money. "Keep it, Sonya, I'll put it on the cuff for you. So we've got four thousand plus twenty-two for a room plus forty-four forty, that makes a grand total of precisely. . ."

"I can pay you for the rum right now."

"Look, kitten, I don't like to haggle with you over every little extra — if you want to pay, pay everything right away!"

"But I haven't got that much money. . ."

"Well then, just so you can see what a good fellow I am — pay me something down, let's say two thousand five hundred."

"I haven't got that much, Uncle. . ."

"That's simply awful, you have eaties and drinkies and roll around in a hotel room without paying a single crown—make a note of it, Sonya! You really are one of those "parasitic elements" they talk about, and the gentlemen at the district court in Jilemnice will take that into account."

"How long could they lock me up?"

"Count on at least a year!"

"A year in prison or half a year with you—it's hard to see the difference. . ."

"Shame on you, Sonya, you can't talk to me like that. Why, I'm your daddy and your mama!"

"And Volrabka's my mama and my daddy, too, right? Only for two years now I've been an orphan."

I passed the rest of Saturday "Jamaican style."

After my Sunday breakfast, also *à la Jamaica* (I had left one more gulp in the bottle), I didn't give a damn about anything. In my wet loden coat and wet sneakers, with the discarded umbrella, I trudged along the road to Rokytnice (the sound of the harmonica coming from the house of the lying witch struck me as a bad joke), a bus splashed me with mud from my soles to the tip of that stupid umbrella, which poured water on me like a watering can, it was like a sieve (from behind, a gift horse smells!), and so I broke it against a cornerstone, threw the fortune-teller over the fence into the cabbage patch (my fate agonized and bored me), and went back to my expensive room to lie down.

In Hrusov a solitary woman can't walk on the road even on Sunday . . . just like any ordinary day.

"We've got a real cold snap, huh?" Volrab greeted me in front of the door. "Yeah, fall is knocking on the window and where, little bird, where are you going to hide? We turned the heat on yesterday, and with heat No. 5 is exactly twenty-five crowns a night."

"So you'll pay seven hundred a month?"

"That's what I said."

"So let's clink glasses on it, boss. On the house!"

"I always like to clink glasses with the help . . . So come here, Sonya, come here, dearie. . ."

I clinked glasses with the boss: starting tomorrow I would earn seven hundred a month . . . Anyway, my husband told me to wait for him here. And it would easier to endure six months here than a year in prison.

In room No. 5, still my room (until 5:00 P.M. according to the hotel rules) I polished off the bottle of rum and for the last time slept as long as I wanted, calm again—or just resigned?. . . Outwardly there isn't any difference between them. And at 5:00 P.M. I packed up my loden coat (still wet), the sneakers (mold was growing on them), the flowered pots and saucers and plates, the double hot-plate—OW!—and I went downstairs to the kitchen.

"Take everything off!" was the first thing my mama and daddy Volrabka said to me, and I had to scrub myself with the heavy brush till I was red all over.

"He did a real job on you," said Volrabka, she sprinkled me all over with baking soda and I had to scrub myself again.

But the kitchen was warm and the dinner filling and good (we ate a pot of undiluted goulash made for a busload of miners who didn't turn up) and after dinner I came across my missing sandal . . . those sandals were, when all is said and done, the best shoes I ever had.

That night Volrab didn't even lock my window, "So you can see how much we trust you," he said— but who would want to take me away with him now. . .

When my four parents had quieted down in their bedroom, I turned on my flashlight under the covers and went on reading the novel by Armand Lanoux, *When the Ebbtide Comes*, right where I'd left off:

> Which of the two is right — Bebe, who doesn't want to think about anything and who lives only in the lonely present, or Abel, who holds onto the past with teeth and claws?
> "Imagine that I belonged to that profession too. At the radio station on St. Ignace Street, they hadn't waited for me in '45, that makes sense. There were others there, untouched by that crazy desire to join up. And so I found a job at old Polyta's, on St. Joachim Street. I told myself, death, that's a commodity I know about. A

dead man does not leave home. It's not hygienic. And then whatever's there is there. We don't complicate things. Ever. And so quick, on the double, we will clean them up nicely, brush them, comb them, paint them, shellac them, polish them till they shine. And then put them in the living room!"

The final verse of Volrab's epic, to be recited at night, orders me:

Cross yourself and sleep like the dead

the first verses, to be recited in the morning, don't give me much time for meditation:

Clean up the kitchen
And scrub the floor.
Scrub up the bar
And the corridor.

they go on remorselessly in the kitchen, the hall, and the guest rooms.

Hard-working girls are beloved by the Lord,
They start with No. 4 for their reward.

Jakub's old No. 4 had always been spartan, now it was even more so, and on the table there was of course no box of candy for me and no letter . . . will Jakub write me again today? . . . If only it were already ten o'clock (and if only a letter had come from Ruda). . .

Room No. 3 has always been occupied by the Baladas, but the wife, Lisaveta, had gone to Usti already to support her husband, who slept until lunchtime (after which he likes to take a nap).

Mr. Ziki goes on paying for room No. 2 all year long, but it's been a long time since he's shown up here. With pleasure, Sonya strode across the soft purple carpet made of sheepskins and again I play with his perfumes and his fancy metal gentlemen's toys in leather cases, I peek into his wardrobe, of course (the study of men is a preparation for my vocation), where once again several more expensive baubles have accumulated, and on the pile of shirts of the finest chocolate-brown cotton (Mr. Ziki is ready for autumn; in winter the pile will be made of wool and of flannel) there lay a woven whip, made of a painfully yellow leather.

Room No. 6 is empty, the doctoral Berkas are already boozing it in some Usti bar or wine-cellar and definitely fighting every night . . . I'd never strike my husband . . . Perhaps not even when he beat me.

And room No. 5—OWWW—is empty, too.

At ten the mail arrives. *I love you and I will come for you*, Jakub has written me again. No letter from Ruda.

But remember, and the kitchen too don't shirk—
Hard-working girls aren't afraid of work.

and she peels potatoes, shines shoes, beats eggs, shapes liver dumplings for soup, cuts the dumplings with a thread, cleans cucumbers as well as Volrab's pipe (but now for money), sugars the pastry slices, dishes out the soup, serves the customers at their tables and smiles prettily at each of them (until I'm forewoman in the Cottex drying room, this will have to do), washes the furniture, polishes the billiard cues, and only has a chance to rest a bit during the afternoon when she works in the bar.

The bar's empty as the grave and for hours all I did was stand around, serve a few beers, and that was all . . . Not till late in the evening did Petrik Metalka come running in (he was on foot because he'd sold his motorbike to pay for his visits to the bar) and with a bang he started off with sparkling wine.

Tuesday (*I love you and I will come for you*, Jakub made the same claim every day, no letter from Ruda) was just like Monday, only Petrik Metelka dashed in at half-past two in the afternoon and ordered a bottle of bubbly, Wednesday was just like Thursday, and Friday was the same as Saturday and Monday—only that more customers began to trickle in and demand increased— this is what it will be like all the time. Six months of this (no letter from Ruda).

"Watch out for that guy," Volrab whispered to me when he

handed me the second bottle of sparkling wine for Petrik Metelka, it was four in the afternoon.

"But he behaves decently and he's our best customer. . ."

"I don't like his eyes, he's got that not quite sane sparkle like that naval cadet who bumped himself off right in our bar. . . And this guy's already sold off his motorbike to pay us and they say he's been stealing damask."

Petrik Metalka's eyes were only a trifle red and they kept gazing at me . . . was it on account of me that he sat there hour after hour "consuming," a good boy with a clean record—was it on account of me that he'd started stealing?—I would have been happy to do something for him, but there was nothing I could do for him and he didn't dare speak to me here . . . Who knows, maybe one day we'll meet at Cottex . . . Who knows, maybe one day we'll go through *that gate* together. . . (no letter from Ruda).

That afternoon I spent two whole hours sitting at the kitchen table (Volrabka had to trim her nails and scrub her paws well, and she was furious at having to serve beer instead of me) designing posters for the *Third Floricultural Evening* (to be held this very Sunday, *August 29, 8 crowns admission, in the starring role the popular Sonya Cechova*), they were hung on our gate and on the door of the Hrusov post office. My boss was pleased, he pressed a can of Spanish sardines into my hand (so his dear Volrabka wouldn't see) and ordered another twenty place cards for the tables, marked RESERVÈ.

I love you and I will come for you, Jakub wrote me (no letter from Ruda), and on Tuesday morning Volrab had another run-in with Volrabka when he decided "to teach me a few things, 'cause our Sonya is really talented."

Carrying a pail, a brush, and two rags, Volrabka was furious at having to clean up the rooms, and my boss explained to me first of all that "a hostess is to an ordinary waitress like a corporal is to a buck private, a nightclub hostess is more like a first lieutenant, and the proprietress gives orders like a major, and there are even ladies like colonels and generals, who have chauffeurs and four poodles on a single leash, and the chauffeur's got to open the limo door for them.

"Sonya, the most you are is a hostess, and only when I close my eyes. Okay, when you're serving one customer and at the table next to him there's another promising customer, lean over for the first one, but wink at the second, and when you serve the second one, do just the opposite, okay, sit here like you're the first customer, this marble cake can be the second, I'm Sonya and now I'll do a fine demonstration for you—"

"Volrab in the role of Sonya" was just tremendous (even better than scrubbing toilet seats), I clapped my hands, Volrab impersonated Sonya to the point that he almost seduced the marble cake, he showed off for a good hour, till the cabbage had burned, and Volrabka gave us a devil of a time about it. But Volrab had developed a powerful appetite for lecturing and he "taught me a few more things" as soon as Volrabka was out of the kitchen. "Let's get moving, our darling'll be back from the rabbits, sit down and watch, now I'll demonstrate how you should work on a boozed-up pater familias. . ." and again Volrab went into a trance (every so often something would burn, and each time Volrabka would give me an increasingly evil eye).

After the posters for the *Third Floricultural Evening* had been nailed up, the bar began to fill up again just like it had at the height of the season. From Thursday on, Postmaster Hudlicky, Ranger Sames, and the veterinarian with the clogged artery, Srol, mingled with the non-residents (no letter from Ruda), who came in in droves and drank heavily, most of all the luckless Petrik Metelka with his endless series of sparkling wines (everyone said he was stealing damask from Cottex and selling it to unknown weavers in Vichov, Rokytnice, Ponikla, and Semily), I performed Volrab's verses in the bar (behind the counter Volrab snorted with delight), and as soon as I went out into the corridor (there was nothing for me to do: I went out there more and more often), two or even four gentlemen would come running out behind me and whisper amazing things in my ear, Volrab always let us whisper like that for a minute or so, then he would hurl himself into the corridor after us, stamp like a bull, and thunder forth: "Not until eight o'clock on Sunday evening, gentlemen! Back to the bar at once, please, I have things to do, and the kitchen'll be busy, too!"

While I was parading through the bar like a peacock, Volrabka was in the kitchen ready to burst, in the morning I had very little food, but the boss would stick his Spanish sardines right in my mouth, until my chin was shiny with oil (Volrabka noticed this and each time she would give me an increasingly evil eye).

On Friday (no letter from Ruda) the customers in the bar hit each other with cuesticks. Petrik Metalka broke someone's glasses, on Saturday he crammed the head of another customer into the kitchen sink, right into the bottles that were soaking there. Then someone called from Prague (could it be that mysterious stranger with the sixteen roses?) and reserved the Bridal Suite for Sunday night. No letter came from Ruda.

On Sunday morning Volrab woke up early, before breakfast even, he wanted to "teach me a few final things," but Volrabka suddenly rebelled.

"I say the girl's going to clean up the rooms!" she shouted, "in a little while you won't be able to tell who's the servant and who's the boss!"

So I took the pail, the broom, two rags and slowly (so that Volrabka would notice—she did) trudged up to clean up the guest rooms, I skipped the bathroom and the WC, since the whole floor was empty — so I didn't really have anything to clean, all I did was glance into the empty No. 4, in No. 3 I let Beda Balada, the thinker, go on sleeping, I only glanced into No. 2 (Mr. Ziki's still out of town) and didn't even stick my neck into No. 6, in room No. 5 all I did was stand in silence for a bit looking at the beds my husband and I had slept on . . . the guitar with its strings cut was still hanging on the wall, like a disemboweled body . . . suddenly I felt empty, as if I no longer felt any pain. . .

Only No. 1, the Bridal Suite, required much attention in order to be ready for that evening, and it's the one nice room here, as if it somehow didn't belong here, almost beautiful, as if it had dropped here out of the sky—

Conscientiously I wiped the two windows and the glass door out to the balcony, the fashionable white furniture, the tall mirror, and the white double bed under the white canopy, on my knees I crawled across the floor and scrubbed every corner — the gentleman deserves it for the sixteen roses, and one likes to serve when there are such beautiful things around.

After lunch my boss let me off so that I could get my beauty sleep for the evening, in his bed (Volrabka gave me an especially evil eye), and when I came back to the kitchen all rested up and rosy, Volrab sent Volrabka to clean out the sty for the new pig (he too would be called Emil) and then put on a demonstration of how to arouse desire in four men at the same time. To entice me, he brought out a can of export frankfurters (for years he'd been hiding the can from his darling), stuck a cold frank right in my mouth, and then began twisting his hips and playing the coquette like a rather prim Carmen— at that moment Volrabka burst into the kitchen and roared louder than I ever could have imagined (even Volrab was surprised, he quickly snapped to, kept mum, and got lost).

"The show's over, Volrab — march to the sty and clean it up yourself! I'll get the girl dressed now. Clothes off—"

I had to carry water to the basin, cold water, put it on the ground, step into it, and raise my hands over my head. And my mama and daddy Volrabka began to scrub me, but with the floorbrush . . . This wasn't for cleanliness but as punishment, and it was, to the point where tears poured from my eyes, Volrabka rubbed the bristles into me and scratched the skin on my thighs until I began to cry out and howl with pain.

"By Monday it'll all be over, and working here'll be as rough as serving in the army. Just don't forget that here you're nothing but a drudge—a drudge and that's it."

And she whipped me with a wet washrag (that *really* hurts)

until I knelt before her on the bristles of the floorbrush and kissed her paw.

Madelon, pour me some wine,
Let's be very merry—

I sang in the bar that evening and played the piano, again in my white dress with the newly resewn flounces, on my lips the revolting taste of colorless machine oil (it extends my kissability) and under my eyelids vinegar (so that my eyes would shine seductively), my body sore from Volrabka's brush and the burning stripes from the wet washrag, with flowers in my hair I sing, play, and offer myself, that is my job and my vocation.

All the tables in the bar are full already and every last chair is taken, the gentlemen are fidgeting impatiently. . .

"After the charming musical overture we go on to the first drawing — there will be more such drawings and each member of the audience will win one! — the floral lottery of our third celebrated floricultural soirée—" my boss Volrab announced, how many of these soirées will I live through over the next six months, which were now dragging out to entire years — and what will be left of me after all those years. . .

"Sonya, step forward, let the gentlemen see what awaits them—" my boss proclaims, and already he's selling tickets for my charm—how long can it last—and for my mouth, he sells them in threes, in fives, in whole dozens (the Rokytnice sexton has hauled in a whole cartload of flowers today) and men's hands are grabbing and snatching them out of the pail.

The first one, Ranger Sames, puts his flowers on the piano (he has maybe fifteen of them), sinks his hard bony fingers into both of my cheeks and stretches them apart until tears pour from my vinegary eyes, and thus he cashes in with his first "pinching operation"—

But all at once he falls backwards and the reddened face of Petrik Metelka appears above him. "Sonya, I won't give you up," Petrik screams, and like a hammer he swings a heavy bottle of bubbly down on the head of my first customer.

There's a sudden uproar in the room, everyone gets up from his table, there's a rumble of chairs being overturned, and already blows are flying through the bar, someone grabs me, I escape from his clutches, I push someone else's face away from mine and run to take refuge behind the bar, the stranger from Prague is arguing there with Volrab, but this doesn't seem to be the time — the first bottle flies into the air, a second hits the chandelier and the shards fall into the tangle of struggling men — Volrab is still arguing with the stranger, at last they come to an agreement, Volrab takes me by the hand and drags me into the kitchen, the stranger covers our retreat.

"Until I get those gentlemen quieted down a bit," my boss says to me hurriedly, "you will stay in the Bridal Suite, half an hour or so — and when this gentleman from Prague knocks on the door, you'll open it and you'll be incredibly, absolutely well behaved and nice to him, understand!"

"But—"

"I don't have time now for any of your lip! Do you want them to flatten the bar and tear you to pieces again? You already know that the only way to hide from them is in one of the rooms upstairs, with one of the gentlemen—so on the double! And for once you'll stay put . . . All I agreed to was half a measly hour—"

From the bar the sounds of shouts and blows. "Take this along and sew up the front of your skirt," Volrabka said harshly, and painfully she shoved her sewing basket right into my side, what could I do?

"We want Sonya!" the men in the bar roared, and they were already pounding on the door — I flew up the stairs and closed the door of room No. 1 behind me (unlocked, but no key to be found!?), the Bridal Suite.

My skirt was torn up to the waist and the side flounce billowed like the sail of a sinking boat, I sat on the white bed beneath the white canopy and once again sewed my white dress, for the second time I am in a guest room getting ready for my wedding—

I don't know how long I was sewing, on the one hand it seemed like a minute, on the other as if years had passed, then outside the door light steps, a knock— I took Volrabka's scissors out of her sewing basket and hid them in my hand.

"Good evening," the gentleman from Prague said with a smile.

"Good evening!" I said without a smile, and in my hand I readied the scissors for a first stab.

"Your safety is seriously threatened."

"But I can look after it myself."

"I doubt it. You must leave this very moment."

"I'd like that — it's been two years now. Only I don't have anywhere to go."

"Please let me take care of you."

"For half an hour you can do whatever my boss gave you permission to do. But the first time you touch me, I'll stick this into you. . ." I showed him the scissors and aimed them his way."

"If you want me to, I'll leave at once and you can lock the door behind me," he smiled and showed me the key to No. 1.

"For the whole half hour?"

"For as long as you wish. For as long as they leave you locked in here. However, I'm afraid that won't be very long."

"I don't suppose so. . ."

"You said that for half an hour I can do whatever I wish. Here is the key — lock yourself in. In a minute I'll knock again. If you want me to, I'll take you away from here."

"Where?"

"To safety."

He placed a key with a tag marked "1" on the glass top of the white night table, bowed to me, and silently left the room.

I jumped up and double-locked the door behind him. If I'd had a watch, I'd have followed its second hand, all sixty of its jumps . . . but without a watch I had nothing to look at, so I gazed at the fashionable white furniture, the tall mirror in the white frame, the white double bed — the gentleman had behaved unusually well, just like a *fairy-tale prince* — under the white canopy and through the two windows and the glass door out to the balcony, I looked out into the darkness.

Machine oil all over my lips and vinegar in my eyes, my skin raw from the brush and all over my body the burning stripes from Volrabka's washrag, downstairs the roar of the impetuous boys in the bar — could things be any worse for me? . . . I opened the door of the Bridal Suite before the stranger even knocked.

The man put his finger to his lips and indicated by a gesture that I should follow him, quietly I followed him downstairs (the racket from the bar was like the end of the world) and through the door out into the yard, he opened the door of his car, seated me in the back, seated himself behind the steering wheel, and we were on our way, the three illuminated windows of the bar flashed past (the middle one was broken), above them the light in the Bridal Suite which I'd forgotten to turn off. . .

Then the gleaming strips of rails when we crossed the tracks, a light at the gas station, the butcher's shop window, the produce store and the grocery store, the lighted gatehouse at Cottex with its barrier lowered — and then there was only darkness and the lighted piece of highway ahead of us, which kept on slipping past.

I wake up in a strange room, leap out of bed, and fly to the window: far below, the roar of a city street, red street-cars clang, cars hum by in both directions, and the sidewalks are full of people. . .

Suddenly I remember everything and fall back on the bed. The free-for-all in the bar . . . the stranger from Prague . . . waiting in the Bridal Suite . . . the ride through Hrusov at night

(I left the light on in the Bridal Suite) . . . and the long trip over the nighttime roads.

Where has he brought me? I spent the whole trip sitting in the back seat looking at his silhouette. I didn't want to talk, I was afraid of conversation, of familiarity, of intimacy . . . and so, when after the long trip the lights of a large city sprung out all over the place, I didn't even ask which city it was, I may be in Prague — had we driven that far? I don't know, I don't have a watch. Anyway, it doesn't matter what city it is.

I am in a hotel . . . He brought me to some sort of hotel, I think a large one. At the reception desk I scrawled my name on a piece of paper, the stranger gave the clerk some money, then there was some sort of enormous lobby all done up in gleaming mahogany (this I'm sure about), I trod after him across the red carpet, then we went up in an elevator. . .

Down on the street, cars and streetcars go by. I'm in a hotel. What's next? But why worry about it: there's always something next. And it's much more comfortable here than in prison.

My (the third already) hotel room is first-category: white furniture, a tall mirror, a conference table with two armchairs, even a desk . . . And you don't go right out of the room and into the hall: there's a small anteroom here with wardrobes built into the walls, and even a bathroom!

I take a bath and a shower just the way I like, with hot and cold water, endlessly, and then I comb my hair (with my fingers, since I don't have a comb). Finally, there's a knock at the door. What will he want from me now?. . .

But it's only a uniformed waiter carrying an enormous breakfast tray. Leaning against the tea kettle is a letter for me, inside is a stiff card with these words:

> *I would be grateful to you if you would have lunch with*
> *me at 1:00 P.M. in the hotel dining room.*
>
> M.M.

And in the envelope were three hundred crowns for me (not even Mr. Ziki had given me so much when he was recruiting

me for his villa in Usti) and next to the letter a white rose with
a sprig of asparagus fern . . . My new master M.M. evidently
has a thing for roses.

So I have time for a walk, until one o'clock — with my
fingernails I pare off the flounces on my white dress so that I
can go out, I run downstairs (I'm on the sixth floor), the hotel
lobby really is all done up in gleaming mahogany and there's a
red carpet here, I place my key (No. 522) on the reception desk
and go through a glass door out of the hotel, on the pavement
outside I turn around once more so that I can find the hotel
again when I come back. *The Imperial.*

There are streetcars here, something I haven't seen for years
. . . they're red and they clang nicely. And the cars! And the
stores. . .

The streets here are all made of glass, and behind the glass
are oranges and bananas, phonograph records in colorful covers, rivers of wool and silk, hundreds of slippers in the same
store, some of them silver, and next door, behind glass, a
hundred cakes, lilies, roses, and orchids, and next door a
window full of gold, pearls, and precious stones.

This is where I want to live!

My new master gave me three hundred crowns, and probably not just for lemonade or ice cream, so first of all some
proper clothes . . . My first husband didn't buy me any—

I bought myself a pretty green dress (green goes best with
my hair and eyes), a plastic comb, nice and cheap, then a shopping net to carry all my things, sweet pink toothpaste called
Perlicka and a green toothbrush. Then for my master a beautiful
white lace handkerchief (I adore buying men handkerchiefs)
and with the rest of the money some refreshments, ice-cold
lemonade like I'd never had before (wonderful!), vanilla ice
cream with whipped cream (topped off with chopped hazel-
nuts!) and—I was still in business—five dekas of chocolate-
covered cherries, and then I flew back to the hotel.

I went up on the elevator to my room, No. 522 (the number
"5" is in it), quickly changed, combed my hair, brushed my

teeth with Perlicka (at Volrab's I used a disgusting toothpowder they had stolen before the war), and on stationery with the hotel crest, which was laid out on the beautiful blue leather table tops, I wrote out my accounts for my master:

August 30	
Received	300.00
Green dress	280.00
Comb	1.50
Toothbrush	2.50
Toothpaste	2.00
Shopping net for all this	4.00
Gift for you	6.00
Refreshments and Misc.	4.00
TOTAL EXPENDITURE	300.00

I combed my hair a little bit more, smiled prettily at myself in the mirror, and went down on the elevator for lunch (my heart in my mouth), my master was waiting for me in the hotel dining room, I greeted him politely, presented him with my accounts and the lace handkerchief, and smiled at him prettily.

"So sit down, please," M.M. said to me, and he smiled himself (quite nicely), he stuck the handkerchief in his pocket, then he crumpled up my accounts and threw them away. "Do you need any more money?"

"No. I've already got everything I need."

"I'll cover your expenses. I like the color of your new dress better than I do the cut . . . but that we can take care of. Green suits your red hair and your green eyes."

"I know."

"An aperitif? Appetizer? Soup?"

"I enjoy taking suggestions."

The suggestions I enjoyed taking were Cinzano *Rosso*, eggs *à la Henri IV*, turtle soup, *filet Orlov*, Emmenthal cheese, sacher torte with whipped cream, and coffee with cognac (*S.-Marikka* rejoiced, *S.-Marie* wrung her hands in despair, *Antisonya* grinned: "At least stuff yourself full before he tosses you out!"

And *Sonya Undivided* knew less than ever what she was getting herself into).

"What should I do now?" I asked.

"Whatever you wish."

"Even go back to Hrusov?"

"Of course. If you like it there. . ."

"I don't like it there at all, but. . ."

"Then don't go."

We laughed. He was around thirty, perhaps a bit younger, but perhaps a great deal older. On the whole he was good-looking: tall, dark, fine hands. Gray-green eyes. Thick, short hair with the first threads of silver. He looked very distinguished, but when he smiled he looked like a boy again . . . He's someone to watch out for.

"You're very kind, sir. But I don't know how long I can . . . this way. . ."

"As long as you wish."

"You're awfully kind, but I. . ."

". . . I make you nervous, don't I? You really have no reason to be. To start with, unwind and relax."

"I'm completely and absolutely calm. . ."

"No you're not. Stop playing with the tablecloth under the table and relax. You keep worrying that I'll want something from you. But I won't. Nothing at all. So don't worry about a thing. Whenever you wish—at any time—I'll take you back to Hrusov."

"No— I mean, maybe it's not so very urgent that I go back so fast. . ."

"Is there anything you might wish to do next?"

"I enjoy taking suggestions."

"Would you care to go for a little drive?"

"Let's go."

We got into his car — I sat right beside him this time, so that he didn't look like a chauffeur — and I went with him for a drive. That's my job here. . .

We drove fast through the city streets.

"I suppose that you've already looked the town over."

"Yes . . . how did you know? Did you follow me?"

"Not today."

"And before that?"

"How else could I have found you?"

"Why did you look for me?"

"Because I like you."

We took a forest highway to some ruins, above the ruins was a tower and at the foot of the tower was a little inn. We drank white wine and all the men stared at me.

"All the men are staring at you," said M.M.

"I know. I'm too conspicuous."

"You're too pretty . . . A phantom of beauty which strayed out of Heaven into Northern Bohemia."

"Thank you, sir. But my appearance causes me a great deal of trouble."

"Like when a princess arrives at a railway station. The travelers gape and forget to take their locals or buy seats for the express."

"If all men did was gape at me, I could put up with it. But so often they're dissatisfied and then—"

"The sexual drive."

"Excuse me?"

"A permanent all-male charge."

"You could put it like that. But who's supposed to put up with it?"

"Tell me something about yourself."

"You mean when I was little?"

"That's a good place to start!"

"When I was little . . . I remember how, once in winter, with Jarunka Slana—that's my best friend—we were making impressions of our ski boots in the snow, I had wavy lines on my soles, while she had squares. Each of us insisted that her impression was prettier, and we started shoving each other away. I'll tell my Daddy on you, Jarunka shouted at me. My Daddy is stronger, I shouted back, although it wasn't true—Mr. Slany would certainly have beaten my Daddy. But because it was *my* Daddy . . . I lost him two years ago. Mama died long before."

"I know. Let's not talk for a while," said M.M.

And he was silent for a long time. I was grateful to him for that. And then he said softly: "If your Daddy could see you . . . he certainly would like you very much."

"You know, I loved Daddy very much . . . he meant the whole world to me. I'd like to find a man like him—"

"You'll find the man you want."

"But I'm looking for the *ideal* man."

"I fully approve."

We laughed and drank some white wine. M.M. was right: only now did I begin to relax.

"If I wanted to leave now. . ." I tested M.M., "would you let me go?"

"Where do you want me to take you?"

"The road to Hrusov. . ."

He paid and actually took me to his car—

"No," I said right away (so he wouldn't seriously take me back to the Volrabs'), "I'm beginning to like it here. What will we do now?"

"Whatever you wish."

"I enjoy taking suggestions."

"Shall we go to the movies?"

"Let's go!"

The theater was large and beautiful, the film was historical— it was called *Angelica*—and it too was probably beautiful, but I didn't pay much attention to it, because the four Sonyas within me had so much to talk about (*S.-Marikka* kept rejoicing, *S.-Marie* was of the opinion that M.M. "was a good man who needs someone to make him happy," *Antisonya* prophesied a mess, but *Antisonya* always prophesies a mess as a matter of principle, *Sonya Undivided* felt good and quite relaxed already).

In the midst of the crowd of people leaving the theater, I nonchalantly took M.M.'s arm (how good it felt to have a man at my side—) and M.M. didn't grumble the way Mr. Ruda Mach did, he led me nicely by my arm (that new rhythm of walking with a man at my side) in that dignified public embrace which symbolizes the fact that a man is protecting a woman. . .

We dined in an elegant little restaurant called The Gastronome, behind a window a cook in a tall white hat was throwing crepes into the air (he flipped them beautifully), as an aperitif we ordered chilled vodka, it glistened like mercury.

"And now you tell me something about yourself," I asked after I'd had some vodka.

"Some other time, perhaps . . . But don't expect anything interesting."

"It just so happens that I already think you're interesting enough."

"Thank you."

We laughed and finished our vodkas at the same time.

"At least tell me your name, Mr. M.M.!"

"My parents gave me too many names for anyone to remember, of which the most congenial is no doubt Manuel."

"That's like out of a fairy tale, and I'm afraid the fairy tale will soon be over . . . I'll call you, quite simply, Manek."

"Manek . . . isn't that something like a little man?"

"Why little? And what else does the M.M. mean?"

"Manek Mansfeld."

"Your name has a lot of *men* in it. . ."

We laughed, drank, and ate. All of a sudden, I felt good being with Manek—

"What would you like to have most of all out of everything in the world — besides your ideal man?" he asked.

"A decent and contented life. To be happy. To have someone who loves me and whom I love—"

"*Besides* your ideal man."

"He always butts into everything, doesn't he. So then: a decent job. To have clothes to wear and never to go hungry."

"That's no problem now. Wish for more."

"Will you fulfil my wish?"

"If you wish it hard enough. . ."

"To sit by my own fireplace, with a fire burning in it. To dance on the deck of a steamer at night on the Indian Ocean. To see Mount Everest—"

"It's a tiny white point the size of a child's fingernail."

"You've seen *Mount Everest?*

"From Sandakf, that's a four-hour journey from Darjeeling and about twelve thousand feet above sea level. We rode out after midnight with the Sikkim Maharajah Raj Ashraf Ram Singh V—that's a comical residuary king to whom the government of Western Bengal has given two free seats and "Red Carpet Treatment" on each airplane starting its flight in Bagdogra. It is the custom to view Mount Everest at dawn. Out of the red strip of dawn in the east the first ray of sunlight flares up and flies through the darkness and strikes the peaks of the highest mountains on earth, and then the sun rises and spreads its golden-red fire over the eternal snows of Everest and its lieutenants Makal and Lhotse . . . On the way back we brought down an old, frozen, sleepy tiger and drank tea with yak butter in a monastery of escaped Tibetan lamas under the tops of the cryptomedias, which look like slender upright clouds, something between a cypress and a cedar. As for dancing at night on the deck of a steamer, it's nice, but first you have to rub on oil to keep the mosquitoes away."

"Oh, Manek. . ."

The wine had made me a little high, I called him Manek and said lots of silly things.

At the Grapevine we were greeted by a racket like an express train passing through a station. Starting right at the doorway we danced out onto the dancefloor . . . Manek danced marvelously and held me tenderly in his arms . . . so tenderly that I might have lost him in that crowd, and so I held him all the closer. He did not resist. If he had tried to kiss me then—I wouldn't have resisted much. Manek didn't try.

We danced without interruption and talked about a million things — that is, I talked; Manek just asked. So attentive . . . and so interested in me — like no one had ever been before.

"Tell me more about yourself—" my new master inquired again.

"At sixteen I began to write a novel."

"About a woman?"

"Of course. The first sentence went like this: I steal down the stairs of the hotel and feel that I have a wild past before me."

"That's a nice, crisp beginning. And what is Mr. Ruda Mach to you?"

"What *was* he. I loved him . . . but I guess I don't have to, now that he's left me, right? He used to read to me from the magazine *Youth World*—all he read was magazines, but otherwise he was great—that a Japanese woman must prepare for her husband a life in which he can spend his free time resting, with a maximum of relaxation, calm, and pleasure . . . he had all that with me and still he left me. He's probably found a new Japanese woman already. Do you long for a Japanese, too?"

"I'd probably be bored. I'm looking for a princess I can love, court, bring flowers to, and think up ever new joys for . . . I'm looking for the *ideal* woman."

"So when we find our ideal partners some day, we'll all be friends, and all four of us will go on outings together, that'll be wonderful. . ."

"It'd be even more wonderful if just the two of us went on those outings. . ."

We went on dancing and embraced one another tightly.

"With you as my partner, dancing is a beautiful thing, Miss."

"Same with me, sir, and you may call me by my first name. It's Sonya."

"Mine is Manek."

To celebrate the rite of familiar address, we had a bottle of magnificent Hungarian sparkling wine, Fortuna.

"Tell me more about yourself," Manek asked insatiably.

"But by now you know everything about me . . . now you yourself can tell what I'm like."

"Inquisitive, a believer in miracles, timid, acquiescent, optimistic, modest, eager, exultant, mournful, greedy, tender, wild, insatiable, and submissive."

"And what else am I like. . ."

"Irrepressible and longing to obey. Untouchable and passionately longing to surrender."

"And what else am I like. . ."

"Indestructible."

"And what will I be?"

"Knocked down and beaten up."

"But in the end?"

"Victorious."

And so I kissed him. He didn't resist, and he responded beautifully.

We danced on in silence—everything had already been said—and in silence we kissed on the dancefloor, in the street, in the parked car, in the gleaming mahogany lobby, in the elevator, and in front of the door to my room, No. 522 . . . and then Manek silently disappeared into his own.

He didn't even tell me when he would come back to knock for me, whether it would be just a minute again, like yesterday at the Hubertus — or actually the day before yesterday, like a hundred years ago . . . I left the door of my room open a crack, he wouldn't even have to knock.

I took great care combing my hair, and since Manek still hadn't come (and so that I would be fresh for him), I lay down on my back and gazed at myself in the tilted mirror. In a little while the man who loves me will come for me.

"What's he like? Tender, understanding, kind, wise, cheerful, dreamy, sad, gentle, refined, clever, cultivated — he is something out of a *fairy tale*. A man who has seen Mount Everest and a *prince who has taken me away*—

I looked at myself in the mirror after that long day which meant more than all the nineteen years before it. Suddenly I looked like a grown woman — I looked at myself in the mirror and my skin glowed softly with excitement.

I woke up in the morning. Manek had not come for me during the night.

I was sorry somehow and at the same time I was burning with gratitude . . . He had promised me security and he had given it to me.

A rough happiness flooded over me, I took a bath and a shower until there was a knock on the door, the waiter was back with a marvelous breakfast, a tea rose from Manek and a letter with a hundred crowns and a note:

> *I would like to have lunch with you in the hotel dining room at 1:00 P.M.*
>
> *Your Manek*

But why should I wait for you till lunchtime, darling, I want to have breakfast with you and be with you all day long, to make you happy, to help you, and to serve . . . When I take money from you, that is my job here and my vocation!

And so I had breakfast and went for a walk, this time in the opposite direction, this city is beautiful all over, beneath a gigantic poster for the film *Angelica*, which we'd seen the day before (a princess in a coach gives her lace-sleeved hand to be kissed by King Louis on a white horse, in the background the red glow of battle) a sign called out *POSITIONS AVAILABLE*, in this city there are a thousand positions for anyone who's not afraid of work, I'm not afraid of it and I'm used to it, *Hiring a large number of saleswomen, earn 900 to 1300* — is it really possible, so much money just to stand around in a beautiful store, where I'd be happy to stand around for nothing . . . *we train unskilled workers*, that's marvelous! *30 shop assistants, earn 1100-1500 crowns and two days off a week*, that can hardly be possible, *Looking for bus and streetcar drivers, lodgings for singles, Looking for a woman to take care of a child. Good pay* — I want to be here in this city and this is where I'll stay.

At the top of the street that climbs past the Hotel Imperial was the gray railway station, and written on it was the word LIBEREC. So it is in Liberec that I shall live.

I still had a great deal of time left, I went into the station, looked at the timetable, and found the train to Hrusov, it leaves early in the morning, at noon, and at night, it's just nine crowns and I have a whole hundred, how quick and easy it would be to go back home . . . But for me *home* is a place I still have to find. I would like it to be here.

In a small quiet shop run by an old lady, I bought a lovely green nightgown, a pale blue handkerchief for my husband and, with my last crown, a needle and white thread — at home I would sew the flounces back on my white dress, to make my husband happy . . . And no longer is this merely my job here and my vocation, MANEK, I LOVE YOU—

And I will stay here with you as your wife — I was moved until I almost broke into tears, but still happy as never before, and so I ran quickly into the Imperial so that I could begin sewing my white dress, this time it must be the third time *I am getting ready for my wedding*—

"Sonya!" someone called to me from in front of the hotel. On the sidewalk stood Jakub Jagr, and his rosy skin was almost white.

"Sonya, I love you and I have come for you."

"But I love someone else and I want to stay here!"

"I have come for you and I am going to take you home right away. Get in—" and he opened the door of a blue van.

"I won't go anywhere!" I cried.

"Ha! Hmm! Nonsense. Snap to it!" shouted an unknown man with a short crewcut, and he turned quickly toward me and grasped me tightly by the elbow.

"Let me go, or I'll call for help!"

"Ha! Hmm! Nonsense. Get in!" the gentleman with the crewcut commanded, and he pushed me toward the car.

"Now not even holy water will help you," an old lady, who evidently belonged to the gentleman and to Jakub, grabbed me by my other elbow and shoved me toward the door.

I shouted, kicked, and scratched with my nails, the three of them surrounded me, dragged me to the back door of the van, and crammed me in as if I were a cow. When they tied my arms and legs with laundry cord, I began to scream, and then Jakub covered my face with a kerchief that smelled sweet and heavy, like something from a hospital . . . and then suddenly I lost consciousness.

BOOK TWO
SONYA UNDER REMOTE CONTROL

The blue van with license number UL-30-85 arrived late in the afternoon in a northern suburb of Usti nad Labem and came to a stop in Valley Street near the blue fence of No. 4.

"Gate!" the man beside the driver commanded, and the driver ran out to open both sides of the low, blue gate and then the garage doors. Mr. Jakub Jagr then sat down again behind the wheel and drove into the garage.

"So what is it now!" shouted Staff Sergeant Jagr, Retired, while Jakub and Mother Jagr remained seated rigidly, in the parked car. "Get out! Take her inside!"

Jakub walked around the car, carefully opened the back door, and said in a cajoling voice: "Sonya. . . Sonya. . . Get out, we're home now. Sonya. . ." Still bound, Sonya Cechova rolled over on her side and employed all the strength in her legs to kick Jakub in the groin.

"Ha! Hmm! Nonsense. Keep calm and level-headed. Mother! Jakub! Both of you help me — Jakub!!" the staff sergeant barked at his son, who was leaning against the gate doubled over in intense pain. "You aren't exactly seriously wounded—ha! Ha! Grab her by the legs. Mother and I will take her arms. Hey-rup! March!"

To the lively commands of the high-spirited staff sergeant, the three Jagrs carried Sonya to the kitchen, where Zlatunka Jagrova was grinning.

"Lower away! Clean and scrub her!" the sergeant commanded his wife and daughter. "If you need any help, we'll be right outside the door! Hmm!"

"I can manage her—" Zlatunka grinned, she grabbed the red down and skin on Sonya's temple and twisted them until Sonya howled and stopped all movement.

"Hmm! Be considerate—no brutality! But if she won't obey, then we're here behind the door. Jakub!"

The sergeant and Jakub stood silently outside the kitchen door, listening to the sounds of water splashing and three women panting. Suddenly a falling object, one blow after another, and Sonya groaning.

"Hmm! What's going on in there!" the staff sergeant barked.

"She kicked the brush out of my hand," Zlatunka announced through the door, "and so I gave her a couple of —"

"Hmm! Proceed!" the staff sergeant shouted, and then silently and with disgust he looked at the way Jakub trembled until the Jagr women unlocked the kitchen door. Sonya was standing next to the smoking washbasin, she was now wearing a blue-and-white striped dress, she was pale as the wall, a red scar on her temple and red stripes all over her arms.

"Hm," the staff sergeant said disapprovingly, reproachfully he looked at Zlatunka (his daughter smiled craftily) and commanded: "Snack time!"

In the hall Mother Jagrova poured white coffee out into five large blue-and-white mugs and cut five slices of poppyseed strudel. The Jagrs sat down to eat while Sonya stood silently over them,

"Eat with us, girl," Mother said to her. "You must be hungry after that trip."

"Sit down and eat, Sonya!" the staff sergeant ordered. "You'll need your strength!"

Sonya didn't even turn her head.

"Want me to sit her down?" asked Zlatunka, and nimbly she reached for the down on Sonya's reddened temple.

"Leave her alone!" the staff sergeant shouted at his daughter. "Hm. Mother will take her to her room."

And when Mother returned, he took the key from her, finished his snack, got up quickly, and commanded: "Jakub! Hmm! To the garage!"

Jakub closed the heavy garage doors behind him and moved dejectedly to the left side of the van (his father always stood on the right).

"Hmm! Hmm!! What's wrong with you!" the staff sergeant shouted at his son. "Get a hold of yourself! Don't stand there like a ghost! Get a hold of yourself—and do it right away! Or I'll let you have it—hmm!"

"Dad . . . I think now . . . maybe we overdid things. . ."

"Ha! Hmm! Nonsense. All is fair in love and war—ha! Everything! Understand! Ha! Ha!"

"But when Sonya. . . I didn't expect she'd be totally opposed to. . ."

"Ha! Hmm! Nonsense. Are you a man? All right! You must conquer her! Mission accomplished. Good! But conquering is the easiest part of war. The hardest is to hold the conquered territory—ha! And pacify it—ha! And this territory is worth it—ha! How she bit—ha! How she scratched—ha! Like a wildcat—ha! Like a tigress—ha! If I were younger, I'd keep her for myself—ha! Ha! Ha! Get a hold of yourself or I'll let you have it! Hmm!"

The staff sergeant went up to his workroom on the third floor, poured himself a large shotglass of cherry brandy, drank it down in three gulps as he paced, then lit a half cigarette in a brown-stained holder made of meerschaum, smoked it as he paced, and sat down to work.

With a pair of long tailor's scissors in his hand he read the newspaper columns with a trained eye, suddenly he shouted a joyous "Ha!" and cut out an article:

A Canadian Air Force STARFIGHTER crashed near Frank-furt Airport. The pilot escaped with light injuries.

He put the clipping into a box marked MILITARY AIRCRAFT (on the table he had more boxes, marked

COMMERCIAL AIRCRAFT, PASSENGER AIRCRAFT, SPY AIRCRAFT, NIGHT FLIGHTS — in each of them a mass of clippings, except for one box labeled SEAPLANES) and with a red pencil he entered a further check along with the appropriate code number and date on his record sheet, to be appended to *The Memorandum of Staff Sgt. Jagr to the Ministry of National Defense on the Destructiveness of Aviation* (after being posted to an aviation squadron for three weeks, Sgt. Jagr had been transferred to the Engineers, with whom he had then served until his retirement), again he grabbed his scissors and newspapers, but unfortunately there were no more crashes, not even a hijacking, not a single premature landing — in a pensive mood he smoked the whole half cigarette in its brown-stained meerschaum holder, then put it out, drank a large shotglass of cherry brandy, bottom up, and with a pair of heavy infantry binoculars moved to the bay window, from which he could see every which way, down towards the ground and up to the airplane routes far above.

Down in the yard, Mother Jagrova was going to empty the bones from Sunday's duckling into the garbage (bones are for the junkman!), "Hm," the staff sergeant said disapprovingly. Jakub was wandering through the garden like a jackass (instead of looking in on his splendidly young wife!), "Hmm!" Sergeant Jagr said with disgust. Zlatunka was marching off along the path, he opened the window and called out: "Where are you going? Back!"

"But Daddy, I just need to run out for some shampoo. . ." Zlatunka called to the window above.

"Hmm! Nonsense. Young girls don't need shampoo. Soap is good enough for everything—just slice a few flakes off of it. Hmm!"

Zlatunka turned back with a look of disgust on her face. When the sound of an airplane engine thundered from the heavens, the staff sergeant checked the time on his pocket stopwatch and with inward hope watched the regularly scheduled jet from Prague to Berlin (he was annoyed by the smoke trails left by jets: when a prop plane leaves that kind of smoke, it means it's all up with the plane) until it disappeared over the horizon. "Hmm!" he said disapprovingly, and he lingered peacefully in his workroom until 6:44.

At 6:45 he went down to the dining room: at the table Mother, Zlatunka, and Jakub, on the table five bowls of steaming soup.

"Hm," he said. "Mother will no longer put bones in the garbage, but in the box for collection. Hm!"

"Yes, bones are for the junkman," said Mother.

"Zlatunka will cut up small cubes of laundry soap for her shampoo!"

"But Daddy— Yes, Daddy," said Zlatunka.

"And Jakub will stop going around like a phantom—hmm! Hmm!"

"Yes, Daddy."

"Hm. Where's Sonya?"

"We invited her to come to the table, but she didn't respond," Mother sighed.

"Should I go get her?" Zlatunka offered alertly, and already she was getting up.

"Hmm! Sit down! Mother will take her supper up to her room."

"Right now?"

"Right now—hm! She's our guest and from now on she will eat with us. Even if she's in another place."

After dinner (no talking during dinner) the staff sergeant made his inspection. Sonya was lying on her back in bed—her plate untouched.

"Ha! Hmm! Nonsense. Eat, Sonya. You must get strong. Don't be angry—hmm. I'll feed you myself. Like this. A nice little spoonful of good little soup—right into your pretty little mouth. . ."

Sonya let him bring his hand right up to her mouth and then bit it as hard as she could.

"Ha! Hmm! Nonsense. It's nothing, let's wait a bit. Only don't be angry. Why, you belong to our family already . . . right? And we like you—nonsense. Ha! Ha!"

"A real tigress!" the staff sergeant said when he went back to the dining room and sucked blood from the ridge of his hand.

"Heehee!" Zlatunka giggled slyly.

"Hmm!" the staff sergeant shouted at her roughly. "At least she's got the spark—ha! She isn't like you—hm! You blimp— hmm! You'd eat up everything right away, sure enough! Hmm! Look how fat your hips are already—at twenty—hmm! My daughter ought to be a tigress—but all she is is a blimp! Hmm! Hmm!"

Back in his workroom the staff sergeant worked hard on his *Memorandum* and licked the ridge of his hand.

At 9:00, Jakub came to announce that so far Sonya hasn't eaten a thing, and then the same announcement again at 10:00. "I'm beginning to have doubts about our success," he sighed.

"Hmm!! At the front I'd have you shot for that! Like a dog— hmm! My own son surrendering—hmm! To a woman—hmm! Hmm! Shot!"

"At first she only shouted, scratched, and kicked. Now she's biting and breaking the skin. . ."

"Ha! Hmm! Nonsense. That's because she has the spark—ha! And how—ha! Ha! A tigress—ha! She's a treasure—ha! Ha! Ha!"

At 10:28, Jakub stormed into his father's workroom without knocking (normally unthinkable) and shouted with joy that Sonya has eaten everything to the last crumb and she is now sleeping beautifully—

"So you see, you sissy—hm. And tomorrow be on your toes! Such a wonderful girl—ha! A tigress—ha! Ha! Good night!"

"Good night, Dad . . . I'm so happy. . ."

"I hope you'll be even happier when—ha! Ha! Ha! Clear out now! Good night!"

The staff sergeant smoked his last half cigarette, put it out, cleaned the meerschaum holder out with a wire, and put it away in its leather case. Then he did ten squats, drank three large shotglasses of cherry brandy, each one bottom up, lay down on his back with the blanket up to his chin, said "Ha!" to himself several times, and fell asleep happy.

At 7:00 in the morning, he got up briskly, did ten squats and, with his pair of heavy infantry binoculars, went to the bay window.

Barefoot and wearing her blue-and-white dress, Sonya was jumping in the wet grass and picking early red apples. Slender, supple, and nimble, her red mane gleamed and her sun-burned arms and calves reminded him of Marikka Rökk in that film of hers—ha! Ha! Ha!

The staff sergeant sharpened the focus on his binoculars and with the white filament in its field of vision he caressed his beautiful daughter-in-law-to-be.

On his chair made of metal tubes Engineer Jakub Jagr sat at his tubular desk, in deep concentration he tapped on his notebook with a green pencil (green: the color of extrapolation. . .) and stared at the 355 square feet of spines of technical books, scifi, and mysteries. Sonya remained a big unknown X.

No longer does she shout, kick, or bite, she eats with us in the dining room, she takes baths, and she walks in the garden— but so far she hasn't spoken so much as a word. Absolutely no progress there . . . What are the psychological motivations and mechanisms of her stubborn silence — WHY AM I SO REPUGNANT TO HER—

The psychological state of a person unjustly imprisoned, of course. But Sonya has been in that psychological state forever . . . at least for the past two years. Her undiluted repugnance to my person is unlikely, why just before the episode with Ruda Mach we had become so close. . .

Sometime later repeat to me once more what you told me this morning, she begged me when I offered her our home that morning at the Hubertus, our second floor, our garden . . . I keep offering them to her every day and Sonya responds with stubborn silence.

If we exclude pure repugnance to my person—in view of the violence of Sonya's conveyance from Liberec, let's still assign that a 15% probability—the only remaining factor of deviation would be attraction to another person. Let's assign this attraction rough percentages of possibility:

Volrab (inertia)	5%
The Stranger from Prague (only a 38-hour aquaintanceship)	10%
Ruda Mach (what's left of the 100%)	70%

However, Ruda Mach deserted her, and why would Sonya (who in any case had enough time to get him back) go off to the Hotel Imperial in Liberec with the stranger from Prague if she still loved Ruda Mach? So Mach's 70% drops to 0% and the probability spectrum of Sonya's behavior is mysterious to the tune of 70%. It's all a mystery.

Let's look at the matter from another point of view. It's evident that the following men, at least, have awakened in Sonya an inclination toward love: 1. Volrab (a father); 2. Ruda Mach (a man); 3. The Stranger from Prague (a cultivated person). So one could readily construct a pattern for Sonya's behavior according to these three models:

1 - FATHER
2 - BODY
3 - SPIRIT

But when I put on overalls, rolled in the grass out back, and laughed out loud (à la 2: Ruda Mach), Sonya was just as silent as when I admonished her like a father (model 1) or when, all dressed up, I employed choice, sophisticated words to invite her to the Usti opera, and after the performance I took her to the Zernosecky wine bar. . .

From which of these three models can we extract an effective principle and appropriate it for myself? The most successful, of course, was the masculine model 2 (Ruda Mach), but how then could model 3 (the Stranger from Prague) win out so quickly? And what is it about model 3 that made him so effective?

Deep in reflection, Jakub drew three little men (he was a technician), on the body of the first, bearded one he wrote the number 1, on the second, muscular one the number 2, on the third one, with spectacles, the number 3, and above them he drew a large figure, on the figure's chest he drew an enormous X and then, after long minutes with his fists on his temples, he gazed at his diagram so fixedly that all four figures began to merge into a single one, *a single one, A SINGLE MAN—*

—and in a flash of discovery Jakub feverishly wrote the formula:

$$X = 1 + 2 + 3$$

X is now a known, and so now I've got it: THIS IS THE MAN FOR SONYA—

Jakub leaped up from his tubular desk, knocking over the tubular chair so that its tubes clanged against the floor, he marched back and forth across his room, then skulked at a more peaceful gait, then slunk, and finally dropped to the floor in utter despair. This is no discovery, this is a banality: such a man would be ideal for any woman . . . that sort of *1 + 2 + 3*, that divine trinity of FATHER-BODY-SPIRIT would be a miracle of a sort that simply doesn't exist — and the young engineer wept bitterly on the floor and beat his fists against the roughly woven, thin, firm blue carpet.

After a long time, he took hold of himself, got up, skulked around the room, then walked, and finally he was marching again: I LOVE SONYA and that's all I know. And instead of further extrapolations, I will get down on my knees before her—

He crossed the corridor and knocked on Sonya's door— Sonya did not respond. Quietly he entered the room and quietly he greeted her—Sonya did not respond. That bronzed Madonna with a strawberry-blond halo, glowing with burning emeralds—

"Sonya, I love you—" said Jakub, and he got down on his knees before Sonya, "and I'll do anything you want me to."

"Anything?" SHE HAD SPOKEN!

"Anything."

"Let me go away from here."

"Anything but that. Please — ask for something other than that. . ."

"All right. Give me my letters."

"But I haven't got any letters of yours—"

"The letters that came here for me in care of you."

"But no letter came here for you—"

"Really?"

"I swear it!"

"I'd like to believe you. What should I ask for myself? . . . At least as much as a soldier confined to his barracks — is that within your power?"

"I promised you anything you want."

"All right then, I want to go for a walk every day. And pocket money, as much as Engineer Jagr's future wife would have."

"She had said the magic words: ENGINEER JAGR'S FUTURE WIFE—

"You can go wherever you want. And I'll give you money, as much as you need. But promise me that you won't abuse your freedom or go away—"

"Idiot. I could go away the first day after our wedding—or are you going to tie me up right after it? Am I your fiancée or your prisoner?"

She had said YOUR FIANCÉE—

"You're free and I'll give you the money right away. May I kiss you now?"

Sonya smiled and, like the princess in the historical drama *Angelica,* she held her hand out to the lips of her kneeling husband.

"And now you can paint the garden bench white," she said over his bowed head.

On the second floor of the Orts' yellow villa, the curtains billowed out imperceptibly, and when they came to rest again, on the window ledge, next to the ficus in its majolica pot, was a yellow watering can.

In a little while, a precisely identical watering can appeared on a ground-floor window ledge of the Jagrs' villa, among flower pots planted with cactuses — Zlatunka Jagrova placed it as a sign to Kamila Ortova that she had received her message (not even Staff Sergeant Jagr himself had unraveled the meaning of this secret telegraphy employed by the two princesses in the white and yellow houses).

Zlatunka glanced at the thick convex crystal of her tiny gold watch: 8:22. Dad is going through the newspapers looking for airplane crashes and hijackings (Staff Sergeant Jagr is as easy to read as the timetable on the wall at the train station), it would take no less than a crash right in our garden to draw his attention, but to be safe she went out the back door of the house, stole along the fence to a loose board (Zlatunka had deceitfully constructed a false secret exit under the gaze of her father's binoculars in order to draw his attention away from a second secret exit, through which she went often and without a worry in the world), quit her familial domain, traversed the clay surface of Valley Street, ran across the concrete highway to the north and, rounding the pre-fab high-rises, came finally to the development's heating plant.

Dressed in a bright yellow dress, Kamila Ortova popped out from behind a pile of wet heating-plant ash, and the two princesses sat down on a low wall. Kamila offered Zlatunka a Peer cigarette from a yellow pack belonging to Daddy Ort, then she helped herself and for a while the girls smoked together in silence.

"I've been making her sweat," Zlatunka said finally, "but when she springs right back. . ."

"For rubber you need a really sharp knife," said Kamila, she blew smoke out through her nose and with the tip of her shoe she kicked away a moldy roll.

"I prefer razor blades . . . Yesterday she deigned to speak to us, and since then they've all been waiting on her hand and foot. . ."

"Even Jakub?"

"Him especially. Can you really still want to marry him . . . after all this?"

"I want to. And when I want something.—"

The two girls smoked together in silence.

"So it looks to me as if you've run out of ammunition," said Kamila. "And that means you've given up the apartment on the second floor—"

"That whore has to clear out. At any price. As soon as possible."

"We have to think of something . . . painful."

"I should be able to come up with something. . ."

"Me, too. You go first—"

"Eggs?" Mother Jagrova was surprised.

"Just the yokes," said Sonya, skillfully she separated the yellows from the whites and poured them into a lemon sauce (the staff sergeant's gastritis was acting up again). "And now just a bit of rind. . ." Sonya grated a heap of lemon rind, sprinkled it into the sauce, let it cook, and with a smile handed it to Mother Jagrova so she could taste it.

"Wonderful!" said Mother. "You know, in all these years it never occurred to me to combine egg yokes and lemon rind. . ."

"And we could mix the whites with carrots and have carrot whip — do you like that?"

"We've never had it—"

"It's quite simple, like this—" and Sonya nimbly washed and scraped some carrots, dribbled in the remaining lemon juice, added the egg whites and some sugar, and whipped it into a froth.

"Isn't that wonderful!" Mother exclaimed as she gulped down an enormous spoonful.

"It'll be even better when we chill it in the fridge and then serve it with lady fingers."

"If I don't manage to get to it first . . . oh, what a treat! And yesterday those cheese-and-nut sandwiches . . . please tell me the recipes."

"Sure. You take twenty dekas of medium-grade flour, baking powder, a smidgen of nutmeg—"

"Good Lord, why am I writing all this down when you're here to stay with us now! You're a wonderful cook — and that's better than the finest dowry . . . Now something does occur to me . . . Come with me—right away, before Zlatunka comes back from school. And quiet, so Dad doesn't know—"

Quietly, the two women went to the dining room, Mother Jagrova unlocked the sideboard and took out a large black leather box. As the lid opened, they could see a long row of silverware sparkling on a bed of blue silk.

"Beautiful, isn't it," Mother whispered.

"Very. . .," Sonya whispered. "May I hold one in my hands?"

"I'm giving all of them to you. Zlatunka was to have them— but I'll give her the engraved ones from Uncle Ada, they're so heavy you can't even eat with them. But not a word about this to anyone till after the wedding!"

"You can trust me, Mother."

"Well then, why don't you go and get dressed — we're going to the tailor's right after lunch."

Right after lunch (the staff sergeant was in ecstasy over the lemon sauce and the carrot whip. Zlatunka ostentatiously turned up her nose at these innovations until her father broke her spirit with countless Hms! and Hmms!, Jakub doesn't come back from the factory until late in the afternoon), Father Jagr started the blue van and personally took charge of the driving, he made Mother sit in back and politely seated Sonya next to him.

"Ha! Hold on tight, Sonya! I'll be driving very fast! Ha! Ha!"

he roared joyously, nervously he put his hand through his thick gray crewcut and every so often he wiped his hands on his trousers — the car pranced around in front of the garage and unexpectedly (especially for the staff sergeant) ran into a bed of poppies.

"Ha! That's a machine for you! Fifty horsepower! Ha! Ha!" Father Jagr rejoiced.

"Careful, Dad!" Mother the backseat driver was alarmed and held her hat tight against her head. At a speed of twelve miles an hour, we hurtled along the concrete highway toward town.

Emphatically better then riding in back bound with laundry cord, like a calf — Sonya smiled at herself in the mirror. I'm going to get myself a bridal outfit—

Mr. Joachim Schwarz, the tailor, is the longstanding purveyor to the court of the Jagrs, and his best customers try on their clothes in his "private comptoir" which looks out on the main square of Usti. He made me a white dress with a long lacy train and he had made to measure (by his longtime supplier Mme. Albina Zwetschkenbaumova in Frydlant) white lacy sleeves that went all the way down to the elbow. . . just like what *Angelika* wore in the film, from the square we could hear the noise of the city, the buzz of cars, and the clang of streetcars — they're red here, like the ones in Liberec. . .

In the tall mirror I can see Sonya the bride, and tears burn my eyes, *for the fourth time I am getting ready for my wedding* —

From the tailor across the square to the shoe cooperative Springtime (we're friends of the manager's, Mrs. Reznikova) for slippers: white slip-ons (for both weddings, in church and at the town hall). White slip-ons (for changing before the refreshments at the Hotel Savoy). Beige slip-ons (they always come in handy). Beige loafers with gold buckles (for the honeymoon). Black slip-ons (for the honeymoon). Red slip-ons (for the honeymoon). Black slip-ons with silver clasps (for the honeymoon). Black mules with fur lining (for the wedding night).

"Ha! Your foot is smaller than my hand!" the sergeant was stirred. "Ha! Ha! Ha!"

From Springtime across the square to the goldsmith's shop, Precious Stones (we're friends of the manager's, Mr. Strunc), for wedding rings (massive, keglike, fourteen carats, the Jagrs had given up three of their great-grandmother's teeth for them, together with 750 crowns) as well as a heavy gold ring with a large amethyst.

As if from one point of a star to another, we crisscrossed the main square, made our purchases, and brought back to the car two crates of sparkling wine, twenty sacks of salted almonds, a hundred bright-colored plastic straws, a pink lampshade, a frying-pan in which, even without fat, nothing would burn, a green bathroom brush with a stand, hairclips, briefs, washcloths, spotcleaner, iodine, band-aids, and three kinds of bandages, and they made an appointment at the hairdresser's and placed their order for a three-tiered cake.

"I'm happy you didn't bring anything with you," the ebullient mother said from the back seat of the van. "I so enjoy shopping and I'd have missed out on it. . ."

"But you brought me here shotgun—"

"Ha! That was really something! The storming of Liberec! A sally in broad daylight! Ha! Ha!"

"But you promised her you'd never say a word about that," the mother said hastily.

"Ha! Hmm! Nonsense. My say is said. Hm," the sergeant said, and in a bravura performance he passed a bicycle (something behind us went bang).

Attempts to go through our blue gate in front of the garage ended, after lengthy maneuvers, in failure (Mother and I each held one of the two garage doors and were forced to listen to no fewer than sixty Hmms!) and the staff sergeant finally resolved to park on Valley Street, Operation Driveway was postponed until sometime later. Hm!

Sonya admitted that it had all made her a bit nervous ("Of course you'd be!" Mother smiled, and the staff sergeant added his "Ha! Ha!") and that she needed to walk a little, she crossed the clay surface of Valley Street, ran across the concrete highway to the north and around the pre-fab high-rises, she finally came to the development's heating plant and disappeared behind the pile of wet heating-plant ash.

I'm sitting here on a low wall shivering all over as if I had a fever, *what is going to happen to me now?* — And then I cry, just as I do every day and every night. Why hasn't my husband Manek Mansfeld, who can *do anything,* been taking care of me here—and why hasn't he answered the letters I send him every day, in the first one I described my imprisonment here in detail for some thirty-two pages, and every day I send him one more despairing supplication—

At the base of the black mountain of ash I shiver and weep until I'm exhausted, and as I do every day I run through the meadow to the village of Skorotice, where in a shop behind the church they sell everything from rolls to Lada sewing machines, I buy a roll and stamped letter paper, then back to my little low wall where I throw the roll away (there are five of them lying here molding), I lick my pencil and write as I've done five times already before:

My Manek,
Come for me. I'm in Usti nad Labem, No. 4 Valley
Street, at the Jagrs'. I love you. Please come for me soon.
Your Sonya

And on the envelope: Mr. Manuel Mansfeld, Hotel Imperial, Liberec.

"Registered, right?" said the woman at the Vseborice post office.

"Registered express."

At 6:44 all of us—Mother, Jakub, Zlatunka, and I—have to sit down to our soup, at 6:44 the staff sergeant comes, intermixed with his chidings ("Hm!" or "Hmm!") he praises me ("Ha! Ha!") and all we hear after that is a fivefold sipping of soup.

Suddenly someone rings — I jump up from the table and run to open the door, MANEK HAS COME FOR ME — but Zlatunka, who's sitting right next to the door, gives me a kick in the shins. "Out of the way!" she hisses, and she opens to someone I've never seen before.

He is short, with a tiny head and an extremely high forehead, he is said to be infinitely talented (Mother has told me about him), he is the second-highest-ranking surgeon at the hospital, his name is Lubos Bily and he's Zlatunka's fiancé (just before lunch I had deprived him of part of Zlatunka's dowry—the silver).

"Hm! You might have left him in the vestibule, since he was late getting here. Hmm!"

"But Daddy—"

"But Dad—"

"Hmm! They don't even let you into the movies during the newsreel. Hm."

No one ventured to open his mouth till dinner was over, and Jakub introduced Dr. Bily to me only after his father had gone off to his workroom.

"I didn't expect you to be so beautiful. . ." Dr. Bily told me when I smiled at him prettily . . . but the smile froze when I looked over his shoulder and caught sight of Zlatunka giving me the evil eye — how much malice can be contained in a single look!

The engaged couple was going to the movies and Dr. Bily invited us (actually he said me) to come along with them, Jakub looked at me beseechingly so that I would stay home with him—but that's just what I feared more than anything, that look from Jakub's sincere blue eyes. We went to the movies in Dr. Bily's American car and parked right in front of the movie house.

In front of the movie an enormous poster proclaimed that the historical film *Angelica* was playing there: the princess in the coach gives King Louis her hand in its white lacy sleeve all the way down to the elbow, *the same sleeve I had bought today—*

"No!" I said. "I wouldn't go in for anything in the world!"

"But we will, won't we, Lubos," Zlatunka said to her Dr. Bily, "and you'll come with us, Jakub—"

The men decided to go to another movie house to see an Italian farce.

"Zlatus, please don't have a tantrum on me now," Lubos Bily laughed. Gray with rage Zlatunka laughed convulsively and from that moment on she was like honey to me — damn the attention I have to give that cunning serpent.

The Italian farce dragged on endlessly, Jakub held my hand in his, my cold and dead in his warm and eager — when we got home I told him I had a terrible headache, double-locked myself in my room and, still dressed, threw myself onto the bed. Lord, another night—

The next morning I stayed in bed as late as I could, so the day wouldn't last so long . . . before night came again, which I fear even more (each evening Jakub comes to knock on my door, more and more often, longer and more insistently). In the morning cooking and peace, after lunch shopping, in late afternoon tears on the low wall behind the black mountain of wet ashes and another letter to Manek . . . *What will happen to me now?*

I loathe this white house which smells of laundry soap, oil, and sweat, this gymnasium with its barracks-like concern for physique, in which spirit is supplanted by nothing but the vigor with which the male officers give commands to the women who man their squad.

I try to be a good soldier, and the staff sergeant is continually thanking me for this. When I found an article in the attic about an explosion aboard a Mexican airplane, he neighed ecstatically "Ha! Ha! Ha!" for a good minute, gave me a drink of cherry brandy, and seemed about to promote me to the rank of corporal: in the kitchen I am the head chef and Mother carries out my orders. And Zlatunka is learning to cook under my command — I don't let her off easy, and her badly peeled potatoes (the girl has two left hands) get tossed back into her lap, even if they're boiling hot — Zlatunka is now like saccharine to me.

Before lunch (Zlatunka can finish cooking it by herself now) Mother takes me for the first time into the bedroom on the second floor. Towering haughtily over the marriage bed is a pile of overly starched superior linen, the cool damask is all ready to soak up Jakub's and my intermingled sweat, the mighty pillows to stifle the moans, and by the door the new slippers with the white fur lining to warm my feet over those couple of steps to my husband.

The worst time is after dinner, when Jakub looks at me beseechingly with his sincere blue eyes.

"I'd like to go work somewhere," I try to engage him in conversation, "I could do just about anything. . ."

"First you should finish *gymnasium* and then apply to the teachers institute. We've got friends there who could help you get in."

"But I don't want to be a teacher, I want to be something practical . . . a nurse, a telephone operator, a salesperson . . . Doesn't the Usti Cottex have a drying room like the one in Hrusov? That's where I'd most like—"

"My wife must go to a school of higher education."

"I like children very much and that's exactly why I don't want to order them around . . . and they'd soon find that out, they'd play all the time and not learn a thing."

"The teachers institute is the only school of higher education in Usti," Jakub said drily, and then he showed me the family gold. Chains, rings, old coins, gold teeth. ". . . it all adds up to nearly ten ounces," he said.

I like gold, but I spent a great deal more time poking through it than my liking dictated . . . all so I wouldn't have to look into Jakub's blue eyes.

"So we've got everything for the wedding," he said. "I'd just like to speak to you about one more thing. Do you feel healthy?"

"Yes . . . of course. . ."

"You know, I'm just. . . Whenever I knock at your door during the night . . . why don't you open it? After all, we could now, already. . . Just tell me quite calmly whether you still might be experiencing some sort of psychological trauma . . .

You understand, an inhibition like this can have a cause that's mental or emotional or physiological or—"

"I'm healthy as a turnip!"

"Great. Dad's letting me have the van Saturday and Sunday. I'll show you beautiful places along the river and in the woods. Lubos is lending us his cottage by the Elbe for the weekend . . . communing with nature, you'll soon get over your psychological block. We'll be there all weekend long, together."

"That would be nice . . . But now I'd like to go to sleep, my head aches so terribly again. . ."

"You're working too hard, in the cottage by the Elbe you'll make a fine recovery."

"You're very kind. Good night."

"Good night, darling. I love you."

"Jakub . . . Promise me you'll never be angry with me."

"I love you."

I kissed him on the forehead so I wouldn't have to look into his eyes.

The next day, after breakfast, I assigned the kitchen tasks, put on the green dress Manek had given me, the dress I was wearing when they brought me here, into my handbag I put my toothbrush, my short white nightgown, a comb, and a hundred crowns (I might well have earned that working here), called into the kitchen to say I was going for a pedicure, crossed Valley Street (not even once did I look back), and on red bus No. 5 I rode through the pre-fab high-rises of the development to the main station and then on the express train to Liberec.

Behind the curtains of the second-floor window of the Orts' yellow villa Kamila Ortova sat at a table reading her lecture notes from Psychology III (in a few days I'll be starting my last year at the teachers institute) and smoking a cigarette from her Dad's golden pack of Peers, and every so often she looked out at the white villa opposite, Jakub's house—

—stolen from me and Jakub by that tramp. I'll never understand how my sober and *rational* Jakub—we're both exactly the same—could slip into such *madness* . . . shouldn't a man be put under guardianship in a case like this? Because his madness does not have tragic consequences just for him, but destroys the happiness and lives of the rest of us as well.

Men are stupid animals. How can I rescue my Jakub against his own will? Ridding him of this madness means ridding him of the tramp—but she keeps installing herself more and more firmly in his house.

Poison her? Zlatunka would gladly do it, and so would I. But, unfortunately, our motives would be quite clear: Zlatunka, to keep the room on the second floor for herself and Lubos Bily (who would vanish nice and quickly without the second floor). And me, to rescue my husband.

If only we could kill her so that no one would know . . . for a very long time . . . Because her wedding would wipe out the motives of us both—

On the much traveled clay of Valley Street, Jakub's figure was growing taller. He was coming home from the plant. The first time he came home from there, he ran upstairs and told me excitedly all about Cottex and the people there—all our lives we two shared everything—and during those years his daily accounts of the goings-on at Cottex meant as much to me as me and my psychology meant to him.

Jakub is coming through the gate and through the garden. *I want that gate and that garden to belong to us both.* He no longer looks at my window, from which I've been watching him since I was little. *I want to look right into his blue eyes again.* And now he disappears into his white house. *I want the house and I want Jakub, too.* MY HUSBAND FOREVER AND EVER, I WILL RESCUE YOU—

When a yellow watering can appeared in a ground-floor window of the Jagrs' white house, Kamila set a precisely identical watering can in the window next to the ficus in the majolica pot.

Then without haste, determined and methodical, she placed

in her handbag a tube of Bromargyl (not too toxic, but its bromide and mercury accumulate in the body), a golden pack of Peer cigarettes and a silver lighter, a silver pencil, and a tiny pocket calendar.

I hurry out of the gray Liberec station and run down the street, red streetcars clamber up the hill and go clanging down it. Out of breath I burst into the door of the Hotel Imperial.

"Is Mr. Mansfeld here?" I ask the clerk at the reception desk, a man I still remember.

"Mr. Mansfeld is traveling," he tells me (he obviously doesn't remember me).

"I stayed with him here two days in late August — I was in Room No. 522 — And I remember you very well—"

"Would you tell me your name, Miss?"

"Sonya Cechova."

"Then I have a letter for you from Mr. Mansfeld."

SONYA CECHOVA was written on the envelope, followed by *to be given to her in person*, inside was Manek's photo and on the back of the photo:

> *I want you to be great.*
> *Will you trust me?*
> > *Your Manek*

"I need Mr. Mansfeld's address right away."

"That's entirely out of the question," said the clerk.

"But I've come all the way from Usti just to see him—"

"Mr. Mansfeld expressly asked that his address not be given to you."

"He told you that?"

"He told me that categorically."

"I've sent letters to him in care of the hotel. . ."

"Every one of them was forwarded to him immediately."

"The first was quite thick—thirty-two pages. And then every day another, ordinary one—"

"Every one of them was forwarded to him immediately."

"If I wrote a letter now — could you send it to him?"

"I would post it tomorrow morning."

"And a telegram?"

"A telegram could be sent over the telephone at once."

"Could you give me his telephone number, at least?"

"That would be against Mr. Mansfeld's categorical wishes."

"So then I'll send the telegram—"

The clerk offered me a pad of paper. With the pen that was attached to the desk I wrote quickly:

> *I am waiting at the Hotel Imperial.*
> *Your Sonya*

The clerk promised to send the telegram at once, refused to take any money and, without argument, gave me room No. 411—even without my citizen's I.D.! *Manek can do anything, even from a distance.*

I passed through the gleaming mahogany lobby and took the elevator up to the fifth floor, I lay down on the couch in my room with Manek's photo in my hand, *I WANT YOU TO BE GREAT*, I want it too if it's what you want, and I will be great if that's what you make me. *WILL YOU TRUST ME?* Absolutely, if you are my husband.

I took the elevator down to the gleaming mahogany lobby and at the reception desk I asked the clerk whether he had sent the telegram yet — he said that he had — and when Manek would receive it — he said, in two hours. So I would see my husband today.

I had an urge to jump on the first red streetcar and ride up and down the line until evening, to go right up to the front and ask the motorman to clang a great deal more, I *love* Liberec — but first I went into the quiet little shop near the station (how long ago it was that I bought a green nightgown here and, for a crown, needle and white thread) and bought from the old lady a dark-red handkerchief for my husband and a white ribbon for my hair, so that he would like me this evening, *for the fifth time I am getting ready for my wedding—*

I walked around Liberec until dark, looked into the Gastronome Restaurant, where I had dined with Manek, stood at the Grapevine Bar, where we had first called each other by our first names and where we had first kissed on the dancefloor. . . At the Imperial's reception desk, the clerk I knew had been replaced by the night clerk, who told me that Mr. Mansfeld had not yet arrived.

I went up the street to the station, on the timetable I found the arrival time of the next express train from Prague and I waited about an hour for it. Manek did not come. But he might have come by car and be waiting for me at the hotel—

The night clerk told me again that Mr. Mansfeld had not yet arrived. I stood in front of the hotel, *my husband has to come any minute* — Manek did not appear, but two other gentlemen did address me (the first invited me for some *veeno*, the second offered me a hundred-note — and when I laughed in his face he offered a hundred and fifty). A lone girl can hardly stand very long in front of a hotel (especially without her citizen's I.D.—) and so I went to see *Angelica* for the second time.

The fair Angelica kept losing and finding her wonderful husband, Geoffrey Peyrac. Geoffrey had fallen into disgrace with King Louis, had hidden from him and had fought against him as a captain of pirates (what does Manek do?), and with mysterious messages and unexpected assistance had kept rescuing Angelica again and again — and even from a distance served her constantly as husband and protector.

The night clerk told me again that Mr. Mansfeld had not yet arrived. I sat in the gleaming mahogany lobby, the guests kept coming in and taking the elevator up to their rooms, at midnight the restaurant closed, I took the elevator to my room, No. 411, and again reread the message on the back of Manek's photo *I WANT YOU TO BE GREAT*, a great woman doesn't whimper in a hotel lobby, Angelica was carried off by pirates, they sold her into slavery, and still she waited patiently for her Geoffrey: *WILL YOU TRUST ME?* Always and in every way.

I phoned down to the reception desk (Mr. Mansfeld had not yet arrived) to say that I was waiting for Mr. Mansfeld in room 411 and that he was welcome to come to my room anytime. Then I bathed, combed my hair, tied the white ribbon into it, placed Manek's photo in such a way that I could see it from the bed, lay down on my back, and gazed at his photo. . .

That's how I was when I woke up in the morning. Manek hadn't arrived.

The reception clerk (again the one I knew) told me that Mr. Mansfeld had not checked in yet, but that a telegram had arrived for me late at night.

Once I'd read it, I had to sit down.

I WANT YOU TO BE GREAT STOP IF YOU WISH I WILL
TAKE YOUR FATE IN MY HANDS STOP YOU MUST HAVE
ABSOLUTE TRUST IN ME STOP GO BACK TO JAKUB AND
WIN BACK HIS LOVE STOP I WILL SEND FURTHER
MESSAGES TO USTI   *M.M.*

Out of the hotel, all four Sonyas roaring inside me, up the street to the station and down to the square, by streetcar to the last stop and then another streetcar to the last stop at the other end of the line, on foot to some sort of forest and then back again to the last stop, by streetcar across the entire city to the last stop, where I've been already. . . When I got there, things began to get clear and then, suddenly calm, I rode back to the Hotel Imperial.

My husband wants me to go back to Jakub Jagr. . .

That's terrible, of course, but: Manek does not demand that I *marry* Jakub, only win back his love . . . which I had lost by running away. I think that's it. *Manek knows everything AND HE WANTS TO TAKE MY FATE IN HIS HANDS.* Why else had I come here to find him?!

All in all, it was stupid for me to have come here for him, maybe it wasn't time yet for us to be together (Manek would have invited me himself, or he would have taken me away from those hellish Jagrs just like he took me away from those hellish Volrabs), maybe Manek's in hiding, maybe he's in grave danger—and I came here to the hotel and went wild when he didn't immediately send a helicopter for me—if that had been necessary, Manek would have done it.

Without any hesitation I will HAVE ABSOLUTE TRUST in you. AND FOR YOU I WILL BE GREAT.

"I'm checking out right away and I'd like to send a telegram to Mr. Mansfeld," I told the clerk I knew. He offered me a writing pad and with the pen that was attached to the desk I quickly wrote:

> *I am yours wholeheartedly stop*
> *I will await your further messages in Usti*
> *Your Sonya*

I paid for the room and and walked quickly up the hill to the station, calm and at peace: I will no longer rush off aimlessly, I will go where my husband sends me.

To win back Jakub's love will not be very difficult, but I always fulfill my tasks one hundred percent: on the way I stopped in the quiet little shop by the station and bought a white handkerchief from the old lady (I had left the dark-red one at the reception desk for Manek) as a gift for Jakub . . . this is my new job and my vocation as long as I live.

I winked at the gigantic Angelica on the gigantic poster (in the background a fiery battle) as if she were a friend: we've got our troubles, girl. . .

The whole trip by express train to Usti I stood out in the corridor, I was too full of everything to sit down in my compartment. . . From the station I took red bus No. 5 to the development and walked through the pre-fab high-rises to Valley Street.

For the first time, as I stood in front of the blue gate of No. 4, I was happy to look at the Jagrs' villa, suddenly their big

white house seemed as tiny as a midgets' cottage. That wonderful feeling that from now on I am on top of the world—
   Today, Manek had given it to me.

"Hm!" said Staff Sergeant Jagr, his hands behind his back and his high-booted legs wide apart. "Is this what you call digging up a flower bed? Hmm! Once more! Hmm! Hmm!"
   Sonya (right after her return, she changed into Jakub's dirtiest overalls, she had to wash all the floors, stairs, and toilets in the entire house, all she slept was two hours in a locked shed in the yard) rubbed her pale, sweaty forehead with the sweaty ridge of her hand and smiled prettily at the staff sergeant.
   "But you can't dig up a bed a second time, Mr. Jagr. All I can do is rake it over and—"
   "For you it's Staff Sergeant, sir, understand? Hm!"
   "Yes, Staff Sergeant, sir."
   "Repeat the command!"
   "The command, Staff Sergeant, sir! Most obediently: dig up the dug up garden, Staff Sergeant, sir!"
   "Right and proper—ha!"
   "Dad, don't you see she's laughing right in your face!" Mother Jagrova cried out in anger and disgust.

Sunday afternoon went well. The guests in the living room of the white villa drank two pots of coffee with whipped cream, ate a plate of hazelnut slices and two blenders full of vanilla ice cream, topped off by a bottle of homemade cherry wine — Sonya ran her feet off (she'd soon lose that laugh of hers!) to serve everything just right.
   "I'm so glad we got together again," said Kamila Ortova.
   "Ha! After all, we are neighbors—ha!" Father Jagr said merrily.
   "And do come again soon, Kamila," Mother Jagr bade her,

and then she gave a command: "Sonya, run and wrap up a bottle of that cherry wine for Miss Kamila!"

"See you again soon," said Kamila, and she got up to leave.

"Wait, I'll go with you—" Jakub blurted out, and he accompanied Kamila all the way to her silver-gray garden gate where, out of breath, Sonya caught up with them, handed over the bottle of homemade cherry wine, and again ran back to the abusive staff sergeant.

"Don't you want to come any further?" Kamila smiled at Jakub.

"I've still got work to do."

"Come any time, maybe after dinner, when you're done with everything . . . I'm always glad to see you."

"Thanks, goodbye. And don't be angry at me anymore. . ."

"I never was angry at you. I want you to know that I've always been fond of you—" said Kamila, and with her head held high she walked into the Orts' yellow villa.

Deep in thought, Jakub went back home. Kamila's persistent interest in me is wonderful—what do we really know about women?—and *thrilling* . . . the way she longs for me so much . . . she invited me to come see her *after dinner*—

The blood beat in his temples, Jakub ran upstairs to his bedroom and, to calm himself down, he did forty push-ups on the firm blue carpet and then took forty deep breaths . . . But even this number seemed insufficient.

Shining through the open window, in the August heat, beyond the graceful swaying of the radiant tops of the apple and cherry trees, was the Orts' yellow villa, where Kamila, the friend of my happy childhood here in our green valley, longs to have me *for the night*, Kamila, my boyhood love — for always LOVE, WOMAN, SEX, and MARRIAGE have meant the same thing to me as KAMILA. . . Now all I have to do is come down the stairs and shout: "I'm going to marry Kamila!" and Dad and Mother would be happy and Zlatunka would be overjoyed and our family and the Orts would live peacefully, without psychoanalysis, kidnappings, or despair, forever as in a fairy tale. . .

All I have to do is cross the garden and ring at my neighbor's silver-gray gate—

But when it's Sonya I STILL LOVE—

Even though she betrayed me so scandalously just before the wedding and spent the night with someone else — is this what I gave her the freedom to do, to the point that I got down on my knees before her. . .

The wedding's been put off indefinitely so we can have an interval—say a month—in which to test her in all sorts of ways . . . even though I already know everything about her. Time to pass from analysis to synthesis. Methodically split Sonya down to nothing but molecules of pure womanhood—the more she suffers now, the better for us both—and then after her meltdown rebuild her via an incandescent synthesis from disconnected molecules into the new person I desire.

How to reach the enormous heat and pressure required . . . when Sonya laughs disdainfully at everyone, as if nothing could ever touch her? By the methods of scientific terror: form a GANG AGAINST SONYA, which will first of all blow up that flighty serving girl.

Jakub leafed through his spiral notebook where the flowchart of Sonya's obliteration and reconstruction was depicted in diagrams and graphs drawn with four different colored pencils, on the left the respective actions taken, on the right columns for commenting on their effectiveness — nothing but filled-in squares of red: today Sonya's subjugation is one-hundred percent.

Jakub picked up and once again studied closely (he was a technician) a color postcard of Prague, according to the postmark it had actually been sent from Prague, to the correct address (*Sonya Cechova, Valley Street 4, Usti n. L.*), with an unusual content, but one that was most acceptable:

Trust Jakub. Everything he does, however strange it may appear, he does for your good.

M.M.

In any event, M.M. is a complete riddle, but the text is of course a welcome one and evidently the actual contents of its message (several times Jakub held the postcard up to the light, felt it over and, in the lab at Cottex, subjected it to all sorts of tests for discovering secret chemical inks and the sort of micro-dots used in espionage, and neither decoding nor deciphering the text of the postcard on the company's Saab computer, with the expert cooperation of the operator—and his friend—Dominik Neuman, revealed any hidden message), and so hand-ing it over to the addressee could be expected to produce a positive pedagogical effect.

At 6:30 P.M. Jakub delivered the postcard from Prague to Sonya and then read to her from his notebook, item by item, her tasks for the next 24 hours:

". . . eighteen: march double-time around the garden. Nine-teen: fill out psychotechnical test No. 376. Twenty: write thirty lines of detailed description of all your sensations during the day just completed. Twenty-one: polish all the shoes in the vestibule. Twenty-two: write a summary of the ninth chapter of van de Velde's *The Perfect Marriage*—"

"Jakub," Zlatunka said caustically, lounging around in her rocking chair, "don't you see that bitch is laughing right in your face?"

"We'll soon put an end to your laughter," said Zlatunka.

In the laundry room, with Kamila's help, she sat Sonya down and used laundry cord to tie her feet to the feet of the chair and her twisted arms to its back, and they wound the rest of the cord around Sonya's breasts and waist and knotted it tightly in back.

"So you think that nothing more can happen to you?" said Zlatunka.

"From you two hardly anything," Sonya said contemptu-ously.

Kamila took a deep drag on her Peer cigarette, brought the

glowing ashes close to Sonya's bare arm and, looking straight into her eyes, put it out against her flesh. Sonya screamed with pain, took a few deep breaths, and then laughed contemptuously.

"We'll put an end to your laughter," said Kamila. "Give those scissors here!"

Grinning, Zlatunka gave her a long pair of scissors and Kamila ran them over Sonya's face. "You've got really long hair, Sonya," she said slowly, "we could shorten it for you a little. . ."

"No," Sonya screamed. "You can't—"

"Really?" Kamila said. She grabbed a strand of Sonya's red hair, pulled it taut, and cut it off close to the skin. Then she took another strand and ran the scissors along it, all the way to the scalp.

"No! No! Anything but that! Please . . . don't do that to me—" Sonya screamed, she shook the chair and tugged at the ropes while her hair, strand after strand, fell to the concrete floor, she snapped at the scissors with her teeth, squirmed, and shouted until at last, in tears, she quieted down.

Naked under my dirty, greasy overalls, barefoot in battered military boots stiff with old sweat, which make me bleed with every step (they're what I have to wear to march around the garden) and shorn bald (that's the only part that really hurt me, but it no longer does at all—hair grows back again), but in spite of it all particularly happy: MANEK HAS TAKEN MY FATE IN HIS HANDS and liberated from fate I now feel completely at ease . . . Like a boat steered in the fog towards a safe harbor by signals from the ether.

From somewhere out of the unknown, Manek guards my course and fixes its direction and its destinaton . . . I trust him absolutely, just like he wanted and just like he needs. Manek writes me every day, only postcards (so that Jakub can pass on them), but it's enough for me to be certain and to be happy to see his daily *M.M.*

When I told Jakub that M.M. was my uncle on my mother's side, I got permission to send him postcards myself. My rigid work schedule allows me only five minutes a day for that (from 9:35 to 9:40 in the evening), but I think about those five minutes all day long. Then Jakub scratches out everything on the post- card that doesn't strike him right, and I have to write it all over again. At first I went through as many as five postcards at a time, but then I mastered the secret language of love. Its secret is to use the simplest of words.

I am incredibly happy, even though it's infinitely worse here than it was in Hrusov . . . how childishly naive and almost good-hearted were the verses of Uncle Volrab compared with Jakub's icy heel—and Volrabka was almost kind (even when she lashed me with a wet rag) compared with Zlatunka and Kamila, those two bitches. Of the two Kamila is worse: color- less, insipid, nondescript, boring, dispensable . . . as if she existed only for my destruction. She comes to see me every day, sometimes even more often . . . Most of the time she comes dressed in sulfur yellow dresses (to me, yellow is the color of cruelty. Hope is green and for that I live), each time as if surprised again that I've lived to see another day.

But life here has an intense zestfulness. My pleasure comes from petty joys which I never noticed before—perhaps I had as a child—and now I have discovered them anew: from the sun on the grass (it's a warm, lovely August), from the striping of golden red pearmain apples, from the scent of the soil, from beams of light in the morning mist, from a warm potato in my hand, from the breeze. . . (I'm allowed to write Manek about all of this.) Today I include in my postcard to M.M.: *From this moment on, I will live a larger-than-life life.*

S.-Marie now plays first fiddle in me all the time, *S.-Marikka* has become quiet, even *Antisonya* has, almost, as if she had suddenly lost all her eternal mockery. And *Sonya Undivided* sings softly all day long with *S.-Marie.*

My task here is to win back Jakub's love. At first I listened to him alone and accepted everything quietly. But suddenly it appeared to me that Jakub needed to pluck up his courage much more than me. I get as much courage from Manek as I could possibly need (an infinite amount), but Jakub has less and less of it . . . The less he has, the more obediently I fulfill his commands and the more prettily I smile at him. Manek gave me the task of winning Jakub's love and it is possible that this will be my final task here. I want to fulfill it as soon as possible . . . How can I speed things up?

Unexpectedly, I got help from Dr. Lubos Bily, the little surgeon with the extremely high forehead. While doing some digging around the trees, I unbuttoned the top of my overalls to cool off a bit, and suddenly he popped out from between a couple of trees before I had a chance to button up again. "You're beautiful, Sonya. . ." he whispered, and then he turned quite pale, as if struck by a wave . . . and from then on he showed up more and more often and stuck around me longer and longer, completely obsessed with the sight of me.

And I was clever enough to arrange for Jakub to see us together from his room (concealed behind his curtains, he watches me for hours on end).

S.-Marikka is encouraging us to use jealousy as a way of awakening Jakub's love.

And *S.-Marikka* is having success: Lubos (Dr. Bily wishes me to call him that) stands beside me wherever I please and as long as I want him to (sometimes he even forgets to visit Zlatunka) and Jakub's curtains often tremble . . . I think I'm doing a fine job of fulfilling my task, and I'm enjoying it . . . it is my job here and my vocation.

For the first time Jakub excused me from having to trot around the garden, now, instead, I read to him every day from van de Velde's *The Perfect Marriage*.

The warm August breeze gently raised the tips of the checkered tablecloth on the garden table, where Zlatunka, Dr. Lubos Bily, and Kamila Ortova were slowing devouring their vanilla ice cream topped with whipped cream. A few yards away, Sonya, in her overalls and army boots, was digging up another hundred square yards of lawn.

The company at the table was quite bored. Slowly Kamila tapped another Peer cigarette out of her father's golden pack, mechanically she reached for her silver lighter—then suddenly she threw it onto the tablecloth.

"Sonya! Run and get me some matches!"

Sonya put down her spade and walked off toward the white villa.

"Why are you banging that spade around like that — is it yours?" Zlatunka squawked. "Pick it up this minute — and do it *on your knees—*"

Sonya smiled, bent over to take the handle of the spade, knelt and picked it up, carefully leaned the tool against the trunk of a tree, and went for Kamila's matches. Dr. Lubos Bily turned pale as chalk, rose violently from the table, and stared at his fiancée, wonderstruck, as if he had just seen her for the very first time.

When Sonya brought the matches and placed them on the garden table, Kamila and Zlatunka lit their cigarettes with Kamila's silver lighter and blew their first puffs of smoke right in Sonya's eyes.

"What are you gawking at? Don't you have work to do?" Kamila snapped at Sonya.

"Clear out and get these matches back to the kitchen on the double!" Zlatunka yelled, and she blew the blue smoke of the Peer export cigarette right in Sonya's face.

"I'll take the matches back myself," Lubos Bily said raspingly, and he took the matchbox off the table and threw them on the ground at his fiancée Zlatunka's feet.

Then he walked slowly over to Sonya, who had already begun to dig again, and tenderly but firmly took the spade out of her hand.

"Let me finish it, I have to have it all done by evening," Sonya said with a smile.

"I won't let you," said Dr. Bily, and he turned to the facade of the white villa and called out, "Mr. Jagr! Kindly come out—I know you're standing behind those curtains!"

The second-floor curtains fluttered reluctantly and in a little while Engineer Jakub Jagr, his ears quite red, appeared between the opened shutters.

"Lubos, what's going on—" said Jakub.

"Not Lubos, Engineer. I'm Dr. Bily to you. I am forced to strenuously advise you that what you are doing to Miss Cechova here falls under the criminal code. I am a physician and I have a professional code of conduct to follow. Will you allow me to make an investigation now, or do you prefer to wait five minutes, when I will have the assistance of the police?"

"I'll be right down—" Jakub was greatly alarmed and in a minute's time he was running across the lawn. "Lubos, I didn't really realize. . ."

"Do you see her feet? Who made her wear those frightful boots, and without stockings? — They last did that in the concentration camps!"

"But I really had no idea. . ." Jakub stammered.

"But it doesn't bother me," Sonya smiled. "And it doesn't even hurt anymore."

"You require immediate care and then a few days of bedrest. I will take you to the hospital and arrange things so you will never have to come back here," Dr. Bily said in a single breath.

"No," Sonya smiled. "I want to stay here with Jakub."

"It might really be better for you, Sonya," Jakub rattled off with dismay in his voice, "if you went with Lubos, I mean with the doctor. . ."

"I want to be with you," Sonya said to Jakub, and she smiled at him prettily.

In a rage, Dr. Lubos Bily cursed abominably, pushed the confused Zlatunka away, jumped into his sturdy American car and, with a hundred-and-fifty-horsepower roar, stormed off down Valley Street in a cloud of exhaust fumes.

Zlatunka flung her cigarette on the grass and beat her fists against the checkered tablecloth.

"Jakub. . ." Kamila said softly to the crushed young engineer.

"Leave me alone," Jakub told her, and he didn't look at her again. For a while he rubbed his sweaty forehead, then he sent Sonya to bed and disappeared into the white house.

A little later he came out again in the company of the staff sergeant, who was nervously plucking his gray, crewcut hair. The two men disappeared into the garage, but their barking made it through the heavy garage doors all the way out to the garden.

Just before dinner, at 6:42, Jakub handed Sonya another postcard from M.M., authorized her to write further postcards to M.M., even letters, and waived his right to censor them.

"Can you forgive me, Sonya?" he asked softly.

"And can you forgive me?" Sonya said with a smile.

At 6:44, Jakub, Mother Jagrova, and Zlatunka were already sitting in the dining room over their four plates of steaming soup and Sonya, wearing an apron, was circling the table, all ready to wait on them.

At 6:45, the staff sergeant entered the dining room, sat down at the head of the table, and commanded sharply:

"Hm! Bring a fifth plate!"

Sonya moved nimbly, but the staff sergeant stopped her short:

"Hmm! Not you, Sonya. Take off that apron and come eat with us—ha! Zlatunka will bring you a plate—hmm! Hmm!"

"Yes, Daddy," was all Zlatunka could say, and then she brought Sonya a plate.

"Tomorrow, Mother will give Sonya decent shoes—hm!" he went on giving orders. "Three pairs at least, for going out—ha!

And send her to the hairdresser's in town—ha! And pay her
three hundred crowns—ha! Ha!"

"Yes, Dad," said Mother. "Three pairs of shoes, to the hairdresser's, and three hundred crowns."

"But, sergeant, sir—" Sonya said with a smile (of the kind
made famous all over the world by the fiery Marikka Rökk in
her film musicals—ha! Ha!).

"Ha! Ha! Hmm! Nonsense. Be quiet and eat. We don't talk
during dinner—hm. From tomorrow on you are freed from
physical work—ha! Two walks a day—ha! And you can help
me arrange my file cards on aviation—ha! Ha! Ha! Eat up now.
Dobrou chut!"

"*Dobrou chut,*" answered the flabbergasted Jagr women,
Jakub said it as if only to Sonya, and Sonya smiled at him
prettily.

Late that evening Zlatunka locked her door and packed her big
brown leather shopping bag with Sonya's green dress, Sonya's
two pairs of shoes and nightgown, one of the Jagr family's blue
bath towels, then she added her own beautiful Italian sweater,
two hundred-notes and then, after a brief hesitation, a third.

She stole quietly out of her room and spent a long time
listening to the familiar sounds of her home — Kamila and I
have lost the game, but that fanatic Kamila doesn't realize it,
from now on then without her and even, maybe, against her —
Zlatunka breathed in with determination, crept to Sonya's door,
and gave it four quick little knocks (Jakub's signal, which she
had overheard).

The door opened almost immediately and Sonya (in her
nightgown) took a step backward. With a finger to her lips,
Zlatunka went into Sonya's room and hurriedly closed it behind her.

"I've come to ask you to forgive me—" Zlatunka spoke with
apparent effort.

"That's all?" Sonya said with a smile.

"I was impossible to you — but it was Kamila who put me up to it! She's incredibly wicked and she goaded me to do what I did . . . She's always playing nasty tricks!"

"Don't you realize I don't give a damn?"

"Forgive me, Sonya . . . It's been hell for you here and I've thought it over and decided to help you go free. Here in this bag is everything you need for the first few days, till you find something—even money!—and I'll get you out myself. For tonight I've got you a room at the Hotel Bohemia and tomorrow morning you can start looking for a job right away—"

"My job is to be here and here is where I'll stay . . . for a while yet."

"But then you'll run off anyway, won't you. . ."

"It doesn't depend on me."

"On whom, then?"

"You wouldn't understand. Take your bag and go. Good night."

The next afternoon Kamila Ortova stood behind the curtains of her second-floor room in the yellow villa, smoking a Peer cigarette (her eighteenth of the day) and closely watching every movement in the white villa opposite.

At Time T (Jakub at work, the staff sergeant over his file cards, and Mother Jagrova just about to go shopping) Kamila placed the yellow watering can in the window next to the ficus in its majolica pot.

When she saw Zlatunka sneaking through the garden toward the secret exit, she looked at her gold wristwatch (Zlatunka was on her way to the heap of heating-plant ash and would wait there at least ten minutes, I'll have to catch up with her during those ten minutes), she took a deep drag from her cigarettte, abruptly put it out, and then shook her head: Zlatunka and I have lost the game, but she's so dense she doesn't realize it, from now on then without her and against her.

Kamila got a firm grip on the yellow shopping bag she'd packed (inside it a linen dress, skirt, pullover, raincoat—Sonya is slimmer than me, but this will do—and in an envelope newspaper clippings and three hundred-notes) and emerged from the yellow villa, went through the silver-gray garden gate and the adjoining blue garden gate, and slipped into the white villa, *into the house which belongs to ME—*

In the kitchen Sonya was decorating a cake with whipped cream, Kamila looked at her wristwatch and quickly rattled off:

"Forgive me, Sonya, I realize how much wrong I've done you, but it was all Zlatunka's plot against you—she would even have murdered you to keep her second floor. You must leave here right away, a great danger is threatening you—and my guilt complex compels me to help you get away. Here in this bag you'll find everything you need for the first few days, even money—and I've cut out some ads about jobs in Teplice, there you'll find work, just what you want. Teplice has spas with a world reputation, it's full of big, lovely hotels . . . For tonight I've made you a reservation in the Hotel de Saxe, near the station."

"My job is to be here," Sonya said with a smile, "and so here is where I'll stay."

"But that would be crazy! After all that we've— that you've gone through here. . . Jakub would never consider you an equal partner. And Jakub will never marry his servant . . . forgive me, but I'm being very candid with you. I know Jakub better than you can imagine — and besides, I'm a student of psychology."

"I'm only doing my job. And not without success, I'd say."

"You've shown a truly angelic patience here — I admit it as I admit your other almost *superhuman* talents . . . But that's just why it would be too bad for you to stay on here to work as a servant, or at best an enslaved wife, don't you agree?"

"Why does this mean so much to you?"

"It's all I've got left in the world. I've invested my twenty years and my whole emotional life in Jakub —You've got so many many more possibilities. Dr. Lubos Bily has fallen in love with you — he's told me so himself. It was his idea that you should settle in Teplice . . . in his gas guzzler he could get there to see you in twenty minutes. And this very evening he'll come see you at the Hotel de Saxe . . . He really yearns to help you."

"My task is to remain here. Take your bag and give my best to Lubos Bily. He's been very kind to me."

By midnight Kamila Ortova had smoked forty-two cigarettes in her room, poring over psychology textbooks, falling into ever deeper confusion, gradually it dawned on her that the girl was a *living miracle*. . . She picked up book after book and in despair she leafed through them.

"*Wundt* (Völkerpsychologie, II, *Mythus und Religion*, 1906, II, p. 308) nennt das Tabu den ältesten ungeschriebenen Gesetzeskodex der Menschheit. . .," that means the oldest unwritten statutory codex of mankind, Sonya *is* in some way strangely *tabu*: "ein natürliches oder direktes Tabu, welches das Ergebnis einer geheimnisvollen Kraft (*Mana*) ist. . .," that means the outcome of the mysterious power of *Mana*. . . "Die Ziele des Tabu . . .," that means the purposes of *tabu* are many: "a) To protect important persons such as chiefs, priests—" that could hardly be Sonya.

"b) To guard the weak—women, children, and ordinary people in general—against the powerful magical force of *Mana* . . ." hm. That's extraordinary—

"c) To protect against dangers such as touching a dead body or eating certain foods." That Bromargyl in Sonya's porridge certainly didn't have any effect—

"Als die Quelle des Tabu wird eine eigentümliche Zauberkraft angesehen. . ." That's it: *magical powers!* "Personen oder Dinge, die Tabu sind, können mit elektrisch geladenen Gegenständen verglichen werden. . .," that is the fact that *persons and things that are tabu are as if electrically charged . . . They are a seat of terrible power, which is transmitted by touching—*"

The wall clock struck midnight, Kamila lit her forty-third Peer cigarette and began to read the chapter on magic.

"The husband should make it his responsibility to insure that the wife take part in his work, that he be concerned about her troubles, that he guide her activity and do away with her uncertainty. . ." Sonya read aloud at Jakub's tubular desk from van de Velde's *The Perfect Marriage*, while Jakub looked rapturously at her glittering green eyes and red hair in the warm, gold light radiating from his chrome desk lamp.

Sonya is wonderful: clever, tender, devoted, diligent, conscientious, obedient, and reassuring, beautiful and affectionate . . . Dad is ecstatic over her, Mom treats her as her own daughter, even Zlatunka says nothing to her now, even Kamila, on the basis of a deep psychological analysis, has announced that there's something *magical* about Sonya. . .

Was she born with all this, or did I have a part in cultivating it myself? Or did she cultivate in me a capacity to recognize it? *That love of which all men only dream—*

"The husband must strive to guide a woman's life, and she will be his beloved and she will be happy, whatever sacrifices are demanded of her. . ." Sonya read, and then she announced suddenly, looking out the window: "Yes, that's the way it is. Just like that, and it's so wonderful—" and then she read on: *". . . so says Mrs. Ferrero, and I do not wish to conceal her heartfelt sentiments from my readers."*

Jakub glanced at the last page of his spiral notebook, where the flowchart of Sonya's obliteration and reconstruction ended on the right with a series of filled-in squares of red: work completed, it's time to dissolve the GANG AGAINST SONYA. With superhuman strength Sonya had overcome them—

"Husbands," Sonya read aloud, *"who should in this respect serve chiefly as guides to their wives, I deal with you in particular because you often lack leadership qualities and even the virtues of a good partner—"* and Sonya repeated to herself silently: "Leadership qualities and the virtues of a good partner. . ." at the same time

looking out the window into the night, her eyes heavy with happiness.

Jakub caressed her with his gaze and again turned back to the last page of his notebook, to the column full of red squares and, on the right, in the column marked *Fulfillment*: SONYA IS THE IDEAL WOMAN . . . and the young engineer thoughtfully noted down at the very end of the last page of his notes concerning Sonya:

$$X = 1 + 2 + 3$$
MOTHER - BODY - HEART

And Jakub put two heavy red lines below the bottom-line formula for Sonya, snapped shut the notebook, and pushed it away. It will be a family souvenir. . .

"Sonya. I love you," he said and got up.

"Really?" Sonya smiled over her book.

"I swear it."

"Once, when things were going bad for me . . . back at the Hubertus when Ruda Mach deserted me . . . you wrote every day on pink stationery that you loved me. Could you write me one more letter like that now?"

"I'll tell it to you a hundred times a day!"

"Yes, but I'd like you to write it to me . . . I can't tell you why, but I need it very much. . ."

Jakub pulled a sheet of pink paper out of the drawer and drew on it a letter *L* a good five inches high, "I'll write I LOVE YOU across the entire page."

"No. Write me that I've won back your love—exactly that—and sign it with your name."

"Sure, if so much depends on it — But could I ask why you need it?"

"Can't a woman have any secrets?"

Jakub bowed to Sonya, then pulled another sheet of pink stationery out of the drawer and wrote on it as Sonya had dictated.

"Is this all right?" he asked when he'd finished.

"Absolutely. And be so kind as to write today's date."

Sonya,
   You have won back my love.
   August 27.
                    Eng. Jakub Jagr

The next morning, in her room, Sonya reread the note and quickly wrote underneath it:

My Manek,
   I have fulfilled your first task and am waiting for more. All I ask is that you not leave me here even a single hour in which I might have to lie to Jakub. Let me leave here and find work in the drying room, which so delighted me at the Hrusov Cottex.
                    Your Sonya

Then she sealed the envelope, addressed it to Manuel Mansfeld, Hotel Imperial, Liberec, ran out of the white villa, and continued running the whole way to the Vseborice post office.

"Express, right?" said the clerk behind the grill.

"Express registered," said Sonya, and she paid and left the post office. I'm finished now with everything here — I ought to be shouting with joy, but instead I feel an immense weariness. . .

If it had taken Sonya just four minutes to run to the post office, it took her a good half hour to drag herself back to the Jagrs', her feet kept feeling heavier and heavier as she nearly staggered into the white villa.

"Is something wrong with you, Sonya?" Mother Jagrova was concerned. "Come here, I'll show you the tablecloths you'll get from us—"

"No, please. I'm awfully tired. . ."

"Of course you are, my poor little girl—you really do look dreadful. . . Would you like to lie down for a bit?"

"I really need to."

Mother Jagrova put Sonya right to bed and placed two

pillows under her head. Then she made tea, and when she brought it in, Sonya was sleeping as if she were dead.

And she slept until lunch, ate a few bites in bed, and then slept until dinner.

When she had woken up a bit, there Jakub was at her bedside with a tray of multi-vitamins, sulfonamide, and hormone preparations, as well as a diverse collection of psychophar- maceuticals and antibiotics, there Mother Jagrova was with a bowl of chicken bouillon with egg, and there Father Jagr was with a bottle of cherry brandy. Sonya took a little of everything and slept on until the next morning.

Listlessly she walked through the garden between the white and yellow villas, yawned and went to lie down, and slept the rest of the day, and then slept like a rock all night long.

In the morning she couldn't even open her eyes, she turned onto the other side and stopped bothering to try.

"Sonya," Jakub's voice came out of the darkness somewhere, "there's a telegram for you from Prague. . ."

In a second Sonya had leapt out of bed, grabbed the telegram out of Jakub's hand, and run to the window. She devoured it in a single glance and then read it over more carefully, word by word:

LEAVE JAKUB TO KAMILA STOP FIND A JOB IN THE
DRYING ROOM AND A NEW PLACE TO LIVE AND BEGIN
A NEW LIFE   M.M.

"Bad news?" Jakub asked apprehensively.

"The best," said Sonya, and looking out the window she asked, "What time is it?"

"Half past seven."

"Morning or evening?"

"Morning. . ."

"Why aren't you at work?"

"I wanted to take you to the doctor. . ."

"There's no need for that. But you can see me off . . . I'll be ready in a jiffy. Now leave me alone."

Sonya threw into her shopping bag: Manek's photo, two pairs of shoes (as always, one for good and one for everyday), a toothbrush, her citizen's I.D. and a comb, two nightgowns (one ordinary and one for Manek), and three hundred-notes paid on account by Staff Sergeant Jagr (my pay for an entire month in a military prison), and she came out the front of the house, where Jakub was already waiting for her in the family's blue van.

"You brought me here in this. . ." she said harshly, and she scratched the carefully preserved polish with her fingernail, "tied up like a bundle—"

"Sonya, that's really very far from the truth. . ."

"It isn't, but that no longer matters," said Sonya, and she looked at the yellow villa next door and at the opposite slope of the green valley, and she went out through the blue garden gate onto Valley Street.

"Wait, Sonya, we'll drive there. . ." said Jakub.

"No. You'll walk me to the bus stop," said Sonya, and in silence she walked in front of Jakub along the clay road, across the concrete highway, and between the pre-fab high-rises of the development to the stop for Town Bus Line No. 5.

She didn't say a word until the red prow of the bus emerged from the turnabout, like the jaws of a kindly dragon, and as it grew larger Sonya spoke hurriedly to Jakub without looking at him:

"It's all over between us, Jakub. Forever. I did like you, but it was never true love. Our marriage wouldn't have been a good one. And I love another man. Marry Kamila Ortova—she's the only one who can handle you. Goodbye forever."

The bus opened its pneumatic door, Sonya hopped in and remained standing in the open door to keep Jakub from climbing up, the two halves of the door hissed and the bus pulled quietly out, through the window Jakub's chalky white face receded and, beyond it, in the hole between the pre-fab high-rises a strip of concrete highway, the roofs of the garden villas on Valley Street and, above them, the yellow-striped Strizek

Mountain in the milky haze. Sunbeams penetrated the mist with the promise of a fine day.

Sonya walked to the middle of the empty bus and, with her eyes closed, went through the streets she knew so well, whenever the bus stopped people got on, rubbed against her, and bumped into her. As if she had only just now fully awakened, Sonya looked with wonder at a woman with coral earrings, at the white moustache of a gentleman wearing a plastic raincoat, at a bespectacled daddy with a little girl in his arms, at a boy in blue jeans and a blue-striped T-shirt (a real good-looking boy), at lovers kissing near the pole at the exit door, at two schoolgirls with pigtails (one had hers fastened with a row of plastic daisies and the other with red ladybugs). Sonya smiled a little, felt the gaze of the good-looking boy in the blue-and-white T-shirt, through the window the mainstreet shop windows flashed past and on the sidewalks people, people, so many people . . . The good-looking boy in the T-shirt began to make his way toward Sonya, he would come with me just like that, Sonya raised her head and somewhere deep within her an extraordinary sort of laughter came to life, rose up through her throat, and seemed ready to choke her, Sonya bit the inside of her cheeks to keep from bursting into laughter and smiled prettily at the good-looking boy, the boy clawed his way through the bus as through a jungle but the bus was already coming to a stop at the main square, Sonya jumped down the metal steps, put her shopping bag down on the pavement, and arched her back in a seizure of gargantuan, cosmic laughter.

And the glittering shop windows gleamed and whirled above the dry but shiny pavement in a fast-spinning vortex, suddenly a spinning disc rose out of the square, spreading in all directions to the ends of the earth, the windows melted into little tears spraying up towards the sun, and since there is no longer anything to fear under the sun, the tears drowned in the eternal blue once they were glassless, the whole world uncoupled and, in that cosmic laughter, overflowed, recoiled, and jerked away like a joyful, naked child, it used its bare feet to push rivers of silk out into what used to be streets, now suddenly transformed into dancefloors and playgrounds, it used its hands to spill gold rings out of what used to be jewelry shops and chocolate-covered cherries out of the suddenly empty sweet shops, it exploded with laughter and the corks popped out of all the bottles, it roared with laughter and all the doors of all the houses lay on their backs and suddenly we are all living in one large doorless apartment and we are all joining in the laughter.

"What are you up to, Miss!" a Security Police officer said to Sonya, who was shaking with laughter and staggering in the middle of Usti's main square.

"But I'm just thinking about the world, Sergeant."

"Officer," the officer said drily. "Do you need anything?"

"No, nothing, just a job and a place to live, but those are funny little things. . ."

"You mean to say you don't have a job or a place to live?"

"By lunchtime I'll have them, you want to bet on it? Just now, for instance, riding with me on the bus was a real nice boy, wearing a blue-striped T-shirt, and if I could catch up with the bus—and I could, by taxi maybe, because I've got heaps of money. I've got three hundred crowns, Sergeant!"

"Officer. Show me your citizen's I.D."

"It's right here. I've got everything I need."

"Till August twenty-ninth employed in the restaurants operated by the Hotel Hubertus in Hrusov on the Jizera," the officer read from Sonya's I.D. (Jakub had fixed it up for me, it was great!) "and since then?"

"I've been employed as a house servant at the Jagrs', Valley Street number four. Now I'm looking for a job and a place to live. I'm trying to start a new life, Mr. . ."

"Officer. Listen here, Miss . . . Cechova, there's something about you I don't very much care for!"

"That's the first time in my life I've heard that from a man. Officer. . ." Sonya (S.-*Marikka*) said, and she smiled prettily at him.

"Well . . . What sort of work are you looking for?"

"In the drying room, Officer!"

"Do you know where to apply?"

"That's just what I was going to ask you."

"The best thing is to apply to the Workforce Referral Office of the People's Commission."

"I'll go there right away. Which way is it?"

"Go up out of the square, left on Fucik Street, then right—I'll go with you part of the way."

Sonya smiled prettily and the officer accompanied her all the way to the People's Commission office.

"Which drying room?" the clerk in charge of workforce matters was a bit surprised.

"Why, the one where they dry handkerchiefs and damasks," Sonya explained. "It's in a great big room and there are drying machines as big as buses, it's wonderfully dry there and there's music, and the girls handle a wet pile of the damasks or the handkerchiefs, two by two. . ."

"That sounds like Cottonola, right?" the clerk guessed, and then she phoned somewhere and informed Sonya that Cottonola would hire her right away for its drying room, at twelve hundred a month, lodging for singles in the singles dorm, working uniform free of charge, inaugural dues three hundred crowns, Saturdays off, young people's band, recreation gratis in the factory's holiday home on the Elbe, and a free pint of milk every day.

"Is it really possible. . ." Sonya whispered when the officer accompanied her to the streetcar (she noticed that he took her two stations farther than necessary), he explained to her how to get to Cottonola in terms more appropriate for a winter campaign across Tibet, and at the same time volunteered the information that every Tuesday and Friday he was on duty in the square until eight in the evening and that he then had twenty-four hours *absolutely* free—

Cottonola is at the end of town at the base of Strizov Mountain: three friendly-looking buildings with large windows from which music poured out of radios and there was a flock of high-spirited girls like in school during recess, and lawns all around, in the middle of one a swimming pool even—this is where I want to be!

But the worst of the horrors were over, and it was with renewed courage that the westward voyage was resumed. When, a week later, another and yet another island was sighted, Magellan knew they were saved. According to his calculations, these must be the Moluccas. He fancied that he had reached his goal. But even his burning impatience, his urgent need to be certain about his triumph, did not make him incautious.

in his magisterial office Engineer Lanimir Sapal was greedily devouring Stefan Zweig's *Magellan*, well concealed in a drawer of his magisterial desk, then he gulped down a roll thickly spread with the cheapest type of processed cheese and drank his daily ration of free milk.

Instead of landing on Suluan, the larger of the two islands, he went to a smaller one, called by Pigafette 'Humunu'. . .

Lanimir Sapal had completed his studies at the School of Chemical Engineering in Pardubice at the age of twenty-one, he was the youngest chemical engineer in the Republic, and after two outstanding months at Cottex's central laboratories he was sent out for a year to Hrusov branch plant No. 08 to prepare to become the youngest director in the field of textile chemistry. However, starved by long years of study, in the course of which he had scarcely eaten two proper meals and in which he had remained a virgin, the promising engineer was seized by such a mighty interest in love and everything connected with it, that over the next five years he had devoted all his concentrated attention to it, every bit of his free time (and a good part of his work hours), and all his financial resources (quite modest, since his loves did not do much for his technical career).

When finally Director Kaska personally caught him being intimate with a woman apprentice inside the pressure kettle on a bed of fine strands of the Egyptian cotton called *mako*, Engineer Sapal was forced to make a quick exit from the mighty

Cottex and to take the position of a mere chief of shop rooms at the tiny Cottonola plant in Usti.

> On Massava, a tiny islet of the Philippine group, so small that only with a lense can one find it on the map, Magellan had one of the most remarkable experiences of his life.

Waiting on New Year's Eve in a borrowed apartment for his girlfriend of the moment to arrive, the failed engineer Lanimir Sapal buried himself in Nikolay Vasilevich Gogol's *Dead Souls*, soon he was roaring with laughter, he ate all twelve of the open-face sandwiches he had prepared, drank both bottles of sparkling wine, roared with laughter, shoved the girl out into the corridor without ceremony when she arrived late, and went on reading until noon on January 1, when he finished the final adventure of Pavel Ivanovich Chichikov, decided to become a writer, and fell asleep happy.

> Again and again his dark and laborious existence had been illuminated by such flashes of happiness, whose intensity compensated him for the stubborn patience with which he had endured so many lonely and care-fraught hours.

Because the Cottonola dorms did not provide the proper atmosphere for creation, Lanimir Sapal obtained permission from the kind Cottonola director to "study" every afternoon in the empty plant library. And already, by January 2 at 3:30 P.M., he had written on the back of his pay slip

Lanimir Sapal
LIVING SOULS

and gazed fixedly at these words until the late hours of the night. Every day he would leave three, five, and even more novels unfinished.

> As soon as, under press of sail, the three large foreign ships drew near the shore of Massava, the inquisitive and friendly inhabitants flocked to the beach.

"Can we pick up our allotment of spools?" a motherly-looking woman in overalls suddenly said to him, and once again Lanimir banged shut the drawer with the novel, but too late.

"Pick them up. But next time don't forget to knock, Mrs. Matouskova."

"We all know you keep a book in your drawer," said Mrs. Simackova, but then she took pity on her terrified boss and added: "but we won't tell anybody."

The job of chief of shop rooms was such an easy one (unlock the shops in the morning, fill out the issue slips, drink coffee with the chief of storerooms, and then again close up all the shops), that Engineer Sapal was well able to cope with it in spite of the burdens of his literary activity. And because he loved women so—he had forty of them working for him—all forty of them loved their boss.

And so in ironed canvas pants from his overalls and a snow-white labcoat (uniforms are laundered free of charge by the plant laundry) over his naked body (you have to wash underwear yourself) every day before the morning coffee break and then again before lunch, Lanimir Sapal strolled through his four shops, settled small arguments, drew in red on the poster showing how much his department has exceeded the expectations of the plan (it was now continually above 100%), talked with mothers about their children, gave advice on marital problems and scolded (quite amiably) the sprightly girl apprentices, handed out the free soap and toilet paper, and ruled his forty souls benevolently and in peace.

> The islanders surrounded Enrique, chattering and shouting, and the Malay slave was dumbfounded, for he understood much of what they were saying. It was a good many years since he had been snatched from his home, a good many years since he had last heard a word of his native language.

Touched, Lanimir drank up his milk and decided that right off that afternoon he would begin to write a novel about a sea expedition (yesterday, after finishing *The Ugly Duchess* by Lion Feuchtwanger, he had gone to the library to start work on a historical pentalogy entitled *The Repulsive Empress*), he repressed his sorrow that so far he had never set eyes on the sea (with his royalties from the novel he will circumnavigate the entire globe) and, thoughtfully chewing a roll, he began to work out the title: *The Defeated Sea* . . . that's weak. *The Downtrodden Ocean* would be better, but there wouldn't be any laughs in that . . . *How I Was a Diver on a Pirate Submarine*—

"Sir, I'm bringing you a new worker—" said the female personnel officer, and once again Lanimir banged shut the drawer with the novel, but too late.

"Next time don't forget to knock—" Lanimir said mechanically, but then he froze.

"Good day, sir," said Sonya Cechova, and she smiled at him prettily.

"What— what—" Lanimir stammered, he passed his hand through his wiry head of hair (quite without consequence) and hastily swallowed several times to no effect.

"The director's sending her to you in place of Majka, the one who ran off to Ostrava," said the personnel officer.

"But that's extraordinarily kind of the director," it pleased Lanimir to no end to inspect his new subject closely and greedily. "I'm Sapal, chief of shops," he introduced himself, and when Sonya whispered her name he gave her his hand with all the courtliness of the young Louis XIV. "You've been working in the film industry, haven't you?" he said with his most radiant smile (his colleagues in the singles dorm maintained that Lanimir had thirty-six teeth).

"In a hotel and in a private home," whispered Sonya.

"I'd be glad to get you into films, I've got several unfinished filmscripts—" said Lanimir, but he stopped himself in time lest he betray his (well known to all) afternoon literary activities in front of the personnel officer.

"But she's supposed to go to the drying room," said the rather slow personnel officer, "in place of Majka, who ran off to Ostrava—"

But Lanimir didn't hear a word she said, he kept hold of Sonya's hand and Sonya smiled at him prettily.

"So if you've said everything you two have to say," said the personnel officer after a rather long interval of silence (but one crackling with static electricity), "I will take the girl to the doctor, to the stores, to the insurance office, to the firemen—"

"Well then, tomorrow morning at six—" Lanimir sighed.

Wrenched out of cascades of inspiration by the siren's honk, he noted down in the columns of expense slips such fleeting observations as *almond fissures in the bewitchingly flaming grass, aureate inclines of unspeakable sweetness, an explosion of Titian gold on the crown of Diana the Huntress*, and many others, he hurriedly locked up the already empty shops (he had never left work so late), and at an economical trot he ran across the dusty street to the singles dorm.

The single men in Cottonola (five specimens in all) inhabited the second floor, in what had once been a two-room apartment (the women had the same space one floor up). In one room confirmed bachelors Vit (chief of the color shop) and Cenek (development technologist) had lived together for years now, while the other's inmates changed several times a year. At the moment Lanimir was living there with lab assistant Pavel Abrt and draftsman Lumirek.

"What an incredible chick!" Lanimir shouted at the threshold of his room.

"That sort of thing hasn't interested me for a long time now," said Lumirek (he was all of sixteen years old) with profound contempt.

Pavel Abrt was already asleep (he could fall asleep in an unbelievably short time after coming home from work).

"Only of course she isn't a chick, but a phantasm! A nymph! A chimera!" Lanimir shouted while kicking off his pants.

"Phooey—!" Lumirek was disgusted.

"Hrr—hrr—hrr—hrr—" Pavel Abrt was a happy sleeper.

Meanwhile, already naked and once again (perhaps for the thousandth time) firmly determined not to throw pearls before swine, Lanimir rushed off to the bathroom (shared by both rooms) in order to use the icy shower to whip himself up to peak performance during his afternoon literary shift.

But in the bathtub, lounging around like a hippopotamus, was the forty-year-old Vit, an enormous tanned muscleman overgrown with black fur from his ankles all the way to the top of his head, where he was beginning to grow bald.

"What a fantastic chick, but also a phantasm, a chimera, and a nymph!" Lanimir announced.

"Where?" said Vit, and he opened his right eye.

"From tomorrow on at my office."

"I'll have a look at her this evening."

"She's reserved for me."

"I'll have a look at her this evening."

"How long are you going to use the bathtub?"

"Till I'm done with my bath," said Vit, and he closed his right eye.

Lanimir sighed and went into the adjoining kitchen (shared by both rooms), where thirty-nine-year-old Cenek was preparing his one and only warm meal: numerous cups of Georgian tea (he got bread and lard from his parents in the country, and salt from Pavel Abrt, who brought it from the lab for all the members of Vit's gang, so that each month Cenek spent—gnashing his teeth—scarcely fifty crowns. That's how he could own a Skoda, but since he was too stingy to pay for a driving school, Vit—for the fifth year—drove the car around with his brood of chicks).

Lanimir set a pot of water on the stove for his daily, extrastrong coffee (a shot in the arm for his afternoon literary séance).

"Why do you boil so much water for nothing, pal?" Cenek was outright angry. "You know how much gas that basin of yours guzzles to get water up to the boiling point?" (Singles share the cost of gas.)

"It's not a matter of *boiling*, but just of *heating up*," Lanimir objected, "and it's the minimum, indispensable volume required for a single cup of Turkish coffee."

"But you poured in a good two hundred cubic centimeters!"

"*Less* than two hundred."

"But a hundred and fifty is enough for Turkish coffee!"

"Sure, but don't forget to take into account the steam pressure, the steam loss at the boiling point—however brief—and the water occluded on the bottom and the walls of the vessel," Lanimir pointed out (unlike Cenek, who was a graduate of a technical school, he held a diploma from a college of chemical engineering).

"Still, there's too much water in there by half," said Cenek, "and the occluded water — that's the water that makes the pan wet, right?"

"Basically. . ." and Lanimir, drinking his literary coffee, expounded to the ever inquisitive Cenek the physical and chemical principles of occlusion, insofar as he recalled them from the Pardubice polytech, and wherever he'd forgotten something he improvised (which was considerably more interesting).

His literary coffee close on the heels of what he had experienced inspired in Lanimir ideas for so many new novels, that without warning he stepped into the bathtub between Vit's powerful legs and loosed the cold water on himself. Vit closed his right eye and submerged.

A few minutes later, Lanimir picked up the key to the factory library and, his hair still damp, he reached his sanctuary. At his entrance, the spines of the books quivered, just as the earth trembles when a farmer sinks his plow into it.

Lanimir Sapal sat at the head of a twenty-four-foot-long table, placed a stack of payroll sheets in front of him, like a sword he drew out a well-bitten pencil, sharpened it against the striking side of a matchbox, and hastily wrote in large letters:

Lanimir Sapal
A PHANTOM OF BEAUTY
A Novel about a Woman

and remained over the sheet of paper until late in the evening.

"So you're the one who's here in place of Majka, who ran off to Ostrava," Sonya was greeted by the dorms' housekeeper, the widow Anezka Sbiralova (more frequently called "Sbiralka" or (most often) "Grannie."

"Yes, if you please," whispered Sonya, and she smiled prettily at Sbiralka.

"One look at you, girl, and I can see you won't be here very long!"

"But I like it here very much, ma'am."

"Just wait till you get your bearings," said Sbiralka, then all of a sudden she bent over to Sonya and hissed sharply: "The men here are no damn good."

"I'll try to cope."

"Well, you've certainly got the figure for it. Bet you won't last. Majka had a figure too and she ran off to Ostrava."

"But why?"

"'Cause the men here are no damn good."

Sbiralka took Sonya up to the third floor and showed her Majka's old bed (a beautiful red daybed and at its foot, her own chest made of light-colored wood), she was to share the room with Ivanka and Barborka.

"Ivanka's a clever bitch," said Sbiralka, "but all the same it doesn't help her much. Barborka is a real broad, but that doesn't help her much either. Because the men here are no damn good for nothing. Marie Junkova and her Petr Junk live in the other room—he's the only one here who got married. He isn't from hereabouts, though, he's from our golden Moravia. But you'll be running away yourself before long. But till then—take off your shoes soon as you come in, don't smoke in bed, clean the tub after yourself, don't keep bags of greasy food in the window—or you'll find out what a shrew I can be!"

Sonya unpacked her two dresses and hung them in the common wardrobe—how many dresses these girls have and how lovely they are!—she put her regular nightgown into the chest (the other, from Manek, she left in the bag), then tenderly she rubbed her hand along her soft red daybed—at last I've lived to have my very own bed!

With her comb and toothbrush she ran into the bathroom, the girls here have a parfumerie just like in a movie, I'll buy lots of perfume too when I'm rich — twelve hundred crowns a month plus overtime!

And I'll bet I can live here for a handful of crowns, Sonya rejoiced in her lovely kitchen with its gas stove — and even a real fridge! For breakfast, tea and crackers are enough, lunch is two crowns eighty at the plant cafeteria, and for dinner you can make do with a bottle of milk and a slice of bread. . .

"You're that new one in place of Majka, right? I live on the other side of the wall, and my name's Marie Junkova," said a beautiful blonde with a smile like a Madonna and with a baby in her arms, behind her stood a handsome brunet (with blue eyes. . .), Petr Junk, her husband.

"Forgive me for poking my nose into all your things. . ." said Sonya (she was just poking her nose into the fridge).

"But everything's yours as well. We're here to welcome you, and we hope you'll like it here with us—" the beautiful Marie Junkova smiled, and the handsome Petr Junk smiled at Sonya too.

The two roommates are first-rate too. Ivanka (before she said a word, she lit a cigarette) is a bit thin, blonde (out of a bottle of peroxide, most likely), has clever eyes and will be a lot of fun. Barborka (she rushed to the kitchen and came back into the room with her mouth full) is a pudgy brunette (probably from the beauty shop), at first glance good-natured, she certainly won't spoil the fun.

Barborka brought in a bottle of chilled *Morella* griotte ("Clink, so we can be friends—"), and before Ivanka had even finished her cigarette (in five minutes) the girls were getting along just as if they'd been friends for two years already.

"He's gorgeous. . ." Barborka sighed over Manek's photo.

"But he must be pushing thirty, right?" said Ivanka, and she lit another cigarette.

"I'd like to get my hands on him," Barborka sighed, and then she went off to the kitchen to spread another slice of bread with lard.

"The guys here aren't worth a damn," said Ivanka, shaking her head with distaste. "But you'll find that out for yourself—"

At that moment in walked a sixteen-year-old boy with a mighty mane of hair, washed, shampooed, laboriously curled, scented, and sprayed — he wore this ornament of manhood like a crown, beneath which his small pale pimply face was nearly lost. He was wearing a bright white shirt with enormous silver cufflinks, supercilious jeans, and gleaming black patent-leather shoes.

"Phew—" he sighed in the doorway, and he disappeared just as he had appeared.

"What was that?"

"Lumirek, from the second floor," Barborka said with her mouth full.

"He retouches drawings in the technical division and he finds the world painful and disgusting," said Ivanka, breathing smoke out of her nose.

"How did he get in here so quietly?" Sonya was surprised. "Does he have a key to our room?"

"We removed the doorlock ourselves," said Barborka, and with her finger she spread the lard all the way to the end of the slice, so her last bite would be as tasty as the others.

"Because those oafs downstairs are so lazy," said Ivanka, "if they had to knock, they'd just as soon stay in their bunks."

In a moment, an older young man with long, slicked-down hair appeared, stared at Sonya for a while, then walked around her to inspect her from all sides, and then, without a single word, vanished.

"That's Cenek, I've been going out with him for four years now," Barborka sighed, "only with him it's no go."

"You made a great impression on him," Ivanka said to Sonya and lit a cigarette.

"But how come he didn't give out a single peep?" asked Sonya.

"Because you completely bowled him over," Barborka said mournfully, and she went off to spread a slice of bread.

Before Ivanka could polish off her cigarette, Cenek and Lumirek came back again, this time with a tall, tanned, powerfully built fellow, overgrown with black fur except for his balding head ("That's Vit, he's their chief and he's going with Ivanka—" Barborka whispered to Sonya), as well as a pale young man ("That's Pavel Abrt, in a little while he'll fall asleep—"), who sat down on the floor in the corner and in a little while fell asleep.

"Lanimir wasn't just feeding us a line," Vit said after some time, during which he had seated himself on Sonya's daybed and, with his head propped up on his elbow, proceeded to inspect Sonya like a connoisseur.

"Lanimir will come this evening," Ivanka told Sonya; "he's at the library now writing a novel."

"Girls, I'd like something to eat," Vit said matter-of-factly, and Barborka rushed off to the kitchen.

The men ate a lot but didn't have much to say. Vit and Cenek talked shop during the few pauses when they weren't staring at Sonya. Lumirek kept pulling his cuffs out and declaring things "a tremendous bore" or simply sticking his nose in the air and saying "Pfff—." And, most exceptionally, Pavel Abrt woke up to eat.

Barborka kept on going to the kitchen and bringing back slices of bread spread with lard, bacon, bloody headcheese, and bottles of beer (but for her Cenek, nothing but weak tea with five cubes of sugar in each cup). Ivanka went on smoking and casting provocative, taunting, coquettish, tender, and various other sorts of looks at Vit — without the slightest perceptible effect. At each man separately and at all collectively, Sonya smiled prettily.

Late in the evening Lanimir Sapal galloped in, grabbed a slice of bread in each of his hands, sat down on the daybed right next to Sonya, asked in detail about the story of her life, and then with reckless abandonment spouted forth volumes about sea battles, about Lion Feuchtwanger, about the mining of emeralds in Zambia, about Sonya's eyes, about physical chemistry, about Sonya's hair, about Françoise Sagan, about Sonya's mouth, about forty ways to write a worldwide 'bestseller,' about Sonya's teeth, about the mystical significance of food in the novels of Rabelais, Gogol, Hasek, and Paral, and when he got to Sonya's shoulders Vit got up, smiled at Sonya and, in the next five minutes, all the men (Pavel Abrt was woken up by a kick from Vit) quickly vanished.

"You made a fantastic impression on them," Ivanka told Sonya with deep admiration. "They were downright *polite* today."

"And they ate much more than they did when Majka came." Barborka was in awe but happy.

After the men's departure, the girls no longer had to be shy, Barborka went to the kitchen and brought back all that was left of the five-pound loaf of bread and all that was left of the two pounds of lard (her Cenek didn't like it when Barborka ate too much), and Ivanka lit one cigarette after another (her Vit didn't like it when Ivanka smoked too much).

The girls bewailed the men's imperfections and polished off the bottle of *Morella* griotte ("If we'd have offered it to the guys there would have been a free-for-all—"), together they ate canned Chinese pineapple ("That would have been wasted on those lazy oafs—") and they didn't let Sonya go to sleep until she'd promised that she would work on those oafs somehow, since she'd made such a stirring first impression on them.

Sonya promised and then asked Ivanka if she could go along to night school with her. Ivanka said, of course she could, and Sonya rejoiced (I can get my diploma here!), lay down on her daybed, sighed with happiness (is it possible that when I got up this morning I was still a servant at the Jagrs'. . .), and fell asleep at once.

At 5:45 in the morning, she stuck her brand new pink card into the time clock at the Cottonola gate, walked along the pool (originally a water basin for putting out fires caused by air raids), crossed herself, went into Engineer Sapal's office, and smiled at him prettily.

In the morning, Engineer Sapal tended to be irritable, even angry (unless—or more frequently—until he'd taken a nap), today, however, he was smooth shaven (all four of his shops were discussing this heatedly and at length) and he was even wearing a new shirt (he hadn't even worn one the time that woman Minister of Light Industry paid a visit to Cottonola), he entered into a long, candid conversation with Sonya, which lasted almost until coffee break, and then he turned her over to her foreman to be trained.

The drying-room foreman is the beautiful Marie Junkova, she chatted with me almost till lunch and in half an hour's time I had it all mastered. And it's just as lovely here as it was at the Hrusov Cottex, where I wanted so much to be. . .

Marecek, a funny old man, wheels wet heaps of damask and handkerchiefs on a cart that runs on tracks, and each time he tells a joke as old as the Austro-Hungarian Empire. And we girls, always two by two (Marie is paired with Barborka and I'm with Ivanka), load a heap into the drier which then does everything itself (it's big as a bus and it takes its time), and then we pick up the dried heaps and place them on a stand, and old Marecek (each time he tells another joke) takes them on to the finishing room.

In the drying room it's warm as a sauna (so all we wear are bras and shorts, Ivanka wears a bikini and I'm going to buy one too) and the light's nice and subdued, like a bedroom, from the jaws of the machines there's a rosy glow, like a fireplace, from a radio there's music the whole shift long (when an announcer starts talking too much, Barborka turns it off and puts on a cassette of nice, swinging hits), what we do is more like ballet than athletics (one can't really call it work), we dance the whole shift through—

A machine has its whims (but it's as if it just wants to tease us a little—it's really good-natured), but it always obeys Marie Junkova like a puppy and keeps on growling peacefully. And the dry fabric smells of ironing and home, of childhood and mama. . .

After the shift is over, I take a shower and, wonderfully rested and refreshed, I take the streetcar to go shopping in town. I buy a new dress, a green bikini for work, De Luxe toothpaste, Renaissance cologne—to rid myself of all that military prison pay from Staff Sergeant Jagr—a pale green handkerchief for Manek and pink stationery for writing, Club butter cookies for breakfast and for dinner a quarter loaf of bread and a bottle of milk — and with what's left of the money ten dekas of chocolate-covered cherries: on Tuesday I get an advance on my seignorial appanage from kind Aunt Cottonola.

The security officer was standing in the middle of the main square saluting me from afar, he would like to go anywhere with me, whatever it took, and the same longing was displayed by some five guys (some of them grown men) in the streetcar, in stores, and on the sidewalk — but men and boys, it's so sweet to be single. . . And I've got a husband already, Manek.

Back home in my room the whole crew of men from the second floor was waiting for me (except for Sapal, who would turn up only after he had finished working on his novel), and big Vit himself made room for me on the daybed (Ivanka hissed with astonishment and Barborka rolled her eyes).

It seemed to me that Vit had shaved closer today than the day before, Cenek wore new shoes which evidently pinched (but he didn't dare take them off), Lumirek was dressed in an unbelievabie shirt with a rich nylon fichu, gold cufflinks (probably from some fair) as large as eggs, and Pavel Abrt dozed off briefly and no more than two or three times — I did nothing, only smiled prettily at them all—and at each of them separately.

But when my cheeks began to hurt from all that smiling (Mr. Sapal had turned up by then and had at once begun to ask me about my feelings, premonitions, and unconscious desires) and since the men did nothing but eat (even more than the day before), I suggested that I sing something to liven up the party.

They all sat dumbfounded — apparently nothing like this had ever happened here before. But then, with lots of enthusiasm, Barborka brought out her cassette player and for a while I sang along with her nice, swinging hits and—since the men were eating even more vigorously—I danced for a while, too. Beyond that I can't report anything — the men frantically tossed down what was left of the provisions in our kitchen (yesterday, at least, we had still managed to save the Chinese pineapple), and colliding with each other they marched out in a state of confusion.

"You're a real enchantress. . ." Barborka told me, and from excitement and hunger she ground her teeth together on nothing at all.

"You really impressed those oafs today," Ivanka laughed, and in high spirits she lit a fat Cuban cigar.

Then all three of us sang for a while and merrily retired to our beds. I have read a lot of novels, largely set in castles, ocean liners, film studios, and worldly Parisian hotels (in which more than half of all novels wearily play themselves out), but never have I read how sweet life can be in nothing more than industrial old Usti n. L.

Moist and troubled was how the final night of that unusual August came in through my window. Trembling in the sky was the orange glow of eternally roaring traffic and its metallic rattle reached my ears like the voice of a faraway storm, the soft rumble of eternally hurtling trains, men singing and, on the other side of the wall, the beautiful Marie Junkova's child crying — the scent of metal, motors, and men is everywhere in this city that never goes to sleep, and it is the scent of excitement, of being thrilled, this city's special scent.

Vit and Cenek lay on their red daybeds in their privileged (just two beds, because steadily inhabited for twenty years) room for singles on the second floor, they stared at the ceiling and they were already on their second hour of talking about Sonya.

"She's. . ." said Vit.

"High-tension," said Cenek.

"That too. She's. . ."

"Electrolytic."

"That too. She. . ."

"Emits electrons."

"That too. She's. . ."

"Electromagnetic."

"Very."

"Will you make it with her?"

"That too. Let's go."

Cenek went to wet his hair under the waterpipe (like someone who puts on a tux covered with medals) and Vit dug some new socks out of his trunk (a tux covered with Orders and a red sash across his breast) and then he played with his trophies for a while: locks of girls' hair and a full box of their shoes: Zdenka, Ola, two Mankas, Hilda, three Veras, Anezka, Trudi, two Helgas, Monika, Barborka, Ivanka, Majka. . .

Vit began to whistle and, in good spirits, he pulled on his new socks.

Cenek came out of the Cottonola gate and looked at his battered pocket watch (he had found it one night at the bus depot, the knob was missing so he had to wind it with pliers, frequently it would stop, but if you tapped on the crystal it would run again for a while): Hell's bells, could it be one minute before or after 2:00 P.M. on the nose? I'm terribly nervous—

Yesterday Vit put on his new socks to impress Sonya and in her room he put his arm around her shoulders — that's the way Vit always begins. And just as I always used to think that was a blast, now it makes me feel nauseous and sad and faint and who knows what else—

Cenek looked at his pocket watch (2:00) and realized that he was about to have another attack. What'll I do, I can't go to Sonya's till three—

In wholehearted pain he unlocked his wardrobe and then the three locks of his cardboard suitcase (two provided by the manufacturer and the third, a padlock, originally the property of Cottonola, Cenek had added himself), he counted his ready cash (28,522.25 crowns), it made his heart bleed to take out 22.25 crowns — he was on the point of putting this gigantic sum back, but the attack made itself known in the form of a stifling constriction of his throat — he quickly locked all three locks, locked the suitcase back in the wardrobe and, at a moderate trot (I don't take the streetcar while I'm paying taxes for my car), he ran all the way to the milk bar on the square (the cheapest place to get it).

The otherwise thrifty Cenek suffered from a maniacal passion for sweets, the satisfaction of his body's desires could exceed by many times his monthly budget of fifty crowns. Therefore, when the passion rose to the level of unbearable agony, he appeased it with scientifically proven anti-alcohol therapy: he stuffed himself so on sweets that for an entire month he could no longer bear to look at them (he figured out that this would be cheaper than eating sweets every day).

In addition, this massive appeasement was (at no extra cost) capable of dispelling depression. Cenek did not suffer from depression more often than twice a year (the last time was when a ticket inspector nailed him riding a train without a ticket and Cenek had to buy it and pay a fine of forty, *forty*, FORTY, FORTY crowns. — Owww!) and in the interests of economy he always made sure that the dispelling of his depression occurred on the same day as the therapy for his attack (so that depression, no matter how deep, sometimes had to wait weeks to be dispelled).

Cenek thought of Vit's new socks and, choking, he ordered ten Linzer tortelets (the most effective sweet substance for 1 crown), gulped them down as quickly as possible (sweets are most disgusting that way), thought of Vit's arm around Sonya's shoulder, and quickly wolfed down ten more Linzers, he still had 2.25 crowns left so he made himself think of Sonya smiling prettily at Vit, in desperation he bought two and a quarter dekas of pure sugar with the money he had left, but it had no effect whatsoever, Cenek dolefully tapped on the crystal of his pocket watch until it finally cracked (it was already starting to crack at the bus station), besides everything else he now had to shop for a new crystal for his watch. . .

And on account of Sonya I still have to gobble down a dairy bar and a whole sugar refinery—

Lumirek firmly believed that correctly chosen cufflinks could win any woman.

Right when he came home from Cottonola he washed his hair with shampoo and tepid beer and, with curlers in his mane, flung his newest shirt with a luxuriant nylon fichu and lace-work on the sleeves over the back of his chair, and like a painter standing with his pallette in front of a fresh canvas, he stood over his shirt and his cufflink collection, which he kept in a ten-pound sugar box.

The beaten silvers and oval golds are out: Sonya has already seen them. Lumirek took out his most expensive pair (imitation Egyptian scarab and nickel) and tried them on his cuffs: they didn't say much.

He picked out one pair of cufflinks after another and evaluated each of them empirically with bowed head and squinting eyes: imitation antique coins, blue saucers, yellow rectangles, black glass, a plate-metal dollar sign — it's a bore, they don't turn out anything decent these days. . .

With a feeling of deep distaste for the world he dug down to the bottom of the box for his ladies' earrings, known as "clip-ons," which can sometimes be used in emergencies: green frogs,

chrysanthemums, ladybugs, cherries, blue prisms, orange fish—
it's a terrible bore when you don't have anything to wear. . .

Tears worked their way into Lumirek's eyes, and he wept for
his miserable life (and his hair that wouldn't dry), and gazing
with rage at that miserable fleabag of a room, through the dewy
veil of his eyelids he suddenly caught sight of something new—

He wiped away the tears with his sleeve, and in a sudden
burst of inspiration picked up a box of matches left by Lanimir
Sapal. They would be just the right size . . . I CAN MAKE MY
OWN CUFFLINKS—

He went down to the basement for a container of silver paint
left over from painting the boiler, in the kitchen he found a
second box of matches and Pavel Abrt's shaving brush (Pavel
was asleep) and painted both of them silver. Then he stuck
those silly orange fish into the button holes of his romantic shirt
and affixed the silver boxes to their tails—it was perfect. And
I'll leave the matches in the boxes, with each movement they'll
sound like castanets . . . I've dreamed up *the first musical cufflinks
in the world*—

Singing fervently, Lumirek used his hair-dryer on his
shampooed hair, then held it in place with hairpins, coated it
lightly with hair spray, and dusted it with aluminum — in his
rejuvenated spirit he kept hearing a hymn of victory I WILL
MANUFACTURE MY OWN CUFFLINKS—

And Sonya won't be able to take her eyes off of them.

The peaceful life of lab assistant Pavel Abrt (eight hours of work
and sixteen hours of sleep—during those sixteen hours, admittedly, he did sometimes open his eyes and eat, while during
those eight hours he often closed his eyes and slept) was
invaded by a peculiar disquiet: the kind curtain of sleep jerked
open during such previously quiet hours . . . Yesterday I even
woke up when Lanimir's alarmclock went off—should I go to
the doctor's?

Pavel Abrt had woken up while Lumirek was using his

shaving brush to paint the match boxes silver. The idiocy of that action (Pavel Abrt considered *any* action idiotic) rocked him back again into drowsiness, but suddenly he was awakened by the fear that he might have slept through the collective visit to Sonya (he had never owned a watch and never gone anywhere by himself).

And fear awakened in Pavel Abrt the so-far unrealized thought of activity, even of cunning: he pretended to go on sleeping (to avoid provoking Lumirek, who might not invite him to come along to Sonya's), but he followed Lumirek's movements closely.

"You're going already?" he cried out, jumping out of bed when Lumirek left the room.

And Lumirek (who was only going to the bathroom for pink nail-polish) stiffened with horror at the successfully galvanized corpse: his whole life he had never heard Pavel Abrt cry out— and not many people had ever seen him jump out of bed either.

In less than two hours Lanimir Sapal had ground out the fifth (eighteen-page) chapter of his latest work *A PHANTOM OF BEAUTY* (about Sonya) and in a "red-hot cloud of creativity" (*viz* Stefan Zweig, *Balzac*) he had hopped along the terra-cotta paving stones of the Cottonola plant library: *I am actually going to write this novel—*

Eighteen pages in two hours, that's forty-five pages in five hours of writing every day, so in a month—if I count Sundays and free Saturdays, when I can write ten hours a day—fifteen hundred pages, and in a year all of eighteen thousand pages . . . Not even Balzac or Tolstoy or all the Dumases together churned out as much literature as I will in a single year, and I'll write for another fifty years and more even—

So today another twenty-seven pages—he counted them, sat down and, on the back of a pay slip, began to write feverishly:

CHAPTER 6

The richly carved, embroidered with twenty-two-carat gold (inlaid with palisander and various shells, African ivory, and jadeite) teak doors of the captain's cabin flew open with a crash and Sonia, in a green crinoline of heavy Lyons taffeta, torn to the waist, in her teeth a dagger of Toledo steel, ran out onto the very prow of the pirates' eight-master.

"From here on out, there's nothing but ocean," John Huston muttered the words sarcastically between his teeth, moving past her with his typical rocking gait, "and in these latitudes there are approximately twelve sharks per hectare. . ."

"The Grand Vizier will have you impaled if you don't bring me back in usable condition!" cried Sonia, her ocular emeralds ablaze.

"If you knew what a sextant was for, chicky, you'd understand that we're sailing full steam toward the isle of St. Calixtus. . ."

"Into the den of the Black and Red Band—"

"And we're as good as there. And there señores De Witt, Ceneka, Lumiretta and Pablo Abrato will sharpen their teeth on your fragile whiteness. . ."

"Lanius will protect me," is all Sonia said to the heaving, shark-infested aquamarine landscape.

"Your Lanius wails now in a leaden cell and

And those rogues are actually going after Sonya, especially De Witt, Lanius (Sapal) suddenly realized, and he glanced at his watch, crammed his papers into his briefcase (my productivity in a single afternoon is not the issue, I'll write for another fifty years—) and he rushed up to the girls' room on the third floor.

De Witt was wearing new socks for the third day running, Cenek's hair was sleek from the water tap, Lumiretta clattered from the matches on his cuffs, and Pablo Abrato was awake— my Sonya is a subject for a most astonishing fictional tome. . .

Vit laid his hairy paw on Sonya's shoulder (this time, Mr. De Witt, we'll come to blows over our *ius primae noctis*—) and Sonya smiled prettily at him . . . O Gods of all continents, isles, and seas, can we leave this splendid meteor to that orangu-tang?!

The second session of the divorce proceedings between petitioner Engineer Zikmund Holy, chief hydraulic specialist at USVLH Prague, domiciled in Usti n. L., Vilova 26, and respondent Aja Hola, née Vesela, presently a bargirl on the premises of RaJ World, domiciled at present with her companion Robert Knapp, was dragging on past 2:00.

Aja wept twice and shrieked three times, Ziki was bored and let his two lawyers talk for him, the young president of the court was all worked up again (Ziki decided that he would give a buzz to his friend Jozek, president of the regional court), Ziki glanced at his platinum datamatic stopwatch (2:16), with a very slight nod to the court he mumbled something and went out of the hearing room into the corridor, crossed to the other wing of the court building, climbed to the third floor, sat on a leather sofa in front of the state notary's offices beside Bertik Lohnmuller, and took from him a box of matches, inside of which a gold Spanish four-doubloon piece shone against a background of blue velvet, Ziki balanced it in his hand, bit into it, and passed a fragment of touchstone around it, nodded his head, dropped the coin into his pocket, and said: "How much?"

"Eleven thousand three hundred. . ." Bertik Lohnmuller announced. "The lady didn't want to sell it and so I had to—"

"That's your business," Ziki silenced him, tapped his index finger against his right breast pocket, and because the heap of banknotes inside did not seem thick enough, he got up and said: "Come with me."

With Bertik Lohnmuller behind him he entered the regional branch of the State Savings Bank (Lohnmuller remained by the door), at window No. 4 Ziki asked for twenty thousand crowns, "Make that thirty—" he corrected himself (why should he have to come here all the time), the clerk filled out a pink slip and Ziki signed it in the lower right-hand corner, he glanced at the cards for his four ordinary accounts (the total balance was over 1,100,000 and roughly as much again would come in over the next twelve months), he sat for a while in an armchair holding the thick cardboard call number in his hand (in his mind he put aside his financial concerns), when his number was called he walked over to window No. 1, asked the cashier to count out eleven thousand three hundred separately, took two packets of hundred-notes, without counting them stuck the thicker pack into the right breast pocket of his black jacket, the thinner into his trouser pocket, and without paying any attention to Lohnmuller at the door crossed the main square to his blue-black Triumph, unlocked it, sat down at the wheel, and opened the handle of the right rear door.

When Lohnmuller got in the back, Ziki looked around and handed him the packet of hundred-notes from his trouser pocket, asked about sapphires (they hadn't arrived yet), listened to a report about a collection of gold louis d'ors and ordered it and any quantity whatsoever of Roman gold solidi, he agreed to meet again on Wednesday, banged the door shut behind Bertik Lohnmuller, and stayed in the car.

He looked at the court building with distaste (he couldn't stand poorly ventilated rooms), in his mind he put aside his divorce business (my two lawyers can trample Aja all by themselves), played with the new coin in his pocket (he jingled it against his pistol), but didn't look at it again (it had ceased to amuse him) and, bored, he watched the security officer in the middle of the square, all of a sudden the figure of a girl veiled the officer from view (he watched her until she passed him, but he only saw her from behind), a beautifully developed girl, long legs and long thighs, a narrow waist and a straight back, hair cut short and passionately red.

Wow! Ziki started the car and slowly drove after the girl, into his broadened field of vision came a police officer saluting, and Ziki nodded slightly in greeting — but the officer was saluting our Sonya! Amused, Ziki smiled, disengaged the clutch, and stopped with the engine running while Sonya chatted with the officer — not more than a minute and Sonya was running after the No. 3 streetcar — Ziki slowly engaged the clutch and drove slowly along behind the streetcar.

He followed it for four stops, and when Sonya got out at Barvirska Street, he went on driving after her, past the battered garages and warehouses there (he recalled precisely what Sonya looked like from the front, he felt mildly excited and indulged himself with a provocative image of Sonya kneeling in her long children's nightgown (which lasted only a few seconds), and made a mental note of her address (14 Barvirska Street) and of the metal tablet by the entrance (*Lodging for natl. enter. Cottonola*).

He floored it and the engine roared with relief (Triumphs aren't made for following streetcars), Ziki shifted into third gear, drove through the Predlice quarter, and glided out onto the steeply rising highway which led to the Klise quarter, on Vilova Street he downshifted and drove through the open gates of No. 26 and through the garden right up to the Villa Cynthia's garage, where Wolf Zahn was using a chamois to polish the windshield of the gray van.

"Marticka was furious again that you didn't want to talk to her," Wolf called to him.

"You don't say."

"She wanted to wait for you in your bedroom."

"That's amusing."

"She wouldn't let herself be dissuaded."

"She's gotten quite steamed up with us."

"I finally had to quiet her down with a blackjack."

"That girl has become absolutely impossible," said Ziki, he took a heap of hundred-notes out of his breast pocket and placed them on the hood of the van, "give these to her in an envelope and then this evening drive her and her suitcase to the station."

"Couldn't I let her stay a few more days? I'd put her in the garden shed—"

"Take her."

"Thank you, sir."

"But I don't want to see her again! And air her room out thoroughly, clean it up, and disinfect it. We're going to have a new little bird. You know her. She's staying at 14 Barvirska Street, in the Cottonola dorm. Go take a look at her and prepare for action."

"Rely on me, sir."

. . .now those oafs on the second floor all want me, every single one of them. Please send me your instructions.

Your Sonya

Sonya wrote at the end of her letter to Manek, it had taken her sixteen pages to describe Cottonola and the dorm in detail, now she slid the pink pages into the pink envelope and wrote the address *Manuel Mansfeld, Hotel Imperial, Liberec.*

"Sonya—" an elegant young lady called from the main hall of the post office—and yes, it was Jarunka Slana, my best friend. . .

We fell into each other's arms and kissed. We hadn't seen each other for so long. . .

"What are you doing here, Sonya?"

"I'm sending a letter to my husband."

"For God's sake, don't tell me you're married?"

"Not yet. And how has marriage been treating you, Jarunka?"

"It's about to hand me a divorce."

"No! You and Dr. Sedivy are getting divorced?!"

"Men are beasts," Jarunka muttered, and she invited Sonya to her apartment.

Jarunka's apartment was a nice 2 + 1 1st.-category co-op on the eighth floor of a pre-fab with a view into a square of pre-fabs. One room was furnished luxuriously with a complete living-room suite, the kind they show in department stores, and the other had bare floors.

"I call it the *T.V. room*," said Jarunka, "and my former husband owes me the furniture for it, the beast."

And Jarunka told about the beast's unbearable selfishness—three months after the wedding he moved back to Mama!—for a good three hours.

"What will you do now, Jarunka?"

"Live. We came to terms, me and the beast—he keeps the car and I get to stay here in this joint. But furnished! So the beast has to buy me furniture for the T.V. room . . . then I can try to forget that I was stupid enough to get married. Listen to me, Sonya, *never* get married!"

"But what if I love Manek. . ."

"After the wedding every guy's a beast."

Jarunka brought out some yogurt and the girls ate it with a single spoon.

"So now I've had my dinner!" Jarunka laughed.

"How are you fixed for money?"

"Awfully. I only make a thousand crowns a month and out of that I have to pay six hundred for this apartment—I'm paying off the mortgage. Hey, Sonya, come be my roommate — I'll let you have the entire T.V. room!"

"I was just going to suggest that you come work with me at Cottonola. You'd get twelve hundred plus overtime—"

"I don't much care for factories. Maybe a little later, if things get worse . . . and then I'd work at a gas station and take in a hundred a day, with no problem . . . Let's work the gas station together, we'll live like royalty together!"

"I'd have to get Manek's permission first."

"He keeps a hold on you, huh? More than Ruda did?"

"Ruda deserted me. Manek's given me a new life."

"Ruda was a jerk, but charming. When I think of his room at the Hubertus . . . But still, all men are beasts."

"They've really hurt you . . . but all of them?"

"I hate them."

Sonya kissed Jarunka on the cheek, and even though she got back to the dorm late that evening, all the oafs from the second floor were still hanging around at their customary posts. As soon as they caught sight of Sonya (she smiled at them prettily), they began to glow (Pavel Abrt even woke up) and began to eat in earnest.

And they ate even more earnestly the next day, when Sonya sang to them, and they fed their faces even more energetically when she danced for them.

In a few days a letter came from Ostrava for Sonya's two roommates.

"It's from Majka, the one who lived here before you!" Ivanka shouted, and she read out loud that, "I liked Ostrava at first, but now I don't like it at all. I had an affair there with someone named Ruda Mach, he was something, but then he started calling me Sonicko in bed, and then he cleared out and was off to eastern Slovakia. The guys here are a bit too lively and I'm homesick for our oafs back there. Girls, if you don't have anybody living there yet, write and and I'll be right back, and have Engineer Sapal keep my place in the drying room, so write me right away, so long! Majka."

"Ruda Mach . . . didn't he used to be your guy, Sonya?" said Barborka.

"Sort of. But not really. Who gives a damn."

"Poor Majka," Ivanka sighed. "She'll be sad when she finds out she can't come back. . ."

"Why can't she?" Sonya was surprised.

"Because we're full up: there's no room for a third girl in the dryer and there's no room for a fourth bed in this room. Poor Majka. . ." said Ivanka, out of sympathy she smoked two cigarettes and asked: "What's that you're writing, Sonya?"

"A letter to Manek," said Sonya, and she wrote sixteen pink pages, on the envelope the address *Manuel Mansfeld, Hotel Imperial, Liberec.*

I took out my red briefcase (I bought it for school) and put in my letter and some notebooks and a textbook and a novel I'd already read, Hermann Broch's *The Sleepwalkers* (I'd fallen most in love with Hanna Wedling) and then I left the building, on the street a car came up behind me right up onto the sidewalk, I squeezed against the wall, the door of the car opened suddenly and a hairy, tattooed male hand pulled me inside before I could get a hold of myself, I saw the grinning face of Wolf Zahn and then Berta Zahnova threw over my face a handkerchief smelling of something sweet and heavy, I'd smelt it somewhere before. . .

I came to my senses again. An unfamiliar room with white furniture, over me Wolf and Berta, and Mister Ziki, too, standing and smiling on a thick yellow rug sewn from sheepskins.

I shrieked and leaped for the door, the Zahns grabbed my arms and twisted them behind me, I scratched, bit, and kicked, but then Zahn suddenly bent over, thrust his head between my thighs, grabbed me by both my ankles, and flipped me upside down so that I was left hanging from his shoulders with my head to the ground, and Berta Zahnova tore off my dress and even my underwear. Then Zahn threw me on a bed, and all three of them went out and double-locked the door.

The heavy door has no handle on the inside, nor is there any on the window, and outside the window a massive concave grill projects out toward the treetops.

In a golden-yellow embroidered robe of Chinese brocade (which had made its way from Hongkong to Woolworth's, a London department store), which opened to reveal a sliver of an exquisite chocolate-brown shirt made of a mercerized Egyptian cotton known as *mako*, which was intersected by a loud, sulphur-yellow tie, Ziki stepped up to the glassed ebony sideboard, with the skillful, silent, and economical movements of a single hand he unlocked and let down the massive door: on the counter thus formed he placed a simply etched glass taken from the upper section of the mirrored shelves, and drew out and uncorked (always with a single hand) a bottle of Spanish wine called Tarragona, in one motion he poured his noontime dose into the glass (precisely the same—a finger's breadth below the top of the glass—as any other day) and with alpaca-lined tongs (always with a single hand) he lowered a circlet of lemon onto the surface of the wine. Sonya is an extraordinary case.

After six days of 'special treatment' (*Spezialsonderbehandlung*), Sonya is as unyielding as on the first day. She's *unbelievable*—

Complete oral starvation with nothing but intravenous glucose, the suggestion of a daughter complex under hypnosis plus psychopharmaceutical aids, a salted whip, an assortment of narcotics, light, heat, and electric shocks, systematic hormonal excitation — with Sonya nothing worked. With Zdenicka, the next-to-last girl, a short period of starvation, a light beating with a rod, and some ice cream on a stick were enough, with the last one, Marticka, all it took was eight ounces of white Cinzano (diluted with ice, no lemon) — Sonya triumphed over all the brain- washing techniques known to the C.I.A. and the Federal Bureau for the Preservation of the Constitution.

And while undergoing the Scottie-Holzenstamm detection system (electro-impulse measuring with a double dose of lithiumdiisooktylhexacarbonchrysoidine) all she talks about is a certain Manek and she claims she's his wife — 'curious,' thought Ziki, and he took a sip of the Tarragona.

The technical literature cited just one case that had held out against the Scottie-Holzenstamm system: a ninety-three-year-old Yugoin from the Himalayas, who was able to emit his I a good 400 miles to a cloister in Lhasa . . . but where would an ordinary Czech girl get such enormous, practically *supernatural* spiritual power?

Five short knocks on the door and in came Berta Zahnova, scratched all over: "She kicked over my last bottle of glucose, sir, and I won't be able to lay my hands on another one today.

She's so exhausted that if we don't give her something pretty soon, she might exit on us—"

"Give her milk, bouillon, toast and, starting tomorrow, gruel," Ziki said tenderly.

It's annoying. All that's left is psychotherapy, and I don't have much faith in it . . . *Extremely* annoying: the Security Police can begin looking for Sonya now that she's been missing for six days, especially that officer who saluted her down on the square—

It's 'shocking,' but Sonya had triumphed. There was nothing left to do but try to eventually win her good will and, through her complete rehabilitation, make it possible to set her free in a state of mutual respect.

Entering without knocking (he could do that only in the most extraordinary cases), Wolf Zahn stumbled in with bloody slashes on both his cheeks, and enraged he announced:

"She threw the hot bouillon in Berta's face and scalded her, sir!"

"'Heaven!' Will we settle with that girl or she with us?!"

"She's quite superduper, sir. . ."

"Did she rough you up like that?" said Ziki, and he pointed a bit queasily at Wolf's disfigured face.

"Only the one on the left. The right one's from Marticka."

"'Damned fool'! You've still got Marticka in the garden shed—get rid of her this minute! Idiot! The police might be here any moment!"

Ziki sipped his wine. Sonya's almost a *miracle* . . . I've never encountered anything like her before and I've encountered all sorts. . . Dr. Menecka, for instance . . . or Isabella from Barbados . . . Ursula von Rottenburg. . .

A sudden uproar in front of the house, Ziki took a sip and with his glass in his hand he went up to the window and looked out between the curtains: a truck had entered the garden, and police in civilian clothes were jumping out of it and coming up to the house.

Ziki took a sip of Tarragona, from the ceiling safe took out his 'emergency' suitcase (packed with a suit, underwear, toiletries, an official and a private passport, both permitting extended visits in all European countries, 300 crowns in Czech currency, 100 east marks and 100 west marks and 50 pounds sterling, under a false bottom eighteen hundred carats of industrial diamonds), he shut the safe (knocks on the door downstairs), drank one last swallow of Tarragona, went down to the cellar, passed through an iron gate past a heap of coke and along a concrete sidewalk at the end of which was his bakelite Trabant auto, in dark glasses (placed in advance on the seat of the car) he drove out onto Sadova Street, left the car near the main station, and on the Vindobona international express he reached his destination at 5:08 P.M., precisely according to the timetable, the station was Berlin-Ostbahnhof, from there a black East Berlin taxi to 'Check-Point Charlie,' then a yellow West Berlin taxi to the Berlin-Tempelhof Airport, and by Swiss Air to London (Heathrow Airport).

From the airport he phoned his friend Randolph S., asking him to make a phone call to Usti nad Labem (which may not be very simple, he may have to dial 'again and again'), and he sent his employer, USVLH Prague (cable: *Ustrevoda Praha*), a long telegram (collect) to the effect that in the matter of the submersible gas burner for the vaporizing apparatus at natl. enter. Cottex, he was making personal contacts with the manufacturer, NORDAC Ltd., pursuant to prior arrangements (with this he gave his journey a legal basis and laid the groundwork for a claim for reimbursement of travel expenses and a per diem in £), he called to make a reservation ("for a week or so") at his favorite hotel, the Kensington Palace, in the *Daily Express* newspaper he checked the cabaret programs, they've never been worse, the season's just starting — and because it was exactly 8:00 P.M., he went to dine at the airport restaurant.

"That girl's a *miracle*," he said to himself after taking a sip of his aperitif (Tarragona with lemon).

A deep-blue five-ton truck rattled out of the industrial quarter of Predlice along the steep highway into the residential quarter of Klise and roared through the quiet, flowery streets, in back Lanimir Sapal, Cenek, Lumirek, and Pavel Abrt held on to the sides throughout the hellish trip, Ivanka and Barborka were jolted around the floor, and in the cab Vit showed Petr Junk the way:

"—take a left and we're there."

Petr turned into empty Vilova Street and stopped in front of the barbwire garden gate to No. 26.

"Should we go in on foot or should we drive. . ." Vit considered aloud after ringing the bell in vain.

"Let's drive—" Peter Junk shouted, and he stepped on the gas.

Six days earlier, from his dorm window, Cenek had seen Sonya get into (". . .something wasn't right—") a low blue-black car (". . .a six-cylinder Triumph, it's got three carburetors. . .") and Sonya did not come back all day. Even Sapal noticed that his newest soul failed to make it to the drying room by the end of the shift. Chief Sapal wrote in the daily log that "Miss Cechova S. to be dealt with by OUNZ (Ivanka and Barborka—Sonya told them everything about herself—deduced that Sonya had spent the night at Jarunka Slana's).

But when she didn't show up that evening, Vit set out after Jarunka in Cenek's Skoda MB and on his return announced to the alarm of all the singles, "Sonya is missing."

There aren't too many Triumphs in Usti nad Labem, but it still took the Cottonola bachelors a good three days (they didn't want to turn to the police except under extreme circumstances, so they wouldn't cause any trouble for Sonya—excepting her unforgiveable absence from the drying room), to find the owner of the mysterious auto.

"It's some Engineer Zikmund Holy and he lives on Vilova Street—" Cenek announced.

"Ziki . . . that's Ziki! Remember, Barborka, what Sonya told us about him—"

"The Lord be with us," Barborka grew frightened, "our Sonya may no longer be. . ."

Twenty minutes later a red Skoda MB parked at the corner of Vilova and Sadova Streets and five men from sixteen to forty in age, one after the other, took a walk around No. 26. The last to come back was Cenek, pale with horror he pointed to what he had found in a garbage can: shreds of Sonya's green dress and her left sandal, charred.

When they rang at the garden gate, the lights in the villa went out and after an entire hour of prolonged ringing the house remained deaf and dark.

"Should we go in on foot or should we drive. . ." Vit considered the next afternoon in front of house No. 26.

"Let's drive—" Petr Junk shouted, he stepped on the gas, the massive front bumper smashed through the barbwire garden gate, and the truck drove into the garden.

Oddly enough, the door of the villa was open and the villa empty (but in the kitchen pots were boiling), both the ground floor and the second floor (in one room a black sideboard was open and on its counter a still damp wineglass with a fresh circlet of lemon).

On the third floor behind a heavy white door (it wasn't locked, but she couldn't open it: it didn't have an inside handle) lay Sonya bound to a bed, wearing a long nightgown (like a child's), by her head a hospital stand with an empty bottle, hanging from its neck and swinging freely was a red rubber tube ending in a hypodermic needle, on the chair a yellow leather whip, and on the damp carpet pieces of glass—

"What have they done to you, Sonya. . ."

"Manek, I knew you'd come—" Sonya whispered and then lost consciousness.

In three days' time (Ivanka sat by Sonya for hours on end without a single cigarette and Barborka cooked till late at night, Marie Junkova furnished some baby food and her baby bottle, out of his savings Cenek bought eggs, vegetables, milk, and chicken, Lanimir read Sonya select passages from humorous novels, Vit forbade the housekeeper Sbiralka to wash the stairs, " 'cause you make such a racket with the bucket!" and on the other side of the wall Petr Junk talked to his wife in a whisper, Lumirek made Sonya a pair of electromechanical earrings which lit up, played music, and rotated, and Pavel Abrt took sleeping pills in order to sleep) Sonya dictated to Lanimir a twenty-three-page report to Manek (while she was gone, all that had come from Manek was a very curt telegram: STUDY FOR YOUR DEGREE EXAMINATION—M.M.).

We sat on daybeds surrounding Sonya and felt terribly sorry she had to go.

The director was sympathetic, but matters involving missed shifts fell under the jurisdiction of the prosecutor (petitions with signatures of all the employees of the finishing rooms didn't help, nor did a thirty-seven-page analysis by Engineer L. Sapal replete with quotations from the fields of law, economics, history, and literature, not even an hour-long visit paid by senior workers Vit and Cenek to the director had any effect), despite all its sympathy, the management of Cottonola could do no more for Sonya than drop criminal charges on condition that Sonya leave. And the telegraphically invited Majka in Ostrava sent an enthusiastic reply *AT ONCE AND FOREVER I WILL RETURN ON FIRST TRAIN.*

And so Lanimir took Sonya's suitcase, Vit and Cenek carried Sonya downstairs, seated her in Cenek's red Skoda MB (Lumirek and Pavel Abrt waved from the open second-floor window, on the third floor Ivanka and Barborka were crying) and they took her to Jarunka Slana's, as Sonya had requested.

"I'll write a pentalogy about you!" Lanimir Sapal promised Sonya (after years of suffering he is publishing the first volume), he kissed her on the forehead and, on the way back, mailed another extended report from Sonya to Manek, already with her new address on the back of the envelope, registered express.

". . . that's it. It'll be all right now," Jarunka Slana said as she pulled off the bandages on Sonya's back, peeled off the last scab left from the shots she'd been given, and spread vaseline on her shoulders. "Now get some sleep and then we'll go out this afternoon," and she smoothed out her glaringly golden hair (à la chrysanthemum), on the run she grabbed a satchel (it was already seven fifteen), took the elevator down to the first floor, and ran off to catch the streetcar.

Jarunka Slana-Sediva hates men. Three months after their wedding Dr. Sedivy marched back to Mama, "because she's the only one in the world who understands me," he said, he took all his things (I haven't got any of my own so far) and got the hell out. He destroyed my life and made a divorcée out of me at the age of twenty—

Beast, Jarunka said to herself as she put her fare, ten hellers short (like every day), into the streetcar's farebox, at the same time smiling at the driver radiantly, they're all beasts and I'll show them—

Jarunka was the prettiest salesgirl in the salesroom of PRIM Fashionable Accessories for Men.

". . .aren't those a little small?" a customer in his prime hesitated over a pair of obviously teensy socks.

"But they're stretch-nylon, they'll stretch to fit your foot!" Jarunka said with a radiant smile, stretching the teensy socks with all her fingers to a pint-size volume (after the first washing, only an infant with an awfully small sole would be able to put them on).

"Well, if you recommend them. . ." the customer gave in, Jarunka wrapped the mini-socks and then rushed to help a young prospective buyer ("some sort of shirt from the West") who had arms stretching below his knees, like a chimpanzee's.

"This is an American original," said Jarunka, opening a dacron shirt 'Made in U.S.A.' (everyone knows that Americans wear their sleeves shorter than anyone else) invitingly across her well-developed chest, "and this is the last one we have. . ."

"Will it f-f-fit me?" the long-armed youth was terrified by what he saw.

"As if it were made to order. But it costs a hundred forty!"

"That d-d-doesn't m-m-matter," the youth said with pride, and he took the shirt (which could have fit a much younger guy, assuming he had a chest like an elderly butcher from Brooklyn).

As with expertly directed whiplashes, Jarunka placed tight socks and shirts, sweaters that strangle, and clothes that constrict the necks, trunks, arms, calves, and feet of the detested male sex (whenever—though not very often—a tormented buyer ventured to come back and beg to make an exchange, Jarunka would crush him with her most radiant smile: "But I thought you *didn't have* a neck like a loaf of bread [a bottom like a ham, feet like dumplings] . . . you don't *really* want to try on something else? We haven't got anything else—" and many a customer went off a second time with the cunningly chosen instrument of torture, since in Usti n.L. fashionable accessories for men are always hard to come by.

So for the most part it was fun (but standing behind a counter gives you varicose veins, and of the less than a thousand a month, six hundred goes for the apartment), so she had to live on a diet of bread, tea, and yogurt, and a twenty-year-old girl also needs to clothe herself and have a good time—

"Those two over there are dying to say something nice to us," Jarunka said to Sonya over their afternoon tea at the Union Café in Vseborice, and with her elbow she cautiously pointed out two old men at a corner table.

"But they're too old even to be our dads," Sonya laughed over her tea (without sugar or anything).

"They've only got a year or two till they retire, and that's the best sort," Jarunka assessed them professionally, "they don't grudge you a crown when they're on their last legs—"

And the eyes Jarunka made to the corner table were so

frequent and so radiant that in five minutes the two near-pensioners joined the girls at their table and Jarunka snapped her fingers impatiently (and hungrily) to the waiter.

"Two Moravian cutlets—each with a double portion of chef salad—and four slices of cake and two Turkish coffees with whipped cream!"

Ecstatic about the girls' appetites and their amiability (Sonya kept smiling at them prettily, and Jarunka radiantly), the near-pensioners ordered headcheese with vinegar and pepper (heavy blows to their gall-bladders—), drank beer after beer (—the same to their prostates and urinary tracts—), and they laced their beers with a little rum (—and to their kidneys).

When they began to tell the girls (a bit incoherently) that "Frantik here has a garden and in the garden a shed and in the shed a crate of suuuch sweeet apples," Jarunka accepted their invitation "to the shed for apples" and sent Sonya to "telephone Dad and tell him we'll be home a little bit late."

"Will you lend us money for the phone?" she said to the near-pensioners with an especially radiant smile, she took a five-crown piece from them and handed it to Sonya.

"Sonya's been on the phone with Dad for a long time now, it seems," she said after a while. "Dad likes to play chess with her every evening and she doesn't know how to say no . . . I'll go and get her—"

And Jarunka ran out of the bar into the vestibule, where Sonya was nervously biting her nails, took her by the arm, and the girls quickly rode off to town in bus No. 5.

"Do you really want to go to that idiotic school of yours?" Jarunka was annoyed with Sonya when they got out on the main square.

"I've got to. Manek wants me to pass the degree exam."

"Too bad, we could go to the Druzba now, it's Thursday, the day they get paid at the glassworks. No problem though, I can go by myself."

"Be careful!" said Sonya.

"Don't be afraid, I can hold my own with those beasts!"

Jarunka grinned, and with a pugnacious spirit she brandished her unusually ample shopping bag (with stiff sides and metal-bound corners, inside were lipstick, a comb, three crowns, and a canvas bag containing several pounds of hairpins: one blow to the head could dispose of any man who wasn't wearing a helmet).

While Sonya was crossing the bridge on her way to night school, Jarunka dropped into the World Cafeteria again, standing at the counter she shoveled down an ice-cream sundae (she loved frozen treats), and shortly after eight o'clock she and her distended shopping bag went down to the underground Druzba Bar.

She went home on the last streetcar of the night, tanked up to overflowing with gin-, orange- and other fizzes, with sparkling wine, and with the most varied cocktails (she loved her alchohol chilled), she found Sonya sleeping with her face down on the kitchen table, by her left ear a geography textbook (*Chapter XXXIX. CONSEQUENCES OF THE SECOND WORLD WAR*), and Sonya was exhaling onto page 18 of the next letter to her eternal Manek—

Poor girl, Jarunka sighed, and tenderly she picked her up in her arms and, half-asleep herself, laid her out on her former husband's daybed, the beast—

Then she pulled the barrettes out of her hair and in her pajamas she smoked a cigarette by the window that looks out onto the square of pre-fab highrises, comforted that all the windows were dark, only here and there in the dark walls of similarly seven-storied buildings the dull glow of a lamp doing its thing above the headboards of double beds . . . there's no way to live with men, sighed Jarunka, and it's even worse without them—in the kitchen she took a long drink of cold water, swallowed a barbituate to help her sleep, and quietly lay down beside Sonya on her husband's daybed.

Sonya slept with her face on one hand, she scrunched up the tip of the pillow with her other hand and smiled happily with her half-opened mouth—she was dreaming again of her Manek.

Lucky girl, sighed Jarunka, and she tried to fall asleep as soon as possible, because nothing spoils skin or youth like crying yourself to sleep.

The last of Manek's commands went *STUDY FOR YOUR DEGREE EXAMINATION* and since then my husband hasn't sent a word to me, even though so much has happened—

—too much perhaps, perhaps everything that can happen to a girl.

Sonya lay on the fugitive husband's daybed with a just-finished history textbook (I'm studying for my degree exam), in a week I'll have mastered physics and then all I have to do is wait till spring for my exam. By then I'll have read another fifty novels or so . . . will that be enough preparation?!

Every morning I wake up in Jarunka's empty T.V. room and do half an hour of exercises (why? I'm studying—), in front of the mirror I comb my hair and make myself up (for whom? I'm studying—) and I go out to look at people (I'm studying).

I go out without breakfast: except for yogurt (she eats it plain and frozen) Jarunka doesn't buy much in the way of food, and I'm saving my thousand crowns from Cottonola (so I can study). I'm happy to go out: in that apartment of shipwrecked love, I feel like I'm on a sinking ship.

It's October 24, a few minutes before eight. Children are going to school. A plain-looking mother comes to a sudden stop next to the sidewalk, opens her car door, watches her little son until he disappears into the school (before he disappears she waves, and I'm gripped by a brief but powerful emotion), and then drives rapidly away. On the other side of the street a teacher has collected a flock of children, suddenly she strides onto the road, with her arms spread wide she stops the traffic going both ways and beneath her arms the children cross the road as if beneath protecting wings.

I go to the greengrocer for nuts, a salesgirl about my age is emptying a crate of apples, and so I have to wait for my breakfast (for an hour sometimes: *she* is working, *I* am not), I tear open the corner of the cellophane bag and pour some peanuts into my mouth. Next door in the dairy store I drink a bottle of milk in a single gulp and return the bottle right on the spot. No one pays any attention to me, in contrast to me everyone here's in a hurry. At the kiosk I buy a paper (I'm studying everything), I read it standing up and soon I throw it away.

I've finished my history lesson, I've exercised, I've combed my hair and made myself up, I've had breakfast and informed myself concerning the latest developments in the Middle East, Peru, and Indonesia — it's just after eight and I'm ready to *shout* from it all—

The nicest time of day is when I watch them work on the highway. The lanes are all done now, and the orange machine which laid them is resting a little beyond its last few feet. All that's left now is to finish the shoulders, to fill the beds for these, stretching all the way to the horizon, with concrete . . . I envy the men their work: it seems endless, but each day they leave behind them a wonderfully solid piece of road. . .

Although the orange machine laid down the lanes almost by itself—the men only served it—they do the shoulders themselves: they shovel gravel into wet cement, they pull their leveling board along it (the gravel disappears and the surface grows smooth), then a vibrating lathe (I read about it in the town library), and finally, on their knees, a trowel, the gravel disappears and the men's road is suddenly as smooth as a freshly baked cake, and that's how they play their day away.

Everyone in the gang is Hungarian (I don't know a single word of Hungarian, I communicate with them only in gestures, but I do manage to understand them: they're men) and handsome down to the last one of them, they walk about as if they were on a golf course, they all take an interest in me (as I in them) and they try to entice me, but honorably, simply, and clearly (oh, Manek. . .), on scraps of paper sacks from their cement they keep writing the figure 2,000, the pay in crowns I will get when I join their gang. I sign that I am still thinking it over (I think of it more and more seriously) and that they should save me a place. There's no hurry, they sign, and they show me my road to the horizon.

I walk in the opposite direction, toward the center of town, and it takes me about an hour since I keep stopping and looking at people. I sit on a park bench, in the sand lie rust-colored chestnut leaves, I sit here all alone, two girls are walking across the grass gathering up the leaves, which keep on falling and falling. Couldn't they wait till they all fall and then gather them all at once? No. This is their job and their vocation. What am I doing? I'm studying for my degree exam. But all that's left now is physics, and then a half-year wait for the spring exam . . . and I'll read another fifty novels . . . is that a job or a vocation? The girls look at me curiously and whisper to one another. I quickly leave.

I am the first visitor to enter the reading room of the town library (every day). What should I study today? I walk by the shelves, take down book after book, leaf through them and put them right back, skim them for five minutes standing up, or sit over them for three hours, I read about the cultivation of fruit trees, about cooking nutritious food, about Ceylon tea, about excavations in Mexico, about catching gorillas, about the Wankel engine, about apartment interiors, about the coronation of the British queen, about viniculture in Soviet Georgia, about Saxon porcelain, about the psychology of a pregnant woman, about breast-feeding . . . have I studied enough?

I have an absurd amount of time left and I walk (it hardly matters where) to the station, for the twentieth time I etch in my memory the departure times of all the express trains to Liberec and Prague (I'm getting ready for a journey—), departures in the afternoon, at night, and in the morning, so that, for example, today I could arrive in Liberec at 4:37, in Prague as early as 2:12—

I trudge back (not home) through the town as it comes to life, where everyone has something to do, they drive their children to school or they help other people's children cross the street, they sell vegetables, milk, and newspapers, they lay highways, they hunt for books in the library, they drive streetcars . . . I'm *studying* OR AM I ONLY DECEIVING MYSELF—Jarunka's mailbox is empty again. M.M. goes on being silent and remote.

In the afternoon Jarunka and I go to the Café Savoy (tape-recorded music and no cover charge), we order two plain teas and before they come we're asked to dance. A few numbers and the two men sit down at our table.

They're both engineers from the glassworks, young and clever. We all laugh together, Jarunka talks about cars (she knows three technical details about Saabs and she gets a lot of mileage out of them), I talk about the Wankel engine (I've studied it in the reading room of the town library), I know its principle and I get a lot of mileage out of it, men like that sort of thing, but we two don't actually talk very much, we mainly listen (the men are delighted), we know how to get along with men (they're something I've been studying for years).

We get up to dance, we sit down and then dance again, with a quick raising of our eyebrows we divvy up the engineers, and then each of us cultivates and takes charge of her own. the one I chose is a quite good-looking and clever guy, we enjoy ourselves (as we did yesterday with the near-pensioners at the Union) and we understand each other (as on Wednesday at the Palace Restaurant and on Tuesday with the dentist at Café Bohemia).

"I'm so glad I met you," my engineer says to me (today at the Savoy) and I smile at him prettily (as I did at the Bohemia, the Palace, the Union, the Hotel Hubertus . . . not to mention the *Hotel Imperial*?)—

"Is anything wrong?" my engineer grows frightened.

"No. Nothing."

"You turned pale so quickly—"

My pretty smile must look silly.

I raise my eyebrows at Jarunka, she's surprised (because

these are really first-rate guys), but she moves smoothly on to a conclusion of our enterprise:

"We're really having a great time with you guys," Jarunka tells the engineers (her radiant smile is absolutely idiotic), "but we haven't eaten anything since morning, so we're in a rush to get home."

"When can we see you again?" the engineers wish to know.

"Let's leave that to chance," we provoke them to take the initiative.

"But at least tell us—"

"No more. We're incredibly hungry and so off we go—"

"But you can have a meal here—"

"I've got just three crowns on me," says Jarunka (at the Bohemia she'd said "five" and the dentist had suggested that she order grated Roquefort), "and you, Sonya?"

"I've just got streetcar fare—"

And so the engineers call the waiter over, Jarunka orders fifteen dekas of ham, two portions of butter, and vermouth on the rocks, I run my finger down the prices on the menu and order three expensive dishes along with a bottle of sparkling wine, Jarunka raises her eyebrows (this is dangerous and even for her it'd be pretty cheeky) and tries to turn it into a joke, I glumly persist in my ordering, the engineers exchange glances, but they don't dare deny me what I want. In spite of Jarunka's stubborn efforts, the entertainment goes downhill. I stop smiling prettily, drink one sip of sparkling wine, get down one slice of Hungarian salami, and mumbling something I get up and leave it all behind. I've got night school, I have to study for my exam, right?

At night school I'm the best student in the class, I get nothing but A's and I know it all in advance, the teachers praise me as a model to my fellow pupils while I stare at the blotches all over my desk to avoid the gaze of the tired mamas and the girls on night shift who haven't caught up on their sleep . . . I've already lost the joy of coming here.

And from school to the movies, to avoid coming as long as

possible to the home that's not a home. I'll write a letter to Manek and start studying physics, in a week I'll have it mastered—and what if M.M. at his comfortable distance goes on being silent another week and even longer, until the men and their highway disappear beyond the horizon—

"I've got something—" Jarunka tells me at night in her kitchen (she's stuffing herself with frozen yogurt and the splinters of ice crackle between her teeth), she puts her finger to her lips and leads me through the foyer into her T.V. room. On the bare floors of the warm bare room (the heat has already gone on) on a checkered blanket lies something wearing striped shorts, it's all hairy and shaggy (except for a face with childlike skin) and it seems to be a sixteen-year-old boy.

"Where did you find it?"

"At the World Cafeteria."

"And what are you going to do with it?"

"I've paid for him!" Jarunka exults and joyfully explains that Krystofek ("Imagine that, his name is really Krystof, I checked his I.D.—") came to Usti without a single crown in his pocket, he has nowhere to live and doesn't know anybody here, and so Jarunka bought him two plates of tripe soup and took him home.

"And what are you going to do with him?"

"Whatever I wish, he's mine . . . I'll send him somewhere to slave away, he'll give me his entire pay, and I'll bring him up like a goldfish in an aquarium — why he's just a silly little animal. . ."

The "animal" is a good six feet tall, Jarunka joyfully shows him off to me, calls attention to how long his hair is (almost a foot), to his powerful legs and arms and, in ecstasy, jabs her finger into his tough white flesh until the boy wakes up and speaks.

"What's up?"

"This is Sonya, my best friend, she lives here with us and you must obey her like you do me!"

"OK," the boy agrees. "Should I get up?"

"But it's nighttime, you simpleton," Jarunka tells him lovingly, "go back to sleep so you can be fresh in the morning. Tomorrow morning you'll be sent to work."

"OK," the boy agrees. "Good night!"

Jarunka got up at four in the morning (I don't think she ever slept at all) and through the thin pre-fab partition I could hear her waking up Krystofek (it took a long time for her to accomplish this), she scrubbed him in the bathtub with a scrub brush, cut his hair and nails, fed him (the door to the refrigerator kept banging for a whole hour), and at half-past five she drove him in front of her like a horse going to market. I began to study physics.

M.M. at his distance went on being silent.

In the afternoon Jarunka drove Krystofek back into the apartment, draped with shopping bags and nets crammed full (she'd hired him out to the town slaughterhouse and talked them into advancing him one week's pay and giving him an interest-free loan on the second week's, as well as a clothing allowance), she'd spent all her own ready cash ("But Krystofek will give it all back to me — right, Krystofek?" "You bet!" said the boy) and she'd bought, among other things, a six-pound loaf of Sumava bread, two pounds of horse salami, seven pounds of pickles, a pair of corduroy trousers (at a bazaar: one leg was shorter than the other and the pocket had been repaired), six yards of flannel (at the bazaar), and at once she began measuring her animal with a tape measure, then sat down at the sewing machine (sewing was what Jarunka was best at), and by nightfall she had turned out a shirt as if on an assembly line. The boy sat and ate and then lay down and slept.

Each day the Hungarians were another two minutes farther away, each day I poured peanuts into my mouth, drank a bottle of milk standing up, read the paper, the encyclopedia, and novels, looked at people, studied for the degree exam (I studied physics more slowly than any other subject. . .) and wrote to Manek every day — M.M. at his distance went on being silent.

Krystofek took to sitting in our room (in the T.V. room all he had was a blanket on the bare floor) in just one chair (it had cost three thousand crowns, by moving a lever it could be tilted to make a bed, but even when untilted it took up a good quarter of the room), which he delighted in tilting and sitting on with his legs crossed.

Jarunka cooked as for an artillery squadron, she spent entire days sewing new gear for her "animal" (out of an old curtain she sewed him a shirt with a fichu even Lumirek from Cottonola wouldn't have spurned) and she gave one order after another, Krystofek ran every so often to the cellar for potatoes, to the self-service market for vinegar or mustard, he beat the rugs, scrubbed the floors, scoured out the bathtub, and washed the windows, and as soon as he finished a task he jumped up on the tilted armchair, sat Turkish-style, and stared at me. Jarunka didn't give him any allowance and forbade him to smoke, the only pleasure permitted him was chewing-gum. Krystofek squatted on the tilted chair, chewed, and stared at me.

M.M. at his distance went on being silent.

It was beginning to get crowded having three of us in Jarunka's apartment. When Jarunka finished clothing her animal, she sat on her daybed opposite his tilted armchair and for hours on end we played a game of rummy known as Vatican, in which you could do anything at all and two hands can take up a whole afternoon, we played five hands of Vatican in one sitting and then I decided to go off to the kitchen to read.

One rainy afternoon I read Gogol's *Dead Souls* and I realized that it wasn't worth reading anything else, I felt a terrible desire to be with people, and so without knocking I burst into the living room — Krystofek stood against the wall, naked as God had created him, his palms against the ceiling, and Jarunka was embracing him with the tape measure.

"I'm measuring him for pajamas. . ." Jarunka whispered.

Krystofek stood there and didn't even blink.

Coming in from school I couldn't unlock the door of Jarunka's apartment: there was a key in the lock on the inside.

"Come back in ten minutes!" Jarunka called to me through the door.

Outside it was pouring buckets (it's already November!), I took a taxi (for the first time in my life) to the main post office and at the grill I presented an urgent telegram:

Manuel Mansfeld   Hotel Imperial   Liberec
I'm in the gutter stop should I come to you or will you come here question mark Please please please exclamation point

                                                        Your Sonya

And I sat there in the hall of the main post office until it stopped raining, then I went to the movies, then the station, and I didn't return until long after midnight. In the living room all that remained was my (that is, Dr. Sedivy's) daybed, everything else—Jarunka's bed, the tilting armchair, the glassed sideboard, the bookcase, the ficus, the rug, the floor lamp—had disappeared (the floor lamp shone through the glass inset in the door of the T.V. room).

In the morning I studied the next-to-last chapter of physics (49: Self-Induction), exercised for half an hour, in the bathroom in front of the mirror (Krystof's toothbrush was reposing in Jarunka's cup) I combed my hair (it had grown out well) and was making myself up when the bell sounded and a delivery boy on a motorcycle gave me a priority telegram from Prague:

ENGAGED IN A SECRET MISSION CANNOT COME IN
FORSEEABLE FUTURE STOP FIND A NEW PLACE TO LIVE
AND BEGIN A NEW LIFE   M.M.

I'd packed my suitcase in ten minutes and left Jarunka a note on the kitchen table: *"Manek is sending me away and so I'm leaving. Regards, thanks, kisses, and I wish you all the best!"* and I left her home behind.

A sack of nuts, a bottle of milk, the newspapers (I didn't throw them away: they'll come in handy in the new apartment), and I ran after the Hungarians, who since yesterday had knocked off another two minutes of highway.

They were happy, they gave me an enormous green pepper, and with gestures they pointed out where I could find the manager.

"And where did you work after being let go at Cottonola?" the fat manager grinned at me (I had never seen him on the highway) when he had finished his telephone conversation with Cottonola.

"I've been studying for my degree exam."

"Well, go on studying, kitten. Five missed shifts, the sack, and then goofing off for three weeks — I'd see you here maybe twice a week, right!"

"But I'm done with my studies and I want to do honest—"

"Clear out!"

I'm standing on the highway with my suitcase, biting into a green pepper.

Engineer Kazimir Drapal (35), the director (and only employee) of the Center for Scientific, Technical and Economic Information (PS-VTEI) and PTK (the technical library) of national enterprise Cottex had done no work at work for many years (no one had noticed).

With a briefcase of quite serious mien (it contained his morning snack, a newspaper, in summer swimming trunks and in winter skates) at precisely 6:30 he arrived at the last stop of bus No. 5 near the Vseborice post office (to do this he had to walk one station in the opposite direction of his journey: on the one hand he likes to walk, on the other hand he likes to ride in the seat right behind the driver), adroitly he always managed to enter the bus first and to sit down right behind the driver.

His briefcase on his lap, he enjoyed looking through the large windshield of the bus, then he got out at the Hvezda Restaurant in Klise (three stations before Cottex), he passed through streets full of gardens and villas (he likes to walk) and at the Cottex entrance gate he punched in at precisely 7:00 (if he had stayed on all the way to Cottex, on the one hand he would have forfeited his walk, on the other hand he would have punched in unnecessarily early).

With his briefcase of serious mien and a gloomy and strict expression on his face, he passed through the Cottex courtyard, climbed to the third floor, right above the cafeteria, and with his personal key unlocked the glass door with its six notices of his own making (he likes to draw):

PS-VTEI	STUDY ROOM	PTK
7-1	7-1	1-3

QUIET!	READING ROOM	RESPECTABLE
7-3	1-3	PEOPLE
		KNOCK!

PS-VTEI and PTK, as well as study room and reading room, were a single large room with two windows looking out on Strizov Mountain (a beautiful view) and another window looking out on the courtyard (a useful view), walls lined all the way to the ceiling with bookshelves, and in the corner by a window two desks: a dark-colored one for the business of PS-VTEI and a light-colored one for PTK (in reality, however, the dark desk served for *correspondence*, while the light one served as an armory for the years-long war which Engineer Drapal had been waging against the Cottex management).

Kazimir Drapal suddenly cast aside both his briefcase and his gloomy expression, for a while he entertained himself with the view of Strizov Mountain (he was reflecting on the similarity of November and March), three times he walked around the room (he likes to walk) and then greedily he read the newspaper from the first to the last line (he pondered over the prospects for legalizing divorce in Italy, he sighed over Indonesia's unsatisfactory balance of payments, he imagined himself as a partisan leader in Angola and then right away cast himself in the part of a Portuguese imperialist, he felt sympathy for the victims of the earthquake in Burma, and he condemned student riots in Tokyo), this all took him about two hours (there's nothing in the papers nowadays!), and then with pleasure he ate his morning snack.

Once more enjoying the view of Strizov Mountain (it's strange that the oak leaves don't fall), he walked three more times around his workspace, then he looked out the window into the courtyard (Look, there's Dr. Lojda talking to Tanicka again, he engraved it in his memory), and with pleasure he seated himself at the light, *de jure* PTK desk, *de facto*, however, his armory.

Engineer Drapal was conducting a years-long war for recognition. According to the ministerial nomenclature diagram, he had the right, as director of PS-VTEI, to request the services of another person, whom *de facto* he didn't really want (his thinking would be disturbed), but *de jure* he fought a prolonged (and well-informed) war over it. Besides this main front, Engineer Drapal had opened up a second front in the war for recognition: according to written agreements (made a number of years before) he was to receive for his PTK functions (which involved practically no work at all) a quarterly supplement of 300 crowns, which to be sure were paid him in the form of a bonus of 100 crowns added into each month's salary, but this way it became part of his salary as director of PS-VTEI, in consequence of which his work as director of PTK remained not only unappreciated, but totally unrecognized.

Glancing into the thick files of his monthly *Report on the Activities of PTK* (for years now he had been copying and re-copying it with only the slightest of changes: no one had read one in years), Engineer Drapal sat down at his ancient Urania typewriter and turned out another edition of the *Report* for the month of October, a modestly revised (in its word order) argument for the necessity of assigning more working forces to PS-VTEI, a further demand for the awarding of a quarterly premium for the activities of PTK, all in quadruplicate (no one had read any of this in years), he took delight in his neat paragraphs on stationery with the letterhead of natl. enterpr. Cottex, even on the pink copies, then he carried his day's production off to the mail room, where he picked up his own mail: a letter from Czechoslovak Television in Prague, a letter from the Pakistani embassy, and sixteen personal letters, he shuffled the letters like cards and looked forward to what he would read in them (he kept looking happily forward to there being something), and then, since it was Wednesday (and because a stroll would sharpen his appetite), he went off (as vice-chairman of the Social and Housing Committee of ZV ROH, entrusted with supervision of the Cafeteria Subcommittee) to check up on the factory kitchen.

The director of the kitchen, Jelinek, obligingly pushed a chair up to the edge of the cutting table, brought out the *Journal* for random examination, and asked:

"Lungs in cream sauce or fried meatballs?"

"A little of this, a little of that. And soup?"

"Cream of vegetable. Real real good!"

"Not for me. What's for dessert?"

"Raspberry whip. Real real spongy!"

"All right," said Engineer Drapal, and he watched with pleasure as Jelinek served him lungs with two dumplings, a fried meatball with two potatoes, and some well-drenched whip—all on small plates—on the edge of the cutting table.

Nodding his head and wrinkling his nose like a connoisseur, he ate with relish all the *samples for inspection and random examination* and made an entry in the *Journal*:

Examination of November 9: Lungs in cream sauce: taste insipid, appearance unattractive, overall within the norms. Fried meatballs: within the norms. Whip: delicious. Quite within the norms and satisfactory.

When signing the *Journal* he reproached Jelinek:

"I've just received six more claims that kitchen personnel are going home with suspiciously full satchels!"

"My God, sir, there isn't any truth in that at all!"

"I will be forced to carry out spot-checks at the gate!"

"My God, sir, and when would that take place?"

"Tomorrow?"

"My God, sir, not tomorrow! There'll be pig liver—"

"Then day after tomorrow. And if anyone's caught I'll take the strictest measures!"

"But that's self-evident, sir, and quite fair. Tomorrow I'll send you some sample livers—soft as butter!"

In conclusion, Kazimir Drapal checked whether all the employees in the kitchen were wearing the prescribed head coverings and the prescribed footwear, thoroughly and with relish he looked the women over (he liked to look at women) and then suddenly he froze: beside the machine for peeling potatoes there was a piece right out of a film magazine—

"You've got a new worker here. . ." he croaked.

"That's Sonya Cechova, they kicked her out of Cottonola and then she goofed off for a whole month. But she isn't a bad worker—and what a looker!"

"Have you taught her the hygienic principles?"

"My God, sir, the moment she got here!"

"I'll do an inspection. Hey, you over there — come here!" and Kazimir Drapal looked the new worker over at length, *mmmm*, he thought, while with a gloomy and strict expression he put questions to her concerning washing your hands, her health certificate, and her previous jobs.

"So you were studying for the degree exam. . ." he repeated, staring at her in wonder.

"Yes, sir. But I've already learned everything and I'll take the exam in the spring."

"Do you like books?"

"Very much, sir. I read everything . . . newspapers, encyclopedias, even novels," Sonya told him, and she smiled at him prettily.

"We'll see," said Engineer Drapal, and he backed out of the kitchen.

"I'll have her bring you the samples," said Chef Jelinek, "Real real delicate!"

Kazimir walked around his workspace a good fourteen times,

and not quite there in spirit, he sat down at his dark *correspondence* desk: Czechoslovak Television thanks him in its letter for his suggestion to broadcast, every half hour, the appeal "Turn down your T.V., your neighbor may not care for this program!" and informed him that the letter would be sent on to the appropriate office, the Pakistani Embassy thanked him for his congratulations on the anniversary of the Islamic Republic of Pakistan, and all sixteen personal letters had the same text:

TAKE WALKS - REFLECT - STRIVE

This is the highest wisdom, deciphered from the secret emerald tablet of the lamasery in Kathmandu (capital city of the Kingdom of Nepal), and it has been sent to you for good luck. It has gone around the world 9x and you should value the good luck it brings just to you. If you govern your affairs according to it, you will have 21 days of good luck. But you must send 10 copies of this letter to people you know and even to people you don't (you may use the telephone book, for instance). In that way good luck will not pass you by. One candy maker in Lima (capital city of Peru) won 600,000 dollars and one librarian in Bangkok (capital city of Thailand) discovered that he was related to the Emperor of Japan, but when he traveled to Japan by ship he drowned, since he had broken the chain. Govern yourself by the highest wisdom, send out 10 copies, and see what happens in the next 21 days. Good luck!

In early spring Kazimir Drapal sent out fifty copies of this epistle (he liked to write letters), but the chain was somehow broken and hundreds of epistles came back to him (he liked to get letters), today he wasn't up to concentrating on his favorite correspondence, again and again he got up from his dark desk, marched around his workspace, and sat back down, absent-mindedly he wrote the Pakistani ambassador thanks for his thanks, and he did it in Dutch (he had mastered nine languages), he tore it out of the typewriter, crumpled it, and threw it away, walked twice around the workspace, imagined Sonya Cechova as his new assistant, swallowed to no effect, Take walks—reflect—strive! he said to himself out loud, and then he swept his *correspondence* into the upper drawer of the dark desk and with determination seated himself at the light one, like an artillery squadron he spread out his thick files on the desk, including copies of his endless petitions, reminders, protests, and analyses relating to the need to supply PS-VTEI with another worker, with eight carbon copies of everything and the cadence of a heavy machine-gun, he proceeded to turn out a monstrous number of documents, as if *at least* 600,000 dollars were at stake, *plus* a castle in Japan.

Through the window where I hand out meals all I can see of the men are their hands and their stomachs. But from these I can learn surprisingly much about them—

They wouldn't take me on as a worker on the highway, and since I need both a job and a place to live, I took the only thing they had available that day at the People's Commission — and now I'm an assistant in the Cottex kitchen.

I peel potatoes, slice bread and dumplings, make puddings — just like for the Volrabs at the Hubertus, but the work here is rather more businesslike — it's all done by machine, you work only eight hours a day, and it's decently paid.

"Don't get the idea you're going to goof off here!" Chef Jelinek raked me over the coals the first thing when they took me to see him, and the whole first day he stood behind me. But he is capable of appreciating good work, and when it occurred to me to decorate the fried meatballs with some left-over pickled red cabbage that would only have been thrown away, he praised me: "Real real nice!" and stroked my head. And when I demonstrated "Mexican goulash" à la Volrab (it looks beautiful, tastes sharp as a knife, and you can whip up a whole kettle of it out of nothing at all), he said, "Real real good!" and threw me a bar of chocolate to be shaved.

"And starting tomorrow bring a satchel!" he added (all the women here carried them and took them back where the ice-boxes are), I took this to be a command and bought myself a satchel like those all the women here in the kitchen carried, and Chef Jelinek beckoned to me then with his finger and in back at an icebox he loaded my satchel with a fine-looking steak, a bottle of Znojmo pickles, and a pouch of milk. "To let you know that now you're one of us!" he said, and he crammed into my satchel a slab of butter ("Real real fresh!").

Through the window where I hand out meals all I can see of the men are their hands and their stomachs, I try to guess what the men look like (I'm studying for more degrees than just the *gymnasium* one), and everyone in the kitchen laughs and shows surprise at how accurate my guesses are.

Nervous, pale, sweaty hands with manicured nails and a stomach like a sink turned inside out—I guess: "His marriage is a failure and he's got a guilty conscience, because he chases young girls and does almost nothing at home."

"Then you know Dr. Lojda?" the entire kitchen is astonished.

"No. And Dr. Lojda has a nervous stomach."

Two brown, boyish arms with tattoos (there were unmistakable marks left from attempts to erase them) protrude from fluttering shirtsleeves, and the hands have thick, roughed-up nails (there are unmistakable marks from attempts to beautify them—most likely made with a pocket knife), hurriedly they pick up a lunch tray and they hold it tenaciously, a flat, hard stomach. I guess: "He was in prison, but perhaps only a military one. He's a bachelor and has no mother. And there's a girl he's fond of."

"How did you know that young Tejnora was in a military prison for three years—" "And that he's single—" "And that he goes out with Uska Kamenikova, from the warehouse—" the entire kitchen is astonished.

"I don't know all that, but young Tejnora is a fine fellow."

Only once did I fail to make a guess: when I recognized the young, well-washed (to a rosy pink) hands, their nails trimmed short, and the firm (and white) stomach of Jakub Jagr.

I live in the Cottex singles dorm: a large hall with massive masonry arches between tiny windows (between the arches a wire is stretched and on it are hangers with the girls' clothes, the few wardrobes there are stand out in the hall) and the only furniture are the rows of iron beds, all of them double-deckers, between them narrow aisles leading to a little square in the center where there's a table without a chair.

Twenty-six girls and women live here with me and the quiet is about what you find at a train station, any hour of the day or night (at Cottex they work straight through in 6-, 8-, 12-, and 16-hour shifts, on Sundays and holidays too), girls come and go, alarmclocks ring and radios clash, and trampling, laughter, shouts, and song resound through the hall.

Few women live here more than a week or two, they move on to better dorms, they go away to other plants and towns, they get married or go live with a friend (the last are the most likely to come back).

Through the iron bars on my bed I can see the girls and women wash, comb their hair, and make themselves up, go to bed (morning, noon, or night) and get up (night, morning, or noon), two by two they boogie to music on the radio or get sentimental and close their eyes, they get letters, good and bad (but not everyone), they write letters on suitcases on their laps (everyone), they snort, they babble, they rave, they weep, and they sleep lying down with their arms behind their heads (these women are right nearby).

Afternoons I stroll through town (I don't have to go to the reading room anymore, and I only go to the library on Thursdays to take out novels) and I look at people (I can never get enough of that), sometimes I have dinner in a restaurant (I get eleven hundred a month: I'm rich) and sometimes I stay home and prepare marvelous dinners with what I bring home in my satchel, evenings I sit on my bed, my suitcase on my lap, and write Manek letters about the new life he's assigned me. . .

I'm starting again for the third time now—

Then I lie down on my back with my hands behind my head and dream of him.

Mornings the men's hands and stomachs, I pass them food through the window—this is my job and my vocation—I feed them and I identify them through the window.

Afternoons I look at them on the streets of the town, they

come out of stores and go into restaurants, they drive cars, streetcars, and trucks, they walk with their girlfriends and their wives, but if they're walking without them, then they're going after them or away from them or they're waiting for them— otherwise they come up and speak to me, or at least stare at me (as do many of those who are walking with their girlfriends or their wives) and I smile prettily at them all (I need them: what would I be without them? And they interest me and make me happy), I already know the security officer who is "on duty in the main square every Tuesday and Friday until eight o'clock in the evening and after that has twenty-four hours *completely* free—" (as he reminds me again and again: I smile at him prettily and manage not to look too foolish doing it), I know the handsome Petr Junk pushing his baby carriage with his beauti- ful wife Marie, I know the hairy Vit from Cottonola hauling Ivanka in Cenek's red Skoda MB and I know Cenek, who secretly stuffs himself with sweets at the milk bar (where they're cheapest), I know Lumirek, gawking at the jewelry store windows and then buying copper wire, for buttons officers' gold stars, and glass Christmas tree ornaments from which to assemble new cufflinks, I know Petrik Metelka, whose ears are red as shepherds around a graceful fifteen-year-old gypsy girl in an outfit made of glossy red artificial leather, a cigarette between her painted, childish lips, I know two near-pensioners from Vseborice who guzzle Plzner at the World Cafeteria, I know the train dispatcher, whom I got on well with at the Palace Restaurant, the dentist who courted me at the Café Bohemia, my young and clever engineer from the glassworks, who sacrificed a good hundred crowns to have tea with me at the Hotel Savoy, I know them all, I know what they want and what they need, what they think of themselves and the sort of impression they want to make, and I know how to deal with them, to arouse them and to pour cold water on them, to listen to them and to manage them without their knowing it, and perhaps even how to make them happy — oh, Manek . . . so that one day they will build me a home.

I smile prettily at everyone, they speak to me or at least look at me (I know that all of them would like to have me), I guess what sort of lives I might have lived with them, and in the evening I lie in bed with my hands behind my head and dream of them all, all those whom I would like to bring together in one husband, my Manek.

Towards morning I was suddenly awakened by tramping, shouts, and confusion: in the bed above me Slavka (a tall, skinny, forty-year-old blonde who sings better than anyone else here) had been seized with sharp labor pains.

Outside the iron bars at the foot and the head of my bed, racing and leaping, were bare women's calves and thighs, bare women's hands reaching toward the bed above me and bearing the groaning Slavka down from her bed, and like the sacred Host they place her on the table, piled high with blankets (all the books, bottles, plates, eating utensils, and framed photos of men have been swept onto the floor), tenderly they wrap her in sheets and blankets and put four pillows under her head — a burning desire to help Slavka grows within me and I squeeze my way through a crowd of trembling, agitated women, I push away warm arms, chests, stomachs, and thighs and am pushed away by them in turn, we all want to help her somehow, any way we can.

And when two male nurses take her off to the health center (we hand Slavka over to them reluctantly: they're only men), none of us can fall asleep and for a long time we don't scatter to our beds, we talk about Slavka (the one who did it to her is married and long gone) and she comes out a saint.

"Her favorite song is the one about a star. . ."

The hunchbacked girl, who has been here the longest and who sleeps right by the door, begins to sing and one after another we join in, the song flows together and gets louder, outside the windows the sun is coming up and the dull glow is coming in through the windows underneath our dresses, which are hanging on the line, those who are coming in from the night shifts and those who are getting up to join the morning shifts stop at the doorway and in the aisles and once again all of us sing the song about a star, about longing and hope.

Over lunch in the plant cafeteria a lot of business can be taken care of — time is more than money, Engineer Jakub Jagr (recently promoted to the rank of manager at the initiative of the plant director himself and entrusted by him with the important task of continuity) set his lunch tray down next to Engineer Ludvik Ludvik (he is important and powerful) and even before the first spoonful of soup he started doing business.

"That could conceivably be interesting. . ." Engineer Ludvik said slowly, "but it isn't clear how you would resolve the problem of continuity within the limits of feasible investment . . . Jagr! Has something happened to you?"

About to put a soup spoon in his mouth (his *open* mouth), Jakub Jagr froze and turned pale, as if he had just beheld a *fata morgana*: through the kitchen issue window he had caught sight of Sonya's hair, now growing back like *flowing, shining copper*— and then her eyes *like warm moist emeralds*—

"I was asking you how would resolve the problem of *continuity* within the limits of *feasible* investment—" Engineer Ludvik Ludvik repeated, quite without effect: in his present state Jakub Jagr couldn't even resolve problems of continuity involving the flushing of toilets—not even if he had had at his disposal *a billion pounds sterling*. Lunch with the important and powerful L.L. ended painfully.

Soaked with icy sweat (however, his temperature was a warm 98.6° Fahrenheit and his pulse 190) Jakub walked back and forth along the dark corridor in front of the cafeteria, in total confusion he neglected to greet Irma Ingrisova (even more powerful than the plant director) and nearly ran into Chief Engineer Ryvola. Jakub, now quite incapable of appearing before his own subordinates, locked himself in the WC (but you can't pace there) and then quite in despair ran upstairs to the plant's technical library (PTK).

"Greetings and welcome—" Engineer Kazimir Drapal blurted out from behind his light desk, he was amazed (normally no one ever comes to the PTK), he got up quickly to wait on (and by the same token evict as quickly as possible) his young colleague who was rising so successfully at Cottex (Kazimir Drapal knows everything about Cottex), "—what can I do for you, Mr. Jagr?"

"I just. . . It struck me simply. . . Have you got . . . a Portuguese dictionary?" Jakub said in total confusion.

"Of course we do, naturally, certainly. I have the large Zimmermann-Jara, the small Dobsinsky-Schmitze, an Italo-Portuguese dictionary of marine terminology, and *Portugal in Pictures*, of course that's in Swedish and from the year 1893 . . . Perhaps it would be best if you were to leave your text here and in the course of . . . let's say two to three weeks . . . or a month I will give you an authorized translation in six copies."

"Y-y-yes, or rather, no. . ." Jakub forced the words out, "I only. . . I only need a couple of expressions . . . What's the Portuguese for continuity?"

"Kontinualisacion," said Kazimir Drapal (admittedly he didn't know Portuguese, but he did know nine similar Indo-European languages and with the aid of an array of dictionaries, as well as his imagination, he might even have translated a Korean patent application).

"Y-y-yes. And *investment*?"

"Investicion," Kazimir Drapal conjectured, without moving an eyebrow.

"Aha . . . and *copper*? *Emeralds*?"

"Kupro," said Kazimir, gazing out the window at Strizov Mountain with a bored look on his face (if the oak doesn't shed its leaves, is the oak not then a coniferous tree? he reflected), and without moving an eyebrow he said "Emraldos."

"Yes, certainly. You've been a great help to me. I have to go now . . . I see you've got a mass of work and I wouldn't wish to . . ."

"I'm really over my head in work!" Kazimir rejoiced (Jagr

would be an immensely valuable ally in my war for recognition and for that wonderful girl in the kitchen) and in a few seconds (he had been doing this frequently and for many years now) he'd piled on Jakub monstrous heaps of his endless petitions, reminders, protests, and analyses concerning the need for an assistant at PS-VTEI, and so persuasive was his insistence that even the accounts inspector would have supported Sonya out of his own pay.

"Yes . . . Of course . . . Certainly. . ." Jakub replied, thinking (like all the others he was caught off guard) how to escape from there, and when no end appeared to be in sight he hastily walked to the door and, with his hand on the handle (like so many others caught off guard), announced: "Certainly you are one hundred percent correct, but you know, where money. . ."

"But it would be practically *free*, for a mere eleven hundred— who would do the job today for that kind of money—"

"Whom would you get for that—" said Jakub, already out in the corridor.

"But I've already found a suitable assistant, and she'd be cheap as an Indian—" Kazimir called out, he was already in the corridor himself, right behind Jakub, who was running down the stairs, "an immensely intelligent girl from the kitchen with excellent qualifications and well-developed talents, a marked interest in technical as well as all other kinds of literature—"

"What's her name?" said Jakub, and suddenly he stopped (one floor down by now).

"Sonya Cechova, and—"

A minute later Jakub was already back at Kazimir's light desk, rethinking the idea (here I'd be able to come see her whenever I liked) he pushed away the files of Kazimir's unsuccessful barbs ("Eleven hundred, you said?" was all he asked) so he could reach the telephone and ask the plant director (his benign protector) to supply an assistant to the staff of PS-VTEI, "who would also be available for assistance with research on continuity."

"Engineer Drapal recommends a young woman comrade,

employed at this time in our kitchen," Jakub said into the mouthpiece, ". . .eleven hundred . . . I think so . . . I would train her myself, if need be . . . thank you . . . The comrade can start on Monday," he told Kazimir and left PS-VTEI, PTK, study room and reading room.

At 3:30 Jakub Jagr walked down Valley Street past the Jagrs' garden fence with its blue gate, and in through the silver-gray gate next door, into the Orts' garden, and entered the yellow villa which was now his home.

In the hall Mother Ortova (his mother-in-law) glanced up at him from her rocking chair (father-in-law Ort would come downstairs from his room on the third floor in time for dinner).

"How's work?"

"Nothing special."

"Kamila's upstairs."

"That's where I'm going."

(The wedding of Engineer Jakub Jagr and Kamila Ortova had taken placed on September 22, precisely on the date already fixed last Christmas vacation).

Jakub climbed the stairs to the newlyweds' living room on the second floor (yellowish furniture of natural oak made illegally by former master carpenter Janecek for an even 30,000 crowns) and kissed his wife Kamila on the forehead (she was smoking again).

"How's work?"

"Nothing special. What are you reading?"

"Apfelbaum's essay on alienation."

"I'm going to take a bath."

Jakub spent two hours in the bathtub (as opposed to his usual fifty minutes).

"You've been bathing for two hours—" said Kamila.

"I was thinking. Are you still reading?"

"If you want, I can put it down and we can play some canasta."

"No thanks. I'm going to take a look at the car."

In the garage (exactly the same as the Jagrs': the two families had built them together) Jakub unlocked the car, to keep from being disturbed (I can only be by myself in the bathtub and in the garage, but my wife even comes looking for me here) he took off the tachometer and all its multicolored wires and, with his face against the steering wheel, he remained there without moving until dinner time.

"What's wrong with you today?" asked Kamila, wearing her nightgown of yellow nylon (the feel of nylon makes me shudder and Kamila will always be like a relative to me), and she lit a Peer cigarette (Father Ort spoils her: he wants to have a grandchild as soon as possible) when Jakub, after an hour's simulation of reading, reached his hand out toward his bedside lamp.

"I've got a headache. Good night, dear," said Jakub, and he turned off the light (from now on I'll be afraid of the dark and afraid that Kamila will turn off her light at the same time as me).

"My love—" whispered Kamila, and she turned off her bedside lamp.

Two days later Staff Sergeant Jagr summoned (with four piercing whistles from the bay observation-window of the white villa) his son Jakub to the Jagrs' garage (the women in the yellow and white villas couldn't breathe for all the suspense), he banged the heavy doors shut behind him and, tugging at his short gray crewcut, he stood on the right side of the blue family van (Jakub had taken his place on the left).

"What's wrong?" he barked in the darkness.

"Sonya," Jakub said with difficulty.

"Hmm!! Hm! Nonsense. Hmm! Hm! HMM! HM-MMM!!!"

The staff sergeant raged as never before. Of course, Dad wants to have grandchildren as soon as possible. It's hard to fool him and even harder to make him happy.

I can't live with Sonya, and even less without her—

"What will I be doing?"

"Everything and nothing!" Engineer Kazimir Drapal cried out in joy, my new boss disappeared behind a row of bookshelves and then reappeared: "Be happy here!" but then he disappeared again behind another row of shelves and reappeared: "We'll be happy here together!" and again he ducked behind a row of shelves and kept walking round and round his maze — it seems that this gentleman likes to walk.

On Saturday Chef Jelinek crammed my satchel close to breaking in honor of my departure: ". . .so you won't forget us up there!", then he gave me a greasy kiss on the forehead and shoved another whole roll of ham salami under my arm ("Real real succulent!"), on Sunday I fed his gifts to the whole singles dorm, and on Monday morning I took over my new position as *documentarist of PS-VTEI and assistant librarian of PTK* for twelve hundred crowns a month, as had been recorded in the letter of appointment.

"Those scoundrels!" Engineer Drapal vituperated over my appointment. "Bandits! Villains!"

"But I'm quite satisfied with the pay."

"Sonya, dear child. It's true, of course, they did give you a hundred more then the official minimum—I won't hide from you that I worked hard for that—but that wretched hundred destroyed my efforts over many years to obtain recognition for a four-year bonus for PTK as well as recognition for PTK as an independent functioning unit . . . Pecuniarily, it comes out exactly the same, but my long-time battle is frustrated, my prestige is besmirched and defiled—" thus lamenting, Drapal ducked behind a row of shelves, but reemerging he again shouted in triumph: "—but on the main front a colossal victory has been won: I now have an assistant! *Victoria! Victory! Victoire! Sieg!*"

"Everything and nothing!" was the answer my new boss gave again and again to my repeated questions concerning what I was going to do there (it was almost time for lunch and still all he could do was shout about his victory), *Take walks—observe—reflect!* I'll tell you the rest when the time comes.

So I began to walk (since that was now my job and what I was paid to do) around the sets of bookshelves (they stand at an angle to the walls, they reach all the way up to the ceiling, and there are fourteen of them in all: all of them are bulging like liver sausage), my boss walked at the same time I did, and when he met me he shouted in triumph and I smiled at him prettily.

It wasn't long before I got a nice grasp of what was what. The first set of bookshelves was boringly crammed with the black (and dusty) spines of bound journals, including the *Chemisches Zentralblatt* (from 1905), the *Referativnij dzurnal* (from 1945), and *Chemical Abstracts* (sporadic issues), the remaining space was filled with stray volumes, such as the *Jahrbuch der Pharmazie* or the *Czech Bulletin of the Society of Retail Druggists and Chemists*. This first set of bookshelves carried the sign SCIENCE AND TECHNOLOGY, written in black ink.

The second set of bookshelves, FOREIGN-LANGUAGE DICTIONARIES (the sign was written in crayon and each language was painted with violet watercolor), was somewhat more colorful and the spines here were tremendous, I was most fascinated by the Tamil-Urdu Dictionary.

"Do you know Tamil or Urdu?" I remarked to my boss as I passed him.

"Take walks—observe—reflect and everything will become clear to you," he said and disappeared behind a row of shelves.

It all began to become clear to me when I discovered that *all twelve remaining* sets of shelves carried the identical sign MISCELLANEOUS (each of the twelve signs was made differently, all they had in common was that they were multicolored) and *miscellaneous* they were: right from the start, alongside the 1944 timetable of the German State Railways was a splendidly illustrated *Woman in Pictures*, and beside it an *Intermediate Theory of Chess,* and then *How to Spend 365 Days a Year, The Beekeeper's Handbook,* and *You Are Becoming a Young Man.*

This last title caught my interest, but hardly had I read that ". . . more than any other time of life, you must now keep your restraint and observe the rules," than out from behind the set of bookshelves (I hadn't even heard the door open) came Jakub Jagr. He said nothing and gazed at me dolefully. But it's the man who's supposed to greet the woman, so I said nothing and gazed at him calmly over my open book.

"Sonya. . ." he finally got out.

"Jakub?"

"How are things with you?"

"Thanks for asking. And you?"

"Always the same. . ."

With deep satisfaction I saw the wedding ring on Jakub's hand—

"You've already married Kamila?"

"Yes. Already. . ."

—the only still unfulfilled command from Manek *LEAVE JAKUB TO KAMILA* was now completely fulfilled.

"Congratulations. And give my best to your wife."

"Sonya, I must tell you—"

"If you would *kindly* allow me, Mr. Jagr," Engineer Drapal suddenly intervened in the conversation after emerging from behind a set of shelves, "*my* new documentarist and assistant librarian has not yet received her training and so *kindly* make do with *me.* What do you need to say in Portuguese *today*?"

"Today—nothing," Jakub grinned with rage. "Only—this is a personal request—translate *I'll come back again!* for me."

"Ich komme nie wieder," said Engineer Drapal, without moving an eyebrow. "'I'll never come again.' Ya nepridu uzhe nikogda—" and went on in other languages until Jakub withdrew from my new workplace.

"Do you know him, Sonya?" asked Drapal, ducking behind the bookshelves and popping back out again.

"I worked at his house as a servant."

"I hope you have no desire to do that again."

"Not the slightest."

"Nor do *I* intend to be his servant. He's a stuck-up technical boor. Conquering is difficult, but more difficult is holding the conquered territory. Until you've been fully trained—until you've read all these books—I'll deal with outsiders myself."

"But *I'd* like to deal with outsiders—"

"Fortunately it's been years since anyone came here."

Fortunately, however, from Tuesday on more than enough people visited our PS-VTEI (my boss seemed surprised) and there were more and more of them (my boss was truly panicked) and in a week crowds of them were standing around our shelves, so that during his walks my boss often had to squeeze between them.

The women came only once, looked me over thoroughly, and went off all fired up. But the women will most likely never love me.

With the men it was easy, I smiled prettily at each of them and in a few days our PTK and PS-VTEI had regular customers, like a bar with a renowned kitchen (and a pretty waitress). They would stand around the shelves (my boss personally carried all four chairs down to the cafeteria) with an Italo-Polish dictionary, the Berlin telephone directory, or the manual *You Are Becoming a Young Man* in their hands and try to strike up a conversation with me.

My boss stood guard over me like a dragon, with his mobility he managed to turn away up to twenty suitors a day (in the same way I managed to have a nice talk with each of them) and in response to my requests he finally set me my first task: to reclassify all the books on the *MISCELLANEOUS* shelves according to field. It was a task that resembled tying sand with straw: on one hand each book was its own field (only the travel guides formed a kind of unit, from *Hiking Trips through the Krusne Mountains* to a city map of Honolulu), on the other hand my boss took around a hundred books a day off the shelves and when he returned them he rarely guessed correctly where they'd originally come from (because, constantly on the move, he covered at least ten yards in the ten seconds he glanced through each book).

Except for Ladi Tringl (a good-looking boy, every day a different pair of trousers stuck out from beneath his labcoat, I counted eleven of them and then gave up) and Ivos Rybicka (a very good-looking brunet), Jakub Jagr came to see me most often, he stood behind me with a book in his hand and once he suddenly stroked my hair—the touch lasted only a moment, but it brought my boss out from behind a set of shelves (he kept an eye on Jakub), he took him by the shoulders and as with a cat into his own puddle he stuck Jakub's nose into *The Automatization of Processes III, Physico-Chemical Tables*, and *Industrial Cooling*.

And so I got to know one Cottex technologist after another and in the short intervals between the last and the next I took a look at the books and placed *Woman in Pictures* beside *History of the World's Volcanoes, Male Anatomy* beside *Let's Build a House*, and longed more and more not only to *learn* endlessly about everything there is, but to begin TO DO THEM—

And so for the first time I smiled prettily at Jakub (he lay in wait for the moment when my boss went off to inspect the kitchen) when he offered me "an interesting, responsible, and important job with the possibility of promotion" in his new division—

"I'd love to!" I said without any hesitation, and Jakub reverently touched the hair on my temple — but then suddenly he jerked his hand away. A man had entered the library, I had so far never seen him whole (only handing out food through the kitchen window: self-assured, composed, calm—perhaps too much so . . . as if he were dozing—and the small belly of a well-fed man of forty. A calm and contented marriage).

Jakub greeted him *very* politely, like a schoolboy caught in the act he muttered something about the invariable aspects of desorption (the newcomer didn't pay any attention to him, he was looking me over quite calmly) and slipped away.

The new man had (in addition to the hands and stomach I already knew) a regular sort of face with gray eyes, half closed as if things didn't interest him very much, on the whole he looked respectable.

"I'm Ludvik," he said (as if it bored him).

"Sonya Cechova."

"My boys have told me about you."

"I hope nothing bad."

"On the contrary. Are you satisfied here?"

"Yes, so far."

"So far?"

"I'd like to get something more out of life. . ."

"Something more."

"A lot more!"

"Yes. Certainly. *Obviously*," he said (as if mocking me?) and asked: "And what are you willing to give it in return?"

"Everything."

"*Everything. . .*" he repeated (as if surprised?), he bowed slightly to me, smiled even more slightly, and disappeared like a ghost.

"Some guy named Ludvik was here—" I announced to my boss when he had returned from his kitchen inspection with a shiny mouth and a mild, all-embracing expression.

"Madre de Dios!" My boss was frightened. "And what did he want?"

"To know whether I was satisfied here."

"And you said?"

"Yes, so far."

"And he said?"

"He wanted to know what I meant by *so far*."

"'For Mike's love!' And you said?"

"That I wanted all sorts of things out of life."

"You'll have everything if you take walks, reflect, and strive—and he said?"

"He said *yes*—"

"Donnerwetter!" Engineer Kazimir Drapal was barely able to

exclaim, and by the end of the shift he had covered a good ten miles of shelves.

The soft, thick nylon curtains on the cream-colored window are open just enough to give Engineer Ludvik Ludvik (L.L.) a view of the treetops. There are only a few last leaves now, brownish red . . . so few you can almost count them. With the ability to count comes sadness. I've been counting all my life, but still I'm not quite sad enough—Huh, L.L. thought, and without haste he stood up, stretched (I used to exercise), and went to take a bath.

He slowly soaped himself, calmly looking at his body, which appeared broken in half by the surface of the water. We start the day by lying in our own filth (I used to shower in ice water—but we didn't have a bathroom then and that's the only kind of water there was), huh.

In front of the mirror he carefully finished soaping and then shaved his face with light strokes. Huh, in the mirror I've looked just the same for years.

He kissed his wife Zora on the forehead (she gets up early, but after breakfast she goes back to bed) and his nineteen-year-old daughter Lanka on the mouth (I love you more than anyone else on earth, more than myself . . . but that wouldn't be very much. Huh!), Zora served him a cup of Indian tea and he plunged a silver spoon into scrambled eggs.

"Just look what Lanka has dreamed up for breakfast again!" Zora complained.

"Why not? It might have an amusing flavor," said L.L., gazing amiably at his daughter's breakfast: orange slices covered with cream and lots of pepper.

"But I don't eat breakfast to amuse myself!" Lanka said rebelliously.

"Really?" L.L. smiled at her (poor girl: she insisted on studying in Prague and had chosen philosophy as her major—huh). "But then why so much pepper?" he asked when Lanka kept pouring pepper on her already well-peppered orange.

"So it doesn't taste so boring!"

"Oranges taste boring?" L.L. was surprised. (Lanka keeps astounding me: I love her for it).

"Like everything!" cried Lanka, and with disgust she spat out the orange, so overpeppered it was inedible.

"Everything? You might be exaggerating a little."

"*Everything!*" cried Lanka, she went to the freezer, got out a frankfurter hard as glass, and bit into it with gusto.

Everything . . . who said that to me? . . . Why, it was that new girl from the cafeteria. She intends to give *everything*.

"How's school?" L.L. asked, peacefully devouring his eggs.

"Like that orange," Lanka said contemptuously, and she courageously ate up her ice in sausage casing.

"So give it up—just like the orange," L.L. proposed to his daughter.

"But Ludvik, what would she do then?" Zora was frightened (Ludvik and Lanka have been joking together for some fifteen years, but it always frightens Zora).

"A place has just opened in the plant cafeteria," said L.L.

"Easy," Lanka said and added jokingly, "Don't rush things unnecessarily, Daddy. Anyway, you wouldn't let me work there."

If we don't intend to give *everything*, what can we expect? At least *a lot?* Or, modestly, at least *something more?* Evidently far less. But what should I really expect?

"Of course not, darling," said L.L., and he wiped his mouth with a napkin, kissed Lanka on the mouth (the taste of ice and youth) and Zora on the forehead (go and rest, my love), went down to the garage, and drove off to work.

Eng. L. Ludvik occupies an unpretentious but influential position at natl. enter. Cottex (he designed it himself and now holds on to it firmly): as Director of Production he functions as the irreplaceable head of a staff of often changing (and variously talented) commanders of an army. The army is a respectable one: 26 branch plants in Bohemia and Moravia and an adjustment center in Prague, the apparatus of the enterprise's directorship (armed with, e.g., a central computer), 22,830 employees, and a turnover of a billion and growing. L.L. with his small (but high quality) division constitutes the operational wing of the general staff.

L.L. likes to count (it amuses him and he's great at it). His telexes spew forth whole pads of numbers which Lada Tringl (production) and Ivos Rybicka (materials) work over and appraise so that Ida Papouskova (secretary, but she has to work, since L.L. doesn't really need a secretary: L.L. has a perfect memory, does not see visitors, and does not drink coffee) spends every day until 10:45 preparing A5 index cards, over which L.L. smokes a Player's Navy Cut cigarette (it was Lanka who showed me how to smoke) and then, soon after 11:00, the management reads the exhaustive appraisal on the cards of everything of significance that occurred at Cottex in the course of the preceding twenty-four hours. Having been asked (in principle only then. For years now only when asked. Years ago I used to argue and fight with them—huh), he would recommend a suitable remedy which either would work (if they followed his advice) or they would later feel sorry they didn't follow his advice (but by then either the deadline hadn't been met or the company ended up a few hundred thousand poorer).

Over the years L.L. had built up a perfect chess-like system of data retrieval and processing, which by a mere glance at the file cards and at the latest telex, and with only a bit of cogitation, enabled him to ascertain, with a high degree of precision, how much hydroxide of soda Cottex 11 will consume by the end of the February, whether it is feasible to transfer a Polish order from Cottex 22 to Cottex 09, and how much cheaper it is to produce an ordinary yard of canvas at Cottex 02 than at Cottex 03, 07, 14, or 26.

After doing away with the central computer and after a corresponding adjustment of the system, even that personal *bit of cogitation* dropped out (I used to like it: it gave me a thrill), so that practically all that remains is to process, in advance, the data churned out by telex (L. Tringl and I. Rybicka take care of that), carry it off to the computation center and bring back the results (I. Papouskova takes care of that), and then go to the management meeting with an A5 index card—so that now all I am is director of a kiddy post office, huh.

Years ago I used to make the rounds of the plants, in a leather jacket (Lanka wears it now to go lying around in the woods) *and knee boots* (I wear them now to go mushroom picking), *I caught workers dozing off behind their kettles or in the cab of a crane* (for years now I've been sleeping regularly from 11:00 to 7:00, no dreams), *spent hours standing by reactors, centrifuges, and especially next to scales* (it's been a long time since I've been on the production floor of any Cottex) *and then with the management, just roused out of bed, stammering in coats tossed over pajamas* (for years now I've only talked to them on the telephone), *dictated how much they could actually supply and, from that moment on, how much they would be supplying* (correspondence with the branch plants is handled by L. Tringl (production) and I. Rybicka (materials), and I. Papouskova submits them to me for my signature). Huh.

"Ivos, what's new?" L.L. asked his materials manager, I. Rybicka.

"Everything normal, sir," the materials manager announced, without looking up from a telex.

"Did you forget to switch those carloads from nine to fourteen?"

"How could I, sir!"

"Lada, what have you got to tell me?" L.L. asked his production manager, L. Tringl.

"Things are buzzing, sir," the production manager announced without looking up from his electronic calculator.

"How about that Egyptian order?"

"It's ours to fill, sir."

"All right, fellows, but you don't seem to be *talking* to me. . ." L.L. said half-jokingly, but more likely half-seriously (if one half can be bigger than another), "tell me something *else*—"

Ivos and Lada looked at each other with surprise.

"What would that be, sir?"

"I mean something pleasant, nice, something *new*—huh."

"Should I tell him?" Ivos whispered to Lada.

"Well, if he wants to hear what's new. . ." Lada whispered to Ivos.

"There's a new girl in the library!" said Ivos, coming to life.

"Drapal snared her from the kitchen and she's a real *beaut!*" said Lada, coming to life.

"Would it be worth my while having a look at her?" L.L. smiled (Huh, he thought meanwhile).

"You bet it would!" said Ivos.

"And how!" said Lada.

Ida Papouskova (in her twenty-fourth year like others at seventy-two) forced a smile.

"I'd like to get something more out of life. . ." that new girl in the library said.

"A lot more!" she said. She's beautiful as a dream (of course, I haven't had a dream in years, and I no longer sleep during the day).

("And what are you willing to give it in return?")

"Everything," that beautiful girl said.

I *did* that, Miss, *for years and years* . . . years ago. Huh.

"Well, sir, what's she like?" Lada and Ivos grinned.

"Young," L.L. announced drily, and he sent Ida Papouskova (she was detestable as an inspector) off to the inspection division for something, and the moment she disappeared he came to life again.

"Fellows, discretely sound out what she would say to the possibility—*in this case the possibility of fulfilling a series of presuppositions and conditions*—of taking the position of secretary in the main production office for—huh—thirteen hundred."

"Goal, sir!" "That'd be wonderful!" The boys rejoiced.

"It's a quarter to one. Ivos—"

"I know—during lunch hour," Ivos said.

"I'm buzzing away already," said Lada, and he turned on his electronic calculator.

And, as with something already disposed of (L.L. had been

disposing of too many things every day, for years now), L.L. forgot about the new girl.

From the bed above me hang two tanned legs rubbing their soles together (the bed used to be Slavka's — she's in the maternity ward now, a young Rumanian girl got it and every ten minutes she throws a cigarette butt down on the floor), I am sitting on my lower bunk with my suitcase on my lap (the one table in the middle of the dorm is overflowing with mugs, glasses, plates, knives and forks, and framed photos of men) and writing a long (twenty-one pages already) letter to Manek, for advice in this my third new life:

Things are all right in the library, but it isn't the real thing, of course, it's play, and NOW I WANT SOMETHING SUBSTANTIAL—I'd say I was already sufficiently prepared.

Jakub continually (by notes, by phone, and—the moment Drapal disappears from the library—in person) tries to entice me to come to his new division for thirteen hundred crowns a month — what I'm looking for is not an extra hundred, but for *life* and *perspective* (is there much difference between them?) — and this morning Lada Tringl asked me (peeping out from beneath his white labcoat were checkered, terra-cotta-colored trousers) whether I would like to be Engineer L.L.'s secretary, in actuality a production manager's assistant, and before lunch Ivos Rybicka came to ask me about the same job (after which he invited me to go dancing with him at the Savoy: I turned him down, but smiled at him prettily). I gave both guys a clear YES (I already knew what it was like to work for Jakub Jagr; now, of course, he would work for me — he told me he loved me), but the days pass and no reply comes to my YES, while Jakub becomes more and more insistent. . .

And so advise me what I should do. When you finish your secret mission, come for me or write me to come for you.

Your Sonya

Sonya finished her letter to Manek, addressed it Manuel Mansfeld, Hotel Imperial, Liberec, sealed it (as she did, another butt flew by), ran to the main post office, sent the letter off by registered express, and treated herself to a small but elegant dinner in the restaurant at the Palace Hotel, danced with six men, paid the waiter out in the hall (so she could leave by herself), and took a roundabout walk back to her dorm where she lay with her hands behind her head (a butt fell past her every ten minutes) and dreamed.

Next morning in the library (with a little anger and lessening patience now) she faced the shelves marked *MISCELLANEOUS* and placed *Factory Farming of Calves* next to the *Newsletter of Refrigeration Technology*, and *Mushroom Atlas* next to *What the Forest Tells Us*.

Kazimir Drapal walked past, he took a book off a *top* shelf, *The Antilles—Pearl Necklace of the Caribbean*, disappeared behind another set of shelves, and then, re-emerging, he called to Sonya:

"Sonya, did you know that the city Port of Spain has a square made of white asphalt? We could take a fine walk there, don't you agree?," after which he thrust *The Antilles—Pearl Necklace of the Caribbean* back onto the *lower* shelf of a *quite different* set of shelves, from which he took *Across Argentina by Highways and Trails* and disappeared behind a set of shelves.

Lada Tringl (peeping out from beneath his white labcoat were dark-blue sailor's bell-bottoms) came early in the morning and Ivos Rybicka (he wanted to know whether I feel a *fundamental* antipathy for men) came just before lunch—no answer again from L.L., while Jakub telephoned me twice to ask when I was coming to work for him and sent me a candy box (cognac-flavored creams) packaged for overseas export and a pink letter telling me he loves me. I placed *A Catalogue of European Watermarks* next to *The Amazon: Mother of Waters*, *A Woman in the Bath* beside *We're Setting Up a Darkroom*, and took a walk into town.

The next day, shortly after lunch (nothing new from Lada Tringl in the morning nor from Ivos Rybicka just before lunch,

while Jakub sent chocolate-covered cherries and his love on
pink stationery, and he telephoned eight times) a telegraph
delivery boy drove into the courtyard on a motorcycle and
handed me an express telegram from Prague:

AT ANY COST GET A JOB WITH L.L. STOP LETTER
FOLLOWS   M.M.

Manek was going to send me a *letter*! — After so many
telegrams I certainly deserved one.

"That telegram of yours cheered you up some, didn't it!"
Drapal said enviously (he liked getting letters, but he never got
any telegrams), and he tried to read it over my shoulder.

"We're going to have to part, Mr. Drapal!"

"No! You wouldn't do that to me — Not after that truly
titanic battle I waged for you. . ."

Just then the phone rang and Jakub, for the ninth time that
day, tried to enlist me.

"No," I told him definitely. "I'm going to transfer to the main
production office!"

"Then this is my Waterloo and my Verdun," Drapal wept
and, for the rest of the shift, he trotted around the bookshelves,
I sat at his dark desk and for the rest of the shift read *Defense
Strategies in Chess*. The most modern opening is to advance the
queen's pawn, which opens the queen on the very first move.

So I went straight from Cottex to buy a sweater with a plung-
ing neckline (one that hugged me shamelessly tight) and in the
reading room of the town library, until it closed, I crammed into
my head all the encyclopedia and dictionary entries dealing
with factory production. From early the next morning I looked
in vain through Drapal's PS-VTEI, PTK, study room and reading room for anything about production that I still didn't know,
and then I spent a good hour modifying my standard-issue
white labcoat so that I could display as much as possible of my
new sweater (inconspicuously I pinned back the labcoat's lapels
all the way up to the shoulders).

The next morning Lada Tringl and, just before lunch, Ivos

Rybicka—but so far nothing from L.L., but I'll show you! And I showed him: long before half past twelve (L.L. comes to lunch precisely at 12:32) I parked myself at the door to the cafeteria, and as soon as he appeared in the corridor I breathed in deeply, drew in my stomach like an old yoga adept, and walked up to L.L. so that my breasts nearly knocked him over—"Good day," is all he said, and he looked at me dimly (as if making fun of me?).

I analyzed this during the remainder of the shift, while walking through the shelves, and then I went straight from Cottex to buy a turtle-neck sweater and a scarf that made me look like a nun, in the town library I went back over everything on production until I knew it backwards, forwards, and randomly, quick as a whip, at the singles dorm I wrote Manek the news and that same evening I sent it from the main post office, registered express.

Early the next morning I had Drapal order for PTK thirty-six books in which there might be something having to do with production (I had noted the titles down at the town library), I personally carried the order to the Cottex mail unit, and I waited at the door until the mail came — I got a whole box of mail, ran to the WC with it, and hurriedly picked through the mass of letters for Drapal (from the Society of the Friends of Cremation, the Mexican Scouts, the Dortmund firm Alles für Turistik, the steering committee for Bridging the Bering Strait, and the South Australian Highway Information Service), until suddenly out popped a gray envelope with my name on it. It was from Manek:

> *My Sonya,*
>
> *From now on I will write to you more frequently. It is now necessary and in our best interest that you should gain maximum influence over L.L., so that he will be obedient to our commands. Together we will employ every possible means, but you should act cautiously and inform me in advance of each new step. Enter his division now, study*

*L.L. in detail and from every point of view, his character,
habits, weaknesses, and lifestyle. Form close contacts with
those under him and let me know everything about them.
Don't wait for L. Tringl and I. Rybicka to bring you a
letter of appointment from L.L. on a silver platter, but
provoke them into acting to further our cause. Enlist other
helpers and give me a running commentary of everything
that goes on. Beginning with your next letter, number all
your reports. Keep our connection a very deep secret.*

*I trust you and will entrust you with this important
mission, the purpose of which I will reveal to you at the
proper time.*

I kiss you,

Your Manek

Maximum influence over L.L. — and I had started out with
that idiotic sweater and my labcoat's lapels all pinned up . . .
like a stupid goose.

Enter his division now — that won't be an easy nut to crack,
but even if it were the biggest coconut from the Indies. . .

Form close contacts with those under him — "Ladicka," I was
saying two minutes later (I had called Comrade L. Tringl out
into the corridor, by telephone), "the trousers you're wearing
today could just as easily be worn by the Prince of Wales!"

"They're just what I wear to go to work in," L. Tringl
muttered happily.

"I'd like to see what you wear on Sundays. . ."

"Then I'll pick out a pair of those to wear tomorrow. . ."

"But you wouldn't wear those to work, surely. . ."

"OK, but then how—" (I smiled at him prettily) "—hey,
Sonya, you'll go out with me on Sunday!"

"I'd like to, I really would—" (I sighed and paused meaning-
fully) "—but I couldn't even think of such a thing so long as
the question of my job with you hasn't been resolved. . ."

"So far L.L. hasn't expressed . . ."

"So I should wait until you bring me a letter of appointment
on a silver platter?"

"Sonya, I'd be terribly happy to, but I really don't know—"

"So think it over and in the meantime iron your Sunday trousers! And send me Ivos Rybicka, perhaps I won't have to provoke *him* into activity—"

L. Tringl shuffled off and a minute later out came I. Rybicka with a smile on his face.

"Sonya, dear, starlet, darling, what are you doing this afternoon and evening?"

"I don't know yet, Ivosek. Do you have any suggestions?"

"Ten thousand. Number One: at five in front of the Savoy."

"You know, I'd go for that—" and I smiled at him beautifully.

"Sonya, honey, scoopsie, doll-face, I'm ready to celebrate, by five I'll be parked in front of the café."

"—if only I had things settled with that crazy old bore Drapal. Couldn't you push a little to help me sit near you?"

"I've been working on L.L. all day long . . . You know, but first you've got to get rid of Ida Papouskova. . ."

"What's she like?"

"A witch."

"Well then. . ."

"She's worse than that, but L.L.'s no barbarian—"

"Then ciao. I didn't think you were as much a wimp as Lada Tringl—but you're even wimpier. At least he's got some *ideas* . . . so forgive me for bothering you."

"So, five at the Savoy. . ."

"Work that out with Ida Papouskova!"

Enlist other helpers— "Sir," I said to Drapal, "do you know who's the best walker in the plant?"

"Me."

"Of course, but I mean which woman?"

"It could be you, if only you—"

"I could *never* cover as much territory as Ida Papouskova. We were just discussing her — she's a *fantastic* walker . . . In other respects they don't speak well of her, but they say she's always *reflecting* and always *striving* against someone—she'll probably get the sack soon."

"Ida Papouskova?" Drapal said thoughtfully, and he disappeared into the shelves.

I wrote Report No. 1 to Manek, then went straight from work to the main post office and sent it off registered express, I spent the rest of the day outside L.L.'s house.

He drove up in a gray Skoda, license no. UL-26-01, parked it in the garage, and disappeared into a gray house. At 5:11 the lights went on in his second-floor apartment. At 7:37 the lights went out, and a little later L.L. came out with a pretty but not very exciting woman (about 40) and a defiantly beautiful girl (probably the daughter and probably 20), went into the garage (I took a thorough look at both of them and then went back behind the telephone booth), he drove out in his gray Skoda, galantly opened the door for his daughter, who sat up front with him (his wife crawled in behind), and L.L. drove off toward the center of town. I rang the porter's bell, asked whether Dr. Spacek lived here, and when it became obvious that he didn't, I began to whimper until the porter's wife took me inside, gave me tea with honey, and jabbered on a good two hours, from which I compiled information to send Manek the very same day by express mail. Report No. 2:

L.L. has lived in this building for nine years. He enjoys a good reputation. No one has anything on him. He only goes out with his family, except on Thursdays to play chess at the Union Café, and sometimes he drives to the woods, but usually with his daughter.

His wife, Zora, is "a good woman through and through" and sometimes she even lets someone else have her turn in the laundry room. She likes to sleep in, but she keeps a clean house, she scours her floors twice a year and sweeps the balcony every day.

Their daughter, Lanka, is a "cute little bitch," she studies something or other in Prague, but "must be goofing off" since "she's always hanging around here." "She drags boys into the vestibule" and "squeals when they cuddle." But she's very fond of her Daddy, L.L., and he "pampers her like crazy."

A perfectly respectable family, quiet and inconspicuous. Every Sunday there's a champagne bottle in their garbage. Manek replied to my letter No. 1 with his telegram NR. 1:

NR. 1 INCREASE PRESSURE ON L.T. AND I.R. TO REBEL
AGAINST L.L. EVEN A STRIKE PERMISSIBLE STOP
INVESTIGATE THE POSSIBILITY OF CREATING A LOVE
AFFAIR BETWEEN K.D. AND I.P.   *M.M.*

Even before I got telegram NR. 1, L.T. and I.R. had been getting it on the chin, but nothing had come of it, however Manek's idea for *creating a love affair Kazimir Drapal—Ida Papouskova* is marvelous (I'm in the hands of a great strategist—).

"Mr. Drapal," I said to K.D. when he emerged from behind a bookshelf holding a tourist map of the Pyrenees, "you're quite a sly fellow!"

"So I am, Sonya, but what do you have in mind, concretely speaking?"

"I've been telling you what a marvelous walker, thinker, and *striver* Ida Papouskova is — and all the time you've known it yourself!"

"Perhaps from you, right? Or could I have read it somewhere. . ." and Drapal reached behind him and randomly pulled from a shelf the books *The Fruits of Knowledge* and *Let's Cook Fruit*, which I had placed side by side.

"But all Cottex has been talking about how much she loves you!"

"Someone . . . me . . . of course, after all, that's obvious . . . So Ida Papouskova's set out on the road in search of Light. . ." and all worked up, K.D. galloped through the shelves, then, on the verge of a nervous breakdown, he ran off to calm down by inspecting the kitchen.

As soon as he had disappeared through the doorway, I called *ex privata industria* (suddenly everything I'd studied, even the Latin from my days in school, was beginning to be useful) Jakub Jagr, and heating him up until the telephone started to burn my ear, I asked him to (". . .if you really love me—") take Ida Papouskova into his new division. And with the help of L.T.

and I.R. (who were eating out of my hand like trained pigeons) I worked on Ida Papouskova to get the poor woman (actually a frightful one) to come the very next morning to PS-VTEI and PTK, study room and reading room, in a waterproof ski jacket, checkered knee breeches, thick wool checkered knee socks, and hiking boots. Hungrily, Engineer Kazimir Drapal took her behind the bookshelves and in a little while they were walking and disappearing among them together, K.D. gushed as he was long accustomed, but from I.P.'s mouth I heard such phrases as "the defile of St. Gotthard," "an earnest night march across the mountains," and "tightrope walking promotes mental concentration"—had I.P. been studying in the town library, too? In any case, the students L.T. and I.R. had done their work fantastically and deserved a reward. I spent a nice evening with them at the Savoy.

And I kept whipping them on (that is my job now and my vocation) to peak performance, just as I did Jakub Jagr, all of which I reported to Manek in letters Nos. 3 to 11 (for which I received Manek's telegrams of praise NR. 2 and NR. 3). In letter No. 12 I informed him that K.D. and I.P. were now calling each other by pet names such as "Iduska" and "Kazimourek" (for which telegram of praise NR. 4), and in my urgent telegram No. 13, I announced the first smacking kiss behind the bookshelves. And of course every day at half-past twelve I pretend to be coming out of the plant cafeteria, L.L. passes me each time precisely at 12:32, says, "Good day," and now smiles at me a little (but peculiarly somehow?).

In telegram NR. 5 Manek expressed his high appreciation for me (YOU'RE WONDERFUL he telegraphed me!), but at the same time his discontent that the conquest of L.L. IS NOT MAKING ANY PROGRESS. In letter NR. 6 he set forth a profound analysis of the remaining possibilities, rejected my proposal from letter No. 9 (to simulate a wrong-number call and in a simulated conversation with a nonexistent friend of mine to mention that I have a crush on L.L.) as technically problematic, as well as my proposal from letter No. 10 (as if by mistake to put a letter to

my friend with the same content into an envelope addressed to
L.L. and, if need be, by a similar oversight to send him a photo
of myself with a text that gives the impression that I am sending
it to a famous photographer from whom I am trying to get a job
as a model) as not serious and obviously beneath L.L.'s level.
But he wasn't stingy with his appreciation, he fully approved
of the suggestion I made in letter No. 11.

L.T. had revealed to me when and to which forest L.L. went
on Sundays, and I was lucky: from my telephone booth I saw
L.L. get into his gray Skoda, all alone.

I hitchhiked to the forest highway and posted myself on the
bridge which, on my tourist map, was marked by a red cross. I
waited there in the rain for almost four hours until I caught
sight of the gray Skoda UL-26-01.

"Good day. This is a coincidence, isn't it?" L.L. said to me
with a smile (but sort of strange?), gallantly he opened the door
for me and like a drowned rat I crawled in beside him.

To my two attempts at conversation L.L. reacted on the lower
threshold of politeness (NEVER IMPOSE YOURSELF, Manek had
wired me in telegram NR. 3), so we went back to Usti in silence.

"Good-bye," is all L.L. said to me when gallantly he opened
the car door for me, but suddenly he added: "You did say
everything, didn't you?"

"Yes!" I replied without giving it a thought, I didn't understand until nighttime (after I had sent off express telegram No.
14), lying on my lower bunk in the dorm (every ten minutes a
cigarette butt flew past me), that he was referring to our first
conversation in the library. But a whole night wasn't enough to
solve the riddle of his strange smile.

The soft, thick nylon curtains on the cream-colored window were open just enough to give a view of the treetops. Lying in bed, L.L. counted the last ten leaves (already wrinkled and brown) and uneasily recalled his dream, a spiral plunge in a blue rotation, and then *a radiant and frighteningly precise picture of the Alpine peak, huge under its eternal snows*, at the base of which Zora and I, on a meadow years ago—huh, thought L.L., and then he got up, stretched, bathed (without even glancing at his body), shaved (Huh—he grinned into the mirror), he kissed Zora on the forehead (why hasn't pharmaceutical research devised anything for wrinkles?!) and sat down to his breakfast.

"Where's Lanka?" he asked, taking the cup of Indian tea Zora handed him.

"She got some idea into her head and took the morning express to Prague," Zora complained.

"Why not. She's in school there after all, you know," said L.L., and he plunged a silver spoon into scrambled eggs.

The Ludviks ate in silence.

"Last week some girl was questioning the porter's wife about us," Zora said all of a sudden.

"A redhead?"

"I was too embarrassed to ask questions."

"She wasn't."

"I don't understand you, Ludvik. . ."

"There's nothing *to* understand. She asked questions and you didn't," said L.L., he wiped his mouth with his napkin, kissed Zora very tenderly on the mouth (I'll never hurt you, my love, he said in his heart, and again he recalled the sparkling snow of the Alpine peak), went down to the garage and, while starting his car, thought about what that redhead might be preparing for us today.

There was more of it today than yesterday: Lada was interceding for her, Ivos was wheedling, and decidedly both of them were *begging*—what is that girl trying to do to my boys?!

". . . and when he—Comrade Drapal—has so much work with his center for scientific and technical information, along with the whole program of the library, study room and reading room on top of it. . ." prattled Ida Papouskova (she certainly isn't going to wear those knee breeches here!) "and when Comrade Cechova is supposed to come here as my replacement—"

"I know nothing about that," L.L. told Ida Papouskova (at the same time freezing both his boys with an icy look), and he ordered her to connect him at once with the director of the Research Institute for Pharmacology and Biochemistry in Prague (he had once been director of Cottex), whom he then asked for something to get rid of wrinkles "that will really do the trick, it's very important for me to have it."

He had hardly put down the receiver when Ida Papouskova announced Engineer Jagr "on a matter of great urgency."

"Couldn't it have been handled on the telephone?" L.L. had greeted the young engineer with some displeasure (L.L. didn't like visits) and had not offered him a chair.

"I need your help for my new division," said Jagr.

"In what respect?" L.L. said as drily as possible.

"I am running into considerable difficulties trying to fill my authorized positions—"

"Refer those matters to the Personnel Department."

"Certainly, but I would very much like to know your views, since it is a question of one of your own subordinates."

"You want to have Papouskova?"

"I am asking you for her."

"Ida!" L.L. called his subordinate, and when she came in (she had been listening behind the door, of course), he said mockingly, "Here's someone else who's interested in you."

"I'd rather go to PS-VTEI," Ida said with unprecedented insolence.

"There's no opening there," L.L. warned her, "but if you want to leave here, I won't hold you a single hour. As soon as I get a replacement, I'll release you and send you back to Personnel. Both of you should apply to that office. That's the whole matter, Mr. Jagr. And Ida, you know I do *not* take visits."

The end of November is somehow desperate: the vain struggle of trees. . . Lying in bed, L.L. counted the remaining leaves in the treetops outside his bedroom window (on Saturday evening he and Zora opened a bottle of sparkling wine and watched television. Lanka had not come back from Prague. When the bottle was half empty, Zora fell asleep), on Sunday only the last four were left and, shortly after breakfast, L.L. drove off to his autumn woods (I have a grove of oak trees there, whose old leaves will keep new ones from growing until spring).

On the way back (it rained buckets, but then I always have liked rain) that girl jumped in, the one who wants to give *everything* . . . what all will she want in return? I gave her a ride. She left a puddle behind on the seat.

On Monday morning (Lanka still had not come home) the tree outside my window was bare.

"Call her in here!" L.L. said to his boys and sighed at their rejoicing.

"I've heard that you're interested in a place in my division," he said drily to Sonya Cechova (he had greeted her, but had not offered her a seat).

"Yes. Very much so," Sonya said seriously (her neck was wrapped: evidently a sore throat from her Sunday hunting expedition).

"Huh. You would get an extra hundred a month here."

"I don't care about that at all. I'd even be satisfied with less pay than I've been getting."

"Oh," L.L. expressed surprise (whenever I'm surprised, I think about and give thanks to Lanka. But she hasn't come back. She'll be coming home less and less—), "and what do you care about then?"

"Work well done. And good prospects."

"Huh. Sit down, take some paper and a pencil, and calculate the following: if five bricklayers build a house in thirty days, how long will eight bricklayers take?"

She figured it out. So she can do word problems, huh — would Lanka have solved it? Not a chance.

"OK. How long will eleven bricklayers take?"

I like the number eleven and all the primary numbers, because they're hard to work with. They're indivisible and they resist . . . She figured it out.

"OK. And how long will a hundred-and-thirty-one bricklayers take?"

"I don't know much about construction and so I would need to know: what is the largest number of bricklayers that can work on the house at one and the same time? If you told me that, I could subtract out the superfluous bricklayers and then solve the problem with the number remaining."

"Very good. Everything has determinate limits, beyond which any kind of increase is nonsensical—right?"

"Yes. Unfortunately—"

"Excellent."

"But who knows? Perhaps we only invent these limits . . . And perhaps they do not exist at all."

"Huh. . ." (But what limits hold, say, for high mountain peaks? Even under a tropical sun don't they still keep their eternal snow. . .)

"Excuse me? I didn't understand you."

"No matter. The job you are applying for requires a *gymnasium* degree, which, I am told, you do not possess?"

"I had to leave school because my father died and—"

"I'm sorry."

"—and I've been studying by myself and will take my exam this spring. I'm *certain* I'll pass."

"I don't doubt it," said L.L., and he got up. "Thanks, and by the end of next month I'll notify you. But don't go walking in the woods alone anymore—don't you have a boyfriend?"

"I've got a husband in Prague."

"You do?" L.L. was dumbstruck, but he got hold of himself right away and drily (but with all propriety) dismissed her.

"Would you like a frankfurter or some Swiss cheese?" Ida Papouskova asked him (she had certainly been listening behind the door).

"A frankfurter . . . but it has to be like an ice cube," L.L. said dreamily.

"Excuse me?" Ida Papouskova voiced her astonishment.

"Or bring me an orange and some pepper," L.L. asked. Ida preferred not to be astonished and now brought what he'd requested. L.L. put a lot of pepper on the orange slices, tasted them, and threw them in the wastebasket. On the one hand there was too much pepper, and on the other hand it needed something to refine, smoothen, and integrate the ingredients — then L.L. remembered Lanka's *entire* breakfast and asked for two more oranges (he'd already had enough pepper) and a half-pint of fresh cream.

"Should I place *The Second Army of the Cross* next to *Crossing Potatoes* or *The Main Crossroads of Buenos Aires*?" Ida Papouskova asked the morning of January 2, she was standing in front of the *MISCELLANEOUS* shelves and she was dressed in hiking boots, checkered knee socks, and checkered knee breeches peeping out from the standard-issue labcoat I'd just turned over to her.

"It doesn't really matter, darling," Engineer Kazimir Drapal answered, he kissed her on the ear as he walked past her, went around three sets of shelves and, holding the book *You Are Becoming a Young Man*, which he'd been studying for a good kilometer, came over to say goodbye to me.

"So long, Sonya, bye-bye. You have matured so much under my influence here that I can now teach you the sum of human wisdom—take walks—reflect—and *STRIVE!*"

"I'll do all of it!" I promised him, and I gave him a goodbye kiss (Ida Papouskova dropped three books on the floor) and left the PS-VTEI, PTK, study room and reading room, crossed the courtyard and, with my formerly "kitchen" satchel (inside, my file of Manek's letters and telegrams, a mirror, comb, and lipstick), went down to the second floor of the administration building (the "White House") and went in the door marked with the black-and-gold sign *DIRECTOR OF PRODUCTION.*

"Good day," L.L. responded drily to my greeting (he didn't smile at me the least bit), and without any transition he dumped a heap of work on me, probably enough to occupy me for twelve hours a day, besides which I was to learn everything Lada Tringl and Ivos Rybicka do ("so that you can step in for them whenever necessary") and, after work was over, study a tome entitled *Principles of Industrial Programming.* When I opened the tome I found long, wormlike derivatives and whole tangles of black, serpentine integrals, both of which I had studied at night school — I admired Manek for timing my studies so perfectly.

Working for L.L. you can always find a moment for fooling around—but just a moment. Otherwise Lada Tringl and Ivos Rybicka do nothing but slave away (I'm amazed that they found the time to visit me in the library), I drudge away like a thresher the whole eight hours (L.L. can't stand overtime) and carry two pounds of work to the town library — back at the dorm all I do is sleep (and all too little of that!) and write my reports to Manek.

"Do you feel you've been working hard enough?" L.L. asked me at the end of the week (in which I had scarcely slept twenty hours all told) and for the first time he smiled at me just a teeny bit.

"How do I look to you?" I asked him (MARVELOUS EXCLAMATION POINT AND NOW YOU WILL TAKE CONTROL Manek challenged me with his telegram NR. 7 the evening of January 2, in which he reacted to my victorious telegram No. 15 I START TODAY, sent the afternoon of the same day).

"Marvelous," L.L. smiled, and he assigned me an additional eleven tasks.

January passed like a single feverish day, I was collapsing with fatigue from the constantly increasing weight of L.L.'s assignments, and I often fell asleep at night school — fortunately this didn't hurt, because I already knew everything required for the degree exam: Manek had planned my studies with the precision of a space-flight.

In a fourteen-page letter, NR. 31, Manek gave a detailed analysis of the results achieved thus far, and in the conclusion he formulated a fundamental strategic guideline for the month of February: AT ANY COST, BY ALL MEANS, AND IN ANY WAY POSSIBLE, MAKE L.L. ACCEPT HIS FIRST ASSIGN-MENT.

"How do you like it here with us?" L.L. smiled at me on the morning of the first of February (now he smiles at me all the time).

"Very much. But. . ."

"But what?"

"Something seems to be missing here. . ."

"What might that be?"

"I don't know how to explain it to you. . ."

"Try."

"You wouldn't understand. . ."

"Let's both try. What's missing here?"

"A bit more life."

"Yes?" L.L. was dumbstruck, but he got hold of himself right away and for the rest of the shift he closed himself up in his office. Lada Tringl went to the dentist's and I worked at his calculator, making it whistle (I can also do Ivos Rybicka's job). At 2:59 precisely (as every day) L.L. said goodbye to us, and to me he added drily, "Tomorrow we're going on a trip to No. 02."

Right onto the keyboard of the calculator Lada Tringl dropped the wet handkerchief with which he had vainly tried to soothe the pain in his dug-up jaw, and then in shock he sighed: "L.L.'s going on a trip—" And Ivos Rybicka explained to me that the last time L.L. went on a trip was six years ago.

In letter No. 46 I sent Manek a word-by-word account of my conversation with L.L. and an evaluation of his astonishing decision, I spent the rest of the day at the hairdresser's (my hair had grown out beautifully) and in my excitement I could fall asleep only thanks to the wonderful book by Dr. Karl Werner,

Hatha Yoga (fundamental yoga exercises), according to Manek's prescription (NR. 23) it will allow me to perfect myself, and it also allows me to fall asleep whenever I want and to remain constantly fresh and efficient.

On the morning of February 2, in the factory courtyard, I boarded an enormous silver-gray Tatra 603 limousine, beside me in back two young engineers from Technology, in front beside the driver L.L., we drove through the slushy late-winter streets (in the square my Security Officer saluted me) and got out in the middle of the courtyard of Cottex 02 in Usti n.L.-Trmice.

"Go and greet the director," L.L. said to the two engineers, he winked at me and we went in the rear entrance. I acted as if the deep puddles on the concrete floors did not bother my high heels the *slightest* bit (L.L. was wearing low boots with corrugated soles), and we passed through an enormous rumbling hall with buzzing reactors, roaring electric motors, and whistling centrifuges, L.L. led me as he might a little girl through a fair, he explained things, picked up lumps of damp fabric, smelled them, rubbed them, and handed them to me, he climbed wet, quivering iron stairs (with my heart in my mouth I climbed after him like a frightened squirrel) onto shaky iron platforms (the highest ones were so narrow and shook so hard, he had to take me by the hand), much of it I didn't understand (I didn't pick it up in school—a pity), only that it was mighty, masculine, in motion and, therefore, all in all fascinating.

When we finally (whenever I looked around, I would ask questions and hold L.L. up) climbed down (I quite daintily, as into the foyer of an opera house) into a puddle on the concrete floor, waiting for us there, between the two engineers, was some sort of frightened little man (later, in the limousine, I learned that this was the plant director).

"Why do you load the Pfaudler with only three hundred sixty pounds?" L.L. asked him drily instead of greeting him.

"I wonder, but we. . . After all, we're loading it right," the frightened little man rattled off.

"How much?"

"But we. . . we're doing it according to regulation."

"How much?"

"But. . . One moment, I'll find out right away. . ."

"It's all taken care of. The correct, increased quantity will be communicated to you today via telephone. By the way, you've got a hippy sleeping in back of the chlorination kettle. Let's go."

"But. . ." the little man was now speaking to our backs (but I did glance back in his direction: he was scrambling up the wet stairs like a *really* frightened squirrel).

"You've made a pretty decent catch with that new assistant of yours," the young engineer laughed when we were back in the car.

"I took her along so she can see what she's actually working with," L.L. replied drily and didn't say another word in the car.

"Thank you, it was really fine," I told him when he said goodbye to us, as usual, at 2:59.

"*I* thank *you*," he said and distractedly (!) smiled.

". . .*and distractedly smiled*," is how I finished my letter No. 47 to Manek. "*Bravo!*" Manek replied in his letter NR. 32, and he gave me plenipotentiary power to enter into direct contact with L.L. whenever I should find it appropriate (in letter NR. 31 he had predicted this would happen in the second half of March), so in March already L.L. would be able to undertake his first assignment, originally scheduled for the month of May.

I found it appropriate to begin at once, and with that goal in mind I went out that afternoon to the largest florist in Usti and bought a potted white cyclamen, back at the dorm I hid it under my bed so that the Rumanian girl wouldn't throw butts on it from her upper bunk (lately she had stopped putting them out before she threw them away), and the next morning I laid it as a trap on L.L.'s desk.

"What's this?" L.L. said, dumbfounded, when he came in that morning.

"A cyclamen. To give this place a *human* touch for a change."

"Y-yes. Certainly. Thank you." He was not only dumb-founded—L.L. was *mystified*.

After a week of the cyclamen's illumination (Manek had suggested waiting ten days, but he gave me the power to decide), I went to town and bought a slender bud-vase, then a white hothouse carnation (insanely expensive) and I installed a second light fixture on *my* desk. I writhed with impatience (Mother Hathayoga was again of great help) for it to begin fading, determined that I would allow it to completely *decay*— but it proved unnecessary to go that far: on February 17, L.L. removed my white carnation and replaced it with his own (a deep pink).

"I GOT A CARNATION" I triumphantly telegraphed Manek at the Hotel Imperial, and he replied in a long letter, NR. 37, which came on the very day that L.L. gave me another (a bright red).

. . .*It's definitely progress*, Manek wrote in NR. 37, *nevertheless, carnations and smiles from your boss are still only acts of pure banality. You must become a great woman to him and thus elevate him. Demand the impossible from him.*

A hard-working secretary gets a bouquet from her considerate boss—but Cleopatra won from Caesar the imperial crown of Rome. Make of him a Caesar, as I will make you a Cleopatra.

For the next assignment, have L.L. give you an apartment.

—in Usti n. L. these days this is almost as improbable as getting a diadem was in ancient Rome . . . "impossible" is just the right word. All the better—

After the February carnations (the last one was a deep red) came March lilies-of-the-valley, then violets (less expensive, to be sure, but more frequent). Something was happening to L.L. (even the boys had noticed it) and not only the fact that we kept taking trips.

On the last and longest trip (to Liberec, where we dined at the Hotel Imperial. . .) L.L. sat, as always, in front beside the driver, I in back where I joked with the two young engineers . . . in Liberec L.L. unexpectedly assigned the younger (and cockier) to stay behind at the Liberec plant and work something out on the spot — on the return trip he sat the older of the two beside the driver and he sat in the back with me.

The highway from Liberec goes through magnificent forests and has an abundance of curves, so I couldn't stay near the door, but kept sliding closer and closer to L.L. On a particularly sharp curve I leaned against him for a second, sighed, and went off as far as I could from him (the back seat of a Tatra 603 has space for three persons).

"It's very fine working with you, but I'm afraid I'll have to leave. . ." I said sadly and sighed again.

"Does something displease you?" L.L. asked with amazement.

"I haven't slept well for a month now. . ."

"From too much work?"

"I can manage it with a hand tied behind my back, and everything else I do in the afternoon at the town library."

"At the town library?" L.L. was astonished.

"I can't work at home. Because I don't have a home."

"Where do you live then?"

"In the singles dorm."

"Oh, an awful roommate, right? She plays her radio or smokes cigars?"

"Some of them are awful and some are quite nice. Some do play radios and others smoke, there's one in the bed above me who day and night tosses down butts, from cigarettes it's true, but she doesn't even put them out."

"For God's sake, how many roommates do you have?"

"Yesterday there were twenty-eight or so. Maybe only twenty-five, or thirty perhaps—the number keeps changing all the time."

"That's what Cottex dorms are like?" L.L. was astonished.

"Can it be that a member of the board doesn't know things like that?" I was astounded myself.

The next morning a real *orchid* landed in my vase and on the morning of March 28 Engineer Kazimir Drapal, in his function as chairman of the Housing and Social Committee (BaS ZV

ROH) in his official quarters (PS-VTEI, PTK, study room and reading room) ceremoniously granted me an apartment in natl. enter. Cottex No. 2000.

("Now start taking care of us, and *right away,*" Ida Papoukova said enviously. "We've got to have an apartment before the baby comes—" My successor no longer stood around the *MISCELLANEOUS* shelves, nor did she take walks, her sandals undone she lolled around in the space between Drapal's light and dark desks. Did this mean that she had done all the reflecting and striving she was ever going to do?

"Woman is the death of the spirit," sighed Kazimir Drapal, he was holding the book *Caring for Infants* and running through the shelves.

On the first of April I moved into my apartment (a self-contained studio on the third floor: two red daybeds, a red rug over a wood floor, a wardrobe with doors covered in white artificial fur, two red armchairs next to a glass-topped table with a stained-glass vase, and on the wall Renoir's painting *Lovers in the Grass*) just like Cleopatra into Caesar's Rome, I tossed my suitcase onto one of the daybeds, washed my hands, and went to the main post office to send telegram No. 62:

CLEOPATRA GOT HER STUDIO FROM CAESAR

"I don't even know how to thank you. . ." I whispered to L.L., extremely touched.

"You didn't get anything you didn't deserve," L.L. replied with the simplicity and grandeur of the real Gaius Julius.

At that moment a telegraph boy on a motorcycle delivered an express telegram from Prague:

NR. 38 CLEOPATRA EXPECTED 15 APRIL 3:00 P.M. AT DOBRIS CASTLE

With one vigorous pull the soft, thick nylon curtains revealed the entire window and L.L. crawled back into bed for a little while in order to enjoy his view of the top of his newly budding tree: an incalculable number of new leaves were burgeoning forth out of the dark wood — of course, in seven months they would once again turn brown, wrinkle, and fall, but *in the meantime.* . . Wonderstruck, L.L. counted the number of dreams he'd had that night: one long and three short . . . Don't cheat on the count, he snapped at himself with a laugh, you staged those short ones yourself.

L.L. got up, did his exercises, bathed (suddenly I don't like my own body), shaved (where did Zora put that lotion for wrinkles?), then he opened the window, kissed Zora on the forehead (forgive me, my darling) and his daughter Lanka on the mouth (there are times when I don't really like being your daddy), let Zora pour him his cup of Indian tea, and plunged his spoon into scrambled eggs.

"Dad, you've fallen in love," Lanka said before Zora could start complaining about her.

"Y-yes?" L.L. was so dumbstruck he almost choked, "How can you tell?"

"Ludvik. . ." Zora was frightened.

"'Cause you're drenched—and how!—with a completely different cologne!" said Lanka, and she burst into laughter.

"It's a present from Kosmopharma," said L.L., and he pushed away the scrambled eggs. I bought it yesterday at the square, quite unconsciously . . . and did I unconsciously put it in the bathroom? And unconsciously use it this morning? And did you just as unconsciously buy flowers and stick them in the bud-vase on her desk? What do a hundred "unconsciously's" add up to?

"From Kosmopharma, you say?" Lanka smirked, the little beast.

"You know, Lanka," Zora intervened, "Dad sometimes does get presents from chemical companies. . ."

"Kosmopharma sent our director a whole case of them and we divvied them up," L.L. said drily (he still hadn't touched his eggs).

"Don't the eggs agree with you, Daddy?" Lanka grinned, my angel and my bitch.

328 | *Vladimír Páral*

"I must have oversalted them today," said Zora, "they make me so thirsty. . ."

"How did you get those red spots on your neck, Lanka?" L.L. asked his daughter.

"Well? Answer your father!" Zora shouted at her daughter.

"From clothespins, Dad. A rum-drop factory sent our school a whole crate of them and we—what did we do? We divvied them up. . ." Lanka finished her sentence with a falling intonation as people do when they end fairy tales.

"You see how insolent she is," Zora started complaining.

"But I'm telling the truth, just like Daddy—" Lanka was enraged.

"Enough of this!" said L.L., and then he stuck a spoonful of eggs in his mouth and courageously swallowed.

"Don't finish if it doesn't agree with you," said Zora. "What else can I make you?"

"Nothing. I'll take some of Lanka's," L.L. said, and he pulled his daughter's plate over, took a whole onion thickly sprinkled with paprika and, like Lanka, bit into it as if it were an apple.

"It's got a bite to it, doesn't it? And it burns, doesn't it?" Lanka said, snickering at her father's torments.

Lanka's jealous of me— L.L. reflected, dumbstruck and enchanted.

The road to Dobris retreated before her in a deferentially broad arc: fenced in by hewn granite pillars festooned with an ornamental black chain, towering over its semicircular ramparts of well-manicured lawns, and majestically laid out among a mass of red walls perforated with long rows of high windows lined with bricks of yellow Baroque stucco, above its grandiose portal were statues lifting a great golden crown into the sky — so Dobris Castle first appeared to me . . . And emerging out of its gigantic gate to meet me was Manuel Mansfeld, my master M.M., Manek . . . my husband.

"Manek—"

"My darling. My Sonya," said Manek, and his dark glasses gleamed with reflected sunlight.

"Oh, Manek, Manek, Manek—"

I wanted to embrace him, but tenderly he pressed my arms in toward my body. "We must be careful," he said softly and whispered, "Inconspicuous, understand . . . They're out to get me—"

Through an open, heavy, metal-sheathed gateway we silently entered an enormous passageway, adorned with a row of stag heads.

"We're with Mr. Jonas," Manek called into the window with the sign VISITORS, and we went on into the castle courtyard.

"Can I kiss you *here*?" I said, and I set my suitcase down on a stone column by the entrance.

"Not until we get to the park," he smiled at me tenderly, "until then we must—"

"I understand," I whispered. "But I hope the park isn't too far away. . ."

"Just over there—" said Manek, and he motioned with his head.

In the middle of the rectangular courtyard, closed off by three wings of the castle and by a staircase with a stone fountain, was a circular lawn with a magnificent oak tree and an astounding Asiatic gingko tree, and between them, through two large glass doors with an ornamental grill, I saw a slice of the park, glowing in the sun.

"I once painted this scene. . ." said Sonya.

"You've been here before?"

"No. But once in school I did a watercolor painting of the Garden of Eden, and over it I did a pencil drawing of a black grill just like this one. . ."

"I'll open it for you," he said, and he opened one of the glass doors and we passed through a white vaulted hall and, with a soft turn of a small gold key, Manek opened the large grill leading into the park.

"This is the French, the English is right beyond it—"

I threw my suitcase down on a bench near the gate, carefully removed Manek's dark glasses, set them down on the bench, and with both hands I drew his thin, tanned face close to mine.

He looked the same as he had last summer . . . a head taller than me, extremely sun-tanned (where had the secret mission taken him?), gleaming gray-green eyes (quite boyish, especially when he smiled), short, thick, dark hair with its first silver threads (how many more since last summer?), combed forward like Mark Anthony in the film *Cleopatra*, and his beautiful hands with their long, slender fingers . . . *were just resting on my shoulders—*

"Sonya, my love . . . You shouldn't cry just now. . ."

I put on his dark glasses (in case I broke into tears again before I pulled myself together), grabbed my suitcase (an expensive one, made of light leather, bought for my trip to join my husband. Inside: the tome *Principles of Industrial Programming*, homework assigned by L.L., but although I had gazed at its wormlike derivatives and tangles of black, serpentine integrals for the entire train trip, I learned nothing during those long hours, not even a single line— and otherwise only a white lace handkerchief for my husband, my toothbrush, comb, lipstick, and a white lace nightgown) and we went to take a walk in the park. The French was large enough, thank goodness, and the English, laid out around a large lake, was even larger, so that as we squeezed our way under the wall, I could now give Manek back his glasses.

"Are you calmer now?" Manek laughed.

"How can I be when I'm with you? And don't put those awful glasses back on, I want to look at you."

"I want to look at you, too. . ."

"But I want more—"

"And I want even more, a close-up—"

And so for a good half hour we squeezed our way under the wall until, giddy with kisses, we finally made it through to the other side.

"That's what we call the *forest steppes*—" Manek said. I gazed at the undulating, fairy-tale meadows stretching all the way out to the woods and the mountains on the horizon . . . and I decided to ask him who were the *we* he was talking about. Across dunes soft as a carpet and last year's thick white grass we walked as if on clouds.

"Watch out for the pond. . ." Manek said, and he took me by the hand.

"That puddle?"

"It's big enough for tall tales . . . As a joke, some fishermen dropped a few fry in there and one of them grew into a fish . . . This was its entire world and it was all alone there . . . more alone than God in the universe."

"That's a frightful idea . . . What if someone had lowered a mirror into the pond?"

"The fish would have fallen in love with its own image . . . Or it would have gone insane."

"Come on, let's go. What happened to the fish?"

"A local poacher unstocked the pond and made a dinner of it. It's out of the question for us to have human relations with fish. Do you like to eat fish?"

"Not anymore."

We came back by a narrow path along the lakeshore, Manek led the way, suddenly he stopped and pointed his arm out over the water. On a silvery rippling surface an old dwarfed tree was growing out from a tiny islet, and above it, high up on grassy ramparts, above the tips of larches and silvery spruces, rose the red walls of the castle and its tower.

"This is our favorite view of it. . ." whispered Manek.

"*Our*?"

Manek did not reply, but kept on walking, we suddenly came upon the tall grilled gate and beyond it, in the English park, a cave furnished like a room.

"Here my brother and I would sit around a fire," said Manek, "and over there, across the lake, the orchestra would play every summer. . ."

The ceiling of the cave was black with soot, and on the opposite shore of the lake a great stone terrace surrounded by a columnar balustrade rose up among chestnut and oak trees.

"Where are your brothers?" I asked as softly as I could.

Manek did not reply, he took me by the hand and led me through the English park back to the French. The surface of the lake, stretched by the water motion underneath, rolled its fish eyes at me.

At the top of a gigantic century-old tree, a bird was flying among the still bare branches, dauntlessly giving its call, our broad sandy road suddenly emerged from the shade into the full sunlight, the trees were radiant, maples (a thousand little bouquets on a single trunk) and thousands of little parachutes (on each chestnut tree), as well as weeping willows (yellow verticals like strokes of golden rain) and in the moist breeze the joyous whirl of young spiny anteaters of damp Chinese silk on all the larches.

In the sunlight the castle looked pinker and more welcoming. Manek stuck his small gold key into the lock and we were through the grilled gate into the white vaulted hall, down the ground-floor passageway into a room with a low ceiling and grills on the windows. It looked like a deserted country hospital, three rows of tables spread with white cloths, at one of which sat a waiter figuring his accounts.

"Rudolf—" Manek said in a low voice, and with his hand he made a special sign.

"I'll be right with you!" said the waiter, and he smiled and winked.

Manek took me by the shoulders and led me back to the white vaulted hall.

"What's in there?" I asked.

"A third-category restaurant. It used to be the servants' hall . . . Now it's where writers and poets bolt down hamburgers and low-cal soups."

"All day long?"

"All day long they tap away at their typewriters like wood-peckers. They've made a 'creative wing' out of what used to be stables . . . Before the war European nobility would gather here, the Archbishop of Prague summered here . . . Our castle has been turned into a factory and an old-age home."

"*Our* castle?" I repeated softly.

Manek did not reply, he gazed silently through a glass gate into the courtyard. The waiter came and brought us two glasses of white wine on a metal tray.

"Thanks, Rudolf," said Manek, and he gave him a hundred-note.

"Anything further, Your Grace?" said the waiter as he gaped at me.

"I told you categorically that I did not wish to be—" Manek reminded him

"Pardon me, Your Grace—I mean: *Mr. Mansfeld,*" the waiter grinned, winked at me, and disappeared down the passageway.

"Rudolf Jonas," Manek said, touched, "our good old faithful servant. . ."

"*Our?*"

"I guess it's a fitting time to introduce myself to you," Manek said distractedly, and he pointed to the mat on the stone floor, so large and thick that it was in fact a kind of carpet, there were two large red letters on it: *CM*, "read it."

"C— M—?"

"That is one of the few authentic objects left here. . ." Manek said, "and these are the initials of our family."

Then it came to me: after receiving Manek's telegram CLEO-
PATRA EXPECTED 15 APRIL 3:00 P.M. AT DOBRIS CASTLE I went
straight from Cottex to the town library and read that "Dobris
Castle was built between 1745 and 1765. The architects, Jul.
Robert de Cotte and G. M. Servendoni, worked in the Late
Baroque style, the park is decorated with statues by the Prague
Rococo sculptor Ignac Platzer. Until 1945, it was part of the
domain of the Princes Colloredo-Mannsfeld; now it serves as a
place of work and rest for the members of the Czechoslovak
Writers Union"—

"So you're—"

"The last descendant of my family."

"And your brothers—"

"They all fell in battle. I am Manuel Leopold Josef Ludvik
Maria Colloredo-Mannsfeld, sole lawful heir and reigning
prince," Manek said matter-of-factly.

I had to sit down at the corner of an enormous dark table.
Lost in thought, Manek paced through the angular white
columns and every so often glanced through the gate into the
courtyard.

"He's here already," he said all of a sudden, "come here and
hide—"

A cream-colored Wartburg drove into the courtyard and
right up to our gate. Concealed behind a column, we watched
a short, stout, white-haired man with a white moustache bang
the car door shut and go into the hall, with short quick steps he
crossed the mat bearing Manek's initials and ran to the
staircase.

"He's after me," Manek said, and he grinned.

"Who is he?"

"A colonel. We must go. But let's not leave the wine behind
for him," and calm and cool, Manek handed me a glass of white
wine.

"Shall we clink?"

Manek looked at his watch, it was five minutes before five. "I never drink before five," he said, and he took me by the shoulders and quickly led me to a small dark- colored car.

We drove around the circular lawn through a gateway in front of the castle and then joined the stream of cars on the highway to Prague.

"Won't he come after us?" I asked Manek when some four cars had passed us on the smooth asphalt (I kept looking back).

"Who?"

"The colonel. . ."

"Rudolf will stall him for at least twenty minutes. That will give us enough time," he said, after a short distance he turned off onto a side road and came to a stop in a small asphalt parking lot.

"Should I take my suitcase?" I asked.

"Yes. We'll hide here till tomorrow."

HOTEL TRIANON was written over the entrance of an elegant yellow edifice, Manek seated me in a high-backed, leather-upholstered antique chair and went up to the reception desk with his red I.D.

After a brief negotiation (I saw him give the clerk a hundred-note) he nodded to me, we went upstairs to the second floor, and Manek unlocked the door to room No. 15. The light-colored period furniture, a tall mirror, glass doors onto a balcony, and twin beds side by side.

"You might want to freshen up," he smiled at me, throwing his black briefcase on a chair. "I'll wait for you down in the bar."

I was grateful to him for this brief moment of solitude. I unpacked our bags; it didn't take long. I took *Principles of Industrial Programming* out of my suitcase, smiled at the wormlike derivatives and the tangles of black, serpentine integrals, which I now know as I do so many other new things—What had I known when Manek took over control of my life? And what had I been— I set *Principles* down on Manek's night table so I could boast of my progress.

My toothbrush, comb, and lipstick on the little shelf above the washbasin, and I put on a little makeup (a good thing I was meeting Manek just now, when my hair had grown back so beautifully), then I opened his black briefcase, stuck his tooth-brush in the sole cup, next to mine, I put his electric shaver on the night table (so he wouldn't have to look for it) and then, full of love, I placed his dark-blue pajamas (brand new) on his bed and on my own I placed my brand-new white lace nightgown . . . How many times have I prepared for my wedding? . . . *This is the last time.*

And then I stood for a while on the balcony and looked at the sloping lawns stretching all the way out to a thin curtain of pine trees, beyond their copper-colored trunks the slender, bright green flames of birches flashed among the mighty dark spruces . . . if I was ever *completely* happy in life, it was at this very moment.

My prince was waiting for me down at the bar, I swung myself up on the stool beside him. Manek ordered a vermouth with lemon and ice and said:

"Work before pleasure. How is the L.L. campaign going?"

I summarized it for him, and Manek asked when L.L. would be ready to undertake his assignment.

"That depends on what sort of assignment it is," I said.

"He helped you get an apartment, compared to that this one'll be a snap . . . You've done fantastically, Sonya."

"You did it with me."

"Cleopatra couldn't have done it better or more quickly."

"You gave me what it took."

"My Cleopatra."

"My Anthony."

"He was defeated."

"But he lived with Cleopatra . . . till death. Manek, when will we two—"

"When the time comes. First, let's get the L.L. campaign out of the way: tame him by any means whatsoever so he'll eat out of our hand, and by the end of May he will have carried out his assignment."

"By *any* means?. . ."

"*Absolutely* any. Cottex has plants as far away as Moravia. By the tenth of May arrange it so that L.L. takes you on a two-day tour with an overnight stay. And then take control of him."

"Oh, Manek, you're ordering me to. . ."

"My Cleopatra. I will tell you something I shouldn't: the assignment L.L. has to perform is fundamental to my *existence* . . . I swear it."

"I accept then and I'll obey."

"Just the right verbs. Let's put an end to this discussion and I'll take you to dinner," said Manek, and he offered me his arm. The feeling of having my husband at my side was so beautiful and so necessary.

I was permitted to choose whatever I wanted from the big leather menu, and I wanted a great deal (it was my wedding dinner), and sparkling wine, naturally.

Manek told of his childhood in the castle, of the outings on horseback in the English park alongside the door of his mother's carriage, of hunting with the hounds in the forest around Dobris, of the trophies his father won racing cars at Monte Carlo, of shooting snipe, spotted thrush, wild duck, and quail, then of his travels across Europe and India, and at my prompting he spoke again and in detail about Mount Everest, how the first ray of sunlight strikes the snowy peak of the highest mountain on earth and turns it to gold and to fire. . .

And (as the level of the wine sank in the bottle) I told him everything about myself, things I would never have revealed even to Jarunka Slana . . . I shared my entire life with him, back to my earliest childhood memories, when I still had both my parents. . .

What I most liked to imagine in bed was that I was a princess with a golden crown, a veil, and a golden star on my forehead . . . My prince (Peta Myrtl from Spalena Street) led me by the hand through the enormous chambers of a fairy-tale castle. My inability to imagine what a castle was like didn't matter very much, but it did bother me that I had to be a queen, and yet even when I closed my eyes there was nothing I could do to imagine what one was like. In fact, this kept me awake at night.

Then late one night Mrs. Janikova came down from the fifth floor with her daughter, Danuska. Danuska was crying and Mrs. Janikova begged Mother to let her leave the girl with us overnight. Mr. Janik had come home drunk again and had beaten them both. I stuck my leg through the door to the hall-way so I could have a look at Mrs. Janikova. Blood was running down her face.

Mother tried to persuade her to stay the night with us too, but Mrs. Janikova only smiled and shook her head. Then she silently closed the door and climbed the stairs again.

I ran to the WC and locked myself in. On its cold chessboard of red-and-white tiles I put one foot on top of the other and closed my eyes, I could suddenly imagine what a queen was like: blood was running down her face and with a smile she was climbing the circular staircase up to her black tower.

Manek tenderly stroked my hair and said quietly:

"The most womanly thing about women is the ability to *give of themselves* . . . the most womanly and the most exalted. Regal."

I kissed the hand that was stroking me.

And we danced and kissed on the dancefloor, in silence now, everything had already been said, at our wedding table we were still drinking coffee and cognac, and at the end of that evening we got up for our final wedding dance . . . before the song ended, Manek was leading me out of the dining room.

"Just one second, Sonya. . ." he said suddenly as we were walking past the bar (as if uncertain?), and he tossed down a double vodka, then another, then a third—

"Manek, don't drink any more. . ."

"No, I just. . ." Suddenly he looked at me almost as if he were *pleading. . .*

In our room, No. 15, the first thing Manek did was throw cold water on his face (his forehead had been glistening with sweat), and then he promptly resumed his usual tone.

"What's this?" he said when he caught sight of my tome, *Principles of Industrial Programming*, on his night table, I had set there as a trap.

"My homework from L.L.," I said with a laugh, "should I read you something from it?"

"No!" he said and, as if he despised the book, he swept it onto the floor and kicked it under the bed.

Then he went out on the balcony and smoked for a long time, alone, and when I finally went after him he frightened me: sweat was running down his temples and the hand holding his cigarette trembled—

"You've drunk too much. . ." I said with quiet reproach.

"Yes . . . Sonya, I. . . I have to tell you. . ."

"Not now. We've said everything already. Come."

He let me lead him back into the room and seat him on the edge of the bed. He stared at his feet and looked so miserable . . . I turned out the light and drew him to me tenderly. Manek, my husband . . . was behaving like a very (this I know from novels) . . . like a young boy. And then he wept like a little boy, I kissed his wet cheeks and told him that it did not, it didn't matter at all, that we were together now for the very first time and that we would be together many more times . . . and I stroked him as a mother does her son, until finally he fell asleep.

The next morning, when he got up, dressed, and went out on the balcony again to smoke, I led him back to my bed again and this time Manek became, in truth and completely, my husband.

"You are a fairy tale and a dream. . ." he whispered, spellbound, and when he dressed for the second time (quite quickly, because we had to hurry), "you are truly my Cleopatra. . ."

"And you my Anthony. Will we be together now?"

"I'll write you," he said (wonderstruck, spellbound, and completely *mystified*), but we had to hurry, I swept all our things into my suitcase (Manek was in no condition even to put his pajamas into his briefcase), we ran to our car (Manek had paid for the room when we checked in), and in a few minutes we were already in the stream of vehicles whistling along the concrete highway to Prague.

"Love. . ." whispered Manek, and he kept repeating the word: "Love. . ."

In twenty minutes we were driving into Prague.

"Which station do you want me to leave you off at?" he asked.

"Prague Central," I said, and since we were almost there, I quickly transferred Manek's things from my suitcase to his briefcase.

"By the tenth of May I'll arrange a two-day trip with L.L. to one of the Cottexes in Moravia, and there—" I said, but Manek suddenly—*furiously*—interrupted me:

"No!"

"But Manek, yesterday you explained it to me quite clearly. . ."

"I'm canceling the order. Absolutely and for all time!"

"Manek, I don't understand you . . . Now, when L.L. is already. . ."

"Not another word about L.L.! I forbid you to undertake anything whatsoever with him . . . anything that exceeds the usual working relationship between a secretary and her boss. I repeat: *the usual working relationship during working hours!*"

"But Manek. . ."

We were arriving at the intersection in front of Prague Central Station. The light shone red, like a warning—

"I'm happy to do what you ask, Manek, very happy. But now you listen to me: give up that secret mission of yours . . . the whole thing. If it's important, tell the police about it. And even if you have to go to prison — I'll wait for you. For years, if need be. Then you'll come for me . . . my apartment's big enough for two people. Even with a baby, if need be. . . And then we'll get a real apartment. I'll find you a job myself—"

The traffic light shone yellow for just a few seconds and then it turned green and we had to go. It was only a few more feet to the station.

"Manek, this time listen to me, the way I've always listened to you—"

In front of the station the redness of a sign called out the command to stop, so Manek stopped, opened the door for me, quickly handed me my suitcase, and mumbled, "I'll write—" and he drove off into the stream of angrily honking cars.

When I got home to my new studio in building No. 2000, I discovered that we had left *Principles of Industrial Programming* at the Trianon, in room No. 15, under our wedding bed.

Arriving at Cottex shortly before seven in the morning, L.L. greeted Lada Tringl and Ivos Rybicka, spent a few moments exchanging jokes with them (there was nothing else to talk about) and went into his anteroom, greeted Sonya, took a sprig of white lilac out of his briefcase, and put it into the vase on her desk.

"Thanks," Sonya said coldly, and she reacted to his attempts to tell jokes and stories just as curtly (and even more coldly). . .

What can have happened to her so suddenly — in shock, L.L. shut the upholstered door to his office behind him. He read the newspapers and the first memo of the morning, it was just 9:12, they won't bring me my A5 index card until 10:45, and then at 11:00 I'll take to the director's office, huh: director of a kiddy post office.

L.L. jumped up from his desk and furiously walked across his office. Well rested, exercised, bathed, refreshed—what good was it all? Just so he could carry a file card to the director's office at 11:00.

In a rage L.L. walked across his office and then stood by the window, drummed on the glass, and gazed out into the court-yard. *A man who just stands by the window*—where have I read that?—*is already a dead man.*

And therefore—now all of a sudden I can grasp it—to Lanka

I'm no longer anything but an object of fun (she envies me . . . but only for the purpose of conversation: she knows me and knows that I am no longer fit for anything). Zora sleeps at my side: what's left for her to do next to a dead man?

L.L. drummed hard on the glass: the last racket I'm still capable of. Why does Sonya look at me with contempt and without any interest now? How else could she look at the director of a kiddy post office . . . who brings her flowers hidden in his briefcase.

It's 9:16: how many more thousand hours will I stand by the window before I die?

A retinue in white labcoats appeared down in the courtyard, Cottex was being visited by the Minister for the Chemical Industry and, after formal greetings in the director's office (L.L. did not take part in official functions as a matter of principle), they would conduct him along a route carefully chosen so that nothing could interfere with the purely ceremonial character of his visit. In the same spirit, they would conduct the meeting in the director's office, the reception, the workers' meeting, the second reception, and the farewells. The minister is a specialist, however, and would have welcomed a more fact-filled and focused show, which even the director of a kiddy post office could have put on for him—

L.L. tore himself away from the window and with a slight shiver he looked at the labeled steel front of the enormous Cottex card file. Here, systematically assembled over the years, is everything about this enterprise, which I helped to found, to which I have given my life, and which I *love*—

(Are things once again as they were many years ago? Yes. And in the meantime? In the meantime it was just something to pass the time.)

—and which isn't well managed.

L.L. breathed in as if profoundly awestruck (to express awe that way is not restricted to young girls), walked up to his desk, took out his note pad as if it were a deadly weapon, walked quickly from the desk to his card file and pulled out one steel drawer after another, and hurriedly covered the paper with tiny numerals. How long it's been since I wrote anything by hand—

When he went out through his anteroom, Sonya did not even look up at him. I think, my queen, that you'll raise your little red head for me when I come back.

The meeting between the Cottex management and the minister in the director's office finished in a boringly ceremonial spirit (the minister had been ostentatiously glancing at his watch), the first ones to grow impatient were looking at the open-face sandwiches on the table, and the director (a decent fellow: but for just that reason he wasn't cut out to be director of a factory) ended the meeting just as they end a mass in church, and everyone began to push back their chairs and get up. . .

"Just one moment—" L.L. said suddenly — for me and for Cottex this will be a historic moment.

"It would be nice if things were the way we've described them, but they're actually quite different," L.L. said drily and deliberately, as if firing a machine gun, the minister watched carefully and with awakened interest, and the other participants were comically aghast as they rose from the table—for many years I have dwelt among you in peace. Now I am declaring war on you.

Glancing now and then at his note pad, L.L. spent the next three minutes puncturing the director's mass as if it were a child's balloon, but it only hissed and deflated, so he put his notes aside and, from memory, factually and mercilessly, he caricatured and ridiculed his three years of ostentatious devotion.

". . .But our employees are waiting to be addressed," was all the director could bring himself to say.

"Good," said the minister and, turning to L.L.: "Could you be prepared to present these matters to me — today is the eighteenth, let's say by—"

"Within twenty-four hours," said L.L. "And that includes the two-hour trip to Prague. And now excuse me. I have to start at once."

When L.L. got back to his office, he called L. Tringl and I. Rybicka into his anteroom, an act dramatic in and of itself, since it hadn't happened in years. Sonya did not look up from her typewriter.

"I knocked our director down a few pegs," L.L. said drily, "I'd like to finish him off tomorrow before lunchtime. You all go wee-wee and ca-ca, and lay in some food. It looks like we'll be here till midnight."

Sonya looked up from her typewriter.

I bought some more plates, eating utensils, glasses (everything for two), a mop, dust rags, soap powder, and a small vacuum cleaner, and now I go straight home from Cottex, straight *home* to building No. 2000.

My studio apartment is the dearest thing in the world to me (my husband isn't a thing, of course) and I spend all my spare time in it (I've spent enough time looking at people), I'm happy now because now I'm getting myself ready: to do cooking, cleaning, and laundry for two. I have a bathroom here, a kitchen, a *large* wardrobe, and two red daybeds. There's more than enough room here for a husband. The only thing missing is a husband.

Suddenly someone rang my doorbell (I even have my own doorbell now!) and when I opened my door, there was a beautiful girl my own age whom I had once seen from behind a phone booth. It was Lanka, the daughter of my boss, L.L.

"You have a nice place here," she said instead of a greeting.

"Won't you come in and sit down?"

"No. I came to ask you to stop bothering my father!"

"What makes you think I'm bothering him?"

"It's the old story of the secretary who tames her boss. First he gives her flowers, then an apartment — What are you going to ask him for next?"

"I see that you've asked me more than I've asked you. All I know is that you're studying something somewhere . . . with little interest or success. This studio apartment is attractive, but it's far from being as fine as *your* apartment. And hasn't it occurred to you that you came into yours much more easily than I did mine?"

"I live in my father's apartment!"

"And I live in *mine*. Relevant information you can send to the workers committee."

"Of course—you're always right about everything!" and she waved at me with her white little hand with its respectably sparkling diamond ring — at least three months' salary for me (I know prices: I've been studying them in shop windows for a long time).

"Your ring is much too expensive, Miss, for you to be in the right."

"Father gave it to me."

"I don't care if it was a lover or a magician who was just passing through. Did you come to tell me anything else?"

"Let me have Daddy . . . I'm so fond of him—" L.L.'s daughter sobbed, and with touching dignity she went out into the foyer.

"Tell your father not to bring me any more flowers," I called after her, "but don't ask me to hit him over the head with them."

Oh yes, I said to myself after she had left and I had begun to vacuum our new rug (a beauty—a warm brown with a quiet pattern—for just four hundred crowns: I picked it out of the second-category pile). Right after I got back from Prague, I asked Drapal to order me *Principles of Industrial Programming* (which I had left behind at the Hotel Trianon), but when it finally came I didn't need it anymore. In May, L.L. was named plant director, and he appointed me deputy chief of his secretariat (he didn't appoint a chief). Two days before that I passed my examination at night school and received my degree (with distinction).

I cheerfully said goodbye to Lada Tringl (beneath his labcoat he was wearing tuxedo trousers) and to Ivos Rybicka (he kissed my hand!), L.L. had his large metal card file carried to his enormous new office, but I left my bud-vase behind for my successor, thus gladly fulfilling Manek's last directive (and Lanka's request as well). As it turned out, I didn't lose a thing: on my new desk stood two-quart and five-quart vases made of gilded crystal.

Since my wedding night I had behaved toward L.L. as coldly as possible, but now that became difficult . . . when we were first alone together in the rather grand halls allotted to the plant director, L.L. said with excitement in his voice: "Now, together, we will make *SOMETHING* of Cottex—will you give me a kiss as an advance against future payment?"

I gave it to him (didn't he deserve it?) and in my letter to Manek No. 71 I provided a good four pages of arguments for what I'd done (but in fact they were very simple: at that moment I *could not help* but kiss L.L.). Manek replied in his urgent telegram NR. 54, of its eighty words a good thirty were categorical prohibitions such as NEVER, ABSOLUTELY NOT, FOR NO AMOUNT OF MONEY, I TOTALLY FORBID YOU, and so forth.

Manek churned out letter after letter and urgent telegram after express telegram, half the text would be a confession of love while the other half would contain the strictest injunctions that I couldn't even set foot out of the house, until finally I got angry (it was when L.L. first collapsed from overwork) and sent off telegram No. 86:

I am at work and I cannot stop working,

to which Manek telegraphed me back:

NR. 84 IS IT NECESSARY TO DO SOMETHING ABOUT THE LAZINESS OF RAILS BETWEEN THE PASSAGE OF TWO TRAINS QUESTION MARK

and in the next letter he told me he might assign me to write a cycle of five novels about contemporary life in Czechoslovakia, adapt them as a 52-part television series, win a following of a hundred thousand readers and five million viewers, become a professional writer, and go live in his castle at Dobris.

When Manek does give me that assignment, I'll fulfill it and it will be relaxing compared to what L.L assigns me.

Every new director has incredible trouble figuring out what he should do—but L.L. was not *everyone*, he knew from the very first day what he had to do to make *SOMETHING* of Cottex. From the very first day we hit up against obstacles, distrust, ill will, lax standards, inability . . . and all sorts of things that people simply didn't know how to do. But how mercilessly he drove himself—L.L. performed superhumanly—as well as others, and with icy calm he reorganized or liquidated whole departments and founded new ones with new people. By the end of May he had collapsed three times from overwork, but by the beginning of June we at least had the apparatus of administration firmly in our hands.

"And now let's begin, as we must: at the bottom," L.L. said to me.

"Do you mean the boiler-room, Comrade Director?" I smiled at him.

"You know, I've never been there. Mark me down for a visit tomorrow morning, at seven o'clock sharp. And at eleven-thirty a two-day trip."

"Where?"

"Out in the field. We'll make a tour of all twenty-six of our legions."

In the course of two days, L.L. wanted to inspect three Cottexes, plants Nos. 03, 04, and 08, and spend the night "somewhere on the way." Not without some joy—because No. 08 is in my very own Hrusov nad Jizerou — I developed an itinerary that allowed us to spend the night at the Hotel Hubertus, and so I called "Uncle" Volrab and ordered his whole hotel, ". . .and the Bridal Suite for our Director!"

"Well well, we're terribly happy," Volrab yelled ecstatically into the phone (I could hear the crack of billiard balls from the bar), "there's a special seasonal surcharge on the Bridal Suite, but your general will sleep there like a baby!"

"We're bringing along our auditor and he will go over *every* surcharge *individually*. And make dinner and breakfast for eight—and no *Sana*, no peanuts, no twelve-day-old meat.

"Good God, you bet, you betchya," Volrab was frightened, "I'd never think of serving stuff like that to a chief general director, all my stuff is fresh and delicate—"

"We'll see. We're bringing the head of the testing labs, an engineer, and two chemistry Ph.D.'s. And our lawyer."

"Good God, you bet, you betchya," the frightened Volrab babbled, "Comrade General Doctor, I swear to you—"

I hung up, laughed, and then decided for the first time that this trip was something I would not mention to Manek.

The next morning at 11:29 I walked at L.L.'s side down to the courtyard, where two limousines, Tatra 603's, drove up: one black (the director's) and the other silver-gray (for the lesser chiefs), in the latter Jakub Jagr was sitting beside the driver and staring at me fixedly through the windshield.

Because two members of our entourage were still not there (Cottex did not adapt readily to the army-like precision of its new director), L.L. ordered both drivers to honk their horns until the two showed up, he took his place on the front seat of his black limousine, placed me next to him, by the window, and despite the deafening din of the horns, he dictated nine items to me which had come to mind during his trip downstairs, then through the car window he dressed down the two tardies, right on the spot he fined each of them fifty crowns and then gave the sign for departure. The gatekeeper, Archleb, nimbly raised the gate and gave a smart military salute. "Give Archleb twenty-five crowns out of each of the two fines," L.L. dictated to me.

After two hours of wild driving, we passed through Liberec (including the Hotel Imperial) and then shot on toward Hrusov, by the same highway Manek had taken when he carried me off that night. . .

"What's the trouble?" asked L.L. (he was watching me in the mirror). "Did something get in your eye?"

"Yes, Comrade Director," I said, and I made myself blink.

Not long after, Korenov flashed past and the New Mexico Motel, there's a river behind it and across the river is Poland . . . and we shot along the narrow asphalt highway where I used to take my solitary walks when I'd been deserted by Ruda Mach, my first husband, the highway I used to walk along in the rain with the worn-out men's umbrella Sekalka had given me, to get out of the way of the cars I'd climb down into the ditch where fragrant grasses and gleaming ferns grew luxuriantly.

"Again?" asked L.L. "Take my dark glasses!"

"No thank you. I prefer to see the original colors."

We were already riding past the home of the fortune-teller who for three crowns had foretold that I would have "much trouble, but also much joy," and that's what happened, and "only with the fifth man will contentment come" — I'll have to count them over again, but already the Hotel Hubertus was coming into view, we crossed the railroad tracks that go from meadow to meadow, past the red gas pump on the square (where, in a cloud of morning mist, my first husband left me with his suitcase and guitar), past the shop windows of the butcher, the greengrocer, and the food store (where I did my first shopping), we honked for the gatekeeper and drove past the factory lawns of Cottex 08 right up to the stairs of the director's office. Director Kaska ran out to open the car door (he was visibly pale, even though he didn't yet suspect how much L.L. had on him in thick black binders I myself had put together), L.L. gruffly refused coffee in the director's office and without delay we proceeded to business. I spent some time alone in the drying room. . .

The large warm hall was bathed in the rosy glow that comes from the openings of the drying machines as from the jaws of friendly dragons, the girls in nothing but bras and shorts, two by two, were feeding the machines rolls of wet fabric, which then, once dry, smell of ironing and home, of childhood and mama. . . Again something got in my eye and I made myself blink. Two half-naked girls raised a roll with an elegant movement of their arms and their entire bodies, so beautiful in the rosy glow — it's a ballet! — they're dancing their job and their vocation . . . I wiped my eyes and went back to the director's office to remind L.L. of the further crimes committed by Kaska, the local satrap, according to the list which was produced in duplicate.

When, late that evening, exhausted as work horses (during the proceedings, poor Kaska required two refills of his anti-asthma medication and he finally had to be taken straight from his office to bed, the next three days his wife answered his home phone), we arrived at the Hubertus, Volrab himself welcomed us on the threshold in a clean (!) shirt, and on all the tables gleaming white cards: RESERVÈ.

"Sonya, darling, so you've come back to your old uncle—" Volrab blared, and he was already calling Volrabka to come out of the kitchen: "Come and see, darling, darling Sonya's come back to us—"

"You've exaggerated things a bit, granddad," I waved aside all his familiarities (luckily L.L. was so exhausted, he didn't notice a thing) and sent "Uncle" for a bottle of vermouth—"not that French stuff you serve to your customers, but the bottle on the lower shelf you keep for Ziki!"

"But you know I only serve the best of everything when we entertain general central directors. . ." Volrab insisted, and he brought a bottle of white Italian Gancia (made in Yugoslavia).

"The local gentlemen showed up when they heard you were back," Volrab whispered to me, "it's true you've reserved the entire bar—see those signs? I did them myself! And every last one of them's got the right French È with the turned-around accent mark!—but if you'll permit me, I'd let them in for just one beer, business is awful bad these days, and clink! clink!— one crown joins another, and right off you've got two!"

The gentlemen were grinning at me from the other side of

the window: veterinarian Srol, postmaster Hudlicky, and forest
ranger Sames, the last was already preparing his thumbs and
index fingers for the famous "kiss and pinch."

"Get rid of them. They've had their evenings, three of them
in fact. This one's mine."

The dinner was, surprisingly, almost good enough to eat, and
the wine relaxed L.L. to the point that he ordered champagne
(the experienced Volrab served only two glasses with it) and
our companions got up and went off to bed (Jakub Jagr gave a
doleful look back at me), in part because they were exhausted,
in part because the situation was obvious.

And then L.L. warmed up when he was telling what Cottex
would be like in future years, I listened to him attentively (I
know how to listen to men) and encouraged him (and how to
encourage them) — to inspire men is a woman's job and her
vocation. L.L. talked late into the night about the great plans he
had and with my intuition (something a woman must have) I
could sense that my L.L. would be a great director.

"For the first time in years I'm drinking bubbly on a day
other than Saturday," L.L. smiled.

"But doesn't this day deserve it?"

"Just this bottle. But in a year's time, at least a case."

"And the following year a tanker and then the whole Medit-
erranean Sea—if you were Caesar, would you give me Egypt?"
I grinned at L.L. (my milk teeth—S.-Marie, S-Marikka, and
Antisonya—had long since turned to steam) as his S.-Cleopatra.

"You would have had that long ago. I would have taken it
for you and invited you to Rome to be the chief of my secretariat."

I noticed that L.L. had suddenly begun to use the familiar
address with me—but does Latin have a formal address? So my
Caesar may use the familiar, at least for ten seconds—

"I'd have thrown Brutus out of the anteroom, as if he were
just a boy. And during working hours I'd have edited your
memoirs of the Gallic Wars—"

I noticed that L.L. had noticed that I had also used the familiar address with him. That was enough — the ten seconds had run out.

"I thank you, Comrade Director, for a lovely day. . ." To soothe a man and put him to sleep is a woman's job and her vocation.

"And I thank you, Miss Cechova. Good night."

"Good night. May you dream about the Mediterranean Sea!"

"Huh," said L.L.—he hadn't said that for a long time—and he went off to the Bridal Suite to go to bed.

Volrab brought me, as an "extra courtesy of the hotel administration," the key to room No. 5, I went to the bar and had a small jigger of rum (that summer I drank it by the bottle), I asked Volrab whether he still locked the kitchen window every night, "But what do you mean, Sonya, you must have dreamed it," Volrab lied heroically and quite calmly asked me whether I "really" wouldn't care to come back to the Hotel Hubertus "for an even thousand c-r-o-w-n-s in cash and up front."

"Go to bed, granddad," I told him sleepily, it had really been too long a day, and I went out into the corridor to the staircase which I had so many times scrubbed on my knees—

At the foot of the stairs, in the moonlight, stood Jakub Jagr, and in his hands (before it had been a suitcase and a kitchen knife) he now had nothing at all. He was being nice, of course, but I was really too sleepy.

"Sonya, I love you—" (before, he'd cried out: "Sonya, should I kill him?" As time was to show, in both instances he was talking big).

"Should I put on the staff sergeant's boots again and run around the garden?"

"Sonya—"

"I know my name is Sonya and not, let's say, Kamila. So have a rum at the bar, write your wife a postcard, and read *The Perfect Marriage*," she told him with a yawn, and then she went off to her first honeymoon chamber to go to bed. Two beds by the wall, as before, the wall still scratched in the spot where Ruda Mach had hung his guitar. . . I remembered that now I have my own apartment, thought about Manek tenderly (I won't use the familiar address with L.L. anymore), and fell right to sleep.

Early the next morning we drove out of Hrusov (the mist rising from the fields below the railroad tracks blurred the road behind us), we carried out inspections of Cottexes 03 and 04 as if they were raids, and with a rich plunder of (well-concealed) millions, which from now on will pour in in even greater amounts (and in the meantime we'll be coming back again), we happily started back toward our home base in Usti.

A man waiting at the door to my apartment showed his official identification as a lieutenant in the Security Police.

"Do you know this man?" he asked me just as he was landing on my red daybed (on the one that was Manek's), and he pulled out a photo of Manek smiling at a model train—

"The picture isn't very clear. . ." I said to gain time.

"Could it be your M.M.?" the officer replied caustically.

"It could be." If he had the photo and knew Manek's initials. . .

"What's his name?"

"He has a number of them. I call him Manek."

"Could his name possibly be Josef Novak?"

I looked at him in silence.

"So go on sending telegrams," said the officer. "But don't forget the position of responsibility you now have. And your duty as a citizen is to *immediately* report anything that could lead us to a crime."

"If I knew anything like that. . ."

"Come and tell us."

"If it would help you. . ."

Ruda Mach woke up in a strange kitchen, rubbed his eyes, and wondered where he'd landed this time, but he was already getting up and looking for the pieces of his clothing, his shirt on a table, his trousers underneath the bed, and his shorts on the chandelier, goddamn it, I've been up to my old tricks again, the kitchen was full of smoke and smelled like a stable, some woman was asleep on a chair, another was coiled up in a knot by the door, and at her feet a shining flashlight.

Goddamn it, thought Ruda Mach, and he dressed quickly, checked his wallet (not a single crown: did those two rip me off or did I shell out that much yesterday? But it's today now and I don't give a good fart), he picked up his guitar, stepped over the woman lying by the door, in the john (they don't have water anywhere else) he drank out of the tank, jumped down from the toilet seat, and ran out—it was a morning out of a painting!

In June the most beautiful place to be is in the mountains, where I was this time last year, Ruda Mach thought as with his guitar in hand he trotted through sleeping Ostrava and remembered Sonya—I'd never had such a beautiful girl before, or since. And anyway, I need some fresh air.

He passed the gatekeeper's lodge (of an immense chemical enterprise) and across its enormous grounds, dug up by truck tires, over the gravel and tracks of a railway siding he came to a gigantic, half-built shed, where for three months now he'd been walling up a hundred-thousand-liter tank, he stripped to his shorts, smoked a fine Simon Arzt Egyptian cigarette, and got to work.

When the siren honked at ten o'clock, he lay down with his morning snack (a pound of smoked corned beef, without bread, and a bottle of beer) on a pile of shavings, soaked with sweat (his shorts felt as if he'd just climbed out of a pool), when he finished eating he got out his wallet and spread it out on his scraped-up knees.

From the left, "pleasure" half he dug out a letter from Jarunka Slana, who was in Usti, then he took out his waxed calendar, with his nail he put an end to yesterday and he thought deeply about the days to come. Above the dug-up plain of bare earth, in the blue sky, a silver distillation tower gleamed like a rocket ready for liftoff.

Finishing half a Simon Arzt cigarette, he went to the office and told the section chief that instead of his current twelve-hour shifts he'd be working sixteen hours starting today, and till ten at night he whizzed through his work at an accelerated tempo, at the station cafeteria he ate four franks and drank four beers, went to his dorm (since Christmas he'd been living in a wooden barracks with forty men), stripped to his shorts, and sat down on a pal's bunk for a game of cards.

But Ruda wasn't enjoying the cards very much, so he sat down by the window and strummed his guitar, suddenly a stone rattled the windowpane and the silhouette of a woman appeared behind the wire fence.

"Ruda. . ." she called softly.

"Oh, it's you, Eliska, my little powder puff," said Ruda, laying aside his guitar, "I'd completely forgotten about you—"

"I've been standing here a whole hour already," said the woman behind the fence.

"Well then, go to bed, it's pretty late!"

"But you promised me . . . And I was really looking forward. . ."

"Next time, Eliska. Bye," said Ruda, and he closed the window and lay down on his bunk.

Finishing a Simon Arzt in bed, he sat up, took out his wallet, dug Jarunka Slana's letter from the "pleasure" part, and once again he read it through carefully. Jarunka writes that Sonya is now a big shot at the Usti Cottex—but big shot or little shot, a skirt's always a skirt, and I'm a guy in pants. Ruda Mach reached for his guitar (thinking of Sonya) and raked his fingers lightly across its strings (his mind made up).

Three days later, with his suitcase and guitar, his pocket stuffed with a thick roll of hundred-notes (his unusually large bonus wouldn't fit in his wallet), Ruda Mach stood on the highway from Ostrava to Bohemia (he was looking forward to the trip), he smoked an expensive Simon Arzt cigarette (he was looking forward to seeing Sonya) and closed his eyes tight in the intense sparkle of a magnificent June morning (the finest joy in the entire world). He stopped truck after truck and asked them all if they were going to Bohemia.

"Where you headed?" the driver of an ancient rattling five-tonner asked him.

"Usti."

"Then you're in luck, I'm going to Carlsbad. Only I've got a lot of pick-ups to make, so it'll be three days before I make it to Usti."

"That's great," Ruda Mach rejoiced, "I like to travel!"

And he climbed into the cab, took his seat beside the driver, pulled his sixteen-times-folded school map out of his wallet, spread it out on his knees, and traced over it with his finger until he found Usti nad Labem (I've never been there, that's good), its double circle indicated that it has a population of more than fifty thousand, so it'd be a cinch for Ruda Mach to find a meal ticket there, and then all around it are mountains (he loved mountains) and a wide, blue river runs right through town, great, I'll sure like it there.

When her big iron alarmclock went off, Anna Rynoltova crawled out of her marriage bed and went to make breakfast, Arno Rynolt lit his morning cigarette, he enjoyed inhaling and letting the ashes fall on the floor (anyway, Anna didn't have anything to do all day, and I have to support her—), he tried to recall the Indian dancers he'd seen yesterday on TV, but Anna's tubercular cough from the other side of the wall (if that hag would only kick the bucket) thwarted his effort, furiously Rynolt got up, pulled a couple of times on his spring muscle builder (years ago he had served as an artillery officer and even after his discharge he worked at keeping himself in shape), but he gave it up when he was overcome by a tenacious smoker's cough (but luckily it gets much better after the morning!) and went to the bathroom.

After a short rinse-off, he spent a long time shaving and then, still in front of the mirror, he massaged his head with birch water and spread over his thick hair (like a young man's!) a thick coating of scented brilliantine, in his forty-fifth year he looked very well preserved and, snorting contentedly, he went off to breakfast.

"Where is that idiot?" he said to Anna gruffly.

"He's polishing shoes in the foyer."

"I thought he was running his trains again!"

"He will, but only when he's done with everything else and you give him your permission. . ."

"Pf—" said Rynolt, and he took a bite of cake, I'm trapped: married to a fifty-year-old tubercular hag with an idiot of a son who, at the age of twenty-three, still plays with electric trains! But it wouldn't be so easy to find another apartment in Prague.

After breakfast Rynolt took his packed briefcase off the sideboard, without a word he went out the front door and unlocked the car door, but before he got in he saw that Anna's idiot had got there first:

"Let me drive, Mr. Rynolt, please. . ."

"No way. Sit down and off we go."

"But you promised me that if I polished all your shoes—"

"You drove on Sunday and you will again soon. Hurry up!"

Rynolt drove slowly through the streets of Prague, yes, in Prague a driver has to keep his eyes open. "Where are you going, you pig!" he roared at a car that had pulled out right in front of him.

"But he had the right of way," Anna's idiot said from the back seat (I don't let him sit beside me), "according to the right-hand rule—"

"Shut your trap! Anyway, I'm the one on the main road!"

"But this isn't a main road. . ."

"Shut your trap or you'll have to take the streetcar, you idiot."

In spite of several minor near-collisions, Rynolt got to his plant without injury and without getting a ticket.

Rynolt's "plant" is actually only an auxiliary to the Usti Cottex, here a mere twenty-two employees arrange and pack Cottex colors into sample boxes or according to the customer's wishes, it is known officially as the "adjustment center," but Rynolt considered himself a "plant manager" and he would defer to anyone who called him "Director."

While passing the gatekeeper (the old hag was knitting curtains again), Rynolt put on an affable expression, which did not leave his face the entire time of his stay in the plant: in Prague it's awfully hard to find anyone willing to work, especially for such miserable pay.

"Today you'll sweep the courtyard!" Rynolt commanded Anna's idiot (no woman would do it), and getting out of the car he went straight to his office (let the idiot drive it into the garage, I can't get the angle right) where two enraged women were already waiting for him (I hadn't paid them for work they hadn't done), affably Rynolt heard them out, then excused them and promised to pay them everything they asked, to find anyone in Prague who's willing to work is awfully hard and it's almost impossible to keep them.

Rynolt soon took care of his own work, in a committee spirit he divided his work so that there was almost nothing left for him, then he strolled through his three divisions and smiled affably at everyone, when Mrs. Brunclikova refused to ride her bicycle to the post office, he smiled at her affably and sent Anna's idiot instead.

Two Tatra six-oh-threes suddenly glided into the courtyard, and Rynolt panicked (that gatekeeping cow with her endless knitting couldn't be bothered buzzing me!) when the bigwig managers from Usti rolled out of the limos, Rynolt already knew the new director, Ludvik, from a conference in Usti, right behind him came a magnificent red-headed kitten and then the poisoners and hatchetmen we know and love.

L.L. had gotten to work before Rynolt had even had a chance

to greet him properly, Rynolt received his first reprimand from L.L. and then that red-headed kitten pulled out some papers and reprimand after reprimand rained down on him, but suddenly Heaven was gracious: the telephone announced that L.L. must go immediately to the ministry.

L.L. and his gang (who were having a fine time waiting for us) jumped into their cars and in a cloud of dust (hadn't that idiot swept yet? That scarecrow couldn't even handle a broom!) burst out of the courtyard, and when the dust had settled a bit, there was the red-headed kitten standing in the middle of the courtyard.

"Sonya Cechova," she said when Rynolt went up to her and smiled at her most affably, "Comrade Director gave me two hours off—won't you show me around?"

"But of course, I'd be very happy—" Rynolt twittered (now I can get a really good look at her—*fantastic!*) and he guided Sonya through the three shops, upstairs and down, but of course there was very little to show her (pouring powder into boxes and sticking on labels), so during the fourth tour of the same shop Sonya suddenly smiled prettily at Rynolt.

"Thanks, that should be enough, Comrade Director. I'd like to be a little bit naughty now. . ."

"I am completely at your service . . . Comrade Chief—" Rynolt said happily, stroking his hair with its caked brilliantine.

"L.L. gave me two hours off and I've only used up a half hour of that. I was born in Prague, you know, and I haven't been here for so many years—"

"As you please . . . I'd be very happy to . . . I'll give you a personal tour of Prague, one you won't forget for a very long time. . ." Rynolt said sweetly, and he took this opportunity to cast his first studied glance in Sonya's direction.

In downtown Prague, I asked Rynolt to stop just before we reached Havel Street and to wait for me in the car — I wanted to go there alone.

The protruding windows of ancient houses with archways (our house is nine hundred years old) smiled down at me and I was suddenly a little girl again, this is the street I walked down on my way to school, this orange mailbox (it was blue then) is where I put Daddy's letters, Daddy always lifted me up in his arms to reach the slot — and now my girlhood street melted away behind a curtain of tears, through which I saw our house, the archway where I used to jump rope, our second-floor windows, and on up past masonry tortured over the centuries, to the dark windows of the black tower which Mrs. Janikova, the queen, would climb — blood flowing down her face (when will *I* climb my own black tower—), then I couldn't see anything anymore, the street broke into burning marbles when out of my family's house came the smell of ironing—

Rynolt must have loaded me into his car, I wasn't conscious of anything at all until I switched to L.L.'s black car and we drove away through the Prague streets of my student years, where Daddy and I would go to the movies, and the park where I had my first kiss—

"Did something get in your eye?" L.L. asked.

I made myself blink when they took me away from my own hometown, which I love and where my husband lives.

We whizzed off along the expressway, L.L. was in a triumphant mood, the minister had approved all his measures, both accomplished and forthcoming, L.L. turned on the radio full blast and to the beat of the music we hurtled northward along the River Elbe, the sun at our back.

To our building No. 2000 — *ours* because L.L. had moved into the second floor, into his predecessor's apartment (it's the director's apartment and by moving in L.L. gained an extra room, and all three are larger and more comfortable than the two he'd had before). L.L. invited me to his apartment "for a glass of bubbly on the occasion of this wonderful day," I thanked him but refused, and tramped up to my own apartment — was I really at home here? What could I do if L.L. decided to start paying me visits?

I don't know if it's good that I'm living in the same building as L.L., that I'm living in his house (like Cleopatra in Rome? Huh!), that we're together in the same building twenty-four hours a day . . . but Mrs. Zora is *sincerely* friendly to me and Lanka . . . I don't know what she's thinking (and I don't have any illusions: why should L.L.'s daughter like me?), but she always says hello to me and she says it first and *very* respectfully. But I no longer like it here like I used to. . .

L.L. wasn't thinking only about his apartment (my L.L. really *is* a great director!), the day after we got back from Prague he asked me to order a car "for twenty minutes from now."

"Where are you going?" I asked him.

"You'll see," he smiled at me, we went out to the courtyard and in five minutes we were climbing up the stairs to my old dorm.

L.L. just sighed when he saw the thirty bunks lined up and arranged around the little square with its table and solitary chair. So much clothing was hanging between the dormer windows that the room was nearly dark, I recognized several of the girls but most of them were new, on my old lower bunk sat a girl with her suitcase on her lap writing a letter on pink paper, on the upper bunk above her my Rumanian girl lay with her bare brown legs hanging down and fsht!—she threw a burning butt past the girl writing below.

"We'll leave *no more* than eight of them here," said L.L.

"And the others?"

"I've found a building in town that we'll fix up for our girls, for the others now and for those in the future — would you see to this matter yourself?"

"I'd be happy to—thanks."

"I'm giving you a free hand with the furnishing. But before you go buying pictures, come and get some advice from me."

"What kind of pictures should the girls have?"

"Pictures of the sea," L.L. said drily, and when we returned to his office he gave me a letter of appointment naming me the chief in charge of his secretariat, with a salary that made me rub my eyes. It was enough to live on even if Manek were unemployed . . . even with our child.

The very same day I was to name all five of my subordinates, by now I knew the Cottex people well enough to make the choices: the elegant and handsome young lawyer ("Huh!" L.L. said in a huff) and four of the ugliest clerks ("Huh!" L.L. laughed), and at once I loaded on the work as L.L. did to me.

Before the end of the working day I wrote Manek a letter, brief as a telegram, No. 99 (after the visit of the security officer, no more telegrams, but I could hardly rescue Manek that way) and on the envelope I wrote, as I had so many times before: *Manuel Mansfeld, Hotel Imperial, Liberec.*

I looked at the white envelope and all of a sudden I felt a wave of anger rise within me: when he writes cables directly to *me*, why to *him*, MY HUSBAND, must I continue to write indirectly, via Liberec (if he wants to stay in hiding, then why does he send heaps of open telegrams?), via the bribed clerk at the Hotel Imperial who, at Manek's "categorical wish" (as he told me last summer), refused to say anything about Manek . . . Had Manek bribed him to act *against me?.* . .

I took the white envelope out of the typewriter, read it over again, crumpled it, and threw it and the envelope into the wastebasket. I don't know how — but not like this anymore.

On the 20th of June Cottex celebrated the 20th anniversary of its founding (my division was busy for twenty hours a day getting ready), the jubilee day was formally opened by speeches from the minister and L.L. in the courtyard, it was a fantastic morning, L.L. got up on a barrel, spoke briefly, to the point and, in general, magnificently (where had he picked that up? As director of production he could hardly manage a few witticisms), all the streets around Cottex were blocked by official cars, and the minister told me I make the best coffee in the world (I smiled at him prettily for that). That evening the jubilee was celebrated in all the rooms of the Usti House of Culture, and the entire town came.

In my first evening dress (green with a deep décolletage, on my neck a sixty-crown gold heart—part of my special bonus—Manek had never given me anything. . .) and in golden slippers I welcomed the guests at the door until L.L. said I was off "till tomorrow." Five orchestras were playing in five halls, young men were dancing with their girls—and all of a sudden I felt so old that I went looking for the bar.

Mr. Ziki suddenly popped up out in the crowded corridor, a glass of vermouth in his hand (with lemon and ice, the way I used to serve it to him at the Hotel Hubertus), and he was wearing a dark-brown dinner jacket and a painfully yellow tie woven from strips of leather.

"I'm glad to see you," Ziki said casually, as if we had just met that week at another dancing affair. I stuck my tongue out at him.

"You're like a Greek peach. . ." he told me, and he rattled the ice in his glass and gazed at the floating circlet of lemon.

"But they have big, hard stones, Zikoun," I told him, and I went off to dance with the minister. Ziki danced with the minister's wife and stared at me over her shoulder.

Then Jakub Jagr came after me, in each hand a glass of cognac: "Drink with me, Sonya—"

"But before, when I was cleaning all your shoes, you used to stand over me and lecture me on the perniciousness of alcohol—"

"Sonya, I love you—"

"Then drink up both glasses. My husband has forbidden me to drink."

Manek had actually done that (in letter NR. 36—I know them all by heart), at least when I'm not with him, but then aren't I always with him? And so I went to the bar and downed a Cuban rum à la Methusalah.

Five orchestras were playing in five different rooms, young men were dancing with their girls, I downed another

Methusalah (does that mean I'm going to drink alone another ninety-nine years?) and danced with all and sundry . . . but the young men were taking their girls to out-of-the-way parts of the corridors, galleries, and stairs, and there they were *kissing*—

I downed another Methusalah and made myself blink, I was beat when I left the party . . . But don't bawl, girlie, and make your life easier, go home in a taxi! The taxi cost me twenty crowns. For that I could have cooked dinner for two.

On the third floor of my Roman building No. 2000, in front of the door to my apartment, Ruda Mach was sitting on his suitcase strumming his guitar.

"Hi, love!" he said as if we had parted the day before, and with a boyish lack of manners he pushed right into my apartment.

"You've got it good here, " he said once inside the door, and he tossed his suitcase onto my red daybed. "I'll like it here," he said, and then he took the thermometer off the wall (a gift L.L. got from a German director in Jena) and hung his guitar on the nail.

"Put that thermometer back this minute!" I shouted, gradually coming to my senses.

"But you won't be needing it! With me you'll always be warm!" Ruda Mach said merrily, and he came toward me, embraced me (I resisted, but he was *much* stronger than me), and gave me a kiss that lasted nearly ten minutes (with my back I rubbed off a good piece of the wall).

"That's enough," Ruda Mach said contentedly. "And now I'd like something to eat! Girl, I've spent three days looking for you!"

And since I wasn't in any condition to say much of anything (I was out of breath from Ruda's kiss and I was massaging my sore spine and shoulderblades), Ruda Mach went into my kitchen and cleaned out the refrigerator.

"That's enough," he said happily. "Girl, for three days all I've been eating is salami and rolls. So tell me what you're up to— and then we can go to bed, okay?" And like a connoisseur he fingered the red daybed (Manek's. But why isn't it *Manek* who's here?) and smiled at me roguishly: "We sure'll sleep fine on this!"

"It's not for you. Clear out!" I said, and I took his guitar off the nail in the wall and tossed it into his lap.

"Whatever you say, but first a little music, okay? I'm all for that, I like music—" Ruda Mach smiled and began to strum his guitar for me. He quietly took off his boots, one boot pushing the other off. I stood with my hands folded, worrying what I should do . . . all alone with this lug.

"Sonya, come here and sit next to me. . ."

"Get lost!" I screamed at him, and I kicked over his suitcase. A heel flew off of my golden slipper, damn!

"Don't kick that like a soccer ball," Ruda Mach said quietly, "or you'll break the present I brought you. . ." and he picked up his suitcase and took out a tiny mirror (worth about three crowns), on the back there was a calendar (Manek had never given me anything—).

"I'll call the police!" I said.

"No you won't. Sonya, come here—" Ruda Mach said softly, and still seated he pulled his shirt over his head, and once again I found myself pressed between him and the wall—

"You deserted me!" I screamed right into his face, and then I struck his face with my fist (he just laughed).

"But now I've come for you again."

"You betrayed me and you left me—" and with all my strength I punched him between the eyes (he just shook it off).

"But now I'm back with you again."

His arms were tough as tires, and he pulled me down onto the rug (a beauty that had cost four hundred crowns, with a quiet pattern, second-category) with a force I could not oppose all *alone*, why am I ALONE, I howled "MAAANEEK—" and I felt a terrible RAGE at Manek . . . I *hated* him, and I stopped resisting Ruda.

"Sonya . . . Love. . ." whispered Ruda Mach (my first

husband), "I wanted to see you so much . . . So tell me, what have you been up to all this time?"

"When was the last time we saw each other?"

"Last summer, in the mountains . . . We were living together in my room, number five. . ."

"Number five, that's right . . . It was five that I liked to clean best . . . And after that the Bridal Suite. . ."

"So tell me, what've you been up to all this time?"

"What have I been up to . . . I don't know myself anymore . . . Maybe I just dreamed it all . . . Yes, this is what I want . . . And tomorrow morning I'll get up, take that leather satchel, and go shopping for two . . . two pounds of bread . . . and ten dekas of cheese . . . but my husband prefers meat . . . Two slices of pot roast and two pounds of tomatoes . . . and beer for my. . . And a white handkerchief. . ."

"Sonya . . . Love. . ." whispered Ruda Mach, and tenderly he took me again. . . Then he fell right to sleep and in a minute he was snoring lightly.

I slept like the dead and dreamt about monkeys.

"Hi, love," Ruda Mach yawned, squinted at his wristwatch (he never took it off in bed), and he was already on his feet, from the bathroom Ruda's joyful splashing in the shower (in a bathroom a man is a song), and when Ruda came back to the bedroom the streaming water glistened on his tough bronzed back and the hard and mobile forms of his muscles and sinews, and it sparkled in the dark growth of his chest (after a bath a man is poetry).

"Give me my shirt—" he muttered (he always wakes up angry), and when he pulled it over his wet body, the water marbleized the fabric.

"Here," he said, and he put a wad of hundred-notes on the glass-topped table, "I'm off to see about a job and when I get it I'll stay with it. So long . . . and buy me some swimming trunks. I'll be home at three."

And then he left. I double-locked the door after him and devoid of any thought I paced through my apartment (how much of it is still mine?), tripped over Ruda's suitcase, fell down, and bumped my knee — until suddenly I came to my senses.

That's it! Isn't it all too much all at once?

How many exams I've passed already. How many times I've gotten ready for my wedding. How many times I've started at the very beginning . . . started with nothing and after three disasters three times become a new person — now I want to BE a new person.

"I'm a woman now, Manek . . . your Spanish Riding School reins are *too* long for me now, I've run around the ring so many times now and all you do is keep turning in place in the middle of the sandy arena with your absurdly long whip . . . I want to have you *in the saddle* now and feel your spurs, eat from your hand, and perhaps even be beaten—but *I CAN NO LONGER BE ALONE.*

AND I DON'T WANT TO BE. AND I WON'T.

Manek, I've already finished your correspondence college, you've taught me all you know. Now *I* have something to teach *you*: love is being together. I have already grown up in your image, now I will bring you back to life in mine, now *I* will lift *you* to it. *LOVE IS BEING TOGETHER.*

L.L. gave me the day off, good. Ruda Mach left me a bottle of milk in the fridge, that should be enough. I showered and drank warm milk, then packed my suitcase, my nightgown: a green one (for everyday now), into my satchel I put my citizen's I.D., all my money, my deposit book . . . and my lipstick, comb, and the mirror with the calendar on the back.

OK. What else should I. . . I took all Manek's telegrams and letters out of the wardrobe and burned them, sheet by sheet, over the bathtub. And I used the shower hose to rinse the black ashes down the drain.

OK. What else should I. . . In front of the bathroom mirror I carefully combed my hair and made myself up.

OK. What else. . . There was a sip of milk left in the bottle, I drank it . . . may the taste remain on my palate and my tongue, so that my first kiss will taste of milk.

I double-locked the door and, with my suitcase and my satchel, I quietly ran down the stairs, I wouldn't have liked to run into L.L. now—

"Miss Cechova," the porter called after me, "the postman left you this yesterday—"

I opened the thick package from Prague out on the street (but how glad I would have been to go back upstairs and wait for you at home), inside was the tome *Principles of Industrial Programming* and a letter from Manek saying that the Hotel Trianon, where we'd forgotten it, had returned the book to him and that he loved me (four pages), but no *COME* or *I'M COMING.*

I crammed the tome into my suitcase, I threw the envelope on the dusty street, and I took streetcar No. 3 to the main station.

BOOK THREE
SONYA 01

I am standing with my suitcase in front of the gray Liberec station, red streetcars climb up the hill toward me and with a clang they go back down, the Hotel Imperial is three minutes down this street. But this time I won't expose myself. During my three-hour train ride from Usti, I had time to think everything over. All that's left is action.

I took a red streetcar down the hill past the glass doors of the Imperial and on as far as the second square, last summer I had noticed another hotel not far from here and I soon found it, it was called the Golden Lion and they had a single room for me on the fourth floor. I unpacked my things and settled in. I will stay here until I've tracked Manek down.

All that's left is action. I made inquiries at the reception desk, and at a specialty shop near the theater I bought the sort of false eyelashes fashion models wear, the blackest, longest, and thickest they had, and a hairnet, then at an office supplies store a large, thick notebook bound in black, a ballpoint pen, and a cheap briefcase made of artificial leather. Then elsewhere on the square a horrible-looking hat with a turned-up brim.

In my hotel room I spent a lot of time in front of the mirror putting on the false eyelashes: they were so long and thick, they sat on my eyes like two big black moths. I put my hair up, fastened it with hairpins, stuffed it into the net, and topped it all off with the horrible hat, which I turned up over my ears and in back — even Manek wouldn't recognize me now.

I blink, with difficulty, so I can get accustomed to wearing the eyelashes, they make my eyes tear up (poor fashion models:

I don't envy them their job or their vocation), and I go on getting ready. On the label of the thick notebook I write, in large letters, *OFFICIAL TRIPS JULY-DECEMBER* and then I start laying out the inside, there have to be a lot of columns, since I didn't buy a ruler I have to make lines using something else, I dig into my suitcase, I find the tome *Principles of Industrial Programming* and, using its edges, I draw lines on the first fifty pages of the notebook, in the columns I've made I use the ballpoint pen to write all sorts of dates, names, and numbers.

Then I lick my thumb, rub it on all the pages, wipe it against the label on the cover, and roll the notebook in the dust under the bed (I did a better job with the rooms I cleaned at the Hubertus), then I go to work on the briefcase I've just bought, it looks much too new so I smear it with the ballpoint pen, spit on it a little, rub it on the floor, trample it, and bend it over my knees, until finally it looks authentic. Then I put in the thick notebook I've worked on so long, wink at myself in the mirror (the false eyelashes really look terrific from a distance), and take a streetcar to the Hotel Imperial.

Chance wasn't on my side: through the glass doors I saw the reception clerk who had refused last September to give me Manek's address, because "That would be against Mr. Mansfeld's categorical wishes." — I remember his face and every word he spoke to me. Presumably he had been on the day shift since summer — evidently a sly fellow whom Manek had chosen to be his collaborator. How much does Manek pay him to conceal his whereabouts from me (and from others?)?

No matter. We will wait until the shift changes, we will wait till evening, till night, or till tomorrow. I walked around Liberec, I had a few snacks in various places, I rested in the waiting room at the station, I drank coffee at the sweet shop, and every two hours I glanced through the glass doors of the Imperial to see if Manek's collaborator was still behind the reception desk. Finally, at half past six in the evening he was replaced by an unfamiliar colleague.

I was determined to obtain Manek's address through three stages of escalation:

1. *Trickery:* "Good afternoon, my name is Makovickova and the Comrade Chief of our audit department has sent me to your hotel," I start off by babbling like a real office drudge, "because one of our comrades is claiming reimbursement for a trip here on—" here I start leafing through my smeared-up ledger, "here it is, on August twenty-ninth and thirtieth, but we don't have an official voucher, and so if you would be so good, I beg you, please tell me if our Comrade Mansfeld was actually here on those days—"

The goal of *trickery* is to get him to show me the guest book (I've never seen one in real life before, but I've seen a lot of them in films), where I could find Manek's address. Should *trickery* not succeed, a further escalation follows:

2. *Bribery:* "Your colleague from the day shift promised to give me Mr. Mansfeld's address for three hundred crowns, I rushed off to get the money but now he isn't here—couldn't you give it to me and take the money for him? It's really urgent and I'm really desperate—"

Either this would have an effect on the reception clerk (I would be smiling especially beautifully at him and batting my eyelashes as well), or he would get an itch himself for the three hundred, or he would go into a rage because the colleague Manek had hired had paid him much less in the past (if he'd paid him at all) — or it wouldn't work, and then I'd be left with the final stage of escalation:

3. *Threat:* "I'm putting an end to your dirty little espionage games! You've been operating long enough now as a dead letter office—but have you declared your take to the hotel book-keeper?! I've sent a lot of letters and telegrams here—now I'd like to know what you did with them. A human life is at stake. Would you like to make an account of your activities as a collaborator? Here's how it is: you tell me now or you tell the police in ten minutes!"

I went through the glass doors into the sparkling mahogany

lobby and stopped in front of the reception desk. The new clerk was a young, good-looking boy. . .

"What can I do for you?" he said very very nicely, and even through my almost opaque eyelashes I could see at once that this boy would do anything for me (and it bothered me that I was wearing such a preposterous hat).

"My office has sent me to verify the official travel of one of our workers," I said and smiled at him *beautifully.*

"When was that?" he said, and he gave me the *sweetest* smile.

"The twenty-ninth and thirtieth of August."

The clerk fished out a heavy file from under the counter (well, there it is: there really is no guest book) and went to sit down at his desk (I'd have needed a periscope to read over his shoulder), he leafed through the registration forms and asked me for the number of the room. I gave him both rooms: 522, where I stayed, and 523, which was Manek's.

"It checks out: both are under the same name and I'll write you a confirmation," said the clerk, and he gave me the most *delectable* smile and began to write.

"For the record it would be good to have all the dates, his address, and soon — I've got a very strict boss . . . and I'd like so much to come and stay here some time myself. . ." I told him and smiled *very beautifully* at him.

"But of course, I'm happy to be of service," said the clerk, and he gave me the most *devoted* smile, finished the statement, stamped it, signed it, put it in an envelope, and handed it to me over the counter.

"You are so very kind. . ." I said to him with a smile of *promise.*

"However I can be of service . . . I've got nothing to do till tomorrow morning. . ."

I pulled the confirmation out of the envelope and rage clouded my vision as I read:

*The management of the Hotel Imperial confirms that on
29-30 August there stayed in rooms Nos. 522 and 523 Mr.
Josef Novak, born 10 February 1937 in Prague, domiciled at
Prague 4, Pod schody 4, and he paid the bill for his rooms
in cash.*

". . .and the nights here are so long. . ." said the clerk with a
smile of *longing* — another bribed scoundrel had tried to trick
me.

"Scoundrel! You couldn't think up a stupider name than Josef
Novak—you could at least have a little imagination, especially
when you lie on hotel stationery—"

". . .? Excuse me?? . . . But I. . ." The clerical swine behind
the counter was playing his part like a great actor. How much
does Manek pay him for this?

Out on the street I pulled off my false eyelashes, hat, and
hairnet and threw them all into my smudged (unnecessarily!)
briefcase . . . in my room at the Golden Lion I was fit to cry.
My husband had raised an unscalable wall against me . . .
Should I go back and wait for another letter from him—while
I'm in bed with Ruda Mach?

Joylessly I began to pack my suitcase (L.L. had only given me
one day off), I dragged it out as long as I could . . . but in a few
minutes everything was back in the suitcase, there were so few
things after all . . . all that was left was *Principles of Industrial
Programming*, the book I always leave behind. . .

ALWAYS? — No. Only at the Hotel Trianon—

Quickly I reached for Manek's last letter, the book had been
sent to him from the Trianon, where we had left it underneath
our wedding bed, and suddenly I recalled our trip to the
Trianon from Dobris Castle, how Manek sat me in the lobby in
a medieval high-backed leather armchair and walked up to the
counter *with his red I.D. booklet—*

How many clerks could he bribe, I kept repeating to myself

the next day (L.L. will have to wait) when I got off the morning express at Prague Central Station.

The taxi driver in the black Volga knew where the Trianon was, and after twenty minutes on a concrete highway and two minutes on a narrow asphalt road between fields I walked into the elegant yellow building where I had spent my wedding night.

The reception clerk was wearing a tuxedo and again it was someone new . . . there certainly are enough of them.

"I stayed here on the fifteenth of March in room No. 15," I told him and smiled at him prettily, "and I left behind a book called *Principles of Industrial Programming.* My boss sent me here to pick it up."

"Just a moment," said the clerk, and he flipped through a notepad and said, "Yes, that's right, we found the book on March 15 and sent it off to the registration address. A bit late, please forgive us, but we always wait a while to see if the guest turns up in person, since we sometimes have trouble when we forward things . . . We sent your book on the sixteenth of June."

"But we ought to have received it by now—"

"You can be sure we sent it *registered mail.* Here's the receipt."

The form gave the Hotel Trianon as addressor, and as addressee: *Josef Novak, Prague 4, Pod schody 4.*

That time we came here from Dobris Castle, Manek sat me in this lobby in that medieval high-backed leather armchair and walked up to that counter with his red I.D. booklet.

"Is everything in order?" asked the clerk.

"Yes, and thank you," I said, and I left the building where I had spent my wedding night, got into the black Volga, and asked to be taken to Prague 4, Pod schody 4.

It was a dark, narrow alley of tall old houses, not a tree in sight, not even a blade of grass, and sooty, pale children of the metropolis were playing in the dust. According to a glass-covered list, the occupants of No. 4 were Josef Vanecek, Jiri Petrak, Miroslav Kindl, Pavel Braveny, Radomil Kucera,

Lubomir Snezny, Valerie Solcova, Arno Rynolt — of course, no Josef Novak.

Arno Rynolt . . . the same name as the head of our Prague adjustment center, the one who drove me around Prague! Could it be him? Well, Prague's a big place.

I let the taxi go, passed through some sort of gate and, in the courtyard, put on my false eyelashes, crammed my hair into the net, and topped it all off with that frightful hat, which I turned up over my neck and ears, and then I went to ask the porter about Josef Novak.

"Yeah, he lives here all right, on the third floor. And Rynoltova's home, she came home from the dairy store just a little while ago," the porter's wife told me most eagerly.

I walked up to the third floor and rang at the door with the card *ARNO RYNOLT*, the door was opened by an old woman with a frightened look.

"I've come for Josef Novak!" I fired off right on the threshold.

"Good heavens," the old woman was startled, "but that officer from the Security Police told me you wouldn't lock him up. . ."

"I've just come from the general. Where is Josef Novak?"

"He'll be back in three hours. Please come in."

Through the dark, jam-packed vestibule into the jam-packed living room (but it was neat) and on to a tiny children's room: on the wallpaper scenes from fairy tales, on the shelves perfectly lined-up toys and books, on top of the wardrobe a great big blow-up pink elephant, and over half the floor a child's electric train set with tiny tunnels, stations, bridges, signal lights, animals, and human figures.

"My son has lived here for thirty-three years," said the old woman. "What harm can a boy do who is happiest playing with his train set?"

I blinked my heavy lashes and it's a wonder they didn't come off.

"Do you have a photo . . . of your son," I said when I'd caught my breath again, "one you haven't submitted to us yet?"

"I've only got one, and the officer gave it back to me already—" and the old woman brought me a photo, the one I had already seen in the hands of the security officer. Manek was smiling at me over his train set.

With an effort I blinked my fashion-model eyelashes.

"I beg you for my son," said the old woman, and she began to moan softly, "he's all I've got in the world now. . ."

"The general has authorized me to close this case," I said after a long time (a hundred years) or a very short one (as when lightning strikes from heaven and then thunder claps). "If you tell me everything, and I really mean *everything*, I can guarantee that we will leave your son, Josef Novak, alone."

"I told your officer everything," Manek's mother said softly. "I'm gravely ill . . . I won't be in the world very long. My husband died when Josef was three. Since then I've lived only for him. I didn't have a happy life . . . and so I tried at least to give him a lovely childhood . . . and to spare him from everything bad. I married again just for my son . . . The first time it was necessary, but my second husband—"

"Arno Rynolt."

"—my second husband doesn't like Josef. He oppresses him . . . and torments both of us. And Josef is afraid of him . . . but he doesn't want to leave me alone with him. He loves me just as I do him . . . He has no friends, he doesn't go out with girls, he stays home all the time with me . . . I have a wonderful son. Please intercede for him . . . He's still just a child—"

"Yes . . . He's still playing games. . ."

"All his spare time. Rynolt keeps him around his plant, mostly to do the dirty work no one else will do, and so Josef has few pleasures: he plays with his train set or drives the car, but that belongs to Rynolt, and so Josef gets it only a few times a year. Josef likes everything on wheels . . . And he reads lots of books, sometimes we read fairy tales together, just like the days when things were good — he's still just a boy. . ."

"Yes."

"If you need to see anything more . . . Please, take a good

look at all his things, at the entire room . . . I'll leave you here by yourself. My son comes home from work in three hours."

"Thank you. I'll take a good look around . . . I think we can settle everything quite smoothly now. Let me just keep this photo for the time being."

I needed it, like a pinch on the cheek, to show me it wasn't just a dream. Manek's mother left the room, and I was left alone in my husband's room—that of a ten-year-old boy.

The train set, the fairy tales, and the blow-up pink elephant . . . a few hundred-notes for the clerk at the Imperial and for the waiter at Dobris Castle, Mr. Rynolt's car, and a few letters and telegrams.

Maybe at least my letters would be there somewhere—

I found them quickly (it's unbelievable how quickly the tiny room revealed its secrets), beneath a well-thumbed, illustrated edition of *ALICE IN WONDERLAND*, which lay at the bottom of a drawer, they were hidden in a black school notebook tied with shoelaces, on its label, written in a childishly uneven hand:

III. B

DRAWINGS

Josef Novak

and inside, all my letters and telegrams stuck between the notebook pages, which were thickly covered with Manek's familiar script.

On the first page, in large printed characters:

MANUEL MANSFELD
THE FOUR SONYAS: A PROFESSIONAL WOMAN

On the very first page my own name caught my eye, and soon I was lost in Josef Novak's fairy-tale romance:

. . .we arrived at Hrusov nad Jizerou. R. ordered me to wash the car so he wouldn't have to buy me a soda, and he and Mama went into the restaurant at the Hotel Hubertus. When it started to rain, I leaned against the wall and through a window I saw Sonya Cechova for the very first time. I decided that she was *the one.*

I was attracted by the absolute randomness of my selection, by the advantageous distance from Prague, as well as by the obviously primitive character of this village waitress. The vessel for holding my great synthesis had to be absolutely empty.

Mother and R. remained in the bar about an hour, during that time I ascertained from the local drunk, Hnyk, who had also taken shelter from the rain, a whole series of exciting facts about the girl I had chosen. Now what I needed was to see her at closer range, obviously without R. or Mama. Therefore, right after that outing to the Giant Mountains, I began to grovel before R. as obsequiously as possible, so that he would lend me his car for my fairy-tale game.

I had my first opportunity to study Sonya Cechova at close range during the First Floricultural Evening. Under the transparent pretense of a floricultural lottery she had to kiss all the customers in the bar, and she performed this task with such devotion, perhaps even relish, that I congratulated myself on my selection.

I redoubled my slavish toadying to R. so that he would lend me the car for a visit to the Second Floricultural Evening, and by telephone I reserved the finest room at the Hubertus. I drove to Hrusov firmly resolved to abduct Sonya, without further delay, to the land on the other side of my looking-glass, but this second "floricultural evening" distastefully turned into a brawl, and the biggest brawler, Ruda Mach, simply picked Sonya up and carried her off to his room, thus stealing her away from me. When I left Hrusov the next morning, all I could do was send a kiss towards her window and reconcile myself to failure.

Under these circumstances, I could hardly continue my undertaking. R. was furious that I didn't bring back the car till Monday morning and that I drove it straight to work, so that he had to take the streetcar: he grounded me for an entire month. Mama had a severe attack of nerves because I hadn't stayed away all night since I did my military service twelve years ago. I read her her favorite fairy tales till she fell asleep, and then I carried her to bed in my arms. Mama keeps getting lighter and lighter.

I tried to patch things up with Vera Provaznikova and to play my fairy-tale game with her. But Vera doesn't want to talk to me anymore, because she despises me for the way I failed her that time at Prevor Gardens. Why is it that every time I do a perfect job of cultivating a girl and getting her warmed up to me, I have to start sweating and thinking of Mama, and then nothing ever comes of it. Maybe I ought to see a doctor.

I wasted the whole summer making another unsuccessful attempt with Jitka Klanska. In reply to her ad in *Young People's Weekly*, I wrote her a sixteen-page letter full of motifs from classical world literature—this caught her fancy. We wrote every day then, but our meeting in Zbraslav Castle park ended in painful failure. I didn't lie to her enough, and the stories I made up were lousy.

Over this entire period, I was getting regular letters from Josef Hnyk, the Hrusov drunk: I had given him a hundred crowns that time in the rain in front of the Hubertus, so that he would keep me informed about Sonya. Greedy for money which, for obvious reasons, I no longer sent him, he kept on sending me information, and from his only half-literate letters I learned how, over the course of time, Sonya lived with Mach, and then how he deserted her.

This new circumstance and my failures with Vera Provaznikova and Jitka Klanska turned my attention back to Sonya Cechova. Of course, her surrender to Mach deprived her of the ideal fairy-tale purity, but at the same time it confirmed her absolute mediocrity and her primitive character. To mold a person out of such common clay is the main inspiration of this romance which, employing literary devices, takes a complete nonentity and synthesizes her into a great romantic heroine, and a living one.

Today's fashionable, snobbish literary criticism may assert that the novel is dead, but I am making this my Great Experiment, and with its publication in novel form I will demonstrate to the world the immortality of the novel as a literary genre, but, even more important, the continuing influence of long-standing motifs of world literature. Should this strike some people as kitsch, I must point out that certain analogous circumstances can be found in Homer, Shakespeare, Lev Tolstoy, and all the great writers. But in contrast to them, I do not merely imagine my circumstances, I invoke them in their full reality.

Hnyk's report concerning preparations for a Third Floricultural Evening gave me the impulse to renew my experiment. I reserved the Bridal Suite at the Hotel Hubertus, begged R.'s permission to use his car and, according to a scenario I'd come up with many years before, obtained the services of the reception clerk at the Hotel Imperial in Liberec for two hundred crowns a month, and reserved two single rooms at the hotel.

Only a couple of days remained, so I had to crawl before R., not on my knees, but this time on my belly, to get him to lend me his car to make the trip to Hrusov that Sunday. I took out all my savings and the hundred-notes went flying out of my hands. I had to give two hundred crowns to Volrab, the manager of the Hubertus, so I could carry Sonya off to my Bridal Suite, from which, according to my great literary models, I could properly and with her consent run off with her to Liberec.

Sonya's consent to running off with me confirmed my hypothesis, and it was in this spirit that I designed my behavior toward her throughout the time of our stay together in Liberec in a composite of the styles of Dumas-Remarque-girls' novels. In this beginning stage I naturally had to develop models that resonate in accord with the reader's subconscious idea of a naive girl.

That happy day in Liberec, I was able, in conversation with Sonya, to utilize my years of reading literature, even travel writing. The strongest impression I made on her was my description of sunrise on Mount Everest as written by Lorenz and Wassermann. According to principles of the most basic psychoanalysis, I first gained her confidence by getting her to talk about herself. My success was so striking that, after twenty-four hours of direct contact, Sonya clearly longed to give herself to me. But again my perennial weakness made its appearance before the final step and I spent the whole night locked in my room, soaked in sweat, thinking about Mama and, in terror, of how furious R. would be when I came back with his car even later than last time.

For that reason I was relieved when, after that terrible night, Sonya suddenly disappeared from the Hotel Imperial. Of course, it would not have been difficult to predict her further development, but at the same time I was sorry to give up an experiment so successfully launched. So I left my photo with the slogan *I WANT YOU TO BE GREAT* with the bribed reception clerk, made arrangements with him to give the photo to her and to forward her letters to me, told him not to reveal my address, and hurried home. R. beat me with a cane and Mama had a terrible attack because of my almost two-day absence from home. She was afraid I might never come back. When I carried her to her bed, already asleep, she again felt significantly lighter.

Entirely in accordance with my suppositions, Sonya eagerly began to write me at my Liberec forwarding address from her imprisonment at Jakub Jagr's. In her long as well as in her brief letters she desperately begged me to carry her away, which was, of course, quite impossible. I must confess that the passion and depth of her feeling exceeded my suppositions, and when I received her telegram, "I am waiting at the Hotel Imperial," I realized that, as in one of the Arabian Nights, I had released from the bottle a djinni mightier than myself.

In order to bring things back into balance, I commanded Sonya by telegraph to return to Jakub Jagr and win back his love. This did not mean the end of my experiment, however, because on the one hand, a merely technically trained and hence only half-civilized engineer in Usti n. L. could never compete with my fairy-tale heroes, and on the other hand, I was making it possible for Sonya to honorably marry Jakub Jagr, who in spite of his limitations seemed to be a decent young man, able to provide her with a home and everything she needed.

To Sonya's further complaints I replied only with postcards bidding her to have trust in Jakub Jagr. But the seed of the great heroines of world literature, a seed I had sown in the soul of a simple village waitress, suddenly sprouted. I began to feel sorry for my seedling, who was suffering under the small-town Jagrs even more perhaps than I was under R., and so by telegraph I permitted her to leave and find a job in a textile drying room, a job she longed for so, and to begin a new life. My actions with regard to her went on being unselfish and honorable, and through my remote control I likewise made possible the wedding of Jakub Jagr to Kamila Ortova, a marriage that Sonya's presence had seriously threatened.

Happy now, Sonya found a job in the drying room of the Usti firm of Cottonola, a job she greatly liked (how I envied her— —), and she also found a group of good friends, so I had little left to do but give fatherly advice and tell her to take the degree exam. And in the same fatherly spirit I commanded her to leave her friend Jarunka Slana, who seemed to be a bad influence on her, and to once again start a new life. If only I could manage to do it myself.

At first I didn't pay much attention to the fact that Sonya had found a new job in the Usti firm of Cottex, which controlled R.'s adjustment center in Prague, where I have been suffering now for twelve years. Sonya's first job at Cottex was as a helper in the kitchen, then as librarian (in twelve days she had gone further at Cottex than I have in twelve years—), but I was thrilled to find out that the powerful L.L., member of the board of the entire nationwide concern and thus a superior of my tyrant, R., was trying to obtain her as his secretary.

For twelve years now I have been trying to extricate myself from dependence on R., at least in terms of my basic subsistence. Naturally I could find a thousand jobs in Prague—but R. would never let me take one, and because of Mama and the apartment I have to obey him. If, however, a superior ordered R. to release me, and in such a manner that R. would have no idea the initiative came from me, I would get eight hours of freedom every working day . . . at least eight hours every day of the new life I granted to Sonya so generously from afar. And in time, perhaps, a new apartment where I could take Mama.

By telegraph I commanded Sonya to get the job of secretary in L.L.'s office—his personal secretary—at any cost, and then I led her toward that goal, step by step, employing numbered instructions in sequence. Thanks to Sonya's comprehensive reports, I was quickly in a position to strategically and tactically command the terrain and to battle, by remote control, for my freedom. True, my manipulation of Sonya thus ceased to be disinterested, but I was asking her for only a fragment of what I had already given her several times. On the whole, my relation to Sonya continued to be honorable, for I had not advised her to do anything that was not in her own personal interest.

Controlled by signals from the world of great amours, Sonya blossomed forth like a true fictional heroine, able to do even the impossible. In truth I had mobilized my own private Cleopatra, and my injections from the fountainheads of world literature even had an effect on Sonya's surroundings, for instance, on L.L., who after many years of lethargy suddenly woke up and, according to the classical slogan "Veni—vidi—

vici," captured the Cottex throne like a fairy-tale Caesar in the realistic circumstances of a provincial center. When in April Sonya received an apartment from him (in a few months she had succeeded where I had failed for twelve years, and Mama for thirty—), I decided to reward her with a meeting.

The winter before, I had come across an army buddy, Rudolf Jonas, now a waiter at Dobris Castle, so I asked him to play a small fairy-tale role for two hundred crowns. For Sonya's complete conquest, I called the Hotel Trianon and reserved a room with twin beds.

I know Dobris Castle and its park from Sunday outings with R. and Mama, and I thoroughly prepared myself for my meeting with Sonya. I read twelve novels that take place in castles and among the world of the aristocracy, from the lending service at work I borrowed a sun lamp and tanned myself for ten minutes every day, I pulled together all my savings and, most important, I groveled before R. so he would lend me his car.

This essential requisite was suddenly taken from me, however. Because I had forgotten to brush R.'s light-colored trousers, which he unexpectedly picked to wear, he refused to give me the car for the day I'd prepared for so long, April 15.

I was tense and anxious all morning, and after hours of torment I finally made up my mind. Before the end of the shift I went to the garage, started R.'s car up, and drove off without his being aware. For the first time in my life I had resolved to disobey R. It was a truly historic day for me. When I touched the starter, I felt like a true Caesar. I cast my die and crossed my Rubicon.

When, in my best suit and with all my savings in my pocket, I sped along the expressway out of Prague, it occurred to me for the first time that the mighty whiplash of world literature across the reflections in a series of mirrors had affected me as well.

Sonya was someone completely different than she'd been the summer before. My remote control had turned her into a fairy-tale princess. As if all the fictional heroines I had fed her with had joined together and come back to life in her, that night she performed a miracle by transforming me, in my thirties, into a man. And like Pygmalion in the fairy tale, I fell in love with my creation.

Sonya has become great and I have shrunk from a fairy-tale prince to the everyday stature of the quite ordinary man in love, of which there are millions . . . and I am happy to be one of them.

If only that age-old fireplace of stories, old, noble, and foolish, ever so deeply human and therefore beautiful, would never go out, but instead become more numerous than they would be if they had actually happened. If only Sonya would keep the fire burning, fanned by the breath I get from those ancient fires, accessible to all who wish to warm themselves.

After my return from Dobris Castle and the Trianon, R. gave me a good hiding, like a dog, and I had to spend two hours kneeling on dried peas. Mama cried all night long, and she was already light as a child in my arms.

Now whenever R. allows me to read, all I read are classical love stories, because on my own I could never write Sonya anything more than *I LOVE YOU,* a thousand times in each letter.

Because for love and for life it's enough to

At this point Josef Novak finished writing his fairy tale. He had stopped in the middle of a sentence, no doubt because he had to run off to brush Rynolt's trousers or get him some beer.

It made me sick . . . all over, but especially my stomach. Incredulously I looked around the little room: on the walls scenes from fairy tales, on the floor an electric train set, and on the wardrobe a blow-up pink elephant . . . As the author Josef Novak wrote: it's enough.

Out of habit (from PS-VTEI, PTK, the firm's reading room and study room) and a bit out of boredom as well, I went over to the boy's bookcase. I caught sight of the book by Lorenz and Wasserman—*The Himalayas, Roof of the World*—the boy had used excerpts from—and on a page he'd marked, I found the following passage underlined with a red crayon:

It is the custom to view Mount Everest at dawn. Out of the red strip of dawn in the east the first ray of sunlight flares up and flies through the darkness, and strikes the peaks of the highest mountains on earth, and then the sun rises and spreads its golden-red fire over the eternal snows of Everest and its lieutenants Makala and Lhotse. . ."

That's the way the boy described it last summer at dinner at the Gastronome Restaurant in Liberec. The man who had seen Mount Everest. . . The book by Messrs. Lorenz and Wasserman bears the stamp of the Prague Library, and beside it are others, novels, encyclopedias, and dictionaries, he had most likely plagiarized some of the ones I used to study for my degree exam . . . It was not I who corresponded with my husband, it was the Prague Library corresponding with the one in Usti.

At the very end of the boy's bookshelf, apparently used very often, an open issue of *World Literature* was lying open, with quotations from surrealists underlined in red:

"It's out of the question for us to carry on human relations with fish. Queneau." The well-read boy had made good use of this in the thinly wooded *steppes* above Dobris Castle, and had, of course, forgotten to cite M. Queneau.

"Is it really necessary to do something about the laziness of rails between the passage of two trains? Duchamp." My boy had plagiarized this in his telegram NR. 84 and had, of course, forgotten to cite M. Duchamp.

"Will someone finally begin to defend the infinite? Aragon." My boy was no doubt preparing to include this in his next letter to me.

I took the boy's red crayon and underlined another quotation for him:

"Cut yourself in half and gulp down one of the halves. Arp."

And to give him some practical advice, I underlined another quote with his crayon:

"If we return to ourselves, it's wise to take roads that are passable. Breton."

And I put Josef Novak's fairy tale back into its black school folder, tied it up, and hid it underneath the fairy tale *ALICE IN WONDERLAND*, where he himself had taken refuge . . . I did it so that Arno Rynolt wouldn't read about himself as the wicked R. and make the boy kneel on dried peas again.

And I left.

Mrs. Rynoltova went along with me to say goodbye, there was fear in her eyes.

"Don't be afraid, Mrs. Rynoltova. Our case is closed. You'll have your son at home now for good."

"Thank you a thousand times," the old woman sighed with infinite relief, "you know, he, my Josef. . ."

"I know. He's still just a boy."

"Yes. I'm very glad you noticed that, too . . . like your officer. Are you taking Josef's photograph with you?"

"What would I do with it? Although. . . let me have it for my souvenir album."

"That's fine, I still have five more copies. I don't know how I can thank you for everything, Miss. . . Miss. . ."

"Names aren't important. And I'm no longer Miss . . . I've been married twice already."

"Really? You're so young. . ."

"I fell into the clutches of unscrupulous men . . . twice already. So goodbye, and don't tell the boy I've been here. He'd only worry unnecessarily, and Mr. Rynolt would whip him again."

I got rid of the false eyelashes and the hairnet and the stupid hat, I stuffed them all into an overflowing garbage can.

The women employees at the Prague Adjustment Center of natl. enter. Cottex like some distraction during their monotonous work (sifting powders into boxes and pasting on labels), and Josef Novak, Rynolt's Simple Simon and, beside Rynolt himself, the only male employee, is an inexhaustible source of merriment for them.

"What's up, Jozifek? Have you found yourself a girl yet?" Mrs. Matouskova screeched at him, and all the women broke into laughter: just imagine that scarecrow Josef with a girl!

"You'll have to pick one who'll let you play with your train set!" the trainee Zdenka burst into laughter (to entertain his employees, Rynolt often gives out tidbits concerning his step-idiot).

"Girls, each of you chip in five crowns and we'll buy Jozifek a scooter!" cries Ivuska, a fifteen-year-old who rarely comes to work (she has a stinking rich father).

"Great idea!" "Girls, seriously, let's all chip in!" "At least we won't have to wait so long for him to bring our morning snack!" the women screeched and laughed.

Wearing a shabby, standard-issue white labcoat over his bare frame and tattered canvas trousers with a rope around his waist, Josef Novak was sweeping the shop floor under the women's feet, he smiled patiently and didn't try to interfere with their fun, until their merry hubbub enticed Arno Rynolt to leave his "Director's Office" and come into the workshop.

"You girls seem to be having a lot of fun," Rynolt said with a sweet (forced) smile, "so then, which of you has a birthday today. . ."

"None of us, Mr. Rynolt," shot back the youngest and most brazen of them all, Ivuska, "but if you'll send out for a bottle, we might let you have a sip!"

"I'll send out, Ivuska, I'll send out," Rynolt prattled affably, "only you finish that Bulgarian shipment for me. Pretty please, girls, the end of the month's only a few days away— And, Mrs. Brunclikova, could you be so kind as to take the bicycle to the post office. . ."

"I don't feel so hot," whimpered Mrs. Brunclikova. "I can't take this scorcher . . . Couldn't Josef do it again?"

"What wouldn't I do to please my ladies," Rynolt jabbered charmingly, "but girls, pretty please, let's take care of that Bulgarian shipment. . ." and he sent Anna's idiot off to the post office on the bicycle.

When Josef Novak came back from the post office, he sprinkled the courtyard to keep down the dust, helped the women carry boxes to the warehouse, ran out to get bread for Mrs. Matouskova and, on the way, got a pack of American Winston cigarettes for Ivuska and five pounds of potatoes for

Mrs. Brunclikova, washed the floor, the showers, and the toilets in the women's room, and burned used wrapping paper until Rynolt called him into the garage by honking the horn.

"Tomorrow you'll paint the barrier!" Rynolt ordered him when the gatekeeper raised it to permit them to exit, the paint had cracked a little, "that's the first thing any visitor sees. Pick up the paint tomorrow and have it done before coffee break, understand!"

"Yes, Mr. Rynolt. Shall I paint it red and white again?"

"No! Pink with silver stars!"

"That would be beautiful. . ."

"You idiot," Rynolt let off steam and with a violent jerk (he had always had trouble changing gears) he burst out of the factory grounds.

When he got to Pod schody 4, Rynolt parked in front, ordered Anna's idiot to wash the car, and went to give Anna a dressing down, all to cleanse himself of those unavoidable pleasantries he'd offered to his personnel (it's damn hard to find anyone to work in Prague and it's almost impossible to keep her), Matouskova wants to give notice and then that gatekeeper, who does nothing but knit, has let it be known that if she doesn't get a raise, she won't be back after vacation.

Josef Novak washed the car with loving care (he had bought the most expensive auto shampoo out of his own savings) until it shone like a mirror, and stood beside it, gazing toward the house, until Rynolt examined his work from the window and with a nod permitted him to play until evening.

Josef Novak ran upstairs to the third floor, he didn't have to ring, for Mama was already waiting in the doorway. While they were still in the vestibule (so Rynolt wouldn't see it) she gave her son a slice of bread with butter and honey and stroked his hair, which was already beginning to gray at the temples.

Once in his tiny room, Josef turned on the electric train set (if there wasn't any noise, Rynolt would be suspicious—he listened to every sound—and would have rushed in at once), and for a while he watched it make its way through the tiny tunnels, past the stations, and over the bridges, and then, since he had adjusted his little railroad so perfectly it could go for whole hours if necessary, he could devote himself to his principal form of play in peace and quiet.

Without a pause, he picked up *Alice in Wonderland*, in which he concealed his writing paper and envelopes, and *Peter and Lucy* and *Anna Karenina*, which he'd borrowed from the city library. He had decided to write Sonya an especially long letter today, the most beautiful in the world.

Hastily (since Rynolt could rush in here, even with the train set going) he marked the white sheet NR. 103 and eagerly began to write:

> *My Sonya,*
> *I love you like. . . and like. . . and more than. . .*
> *And now that you have become great, I will entrust you with an especially important and existentially important task. . .*

By staying light into the early evening, the summer day fooled him good, and he jumped at the sound of Rynolt's voice through the wall:

"Send that idiot out for some beer!"

Josef Novak hurriedly finished the letter, signed it *Your Manek*, stuck it in an envelope, and hid it under his shirt.

Soon thereafter he went down with a jug into the humid air, he felt intensely happy at the sight of a thin strip of dark-blue sky in the chink between the tall tenements, and before he went into the Prince's Inn he stopped at the corner post office and mailed his letter registered express.

I walked away as fast as I could, I don't want to see him again; let it all remain a fairy tale. . .

All I carry away with me is his photo, and one day I will place it in my family album, among the photographs of my sons.

I walked rapidly away from this quarter of tall old tenements. My suitcase struck me on the calves as I hurried along to get away as fast as I could. The buildings made way for a small square, at its its center lime trees were beginning to bloom, a red streetcar rode past and clanged at me so that I would know what route to take from here, and I followed its cheerful voice, here the buildings were more cheerful and on the wide pavements there were more people, women with shopping bags (I want to shop for two), trudging girls and old women, women with baby carriages (I want to have a child, two, three—) and, of course, men.

I reflected on the position in which I found myself, and it started to seem as if it wasn't so bad after all, I'm healthy and not yet twenty, I've passed my degree exam, I know people, I like them, and now I want to live like them.

What I really want: human things. An orderly and satisfying life. To be happy. Someone who likes me and whom I like. My own husband, and to have children with him. My own family. I like this world and I want to do all sorts of things in it. And who knows, perhaps some day I'll even see Mount Everest.

The streets kept getting wider and livelier and there were more and more people on them, until suddenly I found myself on Wenceslaus Square, gleaming cars flowed through flowing rivers of people, the ground floors of all the buildings suddenly turned to glass, and like one rolling river we rippled through traffic lights, the honking of horns, the noise, the music, the vibrations, and the odors, all the aromas here — whenever I'm so happy that I'm moved, I have to name the *aroma* of that moment — this heady aroma here is the aroma of the world.

And I felt men looking at me, I gathered their smiles like

strawberries on a glade in June and I smiled prettily at each of them—no, I've been alone too long, I won't be anymore.

I reflected on the position in which I found myself, and it seemed to me it was a downright excellent one . . . for nearly a year I had been in the hands of a mere boy—still, in that time I had undoubtedly made progress, I'd have to say.

And then I wondered whether it would all have been possible WITHOUT that boy from the tiny room with the fairy-tale scenes on the walls, the electric train set, the blow-up pink elephant on the wardrobe, and the books from the city library . . . With what incredibly simple tricks, with what childish deception he had extracted from me so much I'd never suspected was there . . . wouldn't it have worked even WITHOUT those plagiarized letters and telegrams? Why, that boy had written like an adult: *ALL YOU NEED IS* and I added: TO DO THINGS. There are enough patterns for everyone to choose his own, the libraries are full of books and they can all be borrowed now for free.

If all the girls in the world. . .

And if all the boys and men—

For nearly a year I've been in the hands of a boy, now I want to be in the hands of a real man—so that *I* might hold *him* in my hands and so that we might embrace and always be together. . .

And *HE*, whether he is to be my hero and love, a fatherly protector, or even a trusting child—I will not disappoint him and I will be his wife no matter what: this is my job, my love, and my mission.

We will inform the impatient reader, well in advance, that in the next volume Sonya will pass through a series of vocations and loves (we can't give everything away), that she will travel through Europe and India (and see Mount Everest), and that we are planning to have to her smile prettily another ninety times or so.

ENGINEER KAZIMIR DRAPAL
ENGINEER LANIMIR SAPAL
ENGINEER VLADIMIR PARAL

OTHER CZECH LITERATURE IN TRANSLATION
FROM GARRIGUE BOOKS/CATBIRD PRESS

CATAPULT by Vladimír Páral, trans. William Harkins.
In this novel, Páral employs a twist on the Don Juan story to
look at the attractions and difficulties of freedom in a time
when there are few clear landmarks to help us make decisions.
In the course of his commute, Jacek Jost, a young Czech
engineer, is suddenly catapulted out of his seat and his daily
routine, into a world of infinite opportunities. Jacek's comically
futile efforts to make the necessary choices are full of the excitement, fear, and confusion that accompany freedom. Páral's fluid
style and driving pace do an excellent job of reflecting these
emotions, in a novel much more tightly structured than *The Four
Sonyas*. See the back cover of this book to see what the critics
have said about the novel that is generally regarded in Czechoslovakia as Páral's masterpiece.
$10.95 paperback, 240 pp., ISBN 0-945774-17-6.

KAREL ČAPEK (1890-1938, Chop'-ek) is generally considered
the greatest Czech author of the first half of this century. He
was Czechoslovakia's leading novelist, playwright, story writer,
and columnist, and the spirit of its short-lived democracy,
between the wars. His plays appeared on Broadway soon after
their debut in Prague, and his books were translated into many
languages. Čapek expressed his ethical vision of the world
through accessible, beautifully written, and highly enjoyable
writing. We have published three volumes of his works, and
two more volumes are in the process of being translated.

"Fifty years after his death, Čapek's work has lost nothing of its
freshness and luster." —*New York Times Book Review*

"God bless Catbird Press for calling the attention of Americans to a great writer of the past who speaks to the present in a voice brilliant, clear, honorable, blackly funny, and prophetic."
                                        —*Kurt Vonnegut*
"Imagine discovering the rich, warm humanity of a Dickens or a Gogol, and you have some idea of the impact of this selection from the work of Czechoslovakia's foremost twentieth-century writer."   —*Booklist*

"It's time to read Čapek again for his insouciant laughter, and the anguish of human blindness that lies beneath it."
                                        —*Arthur Miller*

TOWARD THE RADICAL CENTER: A KAREL ČAPEK READER edited by Peter Kussi, foreword by Arthur Miller. This collection of Čapek's best plays, stories, fables, and columns takes us from the social contributions of clumsy people and the mystery of a single footprint in the snow, to dramatic meditations on mortality and commitment. Most of the Reader is newly translated, including the first complete English translation of the classic play, *R.U.R. (Rossum's Universal Robots)*, which introduced the literary robot. "Edited with considerable care and including a number of badly needed new versions of works long to be found only in dumbfounding translatorese, this ... volume brings the voice of Čapek back to life." —*The Nation*
$23.95 cloth, $12.95 paper, 416 pp., illus. ISBN 0-945774-06-0, 07-9.

WAR WITH THE NEWTS by Karel Čapek, trans. Ewald Osers. This new translation revitalizes one of the great anti-utopian satires of the twentieth century. Mankind discovers a species of giant, intelligent newts and increasingly exploits them as laborers. Under a human leader, they challenge man's place at the top of the animal kingdom. "A bracing parody of totalitarianism and technological overkill, one of the most amusing and provocative books in its genre." —*Philadelphia Inquirer*
$9.95 paper, 240 pp., ISBN 0-945774-10-9.

THREE NOVELS (Hordubal, Meteor, An Ordinary Life) by Karel Čapek, trans. M. & R. Weatherall. A unique trilogy of novels that share neither characters nor events; instead they approach the problem of knowing people—of mutual under-standing—through various kinds of storytelling. "Enjoyable philosophical novels can be counted on a hand or two. ... Now, American readers can add to this skimpy list this obscure but thoroughly deserving trilogy." —*Washington Post Book World* "Capek's masterpiece." —*Chicago Tribune & NY Times Bk. Rev.* $13.95 paper, 480 pp., ISBN 0-945774-08-7

COMING IN MARCH 1993 — WHAT OWNERSHIP'S ALL ABOUT by Karel Poláček, trans. Peter Kussi. This 1928 novel takes a pointedly satirical look at the conflicts between a small-time landlord and his tenants. It shows the growth of attitudes that were leading to fascism, with a focus on the prisonhouse of words that hems in all the characters. Poláček was a contempo-rary of Karel Čapek's, and also one of the best and most popular novelists, journalists, humorists, and children's writers of the time. This is the first of his works to appear in English. $19.95 cloth, 240 pp., ISBN 0-945774-19-2.

These books can be found or ordered at better bookstores every-where, or they can be ordered directly from Catbird Press. Just send a check for the appropriate amount, plus $3.00 shipping (no matter how many books you buy), to Catbird Press, 16 Windsor Road, North Haven, CT 06473. If you would like to be on our catalog mailing list, please write to the same address.